Premature Infatuation

Premature Infatuation

LYNN PETERS

SIMON & SCHUSTER
A VIACOM COMPANY

First published in Great Britain by Simon & Schuster Ltd, 1996
A Paramount Communications Company

Simon & Schuster Ltd
West Garden Place
Kendal Street
London W2 2AQ

Simon & Schuster of Australia Pty Ltd
Sydney

A CIP catalogue record for this book is available from the
British Library

ISBN 0-684-81711-X

Typeset in Goudy Modern 13/14pt by
Palimpsest Book Production Limited, Polmont, Stirlingshire
Printed and bound in Great Britain by
Butler & Tanner Ltd, Frome & London

To Pauline Putman

Part One

Chapter 1

I always think that the best part of starting a new job is when you hear you've got it and imagine your bank account swelling with the hefty new salary. And when you've done that the best part is over — which is bad news for me seeing that this job doesn't come with a salary at all, just a minuscule hourly rate, and the only thing that's swelling currently is my bladder.

I've been here ten minutes already. This reception area is full of draughts — I don't know where they're coming from but I can feel where they're going — and this sofa is so low that my backside is touching the floor and my chin is on my knees. I'd read one of the magazines spread out on the table but I'm not sure I could reach it without the aid of a hoist.

I'm far too early. I should know by now because it's happened on my last two assignments. Corinne, the raven-haired siren with scarlet fingernails up to her wrists who runs the agency, likes us to arrive at our jobs early, very early; she thinks it speaks punctuality and efficiency; perhaps she also thinks it's a way of getting twenty minutes extra on our timesheets without having to work for it.

She rang me yesterday and said she knew it was short

notice but she'd be *so* grateful and could I do four days, possibly longer, and I was absolutely perfect for this job (for 'perfect' read 'available'), she'd thought of me the minute she got the booking. I negotiated an extra pound an hour which she finally caved in over, even though it would put me on the absolute top rate and would mean I was getting paid almost as much as Linda who has been her number one temp for years. I was a bit disappointed actually. Previously she's said I was on the absolute top rate already and I'd only asked for more to make her sweat a bit. In my heart, I've been nurturing a suspicion that she pays me slightly less than I've seen her give the jeans-clad boys who wash the windscreen of her sporty little car when it's stopped at traffic lights, but still I've savoured the illusion.

Corinne is fond of saying that starting a new job is a bit like making love with someone new: exciting, stimulating, and you don't know what it might lead to. Personally, I can't see the similarity. At work you have to suck up to the boss, keep your head down and just get on with the job in hand. But when you make love to someone . . . Oh well, she may have a point.

Corinne told me how friendly it is here and how much I'll like it, which is what she also said about the tight-lipped accountant who sent me home at lunchtime because she had told him I was fully competent on a system I'd never even heard of. Corinne is assertive and aggressive which makes her hard to say no to, but she is also transparent. I like that in a person. Now that I have cast myself in the role of secretary, I like to keep things simple.

Not that I am a secretary, not really, though I'm doing the best impression I can. I actually trained as a social worker, wanting to put my social conscience to the test. I did and it got a C Plus, Could Do Better, though that's just my opinion. My boss was very disappointed I was leaving but that could have been because she was a chocoholic and knew she could always find an emergency Mars bar in my desk.

The door to reception opens and the caretaker's grey head appears round it.

'All right?' he says. I nod and he goes away again.

Temping isn't something I plan to do for longer than I have to, but it has its compensations. I have no responsibilities, never take work home and I can take time off for the school holidays or if Joe is ill, or when Sam comes home. And if Sam should take a long-term contract and want us all to live abroad with him – or even go back to America where he was born – which could happen any time, let's face it – then my job commitments won't complicate matters. It suits me. OK, if you want the truth it doesn't suit me at all, but it suits my circumstances. And my conscience. Because there's also Joe, who is only five, to consider and although I plan, ultimately, to work in a situation that will use my intellect and education; in a stimulating and challenging environment with good expectations and an even better salary, I also want to be A Good Mother. Being A Good Mother can really bugger up your career prospects.

These offices don't quite live up to the picture Corinne painted. I walked past the front entrance on this narrow London back street three times before I noticed it: an anonymous little door, dingy and dulled by the constant scrubbing-off of graffiti (which they haven't quite kept up with). No one answered my buzzing on the entryphone but the caretaker let me in on his way down for the milk. Up a flight of narrow stairs is the reception area where I now sit with my chin on my knees. If someone doesn't come soon

5

I'll be adding to the stains on this sofa by peeing on it. I shouldn't have had that second cup of coffee before I left home but caffeine was the closest to Dutch courage I could get. The memory of all that liquid sends a spasm through my groin and I cross my legs.

The reception area isn't much bigger than the lounge in our house, which is to say there's only room to swing a cat if you chop its tail off first, and the high reception desk is made of a substance with all the strength and resilience of papier mâché, though less prestigious. Along the bottom you can see scuffs and digs where people's shoes have scraped against it. Leading off from reception is a corridor lined by offices, the kind which are filing-cabinet grey on the bottom and all glass partition at the top. Inside are ranks of dusty black boxfiles, 'in' trays, 'out' trays, tea trays. If I thought Corinne had meant it, I'd think she had a damn cheek saying I'd fit in somewhere like this.

I learned to type at evening classes and practised by typing up the theses of friends of the absent Sam on his word processor. But now it's autumn, that time of year when happy, smiling faces are turned towards school — well, the mothers' are anyway. Now Joe has started in the reception class I can work full time. In the past month I've been editorial assistant on a motoring magazine, where half the work involved sending out prizes to the winners of the weekly competition, and the other half involved explaining to the losers why they hadn't won. I've worked at the head office of a frozen foods outlet where the bulk of the job turned out to be chauffeuring the marketing manager following his drink-driving ban; and I've been production assistant to the (he assured me) upwardly mobile producer of an independent TV company, though downward and stationary was how he struck me. That's where I'd be now if it wasn't on the other side of town and, what with Joe and everything, too far to travel every day.

The door opens and two women walk in. One of them, fifties, Irish, with short brindley hair like a Scottie dog is saying, 'Just because you hate inequality it doesn't mean you want to be treated like everyone else.' She reminds me of a joke I heard about a pit bull with no teeth. It didn't bite but it could give you a nasty look. I raise one hand and shuffle forward on the deep sofa – not easily done with my backside already at floor level and with the seat sloping backwards – and try to attract her attention. In the circumstances this is not difficult.

'Excuse me!'

The two women look at each other as though I'm a beggar on the underground and they can't decide whether to give me fifty pence or the brush off.

'Yes?' Brindle adopts a superior tone and a helpful smile which doesn't reach her eyes. I grab on to the arm of the sofa and haul myself up while trying to pull my skirt over my thighs. My fingernail catches on one leg of my smooth dark tights and pulls a thread leaving a line across my leg, like felt-tip pen.

'I'm the new temp. I'm supposed to report to reception but there's no one here.' Brindle looks around as though hoping to prove me wrong but the only face that greets her is that of the clock. As it happens that's all she needs.

'It's not nine o'clock yet. We don't start until nine. No one will be ready for you until at least half past.'

'They told me eight forty-five.' I smile slightly: professional but warm. When I'd started at Social Services, they'd welcomed me with open arms: here was someone come to share the heavy load. I posed no threat. They knew intuitively that my skills and abilities were nothing special or I wouldn't be doing social work; I'd be in advertising or the civil service. When you're a temp, on the other hand, you're an unknown quantity. Your skill on the keyboard, mastery of punctuation, spelling and the coffee-making facilities, all these have the potential to strike fear of redundancy and early retirement into the existing staff. Which is why there is but one task which any new temp must deal with first: to overcome the hostility of the other staff. Well, two things actually.

'Could you show me where the loos are?'

Brindle looks at me as intensely as if she's looking for zits. She thinks I could be some down-and-out about to make off with their loo rolls, my black skirt and silk shirt just a disguise.

'We shouldn't really. You haven't been signed in.' I add a hint of the pleading to the winning smile and tilt my head slightly to acknowledge her seniority. She still looks doubtful but she's wavering. All at once her shoulders collapse and I realize she isn't used to the pose of superiority and can't keep it up. Quite possibly the only person in this company she is higher than is me.

'Oh, I suppose it'll be all right. And if you're a masked gunman, come to shoot the lot of them, I'll show you where to start.' She looks at the other woman, not me, to share the joke but I join in the laughter anyway.

Of course, I don't mean to do this sort of work forever. Only until I decide what I really want to be. But for now, this is me: refreshed, retrained, and reborn as a temp. In the short term, anyway. Temporarily.

I've been living with Sam for six years but with his working abroad – he's a site engineer and works overseas, usually two or so months at a stretch – it feels like we only spend about ten minutes of each year actually under the same roof. The upside, as they say, is that if you want to go on having honeymoon sex you have to keep having honeymoons, and with all these eagerly anticipated homecomings, effectively we do. But the downside is that honeymoon sex is the nearest to marriage we ever get. Friends ask why getting married matters so much to me but it's a sign of commitment, isn't it? If a guy wants to marry you, you know you're not just a phase he's going through. But the only time Sam has ever mentioned marriage is in my dreams, unless you include those occasions when he gleefully tells me that someone we know has just split up. (When we last went to a wedding he whispered his own version of the vows into my ear promising – not 'To have and to hold' but 'To have and to spend . . . In fitness and in wealth . . . Forsaking *some* others . . . Till boredom do us part . . .') I asked him once if he was faithful to me, and he said, 'frequently'. I'm not so naïve as to think that getting married would actually make any difference to us but the fact he wanted to, well, that would make all the difference in the world.

My friend Tania jokes that it's being apart that keeps us together but I have a terrifying feeling that might be true for Sam. If he only comes home every few months maybe it's because that's all he wants (when I say this he denies it. But then he avoids saying *anything* that might put me in the wrong mood for having more honeymoon sex). With his being half American and having grown up in the US, he isn't really settled anywhere; he's a bit of a wanderer which is why a job which constantly shifts him around the globe suits him.

But for me, life seems to be a series of leaps between one homecoming and another, with the periods in-between being time that has to be waded through, probably while sentimentalizing over the last visit and planning the next. Contracts keep being extended by a week or a fortnight, eating away at the short gap between. He used to say he'd transfer back over here but each time a new job has come up there's been some reason that this wasn't a good time to do it, and he doesn't seem to say it at all any more. But he's funny and sexy and when he's home making love to me, pinning me against the wall so hard I think we'll crack the plaster – well, I forget how miserable or aggrieved I feel when he isn't.

I switch the machine on and nothing happens. I press enter, return, escape, enter, control, escape, then switch it off then on again. Still nothing. The manual is nowhere in sight and the desk drawer offers only a selection of staples, a leaflet on postal rates and a lipstick with the top missing.

This is the worst of temping. No one tells you anything and they sit you at a desk with a pile of typing and someone else's dirty coffee mug and leave you to get on with it. I lean forward and press a few random keys so that anyone watching will think I'm in control of the situation. Evidently Diane, the senior secretary is watching, but this isn't what she thinks because she gets up from her desk and comes hovering behind me. She bends down so that her face is next to mine and peers at the screen mystified. Then she taps the keyboard. I'm glad to see that it's as unresponsive as when I tried.

'Which disk have you put in?' she says. Disk? Who said anything about a disk? From a box I haven't noticed at the side of the telephone she draws out a black square of plastic (I always wonder why they're called disks when they're square) and inserts it into the machine's ready orifice. The screen sparks into life with a flurry of mechanical notes. It seems to be singing, 'Time to go home,' or is that just me?

'You'll be fine now,' says Diane, like a head girl helping a first former settle in. 'The agency said you were fully conversant with this system.' I'd smile at the tremor of pride with which she enunciates 'conversant', if it wasn't for the panic shooting through me at what that 'fully' might imply. Corinne gave me half a day's tuition but we didn't get much further than how to plug it in. This job was supposed to be more administrative than typing, and I'd hoped I'd just be making coffee and answering the telephone, both skills with which I'm certainly conversant. I can't afford to be sent home before lunchtime again.

Diane shows me where the stationery is kept, where to find the various files and where you put typed letters ready for signing. The procedures are virtually identical to those I've seen everywhere else, but with just enough variants to make you look stupid if you get one wrong. I note down the main points on a pad she gives me. I always like to write down things I need to remember; that way instead of having to search my memory, I only have to search for my notepad.

There are four of us in this small room. Diane, by virtue of her evident superiority, sits at the head, next to the only window and with the best view of the door. Her black hair is cut in a severe and straight bob which emphasizes her angular jaw and with her scarlet lips she has, from the neck up, the eccentric look of a fashion designer. But her dark suit, worn I guess in acknowledgement of the fact she is the most senior of us and secretary to a director (a fact she drops into the conversation early on) sets you right about that. Then there's Suzanne who works for the chief engineer; she's small, thin and watchful, and keeps her head down, scarcely joining in the general chat. Last and by all means least (if you don't count me, that is) is Marie who works for everybody else. She is more homely than the others, and with her apple cheeks, hair the colour of treacle toffee and broad shoulders that were made to carry a yoke, she reminds me of a milkmaid. She wears a slightly too tight short skirt which wrinkles over her thighs and white legs with white stilettoes to match ('If you wear tights all day they rub your tan off,' she tells me. If this is true, then today must be the first on which she has taken her own advice). I am to work for Ed Murray, Head of Sales and Marketing, a mysterious man of whom Diane will tell me nothing because, says Marie, 'She doesn't believe in speaking ill of the dead.' Marie also tells me I'm not to be scared, there's absolutely nothing to worry about, he's nowhere near as bad as people say, and all the other temps, well they probably weren't much good anyway.

'How it works here,' Diane tells me, perching on the side of my desk and glancing at my screen, 'is that, although we each have our own boss, when we're not busy we share the typing for the other engineers and salesmen. They put it in that tray over there, and we just work our way through it. You might as well make a start.' She indicates the communal typing tray. 'Just take out whatever is on the top.'

She goes back to her seat and Marie gives me a sympathetic smile as I approach the typing tray. I soon see why. On the top is a fifteen-column schedule spread across two pages. I can't do tables. Even on the machine we have at home, I can only do Cut and Paste and even then I need the manual. Corinne knows that. She promised me straightforward typing, maybe a little audio.

'It shouldn't take you too long,' says Diane sweetly, seeing me hover over the graphical horror. 'But you can see why we only take people who are experienced on this system.' I sweep it up with a flourish and carry it back to my desk. She's right, it won't take long. In the context of man's habitation of the earth, a fortnight is nothing.

It's unfortunate that I should have to start with such a difficult piece of work because ordinarily I rather like typing. At school, keyboard skills were taken by the same girls who did cookery and sewing while the rest of us were, we were given to understand, destined for higher things. But the drawback to Latin or French or Geography is that you can't gaze out of the window and let your mind roam free while you do them. With typing, especially audio-typing, my particular favourite, you can do just that. While your ears record, 'With reference to your letter of 7 July' and your fingers react accordingly, the higher echelons of your mind are far away in daydreams and fantasies. Admittedly, as yet I have no window to gaze out of; what currently meets my eyes is a wall blank but for a sign which reads 'You don't have to work to be mad here' and a postcard of Torremolinos. But I am not dismayed. In my mind I am in that postcard, on the balcony of the small white house pictured, and Sam, deeply bronzed and with the front of his too-long dark hair bleached by the sun, is with me. His broad shoulders and narrow hips make him look like a youth still though he's almost thirty — just three years older than me. He's wearing his jeans, of course, and a white shirt that he hasn't done up yet, fresh from the shower. As he glances out across the sea he looks pure Hollywood. He moves in behind me as I stand gazing out across the ocean and kisses my neck. 'I love you and I want to marry you,' he says, in his New York drawl.

Against my will, tears fill my eyes and as I turn he crushes me against his strong manly chest. If there is no greater joy known to woman than to be with the man she loves, then a close second is to be fantasizing about the man you love, and getting paid for it.

'How are you doing?' Diane looks up brightly from her electronic typewriter and begins collating some papers on her desk. 'Nearly finished?'

Nearly started would be nearer the mark. The girls who did cookery and sewing would have sorted this out in the time it's taken me to say 'ohmygod'.

Diane collects up handbag and hairspray and heads for the ladies, and when she has gone I suddenly find Marie by my side. 'Move over,' she says, 'I'll show you what we do.' She takes the mouse and with a flick of her wrist a tabulation appears onscreen. I have only to fill in the figures.

'Marie,' I say, as she goes back to her desk. 'Did you do cookery and sewing at school?'

'Oh, very good,' says Diane later peering, as seems to be her way, over my shoulder once again. There's a mixture of chagrin and disappointment in that short phrase, with maybe a soupçon of irritation. 'I take it someone showed you the page layout.'

'Well, we don't want to put her off on her first day, do we?' Marie jumps in with a sweet smile before I can speak. 'We don't want to lose any more temps.'

'Yes, what is all this about the temps?' It seems to me that Marie is itching to tell me something and Diane is anxious she shouldn't. I enjoy the cut and thrust of office politics, it compensates for the tedium of the secretarial round or at least enlivens it, but I don't want to be the centre of it.

'They weren't very good, that's all,' says Diane, adding

meaningfully, 'They couldn't operate the word processor and spent too much time chatting.' She sweeps back to her desk and seats herself, businesslike, in front of her screen. 'Gemma,' she says with a smile that could freeze water. 'They need that chart by eleven.'

'We usually have coffee about now,' says Diane, interrupting my reverie. I look up and realize she's addressing me.

'Thank goodness. I'm gasping.'

'Marie will show you where the kettle and everything is.'

You have to hand it to Diane, she's good. I blink at her for a moment, wondering if I should protest on principle or just accept that, as the newest and lowest in the hierarchy, I get the shitty jobs. While I'm pondering she stares me out, and already I've lost. I stand up brightly, as though there's nothing I'd rather be doing, which actually, given the range of options there probably isn't. I'm losing the battle with the word processor, but with a kettle I know no fear.

'Have you worked at many places?' asks Marie, searching a cupboard for washing-up liquid. A ray of watery sun glints off the scum in the dishwater.

'A few. I was at a TV company last. That was fun.' It wasn't particularly, but it sounds good.

'Gosh, that must have been brilliant. I'd like to work in television.' She swishes the mugs round in the grimey washing-up bowl.

'Why don't you then?'

'Oh, I don't think Gary would like it. He's my boyfriend. Fiancé.'

'Why wouldn't he like it?'

'He thinks they're all on drugs and everything, actors.'

In the three weeks I'd worked for Bernie I hadn't even

seen an actor, only impoverished writers to whom Bernie
offered generous commissions but only in some unspecified
future. Bernie may not have been good for fostering talent,
but he was brilliant at fostering optimism.

'Why listen to Gary? Why don't you do what you want
to do?' She hands me a mug to dry and our eyes meet.

'I am doing what I want to do. I'm marrying Gary.'

Marie and I continue our discussion on our way to get a
sandwich for lunch. I'm not certain whether she has taken
a shine to me or if it's just that she's glad of someone new
to whom she can tell her wedding plans. She gets married
in six months' time. Gary is manager of the fruit and veg
department at Tesco's; to hear her speak you'd think his
job carried all the risks and prestige of a movie stuntman.
She points out to me a wedding dress similar to the one she
is having made ('It's got a different neck and pearl buttons
down the cuffs instead of all that lace – but otherwise it's
identical.' I think she means it's long and white). She has
ordered a size 12 (she's a size 14 but she'll have slimmed
down by then) and points out too the exact shade of peach
of the bridesmaids' dresses. She's having three bridesmaids,
a page boy and a horse-drawn carriage.

Sam says that big weddings are the inevitable result of
what he calls the Cinderella complex: every young girl
cherishes dreams of becoming a princess. He's probably
right, though I don't see why this is any reason to deny
them it. I don't hanker after a horse-drawn carriage but
a long dress and a church would be acceptable. As it is, I
have to make do with my own fairy princess scenario: being
kissed out of a comatose sleep by a returning handsome hunk
like some cut-price Sleeping Beauty.

Marie has been engaged for two years and known her

fiancé for seven. They live within a mile of each other and their parents go to the same church. She tells me what a miracle it is that, with all the world to choose from and all the men in it, Fate places the one who's right for you smack where you're going to meet him, at your table-tennis club. Wouldn't it be terrible, she says, if your real soulmate actually lived in Tasmania, and you never knew. You could spend your whole life searching the environs of Shepherd's Bush and not meet each other.

Marie is one of those people who is always smiling so I can't judge from her expression whether she's being ironic.

'Of course, Fate's not been so good to you, has it?' she says, sympathetically. 'Putting your boyfriend where you could meet him, then whisking him away again.' I was thinking the same thing myself. In fact, setting off for Tasmania to look for one's true love might be rather more enlivening than meeting on a grey January day on the outskirts of Clapham.

'When d'you think you'll get married?' She's still smiling. At twenty-one she can still ask such a direct question with no inkling it could give offence – or that 'if' or 'whether' might be more a more appropriate way of phrasing it.

I open the door of the sandwich bar and Marie follows me in. 'I hope there're some prawn ones left,' I say.

When we get back to the office, a pile of invoices has appeared on my desk but I push them aside. I don't do any work that doesn't come with a 'please' or 'thank you' attached and I'm not a mind-reader. Well, actually I sometimes think I am, but I wouldn't waste my talent on invoices.

Maybe it's a touch of ESP that has made me start thinking about Joe. He had a cold and a cough this morning. I dosed him with Calpol and sent him to school, something I would never do if I wasn't coming to work. I read somewhere that you should always stop what you're doing to show the child the rainbow, because your work will wait but the rainbow won't. This sort of conscience-pricking maxim (probably written by someone whose picture of the average child came from the pages of a Mabel Lucy Atwell story book) seems to trouble me now I'm in paid employment, even though when I'm at home with Joe it would actually need a fork-lift truck to drag him from some psychologically damaging cartoon on TV to look at an uplifting aspect of nature.

'Have you got any children?' asks Marie, apparently an even better mind-reader than I am.

'I can see why you'd feel bad,' she says when I tell her about Joe and my conscience, agreeing, irritatingly, with the maxim writer. 'If I had children I'd want to be there with them all the time. You can't get those moments back can you?' I think of the three months Joe was sick with whooping cough and feel grateful that you can't.

'But you want some time alone with Gary don't you? Once you've got a baby it's never the same. Much as I love Joe, I wish he hadn't arrived on the scene quite so soon.'

'Oh, there'll be plenty of time for us to be alone when they're grown up. No, I want to have children young, so we can be friends.'

I can't think of anything worse for a child than having a parent who wants to be friends with it. Every mother owes it to her child to give it something to moan about. How will it fit in with its peer group otherwise?

I'm just making this point when Diane arrives back with a three-bean salad and a ham roll.

'You're talking about children?' she asks, in a voice that speaks ponies and prep schools but whose parents, I gather, run a fish and chip shop in Penge. 'If you're very young when you have your children, you just end up feeling old sooner than you would have done otherwise. Caroline has taken great pleasure in telling me what an old fogey I am ever since she was five.'

I'm about to ask how old Caroline is, wondering if I can calculate Diane's age from the answer, when Marie says, 'So how old were you when you had her?' It's clear, from her effort to sound casual, that this is something she has been waiting a long time to ask. Diane's carefully made-up eyes narrow very slightly.

'Young,' she says. 'Shall I open a window?'

I'm on the phone to Tania, checking that Joe was still alive when she collected him from school, when the door opens and a man comes striding in. Sharply dressed, with knife-edge creases you could cut yourself on, he is making a beeline for me. Damn. This must be Ed; he would have to catch me in the middle of a personal call. On the other hand, he's younger than I'd expected. And smaller. And smiling. I think I can handle him.

I hiss a hurried farewell to Tania and hang up.

'Hi, I'm Gemma, your new temp.' I extend my hand in greeting and stand up to put myself at less of a psychological disadvantage. He is dark-skinned, maybe half-caste, with a firm jaw and high cheekbones. His hair is cut short at the sides and front to reveal a wide brow. He is slim and of small stature which is just as well. If he were six foot he'd be off modelling on a photo shoot in the Bahamas instead of

gazing into my eyes in this dark backstreet office. I blink as
a delicate scent of aftershave wafts over me. They've been
teasing me, letting me think Ed was some kind of monster.
'So you're Ed.' He throws his head back and laughs. So
does Marie. And Suzanne.

'Jesus, what gave you that idea? Diane, what have
you been telling her?' Even Diane is laughing. I smile
foolishly.

'I thought I was working for Ed.'

'Oh you are, that's the bad news. The even worse news
is that you'll be working for Piers and me too.' He takes my
hand with a flourish. He has slim fingers, the palm is warm
and dry. 'But don't you worry about Ed. If you have any
problems, I'll be behind you.' He pauses for effect. 'A *long*
way behind you.' They all laugh again.

'So who are you then?' My brusque tone pulls him
up a little.

'Sorry. I'm Colin. I thought the girls would have told
you the set-up already.'

'The only set-up I've been told about is the one where
I get to make the coffee.'

'Whoa, sister. You've been here just five minutes and
already someone's been treading on your toes.'

I'd meant it as a joke but I just sound petulant and before
I can cover it up, he has picked up my dirty coffee mug and
is waving it around good-naturedly.

'This lady's our guest, if we don't look after her she
might not visit us again.' He says this, looking in Diane's
direction and for one astonishing moment I think he's going
to ask her to make the coffee. Then, more astonishing
still, I see he means to make it himself. 'There's just
three of us in Treadz right now – that's a new division
the company is setting up, specializing in trainers. We're

separate from Galaxy Leisure – that lot.' He waves his arm at Diane, Marie and Suzanne. 'We're looking to expand so we need our own secretary.' He describes the variety of secretarial tasks I'll be doing, making the job sound far more demanding than the restful audio-typing Corinne had described.

Then he says, 'So have the girls told you about Ed?' He is concentrating on collecting the mugs, not looking at me, but I sense from the smile about his lips that he's expecting to find my reply entertaining.

'Marie said if they told me too much I might go home.' He laughs uproariously which is irritating; it wasn't as amusing as all that.

'Ed's a lovely guy. A real pussy cat. Assuming you like lions and cheetahs and things that maul you if you stand too close.' He laughs at his own joke which saves me having to. 'He's the kind of guy, whatever you do is wrong. If you work fast he says you don't pay enough attention to detail. If you double check everything he says you take too long. The best solution is to accept in advance that he'll find fault with whatever you do, then you won't be disappointed. Oh, and one other piece of advice.'

'What?'

'Get yourself some earplugs. When he starts shouting he can do your eardrums permanent damage.'

'He just sounds like a bully,' I say, not about to be intimidated by tales of the man's immaturity and bad-temper.

'I'm sure he'll like you,' says Marie sympathetically.

'He'd better,' says Colin, balancing the tray in one hand and opening the door with the other, 'the agency is running out of people to send us.'

Chapter 2

———— ◆ ————

Sometimes I think I hate Sam. He rings twice or more a week and his calls invariably unsettle me, make me feel dissatisfied with my life. His regular Saturday calls are particularly poignant. On other evenings, by the time I've eaten, washed up, prepared Joe's lunch box for the following day and got his clothes out, I'm exhausted. It's as much as I can do to stay awake reading his bedtime story. Once he's in bed, the most energetic thing I do is to keep my eyes open.

But on Saturday, waiting for Sam's phone call, the evening seems so long. Joe and I eat earlier, and even though I let him stay up later to watch TV or to play Sorry! or some other interminable board game, by the time he's settled it's still only about half-past eight. Sam always rings before Joe goes to bed, which ought to brighten the weekend but just points up how lonely I am the rest of the time. I spend the day looking forward to talking to him, and the night wishing I'd said something more interesting. Sometimes I think about getting a sitter and going out just to worry him. So that he'll put the phone down wondering where I'm going and who with, the same as I always do with him.

Not that I don't trust him. No, it's all the women he might meet that I don't trust. Sometimes I ask him if he has other women when he's away. 'What do you take me for?' he says, all injured innocence. 'Of course I do!'

It would do him good if I turned out to be not so loyal and reliable as he thought. That would pull him up a bit. I have a fantasy about the area manager of the agency, Corinne's boss. I met him once and he fixed me with a gaze that practically had me welded to the floor and told me what unusual coloured eyes I had. Actually *nobody* has eyes of such a brilliant green, they were contact lenses, I'd have thought it was obvious – but it was sweet of him to say so, and even sweeter of him to invite me to stay while they opened some wine he'd brought in for Corinne's birthday. When their longest-serving temp, Linda came in, with her varicose veins and her roots growing out, wearing a viscose dress she'd bought in Littlewoods – and he enthused over how nice she was looking – well, I realized I'd been taken in. But it didn't entirely erase his appeal and since then he's the one who has starred, quite frequently, in my daydreams.

With Sam being away so much, it's my fantasies which keep me company on long winter evenings or, more often still, on hot summer ones. My latest one is that the area manager, now a one-woman man, comes to visit me at the villa in Hollywood that belonged to Don Johnson in a film I saw, and he (the area manager, not Don Johnson. Though actually sometimes it *is* Don Johnson) discovers me dozing at the poolside in the hot sun, is overcome with desire and wakens me by the touch of his lips on my tanned toes. Looping his thumbs under the waistband of my bikini pants, he draws them down and we make love sweetly and gently under the hot sun, but later when I have to tell him

I love someone else, he gets angry and makes violent love to me on the hard tiles at the poolside and we roll into the pool, still making love and swim together like fishes. When he realizes what he has done, he cries and I comfort him and discover that it is he whom I love after all . . . Sometimes we're in a gothic castle, imprisoned, I forget why, but obliged to make love hourly for the entertainment of the guards, or on the deck of a ship cruising to the Caribbean for no one's entertainment but our own.

Sam would like me to tell him my fantasies but I don't think he envisages them involving someone else, certainly no one as pedestrian as my area manager who, in any case, is currently dating Corinne.

I seem to have a full life but not a fun one. I'm part of that new generation of working women: busy but bored. Underpaid and oversexed. Even if I wanted to play around, who would I do it with? I don't know anyone but Sam who can make my stomach flip over the way he does. In fact, I don't know anyone, period. When you're in regular work there may be potential for a fling among the filing cabinets, copulation on the photocopier, not to mention a quick fax, but as a temp you're in and out too fast (as it were). And there's a distinct lack of male company down at the school gates. The few dads you see look as embarrassed at being there as if they've wandered into the ladies' by mistake.

Besides, as Tania is always so quick to point out, who could be bothered with someone new? Learning how to kiss them, finding out what they wanted you to do, showing them what you wanted done? (Actually, in the gothic castle, showing the area manager what I want done isn't tedious at all.) Tania hasn't had sex for five years, well not with another person anyway, and that's how she likes it. There's a lot to be said for DIY sex, she says. You don't have to dress up for it, you get your orgasms when you want them and whatever happens you still get to keep the house and the kids.

'Hi Gem, what's happening?'

This is how he always greets me on the phone. He doesn't usually ring on a Monday but I guess he's wondering how I got on at the new company.

'Not much. What about you?' I always say that too.

'Is Joe OK?'

I tell him that Joe has a story up on the classroom wall, that Mrs McBride says his handwriting is improving and that Joe has a girlfriend called Melanie. Then Joe comes to the phone and tells him all that over again, plus what we had for dinner and what he's watching on TV right this minute. Then I come back on and tell him about the man I'll be working for who, on the evidence, sounds like he has a face like someone trod on it, or equally, like something you trod in and Sam says this sounds like a good job and I should go for it. I don't think he's listening. Then he says, 'Look, I can't talk for long, someone's waiting for the phone.' He quite often says that too but maybe it's a busy place. On the other hand, why can't he call from places which are less busy?

To get back at him, I say, talking fast, that I wasn't going to tell him this but this man I'm working for, who is actually extraordinarily charming, has had sex in the stationery cupboard with all the secretaries and I think I may be next.

'Yeah, right,' says Sam, laughing, but it may be at something someone behind him said rather than me. 'As long as you're having fun.' It's very noisy where he is, it sounds like a bar.

'So you don't mind if I have sex in the stationery cupboard?'

'As long as it's on the firm's time and not your own. Sorry, babe. Gotta go.'

'Love you, Sam.'

'Yeah. Ring you next week.'

I shouldn't have said that, he hates me saying I love him, especially if he thinks I've said it to push him into saying it. Actually, he does say it sometimes, the times it matters most, when you're making love. Tania says that men will say anything when they're having sex, but I don't agree with that. They might say anything beforehand, but once they're pumping away why would they say something they didn't mean? Sam is just shy of expressing himself emotionally, it doesn't mean he doesn't feel anything.

Thursday morning, my third day, and I'm just taking my jacket off when Brindle Sylvia, the woman I met on my first day and who looks like a Scottie dog, pops her head in. She's an accounts clerk but with pretensions, says Diane (who would know). Her glasses are slung round her neck on a chain and bob against the bosom of her acrylic polo neck as she leans forward.

'Anyone want some Avon?' She holds up a catalogue. 'There's some good offers.' Then she notices me.

'So this is where you are, I did wonder. How are you liking it?' I tell her the job is marginally better than being poked with a stick.

'Poked with a—? Oh saucy!' She winks at me and laughs, imagining innuendo where none existed. She tells the others of our previous meeting as though being first to greet me has given us a special bond.

'What do you think of Mr Murray?'

'I haven't met him yet.'

'That explains why you're still here then!' She laughs, so I laugh.

'You think you'll stay then?'

'If he'll have me.'

'Oh! She's a one, isn't she?' She looks around to share the joke but the others keep their eyes studiedly on their work which puts the onus on me. I smile wanly, trying to convey friendliness while dissociating myself from the perceived witticisms.

'It's very nice here, I've been here almost ten years.' She opens the brochure and points out an item of particular interest to Marie. 'My boss is ever so nice. There's one of them who's a bit of a pet noire, but most of them are very nice.'

'A pet—?'

'It's French. Don't you know French?'

'Not that bit of it, no.'

She hovers but with no one having anything to add to her description of this happy office, she turns her attention to Marie and her special offers. Suddenly she remembers something.

'Oh, you'll never guess, I saw Jed Campion downstairs.' To my surprise, I see Diane stiffen, her fingers halt their rapid motion over the keys as though caught in a photograph. I haven't heard of Jed Campion, but the atmosphere of the room has altered with his name. Marie turns to me to explain, 'He runs the Hong Kong office. He's horrible.' She says this looking sideways at Diane.

Diane starts typing again. 'I wonder what he wants,' she says, turning over the page she is copying from.

'Whatever it is, it's no skin off my back,' says Sylvia,

inspecting a fingernail and beginning to chew at the edge of it.

'No,' says Marie. 'You scratch my nose, I'll scratch yours.'

Marie and I start to laugh. Then Diane asks casually — except that she doesn't sound casual but like an actress with her first talking part who has been rehearsing this line over and over — 'I wonder if it's something to do with Personnel.' Her neck is unaccountably turning red. 'I think I'll just adjourn to the lavatory.' She gets up while Sylvia tries to interest Marie in some gift-wrapped bubble bath, perfect for Christmas.

The first time I ever saw Sam was at a local club. He was onstage, long hair hiding his face, head bent over his Fender Stratocaster.

'Get a load of him,' said my friend, and I thought I'd like to get as much as I could handle. She wasn't talking about the guitarist though, but the blond-haired singer and I couldn't imagine what she thought was attractive about his straggly hair and face pink with acne scars. It was academic in any case, all the band had girls with them, we saw them together in the bar later but as they left, Sam looked straight at me. He doesn't remember that but I do. I knew it meant something.

When I started at social services two years later, there he was, working in the same office block. Social Services had the ground floor, and I used to see him in the corridor or on his way in or out of the building. He smiled or nodded, even though we had never met, unlike the others who kept their eyes on the floor so as not to speak, including some of the social workers I *had* met.

We got together in the same month he signed his first

contract to work abroad. It was January and I was last to leave the office. My pool car looked OK apart from the rust but I'd been warned it was temperamental. When it wouldn't start I thought it was just cold. I turned the key, turned it again, until even its initial faint spark had faded and there was nothing at all but a dull clunk. I lifted the bonnet, knowing that that's what you should do but having no idea what to do with all the stuff under it, and watched as flakes of snow began to land upon the engine. I didn't know whether to phone a garage, get a taxi, or just panic. The car park was empty but for one car and a push bike.

'Got a problem?' *Gad a prablem?* I hadn't heard him approach and now I was also surprised by the American accent. A shiver ran down my back at the sound of his voice but maybe that was just the snow on my neck. Snowflakes were forming a light covering on his dark hair. He turned up the collar of his leather jacket.

'It won't start,' I said, feeling foolish. The independent woman driven into submission by a malfunction of the mechanical.

He leaned across me and tugged on some wires.

'Start her up.'

'She won't start.'

'I mean turn the ignition.'

I got in and turned the key. Clunk. He leaned further into the bonnet, tucking his hair behind one ear, and humming a tune to himself.

'Shall I try the ignition again?'

'Not yet.'

I started out of the car to see what he was doing and because I felt so feeble and useless just sitting there, but as I did so he called, 'OK, try it now.'

I don't know exactly what he did, probably just thawed the points with his smile, anyway it started straight away. He came over and opened the driver's door before I could get out.

'Seems like a loose connection. Should be OK but don't turn her off just in case.'

'I'm so incredibly grateful. I didn't know what I was going to do.'

'No problem.' His jaws worked mechanically on some gum while a slow smile formed.

'I don't know how to thank you.'

'You've thanked me.' He slammed my door shut and was wandering off. I wound down the window as fast as I could, which was not very, the handle was old and stiff. I took a breath in. I hadn't done this before.

'Let me buy you a drink.'

He was already some yards away but he paused and half turned.

'What?'

'Let me buy you a drink. To thank you.' Suddenly I remembered that my hair needed washing and my leggings were the ones that had gone baggy in the seat. 'Tomorrow maybe? Lunchtime or after work?' It felt like a long speech but I was scared to reach the point where I might have to hear myself turned down.

'OK,' he said slowly, walking back to his car. 'Sounds like an offer I can't refuse. Say five-thirty tomorrow?'

He offered me his hand through the open window – then withdrew it again when he noticed black engine grease on his fingers.

'I'm Sam.'

'Gemma.'

'Tomorrow then. I'll wait for you by the entrance.' He

stepped back from the car then and I reversed out and accelerated away. When I stopped at the exit to turn out, I could see him in the rear-view mirror, watching me.

I was late for work the next day. I couldn't find anything to wear which was sufficiently casual for work that would at the same time speak sexuality and allure. I wanted to be subtly understated without being unfeminine. My usual jeans and sweatshirt tended to the androgynous but the less feminine I looked, the stronger I felt in verbal fisticuffs with our more intransigent clients. But I wanted to look more girlie for this paragon of machismo. In the end the decision was made for me. At the last minute I remembered that I was accompanying my boss to court this morning. Jason, one of our younger clients and Mrs Mount's favourite, was up for taking and driving away.

Thus it was that on my first date with the sexiest man I'd ever met, he was dressed in jeans and leather, while I looked like I'd been for an interview at a merchant bank.

He was already at the front entrance when I arrived, and I felt his eyes flicker over me in slight surprise.

'I know, I know,' I said, 'ignore the suit. I've been to court today.'

'What was it — speeding?'

'Juvenile court.'

'Jesus. How old are you then?' I smiled at his joke and he went on, 'I just wondered. Seeing the way you roared off last night in that clapped out old Metro.'

'I'm a very careful driver actually.'

'So am I. Careful there's no police around when I'm speeding.'

We walked to the centre of town to a pub he particularly liked; I was aware of his closeness all the time, his greater height, the leathery smell of his jacket as he moved. When, as we crossed the road, his arm brushed against mine, sparks of pleasure shot through me.

Inside the pub, surrounded by a few solicitors and bank clerks amongst the bedenimed crush, I felt less conspicuous in my suit though at the same time even more concerned that I looked like a solicitor or bank clerk. I fought my way to the bar, ignoring Sam's offer to get the drinks, but as we stood in the throng behind a group of builders and a group of insurance salesmen (well, they could have been) who had been served but just wouldn't move away, it was Sam's proffered fiver which caught the eye of the barmaid. Actually, it was probably Sam himself. I saw her momentary pause as he swept his hair from his face and she looked up at him. He carried our drinks away from the hubbub and when a table fell vacant in a corner next to the log fire he dived towards it, beating another couple by several seconds. He sat down, kicking the chair opposite out from the table for me, his long legs stretched in front of him. Marlon Brando: On the Water Front. Sex appeal with attitude.

'So, Gemma. Do you always ask guys out or am I the first?' Sex appeal with attitude and a forthrightness I hadn't reckoned on.

'No, I don't often ask them. I don't usually have to.' He smiled into his beer at that. 'But if I feel like getting to know someone I say so. I've never been one for sitting at home waiting for the telephone to ring.' If you'd seen how straight a face I kept, you'd have been proud of me. I love meeting new people. You can make up a whole new personality for yourself. 'The fact is, I hate my job and the people I work with. But you seemed quite normal; I thought I'd invest half an hour in finding

out what you're like.' To hear me, you'd think I was
in control here.

'Well, thanks. But wouldn't a better idea be just to leave
your job?'

This wasn't the right response. He should have said he'd
seen me lots of times and been waiting for an opportunity
to speak; his slight surprise at my words made me think
he hadn't noticed me before at all.

'I've only been there six months. It seems defeatist.'

'Six months? If I don't like a job after six minutes I get
the hell out. What is it — worried about your pension?'

Now he was laughing at me. I asked him where he
came from — he was born in America to an English
mother returning to England after his father died when
he was fourteen — and then about his job. He talked about
engineering and about the band he was in, which was only
semi-pro as it turned out, but I didn't mention that I'd ever
seen him play.

He had nearly finished his pint and I knocked back my
lager to catch him up. This wasn't going as well as I'd
hoped but it can be sticky at the beginning, when you're
both feeling your way. Things might look up once we'd
had another drink or two.

'Same again?' I stood up.

'No, I can't, sorry. I have to be out by seven.'

I blinked my surprise. I'd thought we might go on to a
wine bar or for a pizza; now I resented the warm feeling
that had been creeping up my thighs.

I made some sounds suggesting that I was busy too which
sounded unconvincing even to me. Suddenly I was furious
with myself. He didn't fancy me; he'd come along only
because of the novelty of being asked. I'd claimed something
which for him was actually true: he'd calculated that he

could invest half an hour in finding out what I was like. Well, he had and my time was up.

I dragged on my jacket without looking at him, wondering how I was going to avoid bumping into him back at the office. He wasn't even as attractive as I'd thought. He had a red spot on his neck and there were ink stains on his fingers.

I'd forgotten that our cars were parked back at the office. I walked back looking down at my stupid low-heeled court shoes while he talked on about the band and his future hopes for them which I was sure would come to nothing, at least I hoped they would. We got to my car and I turned my back on him to unlock my door.

'Well, thanks for coming,' I said. 'We'll have to do it again sometime.' This was the brush off plenty of boys had given me in their time, I hoped he'd recognize it for what it was. And I wanted to be sure and get it in before he could.

I pulled on the car door to close it but he was restraining it.

'I was wondering . . .' he began. Yes, so was I, wondering how soon I could get away and take refuge in Coronation Street. '. . . have you seen the new Ford Coppola?'

I didn't know if I had or I hadn't. Ford Coppola could have been a film star, a make of car or the the album cover of some obscure one-hit wonder rock band.

'No,' I said, and pulled on the car door again. And now he leant in to the car, bending down slightly towards me, as he spoke.

'It's at the Odeon at the moment. We could go tomorrow.'

I looked at him and I thought: I've had a horrible time, he hasn't even pretended to fancy me, on top of which he's laughed at me. Why is he asking me out? But then I met his eyes, heavy now in the shadows, and I saw he was waiting, as I had waited the day before, to see whether he would be rejected; if he had said the wrong things, put me off, come across differently from how he had intended. Vulnerability lay hidden behind that macho façade, and that, mixed with his musky warm man smell, was a heady combination.

And if that wasn't argument enough, there were his jeans stretched tight over his thighs and crotch, right at my eye level.

I sought about for a casual, laid-back reply, something smart and witty that would also indicate I was just kidding about some of those things I said earlier.

'Sounds like fun,' I said.

Look, I did my best.

Tania tells me that the trouble is that my relationship with Sam is based too heavily on sex, but what better basis could there be? Actually I think she's probably wrong, but we never stop doing it for long enough to test the theory.

When we first met, we always seemed to make love standing up; we couldn't wait long enough to get anywhere to be horizontal. As it happened though, Sam couldn't make the film in the end and it was a few weeks before we spent any time alone together. Sam's band got two gigs and I went with them to see him play. Watching Sam on stage was like being shown your Christmas present but told you can't open it until later.

When we finally got around to going to the cinema the Ford Coppola had finished but by then what was showing was irrelevant, we just wanted a place that was dark and private seeing as we were both living at home. The adverts came on at the start of the programme and Sam put his arm round me and we kissed. I was wearing a woollen scoop-necked sweater with tiny buttons down the front. He undid every one of them.

When we got home I was surprised and delighted to find a message from my mother saying she was babysitting for our neighbour who had just gone into labour and that she would probably be sleeping there.

There should have been no hurry but somehow the unexpected opportunity increased the urgency. Sam kicked the door shut and leant against it, holding his arms out for me.

'Don't you want to go upstairs?'

'Everything I need is right here.' His voice was husky and low and he ran his fingers up my inner thigh in case his words had been too subtle for me.

He pulled my tights and pants down, while I reached forward to stroke the bulge in his jeans, unzipping them slowly. I'd discovered already he didn't wear underwear, now his penis sprang at me like a tiger that's seen its prey.

I started to drag his jeans down, but he was impatient and stopped me when they reached his hips, pulling me to him. I wanted to get his clothes off him and yanked on his shirt buttons to feel his chest but he was lifting me up, curling my legs round his waist. I scrabbled to get my sweater off, to reach the hook of my bra while he held me hard against him. When he slid me on to him, the fit was as tight as a finger to a glove and I came so hard my legs kicked out knocking the telephone table against the wall and scuffing the wallpaper. My mother noticed it when she was dusting two days later; I said I'd tripped coming down the stairs.

Later, lying on my bed and tracing the line of faint hair

that points downward from his navel like an arrow, I asked Sam how many girls he had had.

'A few,' he said, vaguely. Then he laid the flat of his hand against my face. 'But you're the first one I've made love to.'

The first time had been too quick, too urgent, to satisfy what is usually implied by the term. But the second time hadn't. Thinking of the way he clung to me afterwards, whispering against me as we lay on my bed, eyes closed, I knew it was true.

We moved in together just months later and when he comes home after a stint abroad we still make love standing up the first time. It's the equivalent of 'our tune'. Call us sentimental.

The phone on my desk rings, making me jump.

'Are you the new temp?'

'I'm Mr Murray's temporary secretary, yes.'

'I'll decide whether you're my secretary or not. You can type can you?' His voice is deep and gruff, overlaid with more than a hint of impatience.

'Of course I can.'

'And you can do more on the computer than just plug it in?' Well, let's not go mad here, I don't want to make any claims I won't be able to substantiate. But he takes my silence for acquiesence, and goes on, 'Because I've been made a fool of before with that agency – I'm not paying peanuts and I'm sick of being sent monkeys. If you're no better than your predecessors I'll be sending you straight back to the zoo with the rest of them.' There's nothing like a warm welcome – and this was nothing like a warm welcome. I've had friendlier conversations with people who have dialled the wrong number. 'I'm faxing through some notes for a report. I want it typed up and on my desk for when I get back—'

'Which will be when?'

'When you're least expecting me. I want it done properly – no typing errors, no spelling mistakes and no nonsense about not being able to read my writing. I take it Piers is out?'

It takes me a moment to realize we've moved on to a new subject. 'Yes.'

'Well, get hold of him and tell him to ring me at four – not five to, not five past – and inform Colin that if he can't get those outstanding payments in by the end of the month I'll find someone who can. Have you got all that?'

'I think so.'

'"Think" isn't good enough. Have you got it?'

'Yes.'

'I hope so. Goodbye.'

'Goodbye. Have a nice day.' I expect to hear the click of the phone being put down. It doesn't happen and now there's a pause before he speaks.

'What?'

'I said, "Have a nice day."' I try sounding less sarcastic this time.

'Don't get smart with me young lady or you'll be back in the dole queue quicker than you can say you're sorry.'

'I'm sorry.'

He snorts and hangs up.

'Who was that?' says Diane, who has been watching me with the anticipation of a Roman watching a Christian about to be mauled by a lion.

'I'll give you a clue,' I say, making an effort to laugh it off and sounding calmer than I feel. 'I don't think it was Prince Charming.'

Chapter 3

— ✦ —

The next day begins with another set of invoices but I misunderstand what Marie tells me, deleting all the wrong bits and making too few copies, but she is patient with me, helping conceal my errors from Diane. Odd how a job can be undemanding and yet defeat you with minor and unforeseen obstacles. Still, if I'm unfulfilled I just have to remember my time at Social Services to feel better.

I'd wanted to be a social worker since I was at school and Sandra, a girl in my class, got one after she tried to burn down the school. Her social worker visited the school once to take her to see her father who was in hospital, or prison, I forget which; she seemed a powerful and influential figure, the teachers were as in awe of her as we were. But by the time I joined the profession all that had changed. On my first day at Social Services there was a bomb scare, a hoax laid by a dissatisfied client, and that set the tone. Not only did no one treat us with awe and respect, but we were always doing stuff for people who didn't want it done, or they did want it done but not the way we tried to do it. My team leader was Mrs Mount, appropriately called since she was the size of a small mountain or, at the very least, as Dr Johnson put it, a considerable protuberance. She always sat with her legs apart, her thighs being too fat for them to meet, so you could see the tops of her stockings which weren't large enough to roll up much above her knees. She ate Mars bars and shortbread fingers with her tea and constantly explained that she wasn't fat, just big boned, how diets never worked for her, and her size wasn't for what she ate. I discovered quickly that I was in the wrong job and blamed Mrs Mount for my unhappiness though she was just a focus for it, conveniently placed for me to mumble 'fat cow' at when things weren't going well, which was mostly always. I was the wrong personality type, too subjective, too inclined to see the client's point of view, unwilling to concede that my seniors' viewpoint might be superior to my own. As a result I disagreed with most of the decisions that got made and struggled to justify them to my clients. The pathetic hope that Mrs Mount and her superiors might ultimately be right wasn't strong enough to prevent my lying awake most nights worrying about them. There was the case conference at which we discussed a ten year old who kept running away from his children's home to stand outside the council house where he had used to live. Mrs Mount was mystified by this, as though it wasn't perfectly natural for anyone who, until the deaths of his parents, had lived a perfectly natural and unremarkable life along with his four siblings, to want to go back and remember how it used to be. The five children were scattered at various children's homes around the town, but the main solution, Mrs Mount assured me, wasn't to get the kids back together, but to watch the boy more closely so that he didn't have the opportunity to run away. To get on in social work, I used to think, you need to leave your common sense in the car park.

Mrs Mount's favourite foster mother was Jeanie Farmer.

My personal opinion was that someone who washed as rarely as she did had no business caring for our most vulnerable charges, but her lack of hygiene was in her favour since it was vital, I was told, that we didn't foist on to the foster children our own middle-class values. Jeanie Farmer was held up as a model of what we should be looking for in a foster parent, so it must have been very embarrassing for Mrs Mount when, five years later *Mr* Farmer was in court on three separate charges of sexual abuse. If I've one regret about leaving social work, it's that I wasn't in the office when this piece of news broke.

I gave in my notice after just six months but I didn't actually leave for another two years. Mrs Mount said I couldn't possibly give up so soon, think of the other graduates of whom I had deprived a place on their training scheme, and that I just had to learn to become more objective – which was rich coming from the woman who had a soft spot big enough to fill the Old Bailey for some of our juveniles. When I went with her to visit Jason who was being held by the police for driving a stolen car the wrong way down a motorway, Mrs Mount said to him, shaking her head, 'Jason, Jason, what will we do with you?' just as though he'd been caught watching TV past his bedtime. When he called into our office, she would give him money from her purse as though he was a visiting nephew.

But it's due to Mrs Mount that I'm doing what I am now. I used to come from meetings with my seniors and look at Joyce, our team secretary with envy. She never had work to take home, was never on call at weekends, nor did her job, as far as I know, involve her getting punched by an irate father who was being denied knowledge of his child's whereabouts and in an office at the end of the corridor where no one could hear her.

'Isn't it a bit retrograde?' Sam asked when, a few years later with Joe starting at playschool, I first told him I was thinking of secretarial work. But my career didn't seem important. I just wanted to be free to travel with Sam if the situation should arise. I knew several guys who had gone abroad and taken their families with them — so I didn't want to get myself embroiled in some lengthy training course or employment contract that might form any kind of obstacle. I used to think of Joyce who just used to type, answer the phone and drink coffee and had, as far as I could see, no particular commitments or responsibilities to prevent her leaving at a moment's notice. That, it seemed, was the job for me.

Of course, I didn't mention that to Sam, instead dwelling on the incidental advantages of learning computer and keyboard skills and being able to organize my working hours around Joe.

'It's like driving. Sometimes you have to shift down a gear before you can get up speed to get ahead,' I said, using the sort of bullshit that Sam would have used on me in similar circumstances.

'So tell me,' I say to Colin, as I hand him the completed pile of invoices, 'why has everyone got such a dislike for Ed?'

Colin looks surprised. 'You don't dislike Ed, do you Marie?'

'Dislike?' Marie looks up from her screen and contemplates the postcard of Spain on the noticeboard. 'No, course not. Now if you're talking hate . . .' Colin laughs and Suzanne looks up like a mouse sniffing the air, which is about as much joining in as she seems to do.

'Ed's difficult,' says Colin. 'Bad tempered. But he'll be all right with you. He likes women.'

'Oh? And what were the other temps then? Hermaphrodites?' He smiles, leaning towards me to point out an error on an invoice I've missed, his aftershave altering the aroma of my coffee.

'I shouldn't be teasing you, I've only been here a few months myself, don't let me prejudice you against him. Some people like Ed.'

'You mean like his wife and his mother?'

'Yeah, right. But the Managing Director must like him, he took him on.'

'So no one else does?'

'I'll give you one piece of advice. Stand up to him. Don't let him see where you're vulnerable.' It shakes me a little to hear him say 'vulnerable' because he echoes the word that is in my mind as I look at him. Suddenly he looks like a kitten who isn't sure how you're going to treat it. He pauses and we look at each other, thinking our separate thoughts about the mysterious Ed. His expression remains the same but something alters about his brow.

Then he points to the fresh pile of invoices he brought with him. 'Can you do them in the next half hour do you think?' He catches my eye as he turns away and adds with a smile, 'Please?'

Marie reckons the reason Ed sacked the last temp was because she had grey hair and wore glasses, and he prefers a younger model. I can see she means to encourage me with this information, seeing as my hair is demonstrably not grey (it's mid brown with auburn highlights – that's what it said on the box anyway) but I resent the idea of being judged according to my powers of attraction, besides which I'm never quite sure how good they are. (Sam is no good

45

for boosting my morale either. If I ask him if my stomach sticks out he says it's no worse than anyone else's.)

'I don't think that's entirely fair,' says Diane, pausing in the collation of some papers. 'He demands very high standards and he's entitled to, it isn't cheap to hire a temp.' I have the impression she expects me to say something but I let it go and she continues, 'But it's true that he's a bit of a womaniser.'

'He likes them with legs up to their bum,' adds Marie helpfully.

'Well, that is the usual arrangement,' I say, 'but I thought a man had to like women to be a womaniser. From what I hear, he's horrible to everyone.'

'Whatever sex they are,' offers Suzanne, returning hurriedly to her work when she finds us looking at her.

'You're confusing a womaniser with a charmer,' explains Diane. 'He's sadly lacking in the charm stakes, but when he sees a girl he likes he doesn't hesitate. You should see him when reps call in. Remember that one last week, Marie? About twenty, all short skirts and earrings, you know the type. I was down in reception at the time which is how I saw it all. You should have seen him – helping her off with her coat, pulling a chair out for her. Saw her out to the door too, which is when I heard him ask her to go for a drink. She told him where to get off, fortunately, but he's always the same. The only reason we don't usually see it is because he doesn't fancy any of us.'

As she says this, I sense she has taken his lack of interest as a personal slight. Diane is the type of woman who wants all men to fancy her, whatever she thinks of them.

'You'll be all right,' says Marie to me. She seems to alternate between offering encouragement and predicting disaster. Well, I suppose if my legs aren't long enough I could always slay Ed with my superbly honed skills and sparkling personality.

Oh God, please don't let me have to rely on that.

Ed Murray is still in the Midlands somewhere, not expected back for a few more days and it would suit me if he never came back. I like it here. I envy the way Diane leaves a cardigan draped territorially across the back of her chair, and the easy banter which exists between the secretaries and the men who bring their typing to us. In addition to working for Colin, I work for Piers, a salesman. He's tall and thin, and he makes me laugh (not particularly for those reasons). I like the girls too; Marie is fun and even Diane may be loosening up a little. As for Suzanne, well, she's good with a calculator.

They're not like the women I knew at Social Services or even at university: earnest and ambitious, always looking for ulterior motives, worrying if they haven't done the right thing. Unlike those women, Marie and Suzanne rarely find themselves troubled by the constraints of political correctness. They live for today and don't dwell on the repercussions of what this might mean for tomorrow. In fact, they know there's not much they can do about tomorrow because their futures are planned (as their regular consulting of the horoscope charts in *Bella* and *Chat* confirms to them). They don't worry about yesterday either: what's done is done. Suzanne is regarded as the intellectual among them because she buys a daily paper (the fact it's the *Mirror* doesn't influence their judgement; they don't make distinctions of this sort and in any case would be astonished to find anyone of their acquaintance reading a broadsheet, except for the likes of public school boys like Piers and even then they assume they do it as a form of posing). Interestingly, being the intellectual does not, in their eyes, make Suzanne their superior. Intellectualism is just an aspect of personality which affects your tastes: watching 'Panorama' rather than 'Neighbours' is no different, in their eyes, from preferring aerobics to weight-training. The true superior, of course, is Diane, but this isn't only because she is paid more and is older than us, it's also because she wears a suit, can do shorthand and perhaps most importantly, because she knows intuitively that she is better than the rest of us and they (we, actually) take her at her own valuation.

One of the worst things about temping is that you're excluded from the in-jokes. People take a pride in the mysteries and intrigue they've created, and to explain it is to diminish it, besides which it isn't an in-joke once you let outsiders in on it. But my presence of four days evidently qualifies me for admission to the inner sanctum.

'What do you think of Diane?' asks Marie. I know this is leading to something, probably related to Diane's blushing neck of yesterday, and I plan my reply with care.

'She's all right,' I say, treading carefully.

'She had an affair with Jed Campion.' I look as stunned as I can manage considering that Diane's constant blushing at the mention of him has made this pretty obvious.

'I thought he worked in Hong Kong?'

'Not then. He used to be here. Before Ed Murray came, David Renfrew was sales manager and before him it was Jed. She was a temp,' says Marie pointedly. 'His secretary was on maternity leave, and it just happened. He took her on business trips, and all sorts.'

'Does Ed have to go away on business?' It occurs to me that I could end up staying in hotels just like Sam.

Full English breakfasts and clean towels would be a perk worth having.

Marie shrugs her indifference, not wanting to be distracted from the main point of the story. 'Then Jed finished it and tried to chuck her out but she wouldn't leave. We'd never even met her until she came bursting in here with her typewriter under her arm.'

'What?'

'Jed had bought her this state of the art electronic typewriter because she didn't like the word processor, probably couldn't work it actually. Anyway, she considered it was hers so she heaved it down here with her when she walked out. They said there wasn't another vacancy for her but she said she'd be our supervisor and they couldn't get rid of her. Then Jed got a post overseas and a director's secretary's job came up and they gave her that. We're not supposed to know.'

'How did you find out then?'

'The MD's secretary told everyone. Well, she used to fancy Jed herself so she was glad when it all went wrong for Diane. But it was Diane's own fault. Everyone knew what a rat he was, half the staff already thought his last secretary's baby was his.'

'It's got the same amount of hair,' says Suzanne unexpectedly.

'And the worst of it was,' says Marie, getting animated and twisting her hair round her finger, 'Jed had put her on a really inflated salary and she couldn't have got that anywhere else, so she couldn't leave even if she wanted to. What would she have told her husband? And the company couldn't get rid of her because she hadn't done anything wrong.'

Now I was wearing my stunned expression for real. If

I'd just discovered Diane dealt cocaine from her clutch bag I could not have been more surprised, or only marginally. I'd looked at Diane and seen a snob in a suit and all the time there was a heart of passion beating beneath those power shoulders.

'Is he very attractive, this Jed Campion?' I ask. Diane is, if you find that severe arty look appealing. I don't like to think of her throwing herself away on someone who's nothing but paunch and profit-and-loss accounts.

'He's fifty with a beer gut,' says Marie.

'But he must have something.'

'Oh, he has. A Mercedes and a private income.' Thinking of Diane, I can see the appeal.

It's Friday and Piers is having a day in the office to catch up on his correspondence.

'Gemma, can you do shorthand?'

'No.'

'Ah.' I continue to type, gripping the phone between my shoulder and chin just the way you're not supposed to, while Piers who is on the other end gathers his thoughts. This could take some time.

'I've drafted out a few letters but the handwriting's a bit ropey,' he says at length. 'Do you want to pop down here and I'll read them out to you?'

Being a secretary is no job for a feminist, not if her boss is a man, anyway. At every opportunity he will get you running round after him, getting him this, fetching him that. I've already seen one of the men send Marie out for his cigarettes. To be fair this 'pop' here, 'pop' there thing isn't really a chauvinistic element with Piers, he's just lazy. If there's no woman around to run about for him he gets Colin to do it.

'OK, I'll come up if you'd prefer. It's just that Colin's making some coffee so I thought you might like a change of scene from that office of yours. But if that's not convenient—'

The boys' office is downstairs. It only takes a couple of minutes to get there but it means passing ten or so other offices, all with their doors open and their secrets on show, and it's as fascinating as looking in your neighbours' windows when their curtains aren't closed at night. A grey-haired man in a sports jacket is on the telephone, head on hands, looking intense and pressured; a yuppie type is leaning back expansively as though he owns the world but will lease it to you if the price is right; admin assistants are whispering by filing cabinets; Brindle Sylvia is getting her coat on because she is only part-time and leaves at three. She is deep in conversation with the woman I saw her with on my first day who is thoughtfully chewing on the arms of her glasses.

As I pass she's saying, 'It's always been a hobby of mine, history. There's nothing I don't know about Norman the Conqueror.'

The office which Colin and Piers share is next door to that of the still absent Ed. It's what an estate agent would call cosy and everyone else calls cramped. There are two desks in it, two filing cabinets and a table on and under which are piles of boxes with samples spilling out of them. Colin is very houseproud and likes to keep the place neat; Piers prefers disorder and squalor. Piers seems to be winning.

'Here, I'll get another chair.' Colin pulls his chair out from behind the desk for me and brings in another from the corridor. Then he pours coffee for us all while Piers rears up in his chair and flicks through the papers on his desk before him. He hands one of them to me.

'See if you can read it.' There are a few arrows and passages to be inserted but otherwise it's perfectly clear.

'Your writing is better than most people's, I don't know what you're worrying about.'

'I know,' he says, 'and I wasn't worrying. I just couldn't be bothered to walk up all those stairs.' He's watching for my response but he's wheeling his chauvinism on for the pleasure of seeing me respond to it and I can't be bothered. Seeing this he switches to flattery mode instead. 'I knew you wouldn't mind, and you are younger than I am.'

I'm not, and maybe he knows I'm not, but I can't be bothered to respond to the compliment either.

'Don't let him get round you with his flattery,' says Colin, misreading my languor. 'I did and look where it's got me.'

For some reason, I do look at him, and I feel sorry for what I see. With his sharp suit and neat profile, he's still not quite as sexy or attractive as he ought to be. He's too eager to please, like a puppy that comes bounding up wanting to be stroked. He lacks an edge, the hint of danger that comes with, say Sam, and which can be so provocative and exciting. In fact, maybe that's the problem, he isn't exciting. On the other hand, this has its own charm.

'You do realize you're part of Piers' strategy, the same as I am?' Colin is saying.

'Strategy for what?'

'To get us both to cover his back, whatever he happens to be doing.'

'My dear chap—' Piers is laughing, pleased that he's been seen through. We're being manipulated and the fact we know what he's doing doesn't make us any less vulnerable to it.

'He's plying you with coffee — or rather, getting me to ply you with coffee, so that when he rings in with some cock and bull story about being stuck in traffic on the M4 you'll pass it on to Ed, even though you know he's at home with his feet up drinking white wine and watching daytime TV.'

'I don't drink white wine. And I certainly don't watch daytime TV.'

'Only because you don't get out of the pub early enough.'

'I only said I didn't, I didn't say why.' They're both laughing now, this is evidently an exchange of long standing which re-emerges periodically, like in families.

'One of these days——' We never discover the nature of Colin's mock threat because at that moment the door opens. I have my back to it but I catch the expressions on the others' faces. My first thought is that there has been some sort of disaster. I suppose I'm right really.

'One of these days I'll come back and find some work being done.' The deep voice finishes Colin's sentence and I would take the tone for good-humoured but for Colin's and Piers' aghast expressions. It's a powerful sound, though hushed as though the speaker is reining it in, the voice of a big man, and now I sense an ominous note as he continues, 'You all look very cosy. A nice little ménage à trois you've got here. You should have let me know, I'd have got back earlier and joined in.' I look from Colin to Piers, still hoping one of them will suddenly smile with a rejoinder but there's no change to their countenances. For some reason I suddenly remember the home-made soup I made once which seemed quite safe while it sat simmering and bubbling on the stove but which suddenly boiled over and scalded me as I started to lift the saucepan.

It's alarming to sense this hostile presence behind me, not knowing what it looks like and now I stand and turn, determined not to be intimidated, feeling intimidated. I draw myself up to my full height but my full height is only enough to bring my eyes level with his well-developed pectorals.

He is in his early forties, tall and athletic-looking with muscular shoulders and close-cut curly hair such as you see on Greek stone statues, and with a face about as yielding. He looks as though he does weight-training, or more accurately, as though he once did because though his neck is as thick as a pillar he's thickening around the middle with just the suggestion of a gut overhanging his waistband. Silence would fill the room but there's no space with this man's presence in it. His brows are knitted together threateningly as though he's a bull about to charge; he reminds me of the picture of the minotaur I had in one of my books as a child. It used to terrify me, I kept it in a cupboard with the door shut.

Seeing as no one seems inclined to speak, I take a step towards him and offer my hand. 'I'm your new temp, Gemma Millard. We spoke on the phone.' I raise my eyes to look at him but his are still fixed accusingly on Piers. He takes a slow deep breath and I notice the way his broad chest strains at the buttons of his shirt.

'That was you was it? I hope your typing is better than your telephone manner.' His eyes flick over me but he doesn't find anything of sufficient interest to linger. I wish Diane hadn't described him as a womaniser because it makes his indifference even more offensive. Not only has he failed to notice that my legs come up to my bum but he seems ready to point them in the same direction he sent my predecessors'.

'And what are you doing in here anyway? Lost your way *en route* to the typing pool?'

He doesn't wait for my reply but turns his attention to Colin. 'Baxter, I told you I wanted an update on our sales figures on my desk when I got back.'

'I didn't know you were coming back yet.' Colin's voice is scarcely audible, the whites of his eyes brilliant against his dark skin.

'Well, I am and I want them on my desk in half an hour. And if you've got any sense your resignation will be with them. *You*—' to Piers. 'In my office now. And *you*—' to me, 'out.'

He jerks his thumb over his shoulder like a hitchhiker that no driver in his right mind would ever pick up, and stands waiting for us to jump to it, his eyes fixed at a point on the wall above our heads. Now I'm beneath his notice literally as well as figuratively.

I squeeze past him and as I do so he aims a kick at the chair I was sitting on. 'And clear up this bloody room,' he yells. He strides past me to his own office and goes in slamming the door.

Towards five o'clock, the phone rings. He doesn't announce himself. 'Come down now, would you?' There's an abrupt click of the receiver being replaced. I sit there for a moment breathing antagonism down the phone until I see Suzanne watching me. Marie and Diane are both out. Diane has gone home with a tension headache and Marie is out on an errand, probably buying one of the men a present for his girlfriend.

'Was that him?' Suzanne looks at me with her pale

55

mouse eyes. I nod while I get out my time sheet and fill in the remaining entries. Unfortunately, it's Ed who must sign it so I may as well get him to do it now as we're almost at finishing time. 'Don't worry,' says Suzanne consolingly, 'I don't think he's as bad as everyone says. And he can't sack everyone, can he?' With her vast reserves of tact and delicacy, I wonder if Suzanne has ever considered a career in the diplomatic corps.

I get up, noticing as I do so that I must have rested on the keyboard when I answered the phone because I've typed a line of Fs in the middle of the letter I was copying. When I get back I'll add some 'Offs' to go with them.

Then the phone rings again.

'And bring some biros with you from stationery.' He hangs up and I say, 'Die! Dogbreath,' down the phone. Suzanne's expression of horror is momentarily cheering.

Ed Murray's office door is closed and when I knock he answers 'come'. He doesn't look up as I enter. I hate people who say 'come' instead of 'come in'. It may be correct but it's also pedantic (though quite honestly I'd have hated Ed Murray just as much if he'd opened the door singing 'I Just Called to Say I Love You.') Even more, I hate the people who tell you to do either and then, as now, ignore you. He's in the wrong profession, he should have been a doctor.

'Here are the biros.' I place them on the edge of his desk and wait for his next set of orders, holding my notepad like a shield ready to return any spears he might send hurtling in my direction. After a few moments in which I continue to be ignored, I add, 'You wanted to see me.'

'They're there.' He flicks his pen at a pile of papers and goes on writing without explaining what he's talking about.

'Yes, fine. Now while I'm here would you mind signing

. . .' I proffer my time sheet and he raises his eyes to me slowly and with such effort that you'd think he had weights attached to his eyelids. His eyes are as black as the shadows under them and glitter in the light from his desk lamp.

'What?'

'Would you mind signing my time sheet?'

'Yes, I do mind. Can't you see I'm busy?' But despite his words and his expression which clearly implies I have no right to be taking up space on his carpet tiles, he signs the time sheet anyway, though without reading it and in the wrong place.

He hands the sheet back to me and gestures again to the handwritten notes on his desk. 'Piers will sign them when you've finished. I have to go in a minute.'

'Finished?' I stand there foolishly like Oliver only asking for less.

'When you've typed them up,' he says with a great show of patience. 'There's only half a dozen, won't take you long.'

Speed and accuracy aren't things I've yet learnt to combine but even the fastest typist would have her work cut out getting them done in the ten minutes remaining until finishing time. I'd assumed Ed just wanted me to put them in the typing tray for him, or to give them to someone. If I don't leave on time I'll be late collecting Joe which in turn will make Tania late taking Jack to Beavers, plus there won't be time to take Joe swimming which I've promised him faithfully. If you think this doesn't sound like a major problem then you obviously don't have kids. On the other hand, I've always hated people who won't put in a minute more work than they're contracted to do and I don't want to cross this man if I can help it, I still have next week to get through. I prepare to compromise. Undeserving though he is, I honour Ed Murray with my smile of sweetest reason.

'Look, I'm sorry but I really can't stay late – I have to pick my son up. But if you tell me which couple are the most urgent I'll get them done before I leave. I'll finish the others first thing on Monday.'

He leans back in his chair and for the first time he meets my eyes and he's almost smiling. Relief trickles over me like golden syrup.

'So you're booked for next week?'

'Piers has notified the agency.'

He nods, considering. Then he leans forward on his desk as though he's about to take me into his confidence. 'Piers doesn't have the authority to say how many sugars he wants in his tea without he checks with me.'

But I was in the office when Piers telephoned Ed.

'I thought he had checked—'

'You're paid to type, not think.' The smile has been wiped away as fast as if he'd used a delete key. 'I'm away again next week and Piers is supposed to be out on the road selling – so we won't be needing anyone. And as for Colin, who knows what Colin does? He's sweet-talking the typists and plying them with coffee whenever I see him. I'm sorry, but that's all there is to it.' He says this with the air of someone who is actually rather satisfied with the way things have panned out.

'If you need help with these, ask Diana or that fat girl.' He gets to his feet and offers me his hand to shake. 'Thank you for your help this week – not quite sure what you've been doing but presumably there must have been something.' And now the smile is back, but wider. He has very white teeth, like sun-bleached bones. I ignore the proffered hand and he holds the pile of papers out to me. They make a rustling sound.

I don't have a quick temper, except perhaps where Joe is concerned, but I can feel anger rising, not just for myself but for Diane – not *Diana* – whose name he can't even get right, and Marie who isn't fat and whose name he hasn't bothered to learn at all – and for all the other temps who came before me and whose legs don't reach to their bums either – especially the one he sacked with the grey hair and glasses. One of the few things I learned from Social Services was that the least of us has the same rights as the best of us. I prepare to take a stand on behalf of all the others in my position who haven't had the benefit of my education and Mrs Mount's advice.

I pick up his pen and my time sheet and alter my finishing time from five p.m. to four fifty-five, so that now I'm in my own time, not his. 'I'm sorry,' I say, holding up the time sheet so he can see my alteration, 'but I have to leave now.'

'You'll go when I say you can go,' he says with the air of someone stating the obvious.

'I don't think so.'

And suddenly his face is darkening and there's a livid vein standing out on his forehead. If he has a heart attack does it make it more or less likely that they'll ever book me again? Well, it can hardly make it less likely.

'Where the hell do you think you're going?' he yells at my back, as I set off down the corridor.

'Don't ask me,' I call over my shoulder, 'I'm not paid to think.'

Chapter 4

——— ———

One of the great joys of working, I always think, is that you have a ready excuse for why you can't help out at your kid's school. When Joe brought the form home asking for volunteers I happily offered my services, in the almost certain knowledge that I'd never be available.

'Is that Mrs Millard?'

'Ms Millard.'

'Och, Mrs Millard — I'm so glad to find you home. It's Mrs McBride, Joe's teacher. We're desperate for some assistance this morning, poor Mrs Connaught has flu and if another mum can't come in they won't be able to do cookery today and the poor wee bairns will be soooo disappointed.'

The poor wee bairns can sod off as far as I'm concerned. I weigh my disappointment against theirs and find my heartstrings pulled for myself.

'I'm sorry Mrs McBride—' I explain how I have to stay in for a very important phone call, which I'm expecting at any moment.

Unfortunately, it turns out that's fine for her as cookery isn't until this afternoon anyway. 'So we'll say after lunch, shall we?'

She can say anything she likes, but by the time I put the phone down it seems I've not only agreed to bake buns with six five-year-olds, but to stay on until home time and help out in the library as well.

'Settle down, kids, settle down.'

I'm embarrassed at the sudden presence of Chris Trelawny, acting deputy head, come to see where all the noise is coming from. I met him briefly when we came to view the school before Joe started. He's thin and gingery and struck me as mildly eccentric but that may be as much the effect of his goatee beard as the red hat he's wearing which bears the legend, 'Teacher'. His olive green cord trousers are a chalky white in the knees.

'Oh sorry,' he says as I get up from the floor where I'm sweeping up some sugar, and then compounds his *faux pas*, 'I didn't realize the kids had anyone with them.'

I smile wanly. Henry, blond and gap-toothed, has spilled caster sugar and I'm trying to sweep it up, but Kulvinder is jumping in and out of it, kicking it about to the general delight of the other boys. Tamsin, also blonde and with bunches, has been complicating matters by attempting to help.

'I'm fine but we don't seem to have got on very fast.' I sound irritatingly apologetic. Mr Trelawny adopts a stern expression and his voice deepens with severity as he addresses the children.

'I want you all sitting in your places while Mrs—' He turns to me questioningly.

'Ms Millard.'

'—While Mrs Millard gets sorted out. Then when Mrs Millard says – and only when she says – you can come up and watch.'

He stands there with his arms folded, daring the children to disobey while I finish sweeping up the sugar. That done, I'm not sure what to do next. At least while they were rioting it was clear what I had to do (murder them) but now that the pandemonium has been quelled I'm not sure how to proceed.

I shuffle about behind the kitchen counter, rearranging the packets and counting the number of eggs. I had visualized giving each child its own little bowl of mixture but I see now that this is just the effect of my over-exposure to 'Blue Peter' and not something likely to happen in the real world.

'What we usually do,' says Mr Trelawny giving me a hint, 'is to do a big batch of mixture and let them all have a stir.'

'Yes, well I was about to when Henry spilled the sugar,' I say accusingly. I'm not one of his five-year-olds for heaven's sake. He looks a little abashed at that and his arms fall to his sides.

'Of course, yes, excellent. So if you don't need me—'

'Yes, I don't need you.'

He turns a baleful eye on the class and his hat wobbles with every word. 'Now, do as you're told and don't let me hear a rumpus like that again. Or *I'll* be taking the buns home, not you.'

This is a threat the kids take seriously. Even Kulvinder looks suitably cowed.

I've just got in from taking Joe to school on Tuesday morning when Corinne from the agency rings.

'I was trying to get you all afternoon yesterday, where were you? I've got a job for you.' I make a mental note not to let Joe take Mrs McBride a present at Christmas.

'Can you get in to Treadz today? Mr Murray has asked you to go back.' On the other hand, perhaps Mrs McBride deserves two.

Normally when Corinne rings with a booking I feel a little *frisson* of excitement. It's like a mini-adventure, a step into the unknown, to be going armed only with a biro and your bus fare. You don't know who you may meet, what strange rituals you will undertake, how changed and transformed you may be by the experience.

Today, at the thought of Ed Murray, the *frisson* I get is more the kind of constriction of the muscles you get when you want to hit somebody. Anger and indignation are rushing up through my neck like water through a hosepipe.

'If you think I'm going back there to that miserable bastard, you want your bumps feeling. He's rude, he's arrogant—'

'And he wants you back,' says Corinne. 'They've asked for you specially.'

'What — by name?'

'Yes, of course.'

'Then he's confused me with somebody else. He wouldn't want me if I was the last woman on earth — and anyway he's terrible with names.'

Corinne laughs a silvery laugh like coins falling into a cash register. 'It's a two-months' booking. Isn't that just what you wanted? Somewhere to settle down and fit in?'

'You'd need to be a masochist with a death wish to fit in there.' Besides, I've already started looking forward to a week at home. I'm going to collect Joe from school each day, cook him wholesome dinners and be ever ready to show him a rainbow should I see one.

But she has reminded me that I have a bone, if not an entire skeleton, to pick with her.

'Why didn't you tell me how many temps you'd sent there already?' If I was expecting an embarrassed silence I was about to be disappointed. She didn't even pause.

'Darling, it simply wasn't relevant. I didn't want you to go there with a jaundiced view of the company, and they're lovely people, absolutely lovely. Mr Murray can be a *little* difficult occasionally but I knew you would have absolutely no problems at all. And I was right. They love you. They want you back.'

'Sorry, Corinne.'

'Two months, Gemma.'

As though two months of Ed Murray would be an inducement.

'No, Corinne, no way.'

'You drive a hard bargain, but OK. An extra pound an hour but that's my final offer.'

'I'm sorry. Find someone else.'

'Look, think about it. Ring me back in half an hour.'

She rings off, irritating me with her persistence and I march into the kitchen to begin sorting the washing into piles. And then I notice something. One of the rock hard cookies a poor wee bairn gave me yesterday has been abandoned half eaten on the worktop among the breakfast detritus. Even Joe wouldn't eat the cake and he's been known to eat worms. Mrs McBride wrang from me a promise that I'd go in again next week and there, at the other end of the phone is a foolproof reason for being unavailable for the next two months. As I shove Joe's tiny underpants into the washer it occurs to me that while the prospect of Ed Murray is not a pleasant one, at least I don't have to take anyone to the toilet or drink my coffee on my own in the classroom because they don't allow parents, even pressed volunteers, in the staff room. On balance it may be less demeaning to be humiliated by a bully who does it to everyone than to be shown up in isolation by a well-meaning wally in a hat marked 'Teacher'.

I tot up what two months' money will come to and what I can buy with it but I've already made my decision. If Joe wants to know about rainbows, I'll get a book out of the library.

If I'd returned to the office on the Monday morning as we'd all originally expected, my only welcome would have been a fresh pile of invoices from Colin, but because we all thought we had been parted forever, I'm received as a traveller to the bourn from which no employee returns. Marie rushes to find me a chair, my own having gone missing, Piers makes a rare appearance in our office instead of summoning me to his and even Diane adds her own distinctive note to the mood of reunion: 'Such a relief that we don't have to show yet another temp where the coffee things are.'

I'm in jubilant mood myself, because if I've been asked back it must surely be because, now that he has had time to study the report I typed for him and my various administrative tasks of the previous week, I have impressed favourably, despite himself, the bastard Ed. A mere secretary I may be, but while that is what I am, I will be the best there is, and he has been forced to acknowledge it.

'Just one thing,' says Marie, as I arrange a cardigan over the back of my chair. 'Ed told us to get someone who could do shorthand but Corinne didn't have anyone else left. In case he asks, just tell him it was you or nothing.'

*   *   *

Tania opens the door to me, wiping wet hands on her jeans.

'How was it?'

'Compared to being burned at the stake or making buns down at the school, it was brilliant.' Ed is away for the week and hopefully I'll have my feet well and truly under the table before he gets back.

I follow Tania down the narrow hallway and Sophie, Tania's four year old, comes rushing up to show me the potato print she has just made.

'I don't know where you get the patience,' I tell Tania, when I've suitably admired Sophie's efforts.

'I've enjoyed it. We haven't done printing in months.'

Nor have I. Or ever, come to that.

Tania collects Joe from school for me for a small sum when I'm working, and when I'm not she often collects him for free. He's best friends with her eldest, Jack, so Tania says it suits us both, though I can't help thinking I get the best of the bargain.

We live just five minutes from the school. Tania's house is just like ours: a small terraced cottage facing on to the main road. No front garden, just a yard of frontage to stand a flower tub in, not that we do, though Tania has a window box in which a few pansies are struggling for existence. Between her house and mine lives Mr Carruthers who has carved flower beds out of the poor soil and in the height of summer his frontage was a carpet of blue and mauve blooms with hanging baskets to match. But there's little left now to show for all his careful snipping, pruning and watering. Further down the row of houses, others have removed all trace of hedge or fence and set down crazy paving to park their cars on. They have to park sideways, under the lounge window. Anything bigger than a Fiesta and they've no chance. Actually a Fiesta is what we have, but we park it at the side of the kerb, its rusted exterior and loose door trim testament to the living conditions it endures. It's got more miles on it than the space shuttle; I call it the hatchback of Notre Dame in respect of its unbecoming exterior but faithful disposition.

Tania leads us through to the kitchen where the table is covered in newspaper and chunks of potato, and where Tania's other child, Jack is also busy, covered in paint to his elbows. I gaze in horror as a river of dilute cobalt blue drips on to the rug. Tania looks on in pride. That sums up the difference between us: she only sees the activity, I only see the mess that comes with it.

'We've had such a lovely afternoon. We walked the dog and called in at the swings.'

'You've got paint dripping on to the floor.'

She picks up some sheets of newspaper, taking her time, and lays them over the spillage, stamping about on them to soak up the paint.

Tania has small, neat features, and when we were at school she was stunning, but now she looks permanently pale and drained, her eyes pink-rimmed as though she has been crying or is about to start. Oddly, she doesn't look unhappy, only tired. In fact she has an aura of calm and serenity about her. She is resigned to whatever fate has to offer, and perfectly content whatever it should be.

Tania's mousey shoulder-length hair would benefit from a colour rinse but her appearance is something else she seems resigned to. I bought her some mascara and a lipstick for her last birthday, trying to jolt her up a bit, but she hasn't ever used them.

'Joe's got something to show you. Go and fetch it, Joe.' It's a pincushion in the shape of a chicken, although I offend him when I say this as it's supposed to be a duck. Tania does sewing with Jack and Joe's class every Wednesday morning while a friend minds Sophie, and most of the neat stitching round the beak is probably Tania's.

'Isn't it beautiful?' Tania always knows the right thing to say and sometimes embarrasses me by being better with my child than I am. 'And he did the wings all by himself, isn't he clever?'

While I also admire the picture Sophie has made and the painting of something on fire done by Jack, Tania asks me when Sam will be back. She is a single parent, has been since her husband left her when she was pregnant with Sophie (he said he needed more space and found it in the king-size bed of someone from his office), and I think she gets a small amount of vicarious pleasure by thinking about Sam and me. She says herself we're the nearest she gets to romance these days – somehow managing to imply that this is near enough.

'Is he bringing you anything back?'

'Look, it's all I can do to get him to bring himself back.'

'You don't still think . . .?'

She knows that at one time I had wondered if Sam was seeing someone else out there. But that was a long time ago.

'No, he's just wedded to his work.' She catches my eye. 'All he is wedded to, then,' we both say together, laughing.

Tania and I have known each other since primary school though we drifted apart, meeting up again one Thursday afternoon at the local Mothers and Toddlers, where twenty women on anti-depressants met in a bleak church hall to console each other while their infants fought over the Lego, jigsaws and dolls' prams. I took a seat next to Tania and we sat nursing cups of weak tea and conversing in smiles and nods, unable to make ourselves heard over the din of wailing toddlers and their younger siblings. Afterwards we walked home together and I asked Tania in so that Jack and Joe could get to know each other; or to put it another way, so that Tania and I could. We didn't bother with Mothers and Toddlers after that but took it in turns to visit each other: a huge improvement since now it was only Jack and Joe fighting over the Lego and jigsaws, and the only wailing sibling was the infant Sophie. Then Tania moved to live just a few doors away and now we meet all the time.

'Have you and Sam got any plans for when he gets back?' He's due home in a fortnight.

'You know him, he hates to plan ahead.' In fact this is a source of disagreement between Sam and me. He comes home tired of socializing and just wants to stay in, watch TV and play with Joe. But my life is always like that. I'd like a change.

'Wouldn't it be nice,' I muse as I tie Joe's shoelaces and Tania searches for his Thunderbirds lunch box which has gone AWOL, 'to have the kind of man who swept you off to dinner in expensive restaurants, took you to the theatre and for romantic weekends in country hotels?'

'It wouldn't suit me,' she says, and surprises me by seeing the mess and not the activity, for once. 'You show me a man and I'll show you a pile of ironing.' She sellotapes Jack's picture to the back of the kitchen door and gives it a thump to hold it in place.

The week at Treadz has passed without mishap. Ed has been happily engaged at some outlying office, who cares where, and I have had a pleasant and not too onerous time. At five on Friday I take my time sheet down to Piers (who is absolutely definite that Ed has said he may sign it). His room is empty but I can hear his voice being shouted down by a louder one in the next office.

A prickle of antagonism creeps up my neck. I haven't felt this way since I was at Social Services — this sense of frustration and impotence; the powerlessness to win over someone who stands immovably above you in the hierarchy. But Mrs Mount never brought out this level of hostility in me.

I tap at Ed's door and that imperious voice booms out, 'Come.'

I take a breath and stand up straight. I don't want anyone — least of all me — thinking I'm intimidated by this shmuck. I don't bother to smile. I've always prided myself on treating everyone the same — politeness doesn't cost anything, my mother used to say. But then she also used to say my hair would curl if I ate my crusts and carrots would make me see in the dark.

'Hello, Mr Murray.'

My unexpected entry takes him by surprise. He looks at me. And I look at him. Colin and Piers are standing in front of his desk and the chilly atmosphere drops a few degrees further with my entrance.

'What are you doing back here?' he says.

'Working for you.'

He considers this. 'I didn't ask you. Whose bright idea was that?'

'Certainly not mine. But I was told to come back so I came back. That's the sort of person I am.'

He looks doubtful as I hand him the time sheet as though he can't decide whether I'm pulling his leg or not. He reads the time sheet carefully this time, noting the start times, the finish times. Then he turns it over and reads the small print on the back. Colin and Piers glance at each other awkwardly and Colin drops his pen on the floor. Then Ed signs with a broad sweep and hands it back. He looks me up and down like a fashion buyer considering whether to buy this season's designs and deciding that he won't.

'Just so long as you're not the one they've got for the two months' booking.'

I was hoping he wouldn't mention that. 'I am actually. The agency sent me because I'm the best they've got.' Corinne would be surprised to hear that but what the hell.

He heaves a sigh that seems to start in his socks. 'Then God help the others.' He strokes his chin, giving the problem his full attention and fixing me to the spot with the strength of his gaze. 'Two whole months. And last week you couldn't stay an extra two minutes. I'm not fond of slackers.'

There's a pause in which Colin drops his pen again. Ed sits back in his seat and considers the options before reaching a decision. 'Thank you very much, but you needn't come back. And you can tell that agency they've made a fool of me for the last time. Now, Baxter . . .' He turns away, letting me know I'm dismissed. But he's not getting rid of me just like that. I haven't done anything wrong. All the same, I can't see quite what to do. He's ignoring me. Then suddenly he turns back, seeming surprised to find me still here. 'And another thing,' he adds, 'I don't know who asked you back but I'll be wanting to see whoever it is in my office on Monday morning.' He thinks it was Piers' doing. 'I thought I'd made it quite clear that I didn't expect to see you again.'

'I didn't expect to see you either,' I say. His glance doesn't waver but then neither does mine. 'But you know what they say about bad pennies.'

He lifts his chin, considering. 'Oh . . . You may be inefficient and a clock-watcher, but I wouldn't call you a bad penny exactly.'

'Oh no,' I say, 'I didn't mean me.'

There's another pause, a much longer one this time. I hadn't planned to say that, but who cares if I upset him, he had it coming and I was pleased with myself for thinking of it and even more to see his mouth drop open in astonishment. From the corner of my eye I'm dimly aware of Colin down on his knees, purposely failing to find his pen, so he won't be a witness to what's coming next. I wish I'd thought of dropping a pen myself, although I'm on my mettle now, adrenalin racing, preparing to take any of Ed's jibes and bat them back at him. Ed looks from Piers to Colin but Colin is still on the floor and now Piers bends down to help him. Then Ed looks back at me and he takes a deep breath and I steel myself. I'm not giving in that easily and he needn't think I am.

But Ed doesn't speak. Instead he laughs. His head goes back and he rocks back on his chair and his shoulders are heaving up and down. He's laughing. And he goes on laughing.

'Good for you, Gemma. Good for you,' he says, when he can speak, surprising me almost as much by getting my name right as by his reaction. Colin and Piers peer up from the floor and join in, now it's safe. 'Here, take your time sheet. I'll see you on Monday.'

I sweep out, with 'Good for you,' still ringing in my ears.

And that, though I didn't know it, was the first step in the taming of Ed Murray.

Chapter 5

'Thank God for Saturday morning TV,' says Sam, rolling away from me and reaching for the tissues. He means that, short of a power cut or simultaneous strikes on all television channels, Joe will be fully occupied until lunchtime, and we have a lot of lovemaking to catch up on after his latest absence. 'What the hell did parents do when there was only the testcard for the kids to watch?'

'Learn to move quicker,' I say, rubbing the sheet where he has dripped on to it.

He settles down again and I nuzzle into his neck as his arm comes round me. He smells of sweat and yesterday's aftershave. His hair is almost down to his shoulders. I nag him to get it cut, but actually I like the tousled look. His skin is golden which seems odd when it's October and everyone else's tan has reverted to a pale shade of beige.

I take his hand and study it to see if it looks the same as I remember. He has strong hands with long fine fingers: a musician's hands but hinting at the practical as well as the creative. He writes his own songs, gentle ballads to an acoustic accompaniment, and hard raunchy rock numbers that make you want to screw then and there when you hear them. I'm sure he could have been a professional though he himself says he wasn't good enough to give up the day job. He was semi-professional when we met, rushing off to gigs up and down the country after work but his music has been relegated to a hobby since he worked abroad. He's never in one place long enough to get a band organized properly, or the people he meets aren't.

I feel different about myself, in some hard-to-define way, when Sam's home. It's as though I've been holding my breath and now I can let it out and relax. When he's abroad, I manage perfectly well, feel strong and independent. But when he gets back, I realize that impression was just an illusion, a necessary self-deception to make his absence bearable.

I pull the covers back over us, enjoying the damp smell of him that wafts up from the sheets.

The room looks different with Sam in it. Usually I wake to a dull grey light — I didn't realize when I chose blue curtains that the effect would be so cold — but today the shadows are soft and warm as though the sun is trying to break through. In fact, everything is warmer though also smaller. It isn't that Sam is particularly big — he's under six feet and lean with it. But his personality fills the room.

He leans over to switch on the radio on the floor next to the bed, the weight of his body on mine strangely pleasing. Whitney Houston hits a wavery top note which sends a pain through my ear.

'Couldn't we stay quiet a little longer?'

Sam changes stations but turns the sound down only fractionally.

'It's good to have you home,' I say yet again. 'What shall we do today?' He doesn't answer but 'Touch me in the Morning' begins and I take it as an invitation, squeezing his testicles gently. He responds almost immediately. The question of what to do, at least in the short term, seems to have been answered.

We have lunch at the pub on the way into town to see The Sooty Show for which Sam has miraculously acquired tickets. Tania booked for it months ago but, with his usual luck, Sam phoned this morning and got cancellations.

'I don't know why we come here,' I mumble to Sam as we stand at the bar patterned with sticky rings of spilled beer, and observe the scruffy décor. Someone has dropped some crisps where I'm standing and I can feel them crunching underfoot as I move. While Eric, the landlord, pulls Sam a pint and fishes amongst the muddle of boxes behind the bar for smokey bacon crisps for Joe, Joe and I go through to the euphemistically called family room. It's even scruffier than the rest of the pub but at least you can bring children here without breaking the law.

Sam joins us after his usual extended conversation with the landlord.

'That Eric is quite a guy.'

He always says this though if you ask me, with Eric's bloodshot eyes and nose the colour of stewed plums, 'quite an alcoholic' would be more appropriate.

'What did he have to say?'

'Oh . . . you know.' Sam enjoys gossip but lacks any ability to recall it, coupled with the typically male characteristic of never finding out the things you want to know.

'Has she told them who the father is yet?'

'Who?'

'Eric's daughter.' She's sixteen and is leaving school to have her baby. There's widespread if entirely unfounded suspicion that Keith, the barman, is responsible.

77

Sam shrugs. 'Didn't know she was pregnant.' He did know, because I told him during one of our phone calls, which just confirms what I already think: that he never listens.

'Did he mention Grace's operation?' Grace is Eric's wife; better now, no thanks to the surgeon who left a swab inside. There was talk of suing. But Sam and Eric haven't discussed that either.

There's a pause while we wait for our sandwiches to arrive.

'So what were you talking about?'

'Oh, what's been happening. You know.'

Now there's another pause while we wonder what to say next. I asked Sam for all the news of his job yesterday, which is when I also told him about where I'm working. Sam asks Joe a question about school but Joe considers this to be his private domain and increasingly resents questions, however innocent. He just says he likes the sandpit best which is what he said yesterday.

When Sam has been home for a week or so, these silences are merely companionable, but at the outset they're troubling, as though we've lost all that we once had in common.

Joe takes after Sam in many ways. Sam isn't secretive, exactly, but he has many parts to his life which I don't seem to see.

The theatre is hot and noisy and smells of children's sweat and sweets, which would normally be to Joe what water is to fish. But today I'm not the only one not having a good time. Last year Sam got us tickets for the pantomime where he had friends in the orchestra. He took Joe into the pit and backstage to meet Widow Twanky who showed him the coloured bloomers she wore under her hoop skirt and gave Joe one of the packets of sweets they keep for throwing into the audience. As Joe and Sam came out of his dressing room, Aladdin appeared and shot Joe with a water pistol and Widow Twanky gave Joe a pistol to shoot Aladdin back. It was an event which none of us (but especially Jack) has ever been allowed to forget.

But now a terrible thing has happened to Joe: Jack, far ahead of us, is sitting in the front row. Today, if there are sweets to be thrown, it is Jack who will catch them; if children are asked to join in, it is Jack whose eager hand they will spot first.

Now as the lights dim and the curtain rises Joe announces, in a clear voice that carries the length of our row and probably beyond: 'Sooty's crap, isn't he daddy?'

As a would-be performer himself, Sam is a great enthusiast for live theatre (though not to the extent of taking me to any of the West End musicals I drop regular hints about) and regrets that as a child he was never taken himself. It's part of Joe's role in life to make up this shortfall for Sam, though of course Sam doesn't see it like this, maintaining that he is just giving his son the advantages he lacked.

Joe opens his Maltesers and whispers to Sam and I watch their heads, hair the identical colour, as they laugh about something. Joe flourishes in Sam's company. He has the capacity to make Joe smile and bring out the fun in life for him. I just have the capacity to make Joe say 'I want . . .' all the time. Sam should come home more often.

When we first moved in together, Sam was home most of the time. We lived in a downstairs flat, the ground floor of a converted house, with a garden even smaller than the one we have now. But it had a paved patio that caught the sun and a patch of lawn with an apple tree from which Sam hung a baby swing when Joe came along. I'd sit on a blanket on the patio while Sam pushed Joe in the swing. Joe was a fat baby, with deep creases in his elbows and knees, which got sore if you didn't dry them properly, especially in the crevices of his thighs where his nappy chafed. His hair was blond, only darkening as he got older, and he was always happy, always laughing. Sam's mother bought Joe a paddling pool and we'd fill it with two inches of water. Sam used to swing him round by his arms and then lower him with a gentle splash into the water, holding him so he could kick and dance. It was always Sam who played with him, while I brought out cold drinks or icepops or cleared up the toys on the patio.

'Do you remember when Joe cracked his head?' I ask Sam in the interval, while Joe scoops ice cream out of a tub. Sam nods thoughtfully.

It was later that year, and Joe was in the garden toddling along with a pushalong filled with wooden bricks. We were both there with him but we didn't see what happened, probably the pushalong rolled off the edge of the patio or perhaps Joe caught the wheel on something. Anyway he fell backwards and caught his head on the patio where the paving slabs joined the lawn. There was no bump, nothing to see, but he was sick shortly afterwards and then grew sleepy. It was near his bedtime, so this didn't necessarily indicate concussion but we took him to casualty anyway. They found a hairline fracture at the base of his skull.

Sam stayed with Joe all the time he was in hospital, sleeping there while sending me home, insisting on being there himself. I arrived at the hospital early the morning after the accident and there was Joe lying motionless with Sam and two doctors and a nurse standing silently around his bed.

I thought he had died.

'Why were there two doctors?' I asked Sam after he had assured me that there was no cause for alarm.

'I used to play in a band with one them,' he said. 'They came over to see how I was.'

'Yes, I remember,' says Sam now with a grimace. 'Wouldn't want to go through that again.' He aims a playful punch at Joe's head but Joe is oblivious. Sam squeezes my hand.

After the show, we meet Tania and Jack outside and head for the local Burger King (Joe would make burgers his staple diet given the choice, and Sam gives him the choice). In the event, Jack was not invited on to the stage, or to shake Sooty's hand or do a magic trick with him so now as they run on ahead Joe is free to reprise the tale of Widow Twanky and the water pistol.

'He's very good with the boys,' says Tania, as Sam instigates a game of football with an abandoned cigarette packet. But I think we'd both prefer it if he showed the boys how to pick it up and put it in a litter bin.

'It's because he's so immature himself.'

'No, he isn't. It's just men, isn't it? They hold on to what it was like to be a kid longer than we do. It's why they never grow out of train sets and stuff.'

Tania and I overtake Sam and the boys who have paused to examine something we can't afford in a toyshop window, and hurry on to find a table at the burger bar. It's already filling up with children from the audience at the show, some of whom are singing songs, some of whom are crying and most of whom are whining about something or other while the parents shout and make threats.

Sam and the boys return from the queue with enormous burgers and giant-sized cartons of chips. Tania and I usually buy them the smallest of everything and Tania sighs for the precedent which has now been set and is likely to mar our future visits.

'You'll eat it, won't you boys?' says Sam cheerily, setting down frothy chocolate milk shakes. I sigh too in support of Tania and we launch into a discussion of the extravagance and irresponsibility of men in general and the ones we've been attached to in particular. Sam just laughs, saying he knows we don't mean it but Joe leaps immediately to the defence of his patron and ally.

'You leave my Dad alone,' he says, linking his arm through Sam's and pushing a particularly long chip into Sam's mouth. 'We think he's a brilliant Dad, don't we, Jack?'

Jack starts to speak, his mouth full of cheeseburger, and sends a spray of orange gunge in Joe's direction. It's an accident but I think Joe had it coming. To have your nose rubbed in not only your lack of a water pistol from Widow Twanky but also of a dad, demands some sort of response.

'Sam,' I begin, as he lies in bed reading a music magazine, 'why don't you look for a job nearer home?'

'All right.' I swing round from the dressing table in astonishment but it's just his standard answer when he hasn't been listening.

'Sam, put that down a moment.'

'All right.' He still isn't listening so I put down my make-up remover and cotton wool and take the magazine from his hands. He folds his arms across his chest in irritation.

'Sam.' I sit on the edge of the bed by him and kiss his forehead, his cheeks. 'Don't you like it here with us?'

'Of course I do.'

'Then why don't you stay home for longer?'

'How can I? You know what these contracts are like.'

I shouldn't have interrupted his reading, I know what he'll say.

'I mean look for something else. Something nearer home. Or a contract that lets us come with you.'

'There aren't the jobs about.' He adopts a firm jut to the jaw and reaches for the magazine but I move it further from his reach.

'Geoff found one.' Geoff worked with Sam two years ago and has just taken his wife and two-year-old twins with him to Hong Kong on a two-year contract.

'Geoff is married.' He has spoken the words unthinkingly and now they hang in the air like a cloud shielding the sun. He wants to take them back but it's too late. Well, precisely, I say. My point exactly. Geoff is married and married people can apply for married status. If we were married, Joe and I could come with you. We'd always be together. Well precisely, he says. My point exactly.

I don't suppose the conversation would have followed that tack but I don't begin it just in case and it is Sam who speaks first.

'You don't like me working away, I don't like me working away, but that's how it has to be. If I had you both with me, I wouldn't get offered the contracts that I do. You'd price me out of the market. As it is, I'm doing well, we've got everything we want.'

'We haven't got you.' I sound pathetic but I can't help it.

He goes on, 'Anyway, why do you want me here all the time? I'd only be in your way.'

It chills me to hear this. When people tell you they'd only be in your way they really mean that you would be in theirs. I tell him that of course he wouldn't and he rolls away from me, his arm crooked under his head.

But then he says, 'OK babe, I'll make some phone calls,' and grins his slow, sexy grin that can always make me melt, and leans forward to kiss me. But he doesn't kiss me, he lunges past for the magazine. 'Anything to please you,' he says.

I smile as though I believe him.

Chapter 6

'Ed wants you to pop down for some dictation,' says Diane on Monday morning as I'm shaking the rain from my coat.

It's not the most auspicious start to the week. This morning Joe went off to Tania's in tears because I wouldn't let him ride his bike to school and it took surprising reserves of energy to tell him why not; then on the train I asked a youth who was spread across two seats if he'd mind moving his bag and he stood up and pushed his face into mine and asked me if I was going to make him (the people behind me just melted away until I had the compartment almost to myself. The next time I want to clear a space in a crowd I'll know what to do); then I got caught in a downpour and now I look like a drowned rat only less sophisticated. On top of all that, Diane has just reminded me, in her own sweet way, that Ed is still labouring under the happy illusion that I'm a sure thing with shorthand when the reality is that I take notes at much the same speed as Joe reads.

It was only three days ago when I called Ed a bad penny and made my small advance in his esteem, but Friday night moods are different from Monday morning ones and I'm not sure I made a big enough impression on him for it to have lasted the entire week-end.

Ed's office door is open and he beckons to me, pointing to a chair. His eyes rest on my wet hair which I have tried to restore life to with some impromptu finger-drying. The resulting mix of flat bits and sticking up bits isn't entirely what I was striving for; it's a look Johnny Rotten, in his hey day, could have been proud of.

I sit down warily, uncertain of the attitude to adopt.

'Did you have a pleasant weekend?' he enquires.

I'm relieved to see that Ed is too polite to allude to what's on my head.

'Yes, thank you. My partner came home from abroad.' I pause, giving him the option of developing this opener into a conversation but he doesn't take it. 'How was yours?'

'Went to Ireland for the weekend. Very fine. Stayed in a wonderful little hotel – excellent food, and had a rather fine bottle of Bollinger. Do you like champagne?'

'Doesn't everyone? I take it this was pleasure rather than business?'

'I like to combine the two where I can. It makes for a more interesting life, don't you think?' He looks at me expectantly for agreement but becomes distracted by my hairstyle. 'At this company, unfortunately, it's usually more a combination of business and displeasure.' He goes to the filing cabinet and hooks out some files. 'Memo to the sales team,' he begins abruptly, our small talk at an end. 'Tell them there's a meeting tomorrow. Two o'clock in here. Memo to the MD—'

'Sorry – who exactly are the sales team?'

He looks as surprised as if I'd asked who Michael Jackson was.

'How long have you been here now?'

'I know about Piers and Colin. Who else is there?'

'You, of course.'

I feel almost as astonished as if I'd just found out *I* was Michael Jackson.

'We're expanding the sales department and I want some structures in place before we get our new staff. Add this into the memo too: I'll be expecting three ideas for increasing efficiency from each of you.'

My first idea is that it would save time if he bawled the message straight through the wall rather than get me to do a memo for it, but there's no sense in talking myself out of a job which I've only just been given. And besides, it will help justify my presence and hide what I suspect is the real reason for it, which is that I'm only here to add to his empire (a team of three isn't much of a team, but it's a thirty per cent improvement on a team of two). Then he says, reminding me that I might not be adding to his empire for much longer: 'Let's get on with this correspondence.'

He sifts through and takes a pile of letters off the top which he hands to me. 'I've written some of them out already, you can just copy them.' For an instant I think I've been reprieved but he goes on, 'The rest I'll dictate.'

He picks up the first letter and scans it briefly.

'Frears and Son. Dear Mr Kilpatrick, With reference - to - our - recent - telephone - discussion - I - am - pleased-to-enclose-the-specification—'

'Excuse me—'

He does that thing again with his head: the slow rolling up of the eyes with all the disdain and disgust of a Lady Bracknell. I almost expect him to say *A handba-a-a-g?*

'Would you mind going a little slower?'

Lady Bracknell considers the question and thinks not.

'Can't you keep up?'

'I'm a bit rusty. I don't often do dictation these days. Most people generally use dictaphones.' He raises one eyebrow until it threatens to meet his hairline. 'They're very convenient, you can dictate while you're in your car, or in the bath, watching TV . . .'

'I have used a dictaphone, thank you. But it's kind of you to give me your views on the subject.'

I backpedal a little. 'Probably most businessmen just don't have the confidence it takes to dictate straight to a secretary.' I have no idea what businessmen do on the whole but I mean to suggest he is quaintly old-fashioned while sweetening the insult with a compliment. His expression lets me know he understands what I mean all too well.

'Frears and Son . . . Dear Sir . . . With reference . . .' To my surprise he does slow down but within a few sentences he speeds up again. I put off saying anything until my writing has degenerated into mere sweeps of the pen but then I'm obliged to stop him a second time. To be honest, I'd thought I'd be able to keep up, abbreviating the words the way I took notes at college but it wasn't imperative then to have comprehensible abbreviations for things like 'In respect of the foregoing'.

He leans towards me over the desk to see my notepad. I raise it slightly so it's angled away from him but not sufficiently, evidently.

'Let me see that.'

I drop it on the floor but he waits patiently for me to retrieve it, holding his hand out.

'That's not shorthand.'

'It's my own brand.'

'Well, it's not very fast is it? My cat could write faster.'

'Then you should bring her in. Be a lot cheaper.' He looks at me, like Queen Victoria now, not being amused. 'But you shouldn't talk about your wife that way.' I watch carefully for him to rock back on his chair in mirth. He doesn't.

Instead he just stares at me. Then, holding my gaze, he reaches for the phone and dials.

Sod him, then. Well, I've had two weeks here, on pay not far off what the legendary Linda earns, even if I can't do shorthand. But I feel humiliated. Suddenly I'm back at school in the headmaster's office while he rings my mother to check whether the letter exempting me from games all term is genuine. (It certainly was, I wrote it myself.) But this is worse, to have to sit here while he phones Corinne to ask her what the hell she is doing sending out yet another monkey, someone whose shorthand consists of ordinary words with the endings left off.

I hear the phone ringing down the line and then someone answers.

'Piers,' says Ed, still looking at me. 'Bring me in your dictaphone, will you?'

When I get back to my own office, three sets of eyes are on me as I open the door. I go to my desk and start sorting out the pile of correspondence Ed has given me.

'Well?' It's Marie who weakens first.

'What?'

'What happened? What did he say about the shorthand?'

I sit down and call up a fresh document on to the screen.

'Nothing. He's going to use a dictaphone.'

'He never uses a dictaphone.'

'Really? He told me it's the most practical way to deal with correspondence these days.'

'She's making it up,' snaps Diane, tossing her head so that her earrings jangle.

'I am actually,' I say, enjoying the feel of their curiosity coming to the boil. 'He said he hates the bloody things. But he's going to use one anyway. Because how else is he going to get his correspondence done and still keep me as part of the sales team?'

It sounds a bit glib the way I come out with it, but Ed isn't the sort to do anyone a favour so what other explanation is there?

'He must have taken a shine to you,' says Marie.

Well, yes. There is that.

Sam is returning to work a week early – something urgent has come up and he has to go back on Friday. We had the usual row about it but he won't be moved, says he doesn't have a choice. Now I wish I hadn't taken this long booking because we could have had more time together. I had so many things planned – things I wanted to say, not just to do – but he hasn't been here long enough for us to slide back into comfortable coupledom – a week is scarcely time to break the ice – we're still 'him' and 'me' rather than 'us'.

Sam has got a band together with a couple of people he met at the hotel where he's staying. I thought that might be another reason why he wants to get back but as he says, the others are on contract like him so they'll probably be leaving themselves before long. They've got a week's residence at a local night club soon – the vocalist is a good friend of the manager. As Sam says, it'll get them all used to performing together. I'm glad he's got a good social life out there. No, really.

*   *   *

On Wednesday, I'm just finishing the minutes of our inaugural sales meeting when Colin appears at my elbow.

'What are you doing for lunch?'

'Getting a sandwich, same as usual, I suppose.'

'Not today. Today you're lunching with the Treadz team.'

'Am I?'

'I think it's high time we got together, don't you? Reinforced some corporate identity?'

'What, with Ed?'

Colin laughs. 'Be reasonable. It's just Piers and me. Thought you might like to come for a drink and a bite. They do a decent toasted sandwich at the bar down the road.'

I've seen the bar down the road. It claims to specialize in cocktails, and it does so to the same extent that I specialize in shorthand. A closer look at the menu shows chicken, fries, batter in a basket, just like anywhere else.

'OK. What time?'

'Now.'

'Can I come?' interrupts Marie, looking simultaneously eager and offended at not being asked.

'You're not a member of their division,' Diane points out helpfully.

'Honorary member,' says Colin. 'She did my invoices once.'

The cocktail bar is dark and atmospheric. One wall sports a huge martini glass in pink and green neon lights, and each glass table is lit from below giving an eerie glow to our faces. The rose velvet sofa on which I sit is threadbare on the arms, which comes as a surprise when my hand rests against it because in the dim lighting the décor looks sumptuous and elegant.

I hope the lighting will be equally sympathetic to my complexion.

'How did you enjoy the sales meeting?' Piers asks me as I sip a spritzer.

'Interesting.'

'Not exactly the word I'd have used,' says Colin.

'No, it was interesting in lots of ways. Like the way Ed insists on formal minutes being taken when it was just the three of us, there was virtually nothing on the agenda, and almost nothing got decided.'

'Except that we should have another meeting next week. He likes to feel important,' says Colin. Colin's right, but in a way my sympathies are with Ed. He's a man built on the grand scale, his little office and teeny weeny sales team don't do him justice.

'He thinks he's Robert Maxwell,' says Piers, reading my thoughts.

'Well, he's got the face for it,' says Marie.

'Actually, I think he's quite attractive. In an ugly sort of way.'

'How can you think he's attractive?' Marie asks me. 'His face looks like someone slept in it.'

'He's like Charles Bronson. Or Mr Rochester at the end of *Jane Eyre*. He's like a damaged oak tree, bloody but unbowed.'

'How can an oak tree be bloody but unbowed?' says Piers. 'And the thing about Mr Rochester, is that he's a bastard who mellows with the love of a good woman. Ed wouldn't know a good woman if he tripped over one. The only thing he's turning into is an even bigger bastard than the one he started off as.'

'I've never read anything by Jane Eyre,' says Marie, sucking the cherry from her snowball.

Our toasted ham and cheeses arrive then and the subject drops, but even though I disagree with Marie's conclusion about Ed, I support her observation wholeheartedly. His face does look like it's been slept in — it's like crumpled bedlinen, an idea I somehow find provocative. His face shows the ravages of a misspent youth, with a helping of misspent middle age thrown in as well; it's like a diary of his sordid misadventures. And who can resist other people's diaries, especially when they're left around where you can read them?

But Piers was right to say he isn't like Mr Rochester. He's Heathcliff, alone and distraught on the wind-torn moors, his soul lost and seeking the only woman he ever loved.

'I can't believe you're sticking up for him,' Colin is saying, so we haven't completely dropped the subject after all. 'He's such a womaniser. Look at how he flaunts his girlfriend.'

'And his eyes are so firmly glued to your backside, Gemma,' adds Piers, 'it's a wonder you don't feel them when you sit down.' I'm ashamed of myself for feeling pleased to hear this. 'And what about that calendar on the back of his door. I'd have thought you'd have objected to that sort of thing.'

'What sort of thing?' I always sit with my back to the door but in any case he usually keeps it open.

'Well, we're not talking cottage gardens and views of Scotland,' says Piers, enjoying wrong-footing me. 'You should have seen Miss January, cavorting about in the snow with her nether regions turning blue. It brought me out in goose bumps in places I've never even been goosed.'

Colin laughs and Marie turns prim and poe-faced, either at the idea of the calendar or at some dimly perceived vulgarity attached to Piers and geese, or quite possibly both.

'If that doesn't put you off Ed, nothing will,' she says with the air of a prosecutor offering one final damning piece of evidence.

'If what doesn't put her off me?'

Surrounded as we are by the hubbub of music, conversation and on this occasion the rising voices of the barman and a customer who thinks he has been short-changed, you wouldn't think it possible to find yourselves cloaked in a sudden silence. One of my school teachers used to make a joke, 'Silence reigned and we all got wet' only now I see it wasn't a joke because I feel as though a bucket of cold water has been thrown over us, and while we had our fingers poked in a plug socket too.

Piers is the first to rally. It's at times like these when a public school education comes up trumps.

'Ed!' Piers even manages to make it sound like a greeting rather than the exclamation of horror that it obviously is. 'Let me get you a drink.' Whenever a great show of politeness, hypocrisy or play-acting is called for, Piers has all the necessary skills at his fingertips. Conversely, our comprehensive school backgrounds are of no help whatsoever unless you consider being lost for words an asset.

Piers escapes to the bar, making us all regret we didn't think of it first, while Ed draws up a chair from an adjacent table ('Someone's sitting there,' says a girl with doe eyes and an anxious expression. 'Not now they're not,' says Ed.) Ed takes a seat, smiling at our discomfort while silence makes a second attempt to land in our airspace. Colin saves us, though with an embarrassingly honest comment.

'I didn't know you came in here,' he says.

Ed's smile transforms to the demon grin of a man enjoying another's pain and who means to extract the last vestiges of pleasure from it. 'That wouldn't be why you chose it by any chance, would it, Baxter?'

Colin says no, no, of course not, with the defeated air of someone who doesn't even expect to be believed.

'Because that might well be construed as unfriendly. It's the sort of gesture that, some might think, didn't bode well for a man's future prospects.' Colin makes conciliatory noises as Ed continues, 'This isn't a regular haunt of mine but the admirable Diana said you were having a meeting of the sales team so I thought I ought to get along here. You could hardly have it without me, could you?'

'Evidently not,' I say, recovered now from the shock of his unwelcome arrival. 'But we thought it was worth a try.'

Ed considers this but prefers to continue baiting Colin.

'So, Baxter,' he says, 'what did you think of our first sales team meeting yesterday?'

'Interesting,' says Colin.

Walking back to the office, I find myself alone with Ed. Marie has discovered an urgent need to visit the newsagent for Polos, and Piers and Colin set a fast pace. I try to keep up with them but Ed hangs back obliging me to do the same.

'What do you think of Piers?' Ed asks as their figures disappear from sight round a corner. The wine has lulled me into a mood of *bonhomie* and I don't feel like a serious conversation, I want to drift back to my desk and the soft hum of my VDU. Besides which, I don't think he has any right to ask me this; in fact until I've satisfied myself over the truth of the girlie calendar, I'm not sure he has the right to ask me anything.

'I think he's terrific. Lots of fun.' As I say this it occurs to me that fun is not the ideal thing for an employee to be. 'Conscientious. Hard-working. Loyal,' I add. 'He seems to bring in quite a bit of business.' I don't know this but hope it's true.

'He's been lucky. He's got old school contacts who have put business his way.'

'Does it matter how he does it?'

'It matters if he's going to keep on doing it.'

'He will. He's very persuasive.'

'He's very manipulative, if that's what you mean.' He goes on in the same vein, with me trying to support Piers and being corrected at every turn, and then not before time we're back at the dingy entrance to the office and he's buzzing at the entryphone. Tina, the receptionist, answers and lets us in.

'I want to talk about the set up of the new organization, get your ideas on it,' says Ed later, as I enter his office, balancing a pile of files against my chest. 'I was impressed with your ideas at the sales meeting this week.' He pulls out a chair for me and stacks the files on the floor.

I'm not one to turn down a compliment but I could swear that the only things I said at the meeting were: 'How do you spell that?' and 'Not so fast please.' As a temp, you can count the occasions someone asks for your opinion on the fingers of one mitten. He probably just wants to ask me what I think so that he can tell me I'm wrong again.

Ed sits back in his chair and swivels round in it from side to side, like a child riding in one for the first time. 'You could go far. Unlike that dunce Baxter.'

'You're too hard on Colin.'

'Hard on him? I haven't sacked him, have I? How much softer do you want me to be? We're not running a charity here.'

Before I can answer, Colin arrives with coffee and it's hardly diplomatic to continue with him in the room. When he leaves, closing the door behind him, Ed settles back with his coffee.

'Anyway, I didn't get you in here to talk about Colin. No, we're looking at expanding the sales team. There'll be another two salesmen coming, and we'll be moving into new premises on the other side of the city. The office is only half a mile away, you'll still be able to get there with no difficulty. What do you think?'

What do I think of what?

'I think it sounds really exciting. It's always good to be in at the beginning of something.' Actually I think it's better to be in at the end for the big finish but that observation can wait for another time.

'It'll certainly be a good job for the admin staff, especially the more senior one. Lots of responsibility, hard work, lots of liaison—'

'I understand the "job" bit but which part is supposed to be "good"?' It's supposed to be a joke but he doesn't smile.

'Don't you like hard work?'

'No. Do you?'

He raises one eyebrow in mock disapproval. He can look very ugly when he wants to and quite often when he doesn't.

'What I like,' I go on, 'are short hours, long holidays and three-hour lunch breaks.'

'I thought you were so conscientious. Have I got the wrong idea about you?'

'You must have — I aim to earn enough money so one day I won't have to work. So I can lie on sun-drenched beaches reading magazines and getting soused on sangria. If that isn't why you work then I've got the wrong idea about you too.'

Ed is grinning now, a fullness returning to his lips which he now licks, a gesture which would be provocative in other circumstances.

'You're right. Absolutely right,' he says. 'But it's our secret and don't you breathe a word of it outside this office.' He takes a sip of black coffee, grinning with one side of his mouth. He can switch on the charm like an electric light. 'I have to advertise the admin posts,' he says, 'but if you're interested we could talk about it.'

'Then let's talk about it.' I sound like Lauren Bacall. Next I'll be asking him if he knows how to whistle.

He runs through the hours, the job specification, the salary — at which I have to purse my lips to stop from whistling myself. Yet somehow, although his words are entirely businesslike, something in the way he says them makes me feel almost as though he's propositioning me rather than offering me a job. When he has finished he says, as though to confirm it: 'So. Do you think we could live together?' He holds my gaze, checking my response to the *double entendre*.

'Well certainly. But I'd want separate bedrooms.'

He throws his head back and laughs. 'As I say, it has to be advertised. But put in an application and we'll see what we can do.'

Ed can be awkward and obnoxious, I know, but he's not bad when you get to know him. You just have to view him from the right angle — say from the next room. He's like those lions you see in the zoo looking as docile and placid as a fireside rug who suddenly chew the arm off someone who just wanted to stroke them. As long as I don't put my arms through the bars of his cage I'll be OK.

I haven't entirely lost the glow the two spritzers have left in their wake and now the entire day seems bathed in the colours of a summer sunset. I just don't see why everyone has it in for Ed. I pick up my pad and turn to go.

And then I see it.

On the back of the door, immediately behind where I have been sitting is Miss October. She is sitting in an unseasonally leafy glade, a strategically placed fern concealing her hips making her decent yet also more suggestive. She leans forward, tendrils of hair sweeping across her heavy breasts. Suddenly the day is bathed in the colours of Kodachrome.

'I see you're admiring my calendar. There's a lot of nonsense talked these days about pictures of nude women, but photography of that quality really has to count as art, don't you agree?'

I don't agree but I'm not sure how to handle this. The picture isn't quite as tasteless as a centrefold but on the other hand we're not talking Rembrandt either. I don't want to get on my high horse but my feet are itching to get in the stirrups and an angry flush is rising up from my neck at the thought that I've been defending him to Piers and the others. They must think I'm completely stupid. How could Ed be so crass? And to think that while he has been seducing me with his pathetic job offer, he has been comparing my availability with Miss October's. Didn't I read somewhere that imagining a person naked puts you at a psychological advantage? No wonder Ed is always so sure of himself.

'I think it's demeaning. You should take it down.'

'You must be joking! These calendars cost a fortune — this one was a gift from a client. Don't tell me you're a prude,' Ed laughs as he registers my blush.

I'm disappointed in him and embarrassed at having found in his favour so very recently. 'It's just so old fashioned. It's as if the women's movement never happened — it's not just that you're not a New Man — you're not even aware you're an old one.' I want to make a joke of it, and at his expense; shame him into admitting his error of taste, but swallowing back my anger makes my voice strained and unnatural.

'I rather think it's up to me what I hang in my office.' An icy note has entered his voice.

'It's a form of sexual harassment isn't it? It ought to be stamped: Industrial Tribunal, Exhibit A.'

Ed has stopped swaying in his chair. 'So let me get this right.' His mouth has formed a narrow line and his brows are threatening to join in the middle. He speaks slowly and precisely the way I do to Joe when I want to make it very clear how bad he has been. 'You disagree with the way I treat Baxter, you don't like my office décor and you find me old fashioned and offensive to women.' He pauses, allowing his frosty stare to coat my reddening cheeks. 'Is there anything you'd like to add?'

'With your temper?' I say. 'I wouldn't dare.'

I turn to go, noticing with a small degree of satisfaction that a furrow has formed on his forehead deep enough to plant seeds in.

'That secretarial job—' he calls after me, and there's an ugly edge to his tone, 'I think it's already gone.'

'That's fine,' I say, controlling my voice with an effort, '— so has this secretary.'

Climbing the stairs back to my office I wonder if I've been a mite hasty. This walking out of his office is becoming a habit. And it's really of no consequence what men hang on the backs of their doors, certainly not important enough to risk your job prospects for. Nude pictures are the male adult equivalent of the comfort blanket: they soothe and comfort the vulnerable and inadequate. OK, that isn't the whole story, but there's nothing I can do about it either way. And it's not as though he's shipping typists off to the white slave trade or anything. Either I go and the calendar stays, or I stay and the calendar maybe disappears mysteriously one night.

'So you think it'll just blow over? He's not going to make you leave?' says Marie when I tell her what has transpired.

'I'd like to see him make me do anything,' I say, pleased at how convincing I sound.

'Probably if you keep out of his way for the rest of the day, he'll have calmed down by tomorrow.'

'That's the drawback to being a temp,' says Diane. 'You've no security. Say the wrong thing and you can be out on your ear without a by your leave.'

'I didn't say the wrong thing. I said the right thing, he just didn't like hearing it.'

'He's the boss,' says Diane.

'Oh you *can't*,' says Marie, watching me unroll the poster. I'd noticed it in the newsagent's window when we passed earlier – a tasty-looking guy, naked to the waist and licking his lips at the camera. It didn't take me five minutes to dash out and get it and after all, what's sauce for the goose etc. I pin it up over my desk, on top of the postcard of Torremolinos.

'What will Ed say if he sees it?' Marie's eyes are wide at the prospect of drama and disaster.

'Who cares?' I say, satisfied with my small act of rebellion and secure in the knowledge that the day Ed makes his way up to our office is the day pigs sprout wings.

'Watch out for those flying pigs,' says Diane later as our office door opens. I look up, mystified, to see Ed's frame filling the doorway.

'I need some envelopes,' he says gruffly. He hasn't seen me look up so I become immersed in my work, apparently oblivious of his presence, and it is Suzanne who gets up with a sigh and goes to the stationery cupboard.

I can no longer pretend ignorance of him and Marie and I exchange glances, wondering how long it will be before he sees my poster. While he waits for Suzanne he comes over and leans on my chair, bending down to pull off a piece of sellotape that has adhered to the sole of his shoe and flicks it into the bin. As I turn round in my seat our eyes meet.

'I thought you said you were going,' he says coolly.

'I did go. Out of your office.' I smile experimentally but he remains granite faced.

'I warn you,' he says straightening up and looking down at me from what seems to be a great height, 'I don't like to be made a fool of.'

'Oh, I'd have thought you'd be used to it by now,' I smile again, willing him to join in the joke. He holds my gaze and it could go either way. He isn't prepared to concede anything but I see now that he, as much as I, wants to maintain the *status quo*. When Diane said that the drawback to temping was that there's no security what I should have pointed out is that there's no security for the employer either. A temp can be fired with ease but she can also walk out at a moment's notice. Diane and I may have forgotten that aspect but Ed hasn't. He has wandered up here, oh so casual, looking for envelopes, to see whether I'm still here.

Now as he turns to go his eyes meet the bare chest of my monochrome man. He looks at him dubiously.

'You want to take that down,' he says. 'It's demeaning to men.'

'Did you hear the latest on Diane?' asks Marie later in the office kitchen as I wash up the cups ready for tea. She undoes the foil wrap on the egg mayonnaise sandwich she saved from lunch and offers me a bite. She has started to bring in her own sandwiches lately so she can save more money for when she's married.

'She's been caught having sex in the stationery cupboard?' I answer.

'Has she? Why didn't you tell me?'

'No, it's a joke.' Marie takes a large bite and munches irritably. I've disappointed her. 'So what's the latest if it isn't that?'

She takes her time chewing, considering whether to tell me or not while I put the last of the cups on the rack to drain.

'Suzanne saw her with the financial director last night. In his car.'

'What were they doing?'

'Nothing. But it's still odd, isn't it. They could be starting something, you know what she's like. What do you think?'

I don't know what she's like except that she's too good for the likes of the low-lifes who represent management around here, but instead I say, 'I think he was probably giving her a lift. Either that or she was trying to get a rise out of him.'

My joke is wasted on Marie but in any case before she can respond Suzanne calls me to take a phone call.

Back in the office I pick up the receiver, reaching for my notepad with the other hand.

'I'd like to speak to Ed Murray.' The voice purrs. She sounds like a cat stretched out on a hearth rug. A naked cat. Surrounded by velvet ribbons, black chocolate and satin sheets, stretching out its claws.

'I'm sorry, Mr Murray is out this afternoon.' Suzanne saw him getting in his car earlier. 'May I take a message?'

'Just tell him I rang.'

'Who shall I say—'

'Janet Reger.'

She rings off then, leaving me with the receiver in my hand. I replace it and meet Suzanne's gaze. There was obviously something in my manner that caught her attention.

'That was Janet Reger. You don't suppose it was *the* Janet Reger – the underwear designer?'

Suzanne opens a ring-pull can and takes a long swig before replying. 'That's his girlfriend.'

'Janet Reger is his girlfriend?'

Marie arrives with the tea and although it's not her way to give withering looks if it were that's what she would give me now.

'We don't know what her real name is – she rings up and it'll be Scarlett O'Hara, Victoria Secret, Ann Summers. It's their joke. I think it's disgusting.'

So I'm not the only one who has discovered he's not just the dour and bad-tempered old sod he would have us believe.

I wonder what she's like. I can just imagine her – all

lustrous long hair and breast enlargements, and with a full red mouth she probably had pumped up with collagen from her backside. If she ever tells Ed to 'Kiss my arse' he won't know which end to start.

Chapter 7

——— —

I'm just getting on the train home when I see her: Brindle Sylvia, hurrying along the platform, her brown shopping bag knocking against her bulky calves. Her raincoat reaches almost to her ankles, increasing the short stumpy appearance of her legs which her stilettoes only seem to emphasize. She has to stop when the heel of her shoe catches on something. When she sees the train on the platform next to mine she pauses and turns, looking relieved. Bob, who works in shipping, comes running up behind her and she flings her arms round his neck and kisses him as though this is some big emotional farewell. Bob is tall and lanky with fair wispy hair. Standing so close to Sylvia's broad shoulders and hips, they don't exactly look like they were made for each other. He tries to look over his shoulder but she brings him back to face her with one hand against his chin. I had no idea she was such a romantic.

Not that that is all she is. She has a husband and two teenage children; I saw them shopping in Argos last Saturday, her son's acne in full flower.

The whistle blows and my train pulls out, on time for once. Sod's law isn't it, just when there's something you want to watch.

I can hardly wait to get into work next day.

'You'll never guess who I saw at the station last night.' Marie listens, changing into her indoor shoes and sliding her boots under her desk.

'Don't tell me — Billy Connolly.'

'No, of course not Billy Connolly. Why would I see him?'

'He's on at a theatre near here. My mum saw him on the bus. She said he looked much—'

'I saw Sylvia.'

'Sylvia? Not the one in the sitcom with the red hair? What's her name — not Sylvia Simms . . .'

'Not Sylvia Simms, not Sylvia Plath, not Hi Ho Silver.'

'All right, all right, don't get aerated.'

'Sylvia from accounts.'

'Oh her.'

Somehow, I haven't managed the big build up I'd intended.

'I looked out of the train window and there she was kissing someone.'

'It was probably her husband.'

'No, I've seen her husband. It was Bob from shipping.'

'Bob with the crew cut?'

'No, Bob with the spots.'

'It would be. They're all at it.'

'Are they?'

'I thought you knew.'

I can't imagine how Brindle Sylvia has got any man interested, with her stubby legs and her idiosyncratic way with clichés. 'What do you think of Ed?' I asked her during my first week.

'I can't always understand what he means,' she said.

'He starts telling me something and then he goes off on a tandem.'

'I don't know why you don't like Sylivia,' says Marie defensively. 'She's got a very kind heart. Anyway, it was Jean that started it. She had this thing with the accounts manager. They spent so long down in the basement, we thought of having a telephone extension put down there.'

'Or a mattress,' says Suzanne, then blushes when we look at her in surprise. It's not often that she joins in, especially to say something funny.

I've brought a John Grisham with me to read at lunchtime today – Sam has been reading it which is no recommendation in itself, but I can't resist what I've seen him enjoy. I've barely opened it when Diane arrives back. She has bought a ready-to-eat salad from Marks & Spencer, and is gripping a pile of travel brochures precariously under one arm.

'Didn't you say you know Greece?' she asks me, sitting down and skimming the contents page of a brochure with her finger.

'Yes. A bit.' We've discussed hotspots of the world we have visited, prompted by the postcard from Torremolinos on the wall over my desk. Marie favours Spain (it being the only foreign country she has been to. It's her postcard) but Diane favours France (the food! The wine!). Suzanne spends her holidays with her parents at their cottage in the Lake District.

'Where would you recommend?'

'Oh, it's all nice,' I say without enthusiasm and soon Diane is reading for herself what it's like, leaving me to go back to John Grisham. But I find I can't pick up the threads of the story now and perhaps Marie notices, because she begins, 'It's funny you saying all that about Sylvia this morning. Because Sylvia was saying something about you.'

I look up in surprise. Marie is painting Tippex on to the scuffed heel of a white stiletto and sucking on her tongue in a way I've seen her do when she is trying to keep a straight face.

'What was Sylvia saying?'

'That you're always in his office.'

'I'm his secretary. That's how it works.'

'Yes—' she holds the shoe up to see what I think. I think it looks like a scuffed stiletto with Tippex on it but I nod approvingly. 'Sylvia thinks you fancy him.'

Diane's nose pricks up at that. Her black hair is so sleek in this light it looks as though it has been painted on. 'You don't do you?'

'*Fancy* him?' If they knew what Sam looked like they couldn't have asked that question.

'I just think you should be a bit careful,' says Marie, still avoiding my eyes. 'You know he's got that girlfriend. And he's a lot older than you.'

I give up the struggle with John Grisham and close the book and the words on the cover swim. The new-paper smell of Diane's travel brochures, sharp in the nostrils, has been knocking on the door of my memory and now it falls open.

'You want to be careful, he's a lot older than you,' said Rhea. But that was later, at the end of the holiday when she was flying back, leaving me and Rudi alone.

It's our first day. We're newly arrived and I'm lying on a beach reading a magazine I bought at the airport just that morning, and a man with deeply bronzed ankles is walking across the sand towards me. It's hot and my legs are burning, unused to the strength of the sun. Rising on to my elbow for a better look I see the man is wearing faded shorts and a blue shirt with the sleeves rolled up. Rhea and I are nineteen; this man must be almost thirty. Barely young enough to qualify for this holiday for the under 30s. Yet his added years and foreignness are an attraction; he seems mysterious and romantic.

'Hello. You arrive today, yes?' He crouches down in front of me, his knees on a level with my nose. His feet are bare. Rhea sits up, looking interested.

'We got in about an hour ago.'

'I am Rudi.' We've been told that Rudi is our rep. He extends his hand, olive dark, to each of us in turn. 'I am sorry I could not meet you from the airport. A domestic crisis at the hotel.' We've heard about it already from the driver who collected us: the diameter of the drainage pipes is so small that if you put paper down the loo it blocks. Someone did and it had. I hope Rudi washed his hands.

'Tonight we have a welcome party on the beach here. Free wine, moussaka, all the new guests meet all the old ones. Eight o'clock. Then we have fun after, go swimming maybe.'

'Are you Greek yourself?' asks Rhea. He doesn't quite look it yet he is of Mediterranean appearance and his English is halting though perfectly phrased.

'I'm half French, but I have lived in Spain for many years and now here.' He has large, heavy-lidded eyes, and there's something roguish and piratical about him, but maybe that's just the effect of his dark skin and the scar down his left cheek.

'Where did you get that scar?' I realize Rhea fancies

111

him. She puts her hand out to him, almost touching his face. She doesn't believe in wasting time.

'A fight. It was stupid.' He shrugs but his eyes say, 'But it shows I am tough too, no?' Rhea delves deeper but I leave her to it and return to my magazine. I don't think he got the scar from a fight, he probably fell out of his pushchair as a baby, but it's less effective if he tells it that way. I plan to irritate Rhea by giving her my version later.

The party is held under a canopy covered in rushes in the space that connects the two halves of the building, the owner's attempt to turn two small hotels into one larger one. At one end there is the bar, the other is open on to the beach. It is the most romantic setting I have ever seen, but then romance is limited in Tenby and Rhyl especially when you have your family in tow, and they have been the sum of my holiday experiences until now.

The party is less of a meeting of the old guests and the new than a sticking together of existing cliques and forming of new ones. We new arrivals, distinguishable by the red glow of our newly burned faces as well as by our acceptance of the free wine which the existing inmates know to avoid, stand around on the periphery hoping someone will come and talk to us. The old crowd lounge around in groups, laughing loudly and studiedly ignoring us.

'Let's have a walk through the town,' says Rhea, observing that the attention Rudi had focused on her earlier is now being dispensed with equal generosity amongst the women present. He passes among the crowd, and whenever he stops his arm circles the waist of a different girl, who curls against his shoulder and gazes up at him with adoration. When he comes to Rhea she decides to forgive him his fickleness but I move away to the bar. There's nothing less attractive than a man who knows he's attractive.

Despite Rhea's best efforts, we have little personal contact with Rudi during the next week although he is always in the vicinity. When we go on the organized excursions he is there with us, passing round baskets of strawberries on the coach, setting up football matches or building bonfires on the beach for the endless barbecues. When we visit places of interest, the route is by way of private beaches where he insists we can sunbathe undisturbed with our tops off. If you don't take your top off, he teases you for your shyness, but I find that easier to bear than the way his eyes pass over the girls' naked bosoms, observing, comparing. All the men pretend they're not looking, that it's solely from choice that they only sunbathe lying on their stomachs, leaving little holes drilled into the sand in their groin area when they get up. Rudi disguises his interest better than most, but then he has had more experience of it. But it's still there in the way his eyes roll across the girls' half naked bodies.

'He's a Romeo,' I tell Rhea.

'Well, you should know,' she says. She's referring to Nick, my boyfriend of six months who has just dropped me for the girl I'd thought was my best friend. It was Nick I was supposed to be holidaying with: lean and shaggy-haired, the boy all the girls fancied, a younger version of Sam you might say. Rhea is his sister and took up the cancellation. Nick always had a roving eye but, as I used to say, what does it matter if I'm the one he's going home with? Stupidly, I hadn't foreseen that it was only a matter of time before I wasn't the one he was going home with.

Towards the end of our second week, I begin taking walks along the beach after dinner. Rhea has taken up with a computer operator and during this part of the evening I find it expedient to keep out of the way of his friend, a TV repairman from Pinner. On this occasion I've been walking for perhaps twenty minutes.

'Gemma?'

It doesn't sound like the TV repairman but I can't be sure. I keep going.

'Gemma! Over here, behind you.' It's Rudi's voice. I turn and see a figure squatting on a rock. Outlined against the light he looks like a goblin.

I go over to him hesitantly.

'Gemma, what are you doing here on your own?'

'Walking.' Who is he, my mother?

'It is not safe. Let me walk with you.'

'I'm fine.' I don't want him walking with me. In fact, I feel a lot less safe with him than by myself. But he ignores me and falls into step alongside.

We pause to watch the sun setting and, as the rays light up the water, he asks me why I have been so aloof.

'I'm not aloof.'

'But yes. You avoid me. I look at you and you look away. I say, let us do this thing and you say no, I will do that thing.'

Actually, I haven't been aloof so much as bloody-minded, but that has been to irritate Rhea not him. She hasn't been the good company I'd expected, always ditching me in favour of a tight butt and fat wallet, and I'm finished with men. But I'm surprised he noticed me at all. I haven't had that impression.

'Shall we watch the sunset?' It is rather beautiful so I let myself be led to some rocks where we sit.

'You are not like the other girls,' he says, leaning back on his hands and gazing out to sea. This sounds like a line to me and I don't answer. 'I wonder why you come on a holiday of this kind which is so much concerned with, what shall we say, raucous fun. There is much drinking and sex, yet I think those are not things which you are very keen on.'

No, and I hadn't realized Rhea was either but then I hadn't known her that well before we came away. I needed someone to take Nick's place and, my best friend being otherwise engaged, I was just grateful to find anyone to step in.

'Originally I was coming with my boyfriend – he chose the holiday. I didn't know quite what it would be like. But it's been an experience, I've enjoyed it.'

'You are like me, an observer of life.' This sounds like another line. I don't remember Rudi ever observing anything other than naked breasts.

'Oh, come on, Rudi. You're always in the thick of things. You're about as observant as Mr Magoo.'

He raises one eyebrow and looks at me sideways. 'I do not know Mr Magoo but it is my job to be in the thick of things. I must organize, ensure that the fun goes on. There are many men, younger than me, who would like my job so I must be better at it than they can be. But a part of me is always watching, that is my hobby.'

The light changes from orange to pink, and we watch in silence as shadows fill the sky. Despite myself, I am warming to Rudi. He turns to me as the final rays fall away.

'Can I kiss you?' I am embarrassed to be succumbing to him, just like all the others but remembering that first day, how I turned away from him to my magazine as though I wasn't interested, I see how inevitable it was. I've needed someone to take Nick's place in more ways than I realized.

We carry our shoes, walking back through the water, or on the water as it seems to me. Outside my room he kisses me goodnight, a warm deep kiss, like Turkish delight.

I am just getting into bed when there comes a knock at the door. Rudi is carrying a bottle of wine and three glasses, one for Rhea.

But Rhea is still out with her computer operator. She doesn't come back at all that night, which is just as well.

'Was it one of the islands?' says Diane. 'Where you stayed?'

'Yes. And the mainland. We went all over.'

'Where did you like best?'

I liked best the island Rudi took me to on his weekend off. He sailed a boat across and we slept in a cave in two sleeping bags he had zipped together. We were Calypso and Odysseus, I didn't ever want him to go. I don't know what the island was called, or even if it had a name. Or maybe it was just the more remote side of an island we had visited already and Rudi just pretended it was uninhabited and we were alone there.

'So how long were you actually there?' Diane is suddenly interested; she's the sort who can always sense intrigue though she's more diplomatic in the way she puts her questions than Marie.

'A month or two.'

Diane looks both envious and disapproving at the same time. Actually it was four months. Rhea and I arrived there immediately our college exams finished – it was the end of May and wonderfully cheap. We were just staying a fortnight – but I didn't get the plane home when the holiday was over. I fell in love with Rudi in our last three days and I stayed on to see what would come of it.

What came of it was that Rudi was attracted to me only while he was doing the chasing and getting the brush off. Once he had me where he wanted me, he lost interest.

'I could have told you that would happen,' Rhea told me when I got home. 'Don't you know what a powerful aphrodisiac rejection can be?'

But if that was what fired Rudi, what lit my fuse was the challenge of attracting and keeping a man that other women were clearly interested in. It's the uncertainty of knowing where it's all going to lead that turns you on.

'What is it you like about Ed?' Marie persists, determined to bait me for as long as I'll take it.

'He reminds me of someone I used to know,' I say, surprising myself with the reason.

The first indication I get that it's Diane's birthday is when I arrive at work on Friday and find a line of cards already in place on her desk. I feel bad about this. Even though I haven't known Diane long enough to be on card-sending terms my card is conspicuous by its absence.

In the middle of the morning a bouquet of roses arrives. Tina brings them up from reception where they have been delivered and hands them to Diane regally, Tina's face as red with excitement as the roses themselves.

'Oh, how lovely! Are you sure they're for me?' Diane flushes with pleasure as she takes them into her arms like a baby.

'Who are they from?' asks Tina, as Diane opens the tiny white envelope.

'From your husband?' asks Marie innocently.

'Yes! isn't he sweet? I had no idea, and they're so beautiful!' But there was the briefest pause before her answer, and when it came it was all in a rush. Her blush has deepened and her eyes have a strange brightness. She pops the card swiftly into her handbag.

The girls are going to Emilio's, the local trattoria, for Diane's birthday lunch and I'm invited to go with them. Emilio's is done out in red — red logo, red tablecloths, red wall lights. Even the apron of the waiter who shows us to our table is red. So, incidentally, are his eyes but I think that's just coincidence.

The waiter pulls out a chair for Diane and she settles herself lightly, like a butterfly landing on a window sill from which at any moment it may depart. He pulls one out for Marie too and she sits down like a sack being dropped from a great height. Then she wriggles back in her seat, first one buttock then the other, the way children do.

Perhaps Diane is just in a birthday mood, but today she strikes me very differently from how she did when I first started work here. As she orders the wine and suggests what we choose from the menu, it occurs to me that if she adopts a pose of authority and efficiency about her work it's only because she's conscientious and has high standards — not because she's just awkward and sarcastic which is what Marie accuses her of being. If she likes to remind us that she went to secretarial college, has certificates for shorthand, typing and business studies, it's only because she is irritated to see novices (like me, or Marie) starting off in positions not so very junior to hers. I feel sorry for her. To Diane, this is a career not a job. It's understandable that she would wish to maintain a differential.

'I think we should have a toast,' I say when the wine has arrived. We all raise our glasses. Diane laughs, showing perfectly white teeth. Diane once told Marie that she used to have what her dentist called 'a typical fifties mouth' — a network of grey amalgam linked together by insubstantial amounts of enamel. When she laughed she used to cover her mouth with her hand. But last year she spent undisclosed amounts on having her fillings replaced with white porcelain. Marie says she's got more china in her mouth than in the Wedgwood teaset she's saving for her bottom drawer.

'To Diane. Happy birthday,' I say.

'How old did you say you were?' says Marie.

'And I'd like to add something,' I say, passing over Marie so that Diane won't have to dodge giving an answer the way she has been doing all morning. 'I'd like to thank you, Diane, for all your help.'

We drink, or at least, three of us do while Marie pretends to choke and mouths 'crawler' at me — but I mean it. Watching Diane's gift for organization, the meticulous records she keeps, the way she takes an interest not just in the minutiae of her own job, or even her boss's but the performance figures for the company, has been an education for me. I can't see why Diane hasn't been promoted out of secretarial work. But I can see how, if I follow her example and foster the interests of the right people, I might be able to.

Emilio's is filling up now, the warmth and buzz of voices and dim lighting creating an atmosphere of intimacy which a couple of glasses of vino encourages. We're starting to relax now, kicking off our metaphorical shoes, or in Marie's case, our actual ones.

We've been talking about Marie's favourite subject: weddings, and from there we move on to her second favourite — marriage and children.

'Gemma, why didn't you have any more after Joe?' There's a hint of accusation in her voice as she winds

119

her tagliatelle round her fork and watches it roll off again. The wine has brought a blush to her cheeks.

'I still might do. There's plenty of time.' She's putting me on the defensive.

'Oh, but it'd be a very big gap now. They wouldn't grow up as friends.'

'I'm only eighteen months older than my sister,' says Suzanne. 'But we didn't grow up friends. We didn't learn to have a conversation without it turning into a fight until we left home.' No one responds immediately to this. I don't think any of us can imagine Suzanne being sufficiently animated to get into a fight. This is the longest sentence I've ever heard her say.

'It's the way your parents bring you up,' says Marie at last. 'My brothers and me, we've always been close. My mum says they used to wheel me out in my pram, and when I was older and we played games they always let me win.'

'I thought that scar on your eyebrow was where your brother hit you with his Meccano,' says Diane sweetly.

'That was an accident.' The tagliatelle finds its way to her mouth and she chews on it with just a touch of petulance. 'But I don't think it's fair to have just one child.'

'I'm an only child,' says Diane. 'It didn't do me any harm.'

'That's just your opinion,' says Marie.

The subject drifts off to office politics and last night's television programmes, but when the gâteau comes Marie picks up her theme again.

'I want a big family. Four children. More if we could afford it.'

'That's irresponsible,' says Suzanne, jabbing at the air

with her dessert fork. 'The world is over populated as it is. I think they should compulsorily sterilize anyone who has more than two. And fine you if you have more than one.' We're on our second bottle of wine now and at the stage of inebriation where nothing can surprise you. Consequently Suzanne's outburst passes unremarked.

'Four children would completely ruin your figure,' says Diane.

'Oh, is that why you just had the one as well?' Alcohol is bringing out the aggressor in Marie.

'I've never had to worry about my figure. No, I was thinking of you. You are . . .' She sips from her wineglass while she searches for a diplomatic description. '. . . big boned. Generously proportioned. It's very easy for people of your sort of build to run to fat. And even for me – well, you can't see your stomach swell up like a pumpkin without forming some sort of opinion. And pregnancy doesn't do anything for your breasts . . .'

'Mine were rock hard when the milk came in,' I say, remembering. (Diane wrinkles her nose at the description.) After the birth of Joe, my 34B breasts swelled to centrefold proportions, but they were hard and lumpy, white as lard. The skin was stretched over them to a sickly translucence through which you could trace a map of grey veins. They looked like two snowy peaks on an ordnance survey map. Twin mounds of Danish Blue.

'They're badly engorged,' the nurse had said, and she brought me a breast pump to take some of the milk off because the skin around the nipples was so tight that otherwise Joe wouldn't have been able to latch on.

'Everyone's breasts swell a little . . .' says Diane, putting her forkful of gâteau back on the plate and pushing her plate away.

121

My breasts were painful too at first — and at second actually. Once Joe started feeding and my nipples cracked it was unbearable, except that it had to be bearable because I wanted to breastfeed and if you start them on the bottle (they told me) that's *it*, you won't get them back on the breast. I don't know if what they said was true but I was the first among my friends to fall pregnant so I had no one else to ask. With your first baby you believe everything you're told. There's only one thing you know for sure and that's that you don't know anything.

But after the pain of the early days, the feeding routine developed its own peculiar beauty. I knew when Joe would be hungry because I would feel the milk coming in, that tingle in the breasts, feeling them filling as though someone had turned a tap on. As soon as I touched Joe the milk flowed in even faster and I would feel my bra stretching tighter as I lifted him from his cot. By the time I had undone it ready for the feed my nipples would be dripping and my bra soaked with milk. Joe was born in May and on fine days I'd sit in the garden to feed him, or else in the patch of sun that came into the sitting-room of our flat in the mornings.

By the second or third month I was growing proud of my new breasts and looking forward to the time when I'd lose some of the hugeness and settle back into some sort of compromise. 34C was what I was hoping for.

'It's so good to see a mother willing to breastfeed,' said the health visitor when I called in at the clinic one day.

'Oh? I thought most women breastfed.' It hadn't occurred to me not to. I'd assumed bottle-feeding was just for those who had problems.

'Well, some do, of course. But it ruins your breasts doesn't it, and I suppose it puts them off.'

'What do you mean "ruin"?'

'Oh, well no, not ruin, I suppose. But they go smaller don't they? And floppier. More inclined to sag. But that's not important is it? The important thing is you've done the best thing for your baby.'

Was it the important thing? As I stood in the clinic looking around at all the happily gurgling babies, a proportion of whom, statistically, must have been seriously disadvantaged by their vain mothers, I wondered how it was that I couldn't tell which was which. None of the babies gave any indication of knowing that they hadn't had the best thing done for them.

Sometimes now, when I'm hooking up my 34B (which hangs forlornly empty) or my 34A (in which I look as flat as two drop scones), I hope that Joe will appreciate the sacrifice I made for him. Sam certainly doesn't.

'It must be lovely to be pregnant,' Marie is saying.

'I certainly felt very well,' answers Diane, 'the best I've ever felt. People said I glowed.'

People said I looked fat and shouldn't put on so much weight. My cheeks swelled out like a hamster's.

'It's the hormones,' adds Suzanne.

It's also the food. Or it was in my case. I developed the most ravenous appetite. Anything, everything looked good. If it was fit for human consumption I wanted a portion. Maybe seconds. With custard on it.

'It's awful being fat,' I say, unable to contain my unhappy memory any longer.

'I wasn't fat at all.' No, Diane wouldn't be. 'People said they wouldn't have known I was pregnant – except for the glow. I had a little round bump in front and that was all. I didn't put on weight anywhere else.'

'I thought you said you swelled up like pumpkin.'

'Well, everyone does at the end but it's only for a week or so. But before that I was fine. I was still going to keep fit up until I was six months.'

Marie and Suzanne express awe and admiration and I refill my wineglass. I'd like to catch the waiter's eye, it's time we were getting back. But two of them are discussing the merits of a blonde girl at a table in the window whose skirt has ridden up her thighs and are too busy to notice me.

'I had a home delivery,' Diane is saying. 'My GP wasn't keen at first but he could see I was in tip-top physical condition so eventually he agreed. The midwife was excellent, she became quite a friend.' She smiles fondly at the memory and I trace patterns in the crumbs that dropped from my bread roll.

'I'd like a water birth,' says Marie.

'Oh yes, that must be wonderful. Of course there was no facility for that then, but we had soft lights and music playing so Caroline was born into an atmosphere of harmony and peace. I do think that's important.' Marie and Suzanne chime their agreement, so I add mine though I wouldn't know really, Joe having been born into an atmosphere of noise, mayhem and chaos. He was a face presentation, as they call it, and had to be turned in the womb during delivery. It was an extremely difficult procedure they told me afterwards, as though I hadn't been in the room when they did it. It was painful too. I'd been given an epidural but they forgot to top it up. Later, when it was all over and Joe had been whisked away for examination, I asked if I could have something for the pain.

'Pain?' the doctor said. 'Are you in pain?' She was sewing me up at the time. I'd like to see her having needles shoved up her nether regions and not want something for pain. But she didn't know then about the epidural. They had been in such a panic about Joe that the topping up of it got overlooked.

'Did it hurt much?' But Marie is asking Diane, not me.

'Just a little, but if you have good breath control it's fine. Of course my yoga helped with that, but I was scrupulous about attending the antenatal classes too.'

'Well, that's what I think,' says Marie, with satisfaction and an air of wrapping up an on-going argument. 'Every time you see some woman giving birth on telly she's screaming and yelling and there's blood everywhere. And I say to my Gary, if it was really like that no one would have kids at all, would they?'

'That's like saying once you know how awful a hangover is you'll never drink again,' I say acidly.

'No, it isn't,' says Marie stubbornly.

'It's exactly the same. At the time you forget that one leads on to the other. Just like with sex — at the time you have it you're not thinking about being pregnant. Once you're pregnant, it's too late. But it is painful and that's one of the many reasons that people like me don't have a second one.'

Marie considers this doubtfully. 'But on telly they do exaggerate, don't they?'

'No, Marie, they do the opposite. Because if they showed what it was really like everyone would switch over and watch "Come Dancing".' I let the magnitude of this image sink in before I ask, 'Shall I tell you about Joe's birth?'

'I think we should get the bill,' says Diane, looking round for the waiter and attracting him immediately.

'First of all, they shave you.'

'Shave you? Shave your legs?' Marie looks mystified.

'Oh Marie, work it out.' Suzanne is getting tetchy.

'Then they make you wear one of those hospital gowns that do up at the back, except that they don't do up so your backside is all bare. When you have a baby you leave your dignity in the changing room with your knickers.'

'Gemma—' Diane taps at her watch but we've had her angle on the glory that is childbirth, now it's my turn.

'Then you get to the birth. It felt like I was having a boulder pulled out of me. A boulder with spikes in it that was trying to get out through the neck of a bottle. Then they do all this stuff with forceps and you want to push but you mustn't and when you don't want to they tell you you should, then your baby's born and he's all bashed and bruised from the forceps and you can't hold him anyway because they have to rush him off in case there's something wrong with him. Then everyone goes off and leaves you and they bring you a cup of tea but they put it where you can't reach and you can't move to get it because you're still wired up to the epidural.'

'It sounds horrible,' says Marie faintly.

'Oh no. It was all peace and harmony.'

Suddenly I'm aware of how quiet Emilio's has become. Faces from other tables are pointed in my direction; they're sitting still, cutlery clutched in their hands, not eating. Marie and Suzanne are looking down at their plates. I have the impression I may have spoiled their appetites a little.

'Well, Gemma. If there's nothing you want to add perhaps we should get back.' Diane starts dividing up the bill which must have arrived while I was talking.

Actually there is something I want to add. I forgot to mention that Sam was at the birth and passed out in the middle of things. He had to be carried outside. But I'll save that for another time.

Chapter 8

I've been working for Ed for two months now — I toasted myself in coffee this morning to celebrate. We moved into our new offices just round the corner from Head Office three weeks ago and I love it here. We have more staff and I have more money, being employed by Treadz now, not the agency. It was a big decision, becoming permanent, but Ed was so conciliatory regarding the time I could take off for school holidays, even saying I could work part time if there were any problems, that I couldn't say no. I thought some of the admin staff might have objected to me walking straight into such a nice little number but I think the consensus was that it wasn't a nice little number at all and that actually I'd drawn the short straw. Even Diane who, you might think, would resent my sudden rise seemed enthusiastic but I think she, like the other secretaries, was so relieved to have Ed so completely off her hands that she was filled with nothing but gratitude. She even took me to the wine bar to welcome me into the ranks of the élite which, as director's secretary, I have apparently joined.

I like Ed, and if he's as much of an awkward sod as ever, well, I've got the measure of him now. And he does intrigue me. I love the way he slinks into his office, shutting the door, when his girlfriend rings; the way his shoulders drooped the one time he got a call from his wife. (Her voice carried down the phone to the other side of the office. Ed shrunk into himself the way Colin does when Ed bellows at him.) We've had the occasional drink after work, usually with one of the new salesmen in tow, and that small amount of socializing seems to have nurtured our relationship.

Don't get me wrong, I don't fancy Ed. He has lines under his eyes with dark shadows as though they've been smudged with newsprint, and his broad shoulders can make his suits look untidy. His face looks lived in, and by someone who ought to get a cleaner in to tidy round. But if I'm not attracted to him, maybe I am attracted by him. He makes me feel he values me and I like that. He discusses with me details like the marketing strategy, making me feel respected and significant; I like being where he is, he gives coming to work a purpose. Sam doesn't always notice what I wear any more, but Ed does – when I arrive in the mornings, I see his eyes flick over me, lingering on my legs. I've swapped my business-like image for that of – well if not the *femme fatale*, certainly the *femme* seriously-wounded. He's a wonderful boost to my morale.

Quite spontaneously we discovered a rapport. We've stopped sparring (or stopped sparring exclusively) and have become, if not friends exactly, well, confidantes, perhaps. One day he was still spikey and tempestuous; the next he was my buddy. These days I find it a challenge to see how I can restore his mood when he arrives from home bringing an atmosphere that hangs around him like a cloud. I joke that he looks harassed or hungover and he responds.

It happened just after we'd moved here in mid November. Ed is in charge of developing the sales and marketing strategy for the company's revolutionary training shoes. The soles are made of some new kind of rubber that put a spring in the step (according to the promotional literature in our mailshots) and the linings have been coated with a special anti-pong agent (the promotional literature puts this slightly differently). We have a new logo, new furniture. Even a few new faces. The parent company retains overall control, but on a day-to-day basis the buck stops with Ed. He's a director now.

My office, which is only slightly smaller than the one Ed used to have, is next to his and leads directly off the large outer office where Colin and Piers sit with the new salesmen: Kev, who is twenty-two and will be a millionaire by the time he's thirty (he says); and Les, fifty, who wears tweed jackets and chain smokes. Les thinks my tight skirts are exclusively for his benefit and is mystified that I have twice turned down an invitation to lunch. Marie, who ultimately got the job of junior secretary, sits out there with them, and in reception we have eighteen-year-old Debbie. She has no qualifications of any kind and isn't very bright but she has big eyes and a bosom you could balance a tray on — which evidently are qualifications of a kind because the male consensus was that she was the ideal candidate.

On this particular morning I had collected the mail from reception as usual, and was taking the opened letters into Ed's office — on the door of which, incidentally, calendars of nude women no longer hang — when I was surprised to find him there already. Ed is a reasonable timekeeper but I like to get in first to sort out the day's work and glance through his appointments so I'm prepared for when he starts shouting that he's lost something.

Oddly, he was wearing the same coloured shirt he'd had

on the day before: blue cotton with a button-down collar. Same tie too. I had never consciously registered what shirts he wore but now it struck me that he never wears the same colour on consecutive days. He was even darker than usual around the eyes. When he stood to take the letters from me I saw his trousers needed pressing.

'I like your flared knees,' I said. 'Has she thrown you out, at last?' He threw his head back and laughed. Then he got up to close the door.

'How did you guess?'

I hadn't guessed actually. I thought the likeliest thing was that he had been out on the razzle. My jokey insult was just meant to imply that no woman in her right mind would keep him around for long. But he was so impressed with my powers of intuition that it would have been unkind to disabuse him.

'I didn't have to guess. We women just know these things.'

'Have you been listening at doors again?'

'I don't have to listen at doors. I just have to look at you. Your most secret thoughts come up on your forehead like subtitles.'

He sighed and sat down, pulling at his trousers where the creases ought to be.

'Then you'll know that I spent the night at a friend's. When I got back yesterday, she'd changed the locks.'

I didn't know how to respond to this so I stuck with banter.

'What took her so long?'

He smiled wearily and stirred the cup of tea on his desk, batting with his spoon at the grains of milk powder that hadn't dissolved.

'Don't know anyone with a spare room do you?'

'Hasn't Janet Reger got a spare room?' By mutual consent this is how we now refer to his girlfriend.

He sighed and his head drooped between his shoulders blades, like a defeated animal.

'She's got a very nice house. Right on the Thames. Three bedrooms — and she doesn't want me in any of them.'

I pulled up a chair and sat down wondering how we had got into this territory. It's so difficult to know how to handle the confessional and I wasn't sure what to say. One of my old friends, Laura, used to do this to me. She'd call round, throw herself on the sofa, burst into tears and embark on detailed descriptions of the latest episode of ill treatment she'd suffered from her boyfriend. She was fine as long as I just listened and poured brandy into her but if, trying to be supportive, I said anything like 'I always thought he was wrong for you,' then she'd go berserk, shouting that there was no point in telling me, I never liked him anyway. Once when she'd said she was going to leave him and I said if she felt like that she could always move in with me, she accused me of being jealous and wanting them to break up.

So seeing as whatever I said was likely to be miscon- strued, I just asked what I wanted to know.

'Why doesn't Janet Reger want you in her house?'

He shrugged. 'She doesn't want to get involved.'

'Not get involved? She rings you every day!' This was an exaggeration but only slightly. 'How often would she ring if she *was* involved?'

He bristled slightly, the way Laura used to when I thought I had been particularly helpful. 'You don't understand,' he said mournfully. 'She's been hurt before. She's very sensitive. She needs space.'

I always think that 'I need space' is a roundabout

way of saying 'piss off' but it didn't seem diplomatic to say so.

And to be honest, I was impressed. Here was a man who not only acknowledged that a woman's feelings might differ from his own but who was ready to talk about them too. So what if he had to resort to clichés, it was a start.

'Sometimes we all need space,' I answered, resorting to clichés myself.

'I'm sensitive too, you know. And I've been hurt, she knows that.'

It always amuses me when people assume that being sensitive means just acknowledging your own feelings, not appreciating other people's. But being sensitive myself, I didn't let this show.

'Have you been hurt?'

He looked at me and the side of his mouth twitched. He hated any suggestion of interrogation; I should have known better. But he answered anyway, well kind of.

'Yes, I've been hurt. Badly. My wife threw a *coq au vin* at me once.'

We both smiled at that as though it was a joke but I have to admit I kind of hoped it was true.

'How would you like to go out for lunch?' Ed asks unexpectedly, his head appearing round my door.

It's ages since I've been taken out to lunch, apart from the uncharacteristically generous gesture of Diane's when I got this job. It would be nice to go out but it's not always easy to know with Ed what you're being offered. This could turn out to be a tête-à-tête to discuss some detail of office politics, a drink and a sandwich with all the staff in tow − or he could just mean he's giving me an extra half hour away from the office because he wants something delivered to the other side of town.

'What do you have in mind?'

'Just lunch – nothing fancy. I've asked Roger Hayward and I thought you might like to meet him.' Roger Hayward is our new accountant, he's starting next week and is an old friend of Ed's. 'But don't do me any favours.'

'Thanks, I'd love to come.'

'Then get a move on. We're already late.' He's wearing a tie decorated with a geometric pattern of greens and yellows which seems to bring out the wolf in his eyes. He licks his lips as though tasting the blood of a carcass on them.

Ed opens the door to the pub and I hover for a moment on the threshold. It's one of these mock-Tudor places, all oak beams and red velvet, though Chris Rea booming from the juke-box sets you right as to which century you're in. The atmospheric gloom makes it difficult to see initially but soon my eyes grow accustomed and I make my way down the steps. Ed pushes his way through to a booth in the corner where a man sits watching two women at the table next to him. Ed has told me that he used to work with Roger Hayward some years ago. The new salesman, Les, is also an ex-colleague of Ed's and I wonder if it's coincidental that Ed should be populating the office with his old mates. If you have a personality like Ed's, it's probably the only way to proceed.

As we approach, Roger Hayward stands to greet us, holding out his hand to me.

'So this is –?' He looks at Ed expectantly.

'Gemma, my PA,' says Ed quickly as though he thinks Roger Hayward may say something indiscreet.

He shakes my hand warmly, if moistly. He is short and sharply dressed, with a balding pate which is caught in the soft glow of a wall light. 'We've spoken on the phone, haven't we?' I don't think we have, he may be thinking of Marie or more likely Debbie, our receptionist. Recalling how she pouts at the men like Marilyn Monroe singing 'Happy Birthday Mr President', I'm not thrilled to be confused with her.

'Gemma is my own personal Wonderwoman, she can help with anything you need to know,' says Ed with a surprising and not entirely convincing enthusiasm.

'You're a lucky man,' says Roger looking me up and down as though I'm about to be offered for sale.

'But just watch your step, she's got a tongue like a whiplash.'

'Shouldn't worry you then,' says Roger, laughing and making me feel I'm missing something.

'Anyway, to business,' says Ed. 'This hostelry isn't of the finest but they've an excellent choice of beers, and though I can't entirely recommend the food, they do a very acceptable beef in red wine.'

Knowing Ed to fancy himself as something of a gourmet I'm disappointed to have been brought somewhere where the food is only 'acceptable', but the avid discussion of real ales that ensues explains why we've come to this particular establishment.

They do the male thing of tussling over who will get the first round, reminding me of two stags locking antlers in a mock battle. Ed wins and we watch his retreating back, casting about for something to say to each other. Roger strikes gold first.

'So. How are you liking working for Ed?'

'Oh, very much.'

'He can be a bit of a bugger, old Ed, but he's a good bloke.' Roger is the only person I know besides me who thinks this and I warm to him instantly though, as it turns out, temporarily. 'We worked together in Birmingham years ago, I'd just qualified and Ed had just come back from abroad to get away from some woman . . .' He laughs, recollecting.

Looking up, I see there's a long queue at the bar. I hope Ed won't come back before Roger has had a chance to dish the dirt. But Roger turns out to be less of a mine of information than a pothole. He turns the conversation to himself and talks on happily brooking no interruption. But then, after a short pause in which I resist the temptation to ask him anything, lest it starts him off again, he says, apropos of nothing, 'So you're not seeing Ed, then?'

He takes me completely by surprise. 'No, of course not.'

'Sorry, sorry,' he wafts his *faux pas* away with his hand, 'I just thought, with him bringing you along and knowing what he's like and everything . . .'

'What is he like?'

He focuses on a dirty glass on our table and grins confidentially. 'I'm sure you've found out, an attractive girl like you.'

'I know he has a wife and a girlfriend, if that's what you mean,' I say, archly, irritated at his assumptions. 'But I've never met either of them and despite what I keep hearing about him, he's been the model of decorum as far as I'm concerned.'

'Well, I'm glad you've told me,' Roger straightens up and pulls his white cuffs down his jacket sleeves so the right amount is showing. 'I like to get the feel of staff relationships before I join an organization, and I just thought . . .' He twiddles with one of his cuff links. 'He has obviously quietened down from when I knew him. Thanks for warning me. I wouldn't want to say anything to embarrass him.'

We sit in silence then, observing the other drinkers and it's a relief when Ed returns with the drinks though my delight is short lived. Roger turns his attention to Ed as he places the glasses on the table.

'So. What are you driving now?'

'I've got a BMW – the 2.8 litre 3 series; picked it up last week. Not a bad little motor. Nought to sixty in seven with a . . .'

I look from one to the other like a spectator at a tennis match.

'Wise choice. I used to have a Cavalier which was fine in itself but it didn't have the *i* on the back. So no one driving behind you knew that's what you were driving. I wouldn't make that mistake again.'

'Well, exactly, people judge you by what you drive . . .'

For 'people' read 'men' I thought. The two women at the next table are leaving already and I have a sudden urge to join them. I'm so bored I almost wish I'd gone shopping for duvet covers with Marie. I glance around the table for a beer mat to colour the o's in on but there isn't one.

The food arrives and they're still discussing what they drive – miraculously without even mentioning the colour. I push my way back into the conversation, hoping to shame them into taking the conversational vehicle in a new direction.

'I come in to work by bus and train,' I say.

'What?'

'I travel by bus. Nought to sixty in forty-five minutes but very reliable. If it breaks down you just get off and get on another one.'

They're both looking at me, nonplussed.

'But I only get the single deckers. People do judge you by what you ride in.'

'I'm glad you've met Roger,' says Ed as we watch his portly but carefully tailored frame disappear through the double doors. 'He has a few rough edges but he's an excellent accountant. Between us I think we'll run a very tight ship.'

I can't think of anything to say to that. Despite the fact Roger has been introduced as a friend, I thought it was obvious that the man has a black hole where his personality ought to be. 'I was surprised his children are so young,' I offer, searching for neutral territory.

'It's his second marriage. He's got teenagers by his first wife. She was a friend of Maxine's.'

'How long have you and Maxine been married then?' So it *was* worth coming after all. Without any manipulation at all, the conversation has led to the very question I've been wanting to ask.

'Fifteen years.'

'Gosh. Fifteen happy years.'

'Fifteen happy minutes more like.'

'Then why . . .' No, even I can't ask, on such a throwaway remark, why he doesn't get divorced.

'We should have split up years ago but it'd kill her.'

Seeing as Ed is living in a bedsit in Battersea ('While I sort myself out') since Maxine changed the locks, I don't quite follow the logic of this.

'Oh, we have our ups and downs,' Ed goes on, 'but underneath it all, she needs me.' (I translate this as, 'But underneath it all, I need her.') 'The trouble is she thinks I'm a one-woman man and I'm not, never have been. I told her that when we met.'

'Yes, but every woman thinks they can change that.'

'They wouldn't change me.'

'Not even Janet Reger?'

He looks at me hard, making me feel I'm somehow taking her name in vain. Then he stands up abruptly and starts pulling on his coat.

'I'll see you back at the office. I need to go somewhere.'

God, he's so touchy.

After lunch I call at the printer's and when I get back to the office it's to find Debbie standing guard at the door to reception. Her black-ringed eyes are as round as conkers and her white face is more than just the result of too much make-up.

'Don't go in there!' she warns me.

Ed's bellowing voice hits me in the face, though thankfully it's not me he's shouting at. 'I told you Tuesday and I meant Tuesday!' There's a crash as though a chair has fallen over.

Quieter voices, one of them Colin's, are raised in ineffectual opposition.

'Debbie, what's going on?'

'He says Colin forgot to do something, and Colin said Ed didn't tell him to, and it's made Ed mad.' Debbie is whispering though there's little chance of anyone hearing us over the commotion.

'Get on the phone now and give them an ultimatum!' Ed's voice is as loud as if he were in the room with us.

'I'm going to look for another job,' says Debbie sadly, delving into her V-neck sweater and hooking a pendant out of her cleavage.

'Cover me, I'm going in,' I say, but Debbie doesn't think

it's funny and when I open the door to the main office I don't think it's funny either.

It looks like a war zone. Filing trays have been upset, two chairs are on their side and a pile of papers has been knocked to the floor. Les and Kev are both at their desks bent over their work — for the first time I fully understand what 'keeping your head down' means. Colin is leaning on his desk, determined to stand his ground but Piers is in my office taking cover.

'Ed.'

He looks at me in surprise, not having noticed my entrance.

'Ed, it's OK, I'll sort things out. Calm down.'

'Don't you bloody tell me to calm down.' He looks at me threateningly, trying to find something to blame me for. But he does calm down. As I look at him, his breathing becomes more shallow and he bends down to pick up one of the upturned chairs. Then he strides into his office, closing the door behind him.

The row casts a pall over everyone which isn't much relieved by a visit from Brindle Sylvia, calling to see if she can interest anyone in something from her catalogue. When I emerge from my office to get a cup of tea she is sitting with Marie on the sofa in reception (a sofa without stain and from which it's possible to rise without the aid of a hoist) and pointing out to her a set of kitchen knives she could buy for only eighty-five pence a week.

'How do you like us, Sylvia?' I ask, dabbing with my finger at a ladder I've just seen in my tights. I caught them when I picked up the chair Ed had kicked over. Though we've been here several weeks, it's Sylvia's first visit as she's been away at her timeshare in Spain.

'Very smart, and I don't dislike this carpet either.' The

carpet is dove grey with a charcoal fleck and a pile that is as yet entirely unflattened by the passage of busy feet. Nor have assorted liquids been spilled upon it and inadequately mopped up. 'And this no smoking policy you've got – I wish we had it in our office. That Glenda at the next desk from me – smokes like a fish.'

'What sort of fish?' I ask. 'A haddock?' Sylvia looks mystified so I go on, 'Why don't you ask her to smoke outside the office? That's what Ed did with Les.' Les spends half his life puffing away outside in the hall by the lifts.

'Is he one of the new ones? I saw him. Very nice. Asked me if I wanted to buy any Tupperware.' Les's wife runs Tupperware parties and Les adds to her business where he can. 'I thought I might ask to see what he's got.' She claps her hand over her mouth and giggles at the innuendo.

'I don't know what gets into you, Sylvia,' says Marie in mock reproof.

'At least you didn't say "who"!' Sylvia is almost convulsed by her own wit now.

'That reminds me,' says Marie without explaining why it should. 'Janet Reger rang. She said would Ed ring when he'd got a minute. She's amazing, isn't she, with that voice? No wonder he's so keen.'

Without warning I feel a black mood of irritation descend. It must be Brindle Sylvia with her stupid jokes. She's the only person I know who can make the typing of minutes a tempting prospect and, forgetting my tea, I return to them with gratitude.

'Ah, Gemma. Hi!' Colin is sitting at my desk and looks embarrassed at my sudden entrance, as though I've caught him cheating in an exam though there's nothing in my office that he's not allowed to see. He's holding a letter in his hand.

'Is that something you want me to deal with?'

'Uh? No. It's er, I was just looking for an envelope.'

'There are plenty in the stationery cupboard.' I take one from my drawer and hand it to him.

'It's quiet in here, I wanted to be on my own for a while.' He folds the letter, making sharp, even creases, then scribbles a name on the envelope and hands it to me.

'Will you see Ed gets this?'

'What is it?'

'You know what it is.' I turn it over in my hands, going over the options. He's talked about giving notice before but then Ed talks of sacking him with the same frequency most people say 'Good-morning.' I didn't think either of them was serious but then the row of this afternoon has brought things to an all-time low.

He screws up a piece of paper on which he has been doodling and tosses it into the wastepaper bin. It hits the top edge but drops in. 'You know what happened earlier. He does it all the time – he makes a decision – it backfires and he looks around for someone to blame it on. And it's usually me.'

'I'll speak to Ed.' I'm surprised at the *frisson* of excitement I get at the prospect of interceding. 'He wouldn't want to lose you.'

'Only because he'd have to find a new scapegoat.' Colin leans back in his chair and gazes unseeingly at my desk calendar.

It isn't just Ed's heavy handed approach that's the problem, though that's bad enough. Colin's resentment comes from several sources. Before the new staff were recruited he told Ed he wanted to apply for a salesman's

141

job. He has almost none of the qualities a salesman needs: he's too sensitive, too easily hurt, has too much soul. As I told him when we talked about it, he'd be brilliant at selling if the product was good because he's so sincere that everyone would believe him. But a salesman has to make you believe it's a good product even when he knows it's crap and overpriced into the bargain. Ed told me a salesman should be brash, flash and focused on cash. That hardly describes Colin.

But Ed is such a coward. He told Colin he would think about it and the next thing we knew, Kevin and Les were arriving and that was the end of that.

'Out of the blue he brings in these new guys. And I'd got more experience than Kevin – he's only just starting.' That's true but Kev was born to sell. He's frighteningly plausible and with charm so thick you could spread it on toast. Clients love him. And not just clients. Debbie plays the coquette with astonishing gusto considering she probably doesn't even know what a coquette is. When he enters reception she stands and cocks her breasts at him like two handguns ready to go off.

I pull up a chair and sit opposite Colin. He smells of pine kernels and mint. As always his suit looks fresh from the tailor's, pressed into surrender while his shirt collars have the sharp edge you usually only see when they're still in the packet.

'What would you like Ed to do? What has to happen to make everything OK? An apology? Another chance at selling?'

He shrugs that it's too late and I tell him he's wrong and how everyone depends on him but as he listens to my wilful misrepresentations of his current situation, I see him in my old job at Social Services, seated by Mrs Mount, understanding her craving for chocolate and her bizarre views, able to temper them with common sense without it leading to conflict. He's in the wrong job here, with us. He should be in an environment where his sensitive nature would be an asset not a disadvantage. He might not be ideal for the teenagers — they'd run rings round him — but younger kids would find the child in him. Old people would mother and adore him and agree to whatever he suggested. Those in need would know they'd found a sympathetic ear.

Of course, I don't say so. I like Colin. And you never know when you might need a sympathetic ear yourself.

'You can't afford to throw your job in,' I point out. 'What about your mortgage? What will Nina say?' Colin's partner has ambitions for him. She wants him to be a hotshot executive with a company car and prospects.

He doesn't answer and I lean forward and squeeze his hand.

'Leave it with me. I'll speak to Ed.'

Ed returns from the bank but before I can speak to him about Colin, I hear Marie relay the message from Janet Reger. In his eagerness he almost runs to his office and slams the door.

Chapter 9

———— ▪ —

Tania slips into the water with the ease of a fish and ducks her head under.

'It's really warm today.'

I dip my toe in then sit on the poolside dangling my legs in the water. It's the temperature of body heat, probably so that when the kids start weeing into the water no one will notice.

Jack and Joe are at the far end of the pool in a sulk. They want to go into the big pool but Tania has Sophie to consider so for now we're all in the toddler's pool.

'If you want to swim, go ahead,' Tania offers, 'it doesn't take both of us to mind the kids. Or the boys could go with you.'

But I hate to swim. In Corfu, with Rudi, it was different, and in the few resorts on the Mediterranean that I've visited with Sam. But in none of those places was I surrounded by dozens of screaming kids and almost as many blow-up animals. If there's one thing guaranteed not to aid my swimming enjoyment it's being butted in the rear by a pink rhinoceros.

'Why don't you let me stay with Sophie and you swim with the boys?' I ask Tania, making it sound as though

I'm doing her a favour. I've seen Tania dive off the highest board. She loves the water. But she says no, so I stay sitting on the edge of the pool feeling the water seeping through my costume while Sophie splashes me in her waterwings, periodically shouting 'Look at me'.

'Hulloo there!' I recognize the deep Scottish brogue but don't immediately identify it with the heavy breasted woman heading this way. Partly this is because I've taken my contact lenses out and now any object more than two feet away is just a fuzzy shape that either moves or doesn't, partly it's because I'm not always good at placing people out of context. I know this woman: know I've had conversations with her, some of which have been as irritating as a stone in your shoe. But I can't recall whether she's an ex-colleague from work, the mother of one of Joe's friends, or a checkout assistant at Kwiksave.

'I didn't know you liked swimming, Mrs Millard.' There's only one category of person who still uses a title and your surname. Mrs McBride, Joe's teacher, squats down next to me.

'You should join us for the children's swimming club. Great fun.'

I make a mental note to look up 'fun' in the dictionary but I don't expect running the children's swimming club to form part of the definition.

'It's not really my sort of thing, Mrs McBride.' My sight is good enough to see that she doesn't shave her legs and has varicose veins. The backs of her thighs are fluid and collapsed; gravity has got the better of them.

'Now where would we be if we all thought that?' She smiles but still manages to let me know I'm being reproved.

'And I can't swim very well. A length is about my limit.'

'Then here's your chance to learn. We meet on Wednesdays, three-thirty, in the playground.'

She makes me feel so guilty I almost say yes. But only almost.

'I work, Mrs McBride. Perhaps when I've got some time off.'

I expect her to look resigned or annoyed but her expression doesn't alter. She knew I'd turn her down; she was going through the motions. Probably she gets lucky sometimes.

'And what about you, Mrs Donahue,' she says to Tania. She won't get lucky this time either; Tania has a ready made excuse in the form of Sophie who would be too young to go.

Only then Tania says she would love to join in when Sophie starts school next year. 'In fact, I'm wondering about training as a teacher.'

I can't believe what I'm hearing. I didn't realize Tania had masochistic tendencies.

'Good for you, Mrs Donahue. The teaching profession is crying out for people like you — in fact, Mr Trelawny was only saying to me last week how well you're doing. And I've seen how you relate to the children in your sewing class. I think you're a natural.'

Tania smiles shyly and looks away but I can see how delighted she is with the compliment.

I wait for Mrs McBride to comment on my own skill but she doesn't say anything. 'It's certainly not everyone who has the knack with children. I know how tricky kids can be from when I've done cookery with them,' I say, to prompt her.

'Oh, I was so grateful for that day you stepped in,' she says kindly, reminding me that it was just the one day. 'We

147

don't all have the same talents, of course, but I'm sure the children appreciated your efforts.'

'Do you think all women's thighs go like that?' I ask Tania, as we watch Mrs McBride's thighs go jiggling off toward the adult pool, her back displaying the remains of last year's tan and, judging by the strap marks, last year's swimsuit. Her buttocks are like chicken skin, pink and dimply: empty sacs, drooping down from the legs of her swimsuit. I can't disguise a pang of hostility in view of her less than fulsome praise of my teaching ability.

'No, not everyone's,' Tania says consolingly. 'Only yours.' I drop into the pool next to her, making as much of a splash as I can without getting my hair wet.

'Tell me about Colin,' says Tania as we cling to the bar at the side of the pool, kicking our legs out to strengthen our stomach muscles. Sophie has made a friend of a precocious five year old with pierced ears, and the dad of a classmate of Joe's has arrived with his children. He stood at the poolside briefly to greet us and when I looked up I could see, down the leg of his swimming shorts, the net inner lining supporting one heavy but perfectly formed purple testicle. Jack and Joe have followed this man and his brood into the big pool and Tania and I have abnegated responsibility for our boys to him (whether he knows it or not).

'Why are you asking about Colin?' I've hardly mentioned him.

'I like the sound of him. He sounds soulful and compassionate. And you like him, don't you?' She looks up at me from under her lashes, less pale now the water has wetted them.

'Of course I like him. He's a very nice bloke.'

Her expression suggests I'm saying less than I mean. I know the kids can sometimes prove a distraction but I can't think of anything I've said that could have led her to think I was brewing any feelings for him. Tania shrugs and asks for details of the latest unkindness Ed has shown Colin, and now I see what has happened. When I've told her about how he attacks Colin, she's assumed I was focusing on Colin, whereas really I've been telling her about Ed.

'You don't mean to tell me you fancy Ed!' Honestly, you'd think I'd said Hitler or someone.

'Tania, I don't fancy anyone. It's just that he's a challenge . . .'

'A challenge? He's a bully, you mean.'

'He isn't a bully, it's just that he gets frustrated easily . . .'

'You mean he's childish as well? If he can't get what he wants he throws things about and ends up drumming his heels on the floor?' I've thought this myself, but it's different now it comes from Tania. I kick off to do a width, change my mind and come back again, needing to take out my irritation with Tania on Colin.

'Colin is very sweet, you're right, but he's also . . .' Sophie and her friend take a running jump into the pool so that we have to turn our heads away to avoid the spray. '. . . Wet. He's a bit wet.'

'That's not very nice. I thought you said he was sensitive.'

'Too sensitive. That can end up like being wet, can't it. Or damp anyway. Maybe he's just a bit damp.'

Tania chews at a fingernail thoughtfully.

'You don't call someone you like "wet". I thought you were friends.'

Strange; until Tania says this I haven't thought of Colin as a friend; I haven't thought of him at all. He's good looking but he's not, you know, sexy. He dresses well, and he has beautiful eyes but he's, well, safe. There's no hint of danger such as you get, say, with Sam or Ed.

Some more children arrive all laughing and shouting at each other and for a moment the din echoes round us, shutting out all other sounds. A lifeguard in the big pool blows a whistle.

'Is Colin with a partner?' asks Tania when the sound has quietened a little.

'I hope you're not going to interfere,' says Tania when I tell her and complain about women like Nina who are always trying to make their men do what they want them to.

'Which isn't something you'd ever do,' she says sarcastically. She purses her lips and hard lines form either side. They'll be wrinkles when she's older. I must look in the mirror and see if my mouth does that.

'He can do better than her.'

'God help Joe's girlfriends if this is how you react about a guy you say isn't even your friend.'

'He needs someone to watch out for him, that's all. He's been sucked in by this woman; I bet she just wants a meal ticket then she'll start sprouting kids like Grandma Moses.'

'Who's Grandma Moses?'

'I don't know, but she obviously had kids.'

Tania sighs again. 'Just keep out of it. And he must like being pushed around or he wouldn't stick with her. Some men are like that. Probably you're right, he's a bit wet.'

But I'm not having Tania finding fault with poor Colin. Who does she think she is — me?

'He's just shy. Sensitive. Once someone like that falls for someone, they're incapable of seeing the truth about them.'

'Gemma, you don't have to be shy and sensitive for that to happen. Of all people, I'd have thought you'd have known that.' Is she getting at me over Sam or Ed – or both? 'So what is he going to do, this Colin? Do what his girlfriend says and leave – or do what you say and stay?'

In view of Tania's totally inaccurate reading of the situation I don't tell her about the career for which Colin is really suited, and into which I will steer him when the time is right.

Anyway on the subject of careers – 'What's all this about you going into teaching?' I'd always thought if she were to qualify as anything it'd be full-time earth mother.

'I haven't decided anything. But it seems the obvious choice – that way I'll always be home for the school holidays.' I start to say that you can't choose a job for the holidays but she silences me – 'And I really like it. It gives me a buzz when you're showing a kid something and suddenly they can understand how to do it and they couldn't before. Especially the ones who couldn't do much to start with. I know there's all this about the low pay and low morale but it's very rewarding, teaching. I'm wondering about maybe going into special needs.'

It surprises you when friends disclose depths you never guessed at. Undiscovered shallows I'm used to, but they're mostly my own; and the only special needs I've ever been interested in are mine and Sam's. What with the soulful Colin and tender-hearted Tania, I seem to be surrounded by masochists with bleeding hearts.

'So you don't think you'll go back into the bank then?' Of course I know she won't, the big mystery is how she got into it in the first place. It seems an unlikely career for someone who spent a year hitching round Europe on her own when she left university, but then she's given to

151

being unpredictable – and what's less predictable than that someone like that would want to be a bank manager?

'I didn't want to go into the bank the first time,' she says, reading my thoughts perhaps. 'The idea was that I'd work there for a few years so we could get a low mortgage for the house. It seemed a good idea at the time.'

I can see it would have seemed a good idea to her bloke but I'm less certain why Tania should have fallen for it. Anyone could see that Darryl's view of a good idea was what was best for Darryl.

She shrugs. 'Don't tell me you think Sam is any different?' But that isn't fair. Sam does what he perceives as being best for all of us. The fact I happen to disagree doesn't mean he isn't putting us first. But Tania goes on, 'It's like I've just said. You fall for someone and you're incapable of seeing the truth about him.' I don't believe that either. I love Sam for what he is, not what I imagine him to be.

As she finishes, and before I can respond, Joe and Jack come running back followed by some other boys and the dad we had seen earlier. Seeing our boys come over to us he raises a hand in greeting. He's older than us, maybe late forties, with greying temples and a hairy belly pushing over his navy trunks. His legs look too thin for his torso, like a toffee apple on two sticks. It's rare to see a father at the pool, particularly with boys this young, but his age probably accounts for it. Either this is his second marriage or he's the ex-husband. (Ex-husbands are like old rock stars – they keep coming back older and fatter). Men Sam's age are too busy with their careers to spend this much time with their kids; even if they don't work away, like Sam, the hours they work are too long to allow it or they just underestimate how fast children change; how soon it will be before – far from wanting their dad to come along – they're thinking they wouldn't be seen dead in public with him. Older men know how fast it all changes. A second marriage is a chance to fill in the gaps they left first time round.

The man is coming round the pool to speak to us, his large feet making a flapping sound as he steps through the puddles. 'How old is Ed?' asks Tania, apropos of nothing. But without waiting for an answer she slides into the water slowly.

It was Tania's suggestion to bring the kids swimming this weekend. She says it's so Joe won't miss his dad so much but really it's so that I won't.

Sam should have been home for a few days in November but it has had to be postponed again and he phoned yesterday to say he won't be home now until Christmas Eve.

Sometimes, in the middle period of each three-month stint of Sam's, I wonder if I miss him at all. I'm acclimatized to single parenthood by then; shopping for two instead of three, watching TV alone, going to bed early to read. We develop our own routine, Joe and me, and Sam is just a voice at the end of the phone. But the first few days after he's gone, or approaching his return, it can be unbearable. I think about him all the time; I can smell him, have imagined conversations with him, I dress in the mornings in the things he finds appealing, just as though he'll be seeing me in them. Sometimes I almost pant for him. From day to day I've been expecting him to say he was on his way and now he's not coming I feel like an athlete who has reserved his energy for the last lap and then found there's one more to run.

'You might as well be dating,' says Tania wryly, 'always waiting for the phone to ring.'

It's never possible for outsiders to really understand the dynamics of a relationship and Tania bases her opinion of ours almost entirely on what I tell her about it when Sam is away. But she doesn't see us together when he's at home. You talk to your friends about your quarrels but try describing your making up and watch their eyes glaze over. 'Man bites dog' is news, but 'Dog forgives man and they live happily ever after' lacks a certain dramatic element.

This is what I'm musing on as I scrape the mud off Joe's wellingtons in the kitchen. A sudden shaft of sunlight pierces the grime on the windows and at once I'm back there though there was no grime on the plate-glass windows of our six-berth caravan.

May, just this year. We're sitting looking out of the window of a caravan — 'mobile home', the owner said — across dunes to the sea on the west coast of France. It's as hot as a greenhouse, with all this glass, and the dust is dancing in the sunlight like fireflies. Sam knows someone — he always knows 'someone' — who had a cancellation and we've got the caravan for half price. Joe has made friends with the older kids at the next van and is playing swingball with them, getting frustrated because he can't hit the ball as hard as they can. Sam is reading some kind of pop biography and I am playing house — tidying the lounge area by throwing sweaters, toy cars, board games — into the overhead cupboards. I love it here, the housework takes about fifteen seconds. The smallness of our town house terrace is an irritation and is the reason, I always say, that it's always a mess. But the confined space of the mobile home has its charm. There's nowhere for dirt to hide. You could clean it from top to toe and be done in less time than it takes to get the limescale off the taps at home.

'Do you want to go into the town today?' Sam asks this

every day but so far we have travelled no further than the beach. I look out the window and consider the weather. The deep cobalt sky is radiating heat. Above the track that leads to the camp shop wavey lines of iridescence sway and shimmer.

'After we've been to the beach.'

Sam laughs. Every day I give the same answer. When it rains, then we will visit the town, but after a week it seems more likely that the tedium of routine rather than the weather will drive us further afield.

Collecting everything we need for the stroll across the dunes takes a lot longer than tidying the caravan does. Buckets (two), spades (three. Joe insists that Sam and I have one too), moulds in the shape of fish or boats, and little flags to stick in the top of sandcastles; then there are books for Sam and me, a blanket to lie on, sunhats, sunscreen, towels, more towels . . .

'Aren't you ready *yet*?' asks Joe.

At lunchtime I walk back by myself and buy bread, pâté and cheese from the camp shop. The shop is cool and the assistant tries to engage me in conversation but the heat has deadened my responses and I can manage only the briefest reply. With my guard down, I find myself seduced into buying yet more sunscreen, a new sunhat for Joe and some twinkly coloured things for tarting up sandcastles which suddenly strike me as irresistible.

'I thought you were only going for cheese.' Sam is bemused to see me struggling towards him weighed down with purchases which, with all the stuff we brought from the caravan, would be enough to fill a pantechnicon and will require one if we're to get it back there. But he's too sleepy to enquire how much over the odds I have paid for the inedibles from the camp shop.

Sam is tanning by the minute; he looks darker now than when I left him, the whites of his brown eyes glittering against his glowing skin. He yanks the top off a beer and takes a swig, sighing with satisfaction as he offers it to me before collapsing on to his back. I give Joe a piece of baguette filled with cheese and he crouches down with the remains of it, digging a hole, putting the sand in sandwich. He's deep in concentration and giving voices to the play people he has brought with him. A few yards away two kids, aged about seven, are fighting over a bucket: with a yell one falls backwards as the handle comes away in his hand. He cries and his mother runs to pacify him. In the other direction the legs of two teenagers project from behind a rock, no, forget them, but beyond are two young parents arranging the sunshade over their baby's recliner. A girl, about Joe's age, is running up to the water's edge and running back squealing as the waves come in. Families. The beach is full of families and that's what we are, now, the three of us. The sun is high overhead, and the air is still and hushed as though the world has stopped turning. I want to hold the moment but the one thing we didn't bring is the camera.

'Sam?'

'Hmmm?' He has lain back, his wrist shading his eyes, revealing the dark, damp hair of his underarm. Beads of sweat gather in the dip of his chest and begin to run down the valley that leads to the tuft of hair protruding from the waistband of his shorts.

'Sam, I wish it could always be like this.'

He reaches for my hand without looking up. 'It can be.' For a moment, just a moment, my heart skips.

But not really, not seriously. See how well I know him?

'We can get this caravan any time we want, babe,' he says. 'We just have to let the guy know.'

Chapter 10

‘Can I speak to you about Colin?’ Ed is signing some letters which takes a minimum amount of attention so this is as good a time for me to get him as any. Last week Ed was away on the Thursday and Friday so today is the first opportunity I've had to talk to him.

‘You've got thirty seconds before I have to go into a directors' meeting – but I should think that's twice as much as you need to say anything about him.’ He grins at me, satisfied with his latest put-down of Colin.

‘He's given his notice in.’ I don't smile but I'm just as satisfied to see the smug expression drop from Ed's face. He adopts a ‘What did I do?’ expression.

‘What's got into him now? If he's after more money, he can whistle for it. I gave him more than he's worth when we moved here.’

I pull up a chair and sit down adjacent to him. ‘Then you'll be glad he's going.’

‘Yes, well I am.’ He sighs. ‘It's just the hassle of interviewing for someone else, having to cover till we get someone . . . Have you tried talking him out of it?’

‘I'm not the one who throws chairs at him.’

‘He wants to learn to duck quicker. Anyway, I didn't

throw it at him, it fell over. I was mad, that's all. I had no idea he'd be so easily upset.'

'We were all upset. If my son carried on like you did, I'd slap his backside and send him to bed.'

'Well, try it out,' says Ed, opening his arms wide and offering himself up to the experiment. 'I'm game if you are.'

I ignore his attempt at levity. 'And I have to tell you that Debbie is also looking around for another job and that if Colin goes Piers almost certainly will.'

'Piers?' Ed drops his arms and looks almost hurt. 'I thought he was getting on rather well.'

'Only last week you told him if he didn't pull his socks up he'd be out on his ear!'

'Figure of speech. You have to keep behind these guys if you don't want them slacking.'

I heave a sigh and we sit looking each other, divided by our different perceptions of the problem. Then Ed says, 'Go on then, Miss Know-it-all Knickers, let's hear your solution.'

I expand on my hopes that he will speak to Colin, acknowledging Colin's undoubted strengths and agreeing to be more amenable in the future. I leave out my private vision of Ed prostrate on his knees and begging forgiveness as a scenario unlikely to achieve fruition, pleasant though it is to contemplate.

Ed's expression makes it clear that my first scenario is as unlikely to come true as my second.

'Here's what we'll do,' he says, getting up and gathering the files he needs for the directors' meeting. 'You can tell Baxter I won't accept his resignation – he goes when I say he can go and not before. And you can tell him I won't be throwing any more chairs about – in future I won't chuck anything that might break if it hits him.' He takes a pen from his desk drawer and leans his thigh against it to close it. 'Now is that all?'

I suppose it is. I return to my office not knowing if I've helped Colin or just given Ed another stick to beat him with.

The Tuesday progress meeting has become a regular item. It's much more impressive these days and now there are more of us there seems some point to the typed minutes with their 'Action' column. Now Colin, Les, Kev, Piers — and even I — have tasks we have to complete and report back on. Which means that it is no longer only Colin who's the brunt of Ed's temper.

We're sitting in a loose circle around Ed's desk, at a slight disadvantage with our hard-backed chairs and nothing to rest our files on.

Ed is going through the sales figures for the new product. It's early days but that's no reason not to start seeing some results, as he tells us. He skims down the page and then stops as though transfixed. We all tense — except, ironically, Kev, despite his being the object of Ed's irritation.

'I thought you were going to try some retailers in the West Country?' Ed's eyes narrow and he looks at Kev accusingly. Les shifts uncomfortably in his seat but Kev refuses to be intimidated. His papers are on the floor, he doesn't need to refer to them and he leans back in his chair, his legs spread as wide as they'll go, his arms wrapped round the back of it.

'I did but I only had time to get to a couple because you wouldn't pay for me to stay over.' Kev is heedless of the danger he is in.

'That's because you *were* only seeing a couple. If

you'd set up a series of appointments, we could have run to it.'

'But I couldn't set them up till I'd been down and seen what there was.' He smiles the smile of sweet reason.

'If it'd been me, I would have gone down for three days, scoured the area, and not come back until I'd got those orders.' Ed isn't smiling, he's leaning forward over his desk, one fist gripping the week's sales figures. He means Kev to see that he's the boss.

'That's what I would've done too. But you wouldn't pay for me to stay over.' Kev stops rocking on his chair and brings it to a halt. He looks around for support but everyone but me has their eyes on the floor and the only reason I'm looking up is to be ready to take down Ed's next pronouncement.

'Action: Kevin. Go down to the West Country next week, Monday to Wednesday. And I want to see those orders on my desk Thursday morning. Or the hotel bill comes out of your pay.'

Kev is still smiling, scrutinizing his fingernails. Despite Ed's tone he knows he has won this one. Already Kev has made the same discovery I have: stand up to Ed and he capitulates. I will Colin to make the same observation but the muscle twitching in his face shows he's too preoccupied waiting for his own cue.

'Les.' Les jumps in his seat at the sound of his name but in fact he has nothing to worry about. Ed is satisfied with his progress; his years of experience show. Les is doing better than expected – and Ed always expects a great deal. Les is grinning now, displaying tobacco-stained teeth, his pink face clashing with his sandy hair. He looks seedy and shifty, more like a bookie than a top salesman.

While Piers gets a dressing down, I sip the coffee Marie

has brought us. We have proper china coffee cups with matching saucers now, not chipped mugs that we've brought in ourselves. Everyone complains that the cups don't hold enough but I like the veneer of civilization that the blue-white porcelain gives.

Piers is smiling with one side of his face, supercilious and irreverent, his chin lifted in defiance. But two dots of pink light his cheeks. A smart remark will not go down well with Ed and it's the only response he knows.

'Colin.' Colin raises his eyes and that muscle twitches in his cheek again. I think Ed has left him till last on purpose, knowing the agony he will be in. He leans back in his seat and swivels from side to side looking Colin up and down. There's a long silence. Colin swallows. I watch his Adam's apple bob up and back down. If he wasn't so dark skinned, the fleck of green in his paisley tie which matches his suit would probably also match his pallor. 'You need to keep a closer check on the invoices. Marie isn't as accurate as Gemma, she needs watching.'

I almost gasp at this obvious untruth but Colin just nods. His knuckles are white as he grips the chair. 'And I want you to start preparing for the mailshot, we'll need more temps in for stuffing—' He pauses, daring someone to crack the inevitable joke but we disappoint him and he continues – 'the envelopes. You better check when you can collect the leaflets from the printers. Check what each envelope will weigh with the sample in it too, and what the postage will be. We don't want a repeat of last time.' It was before I joined the company, but I understand a mailshot went out with letter-rate postage because no one had thought about how the enclosed samples would increase the weight. Recipients had to pay the shortfall and there were numerous phone calls and letters of complaint. The mistake was Colin's predecessor's but Colin stands accused by proxy.

There's another pause and Colin swallows again. As usual Ed is saving the best till last. Making Colin wait. Making him suffer. He opens his address book and jots down a phone number on his pad and looks at it thoughtfully. Then he swings his chair back to the front of his desk and shuts his folder with a flourish.

'Other than that Colin, good work. Keep it up.' He sits there, daring us to comment on this unexpected praise.

'I hope you noticed how I handled Baxter,' says Ed when the others have left, clearly pleased with his effort, minimal though it was. He stands up and wanders over to the window, leaning on the sill to look down at the traffic. His office gets the sun all day but in this position he is blocking it so that a shadow falls across my papers. From this angle I can see he has the start of jowls. I wonder if Sam will ever develop jowls. But he's too long and lean, I can't imagine him with sagging flesh anywhere. 'Not that it'd be such a loss if he did leave. It's people like you we need more of – bright, full of ideas, capable.'

I take another sip from my cup trying not to look as though this is the most I've been praised since Miss Freeman at my junior school told me I was good at spelling.

'You're wasted as a PA. Tell me, where do you see yourself in ten years' time?'

With the glow his words have produced I'm tempted to say 'Working here with you,' but the image of what I'll be doing is speedily followed by a vision of how I'll be looking. In ten years' time I'll be thirty-seven – nearly as old as Ed is now. I could have jowls myself by then.

'I'd like a job related to psychology – that's what my

degree is in,' I say, focusing on the practical rather than the personal with relief.

Ed turns to face me, his arms folded across his chest. 'That's how you understand people so well.' He would think that, when he understands them so little. 'Well, it's a flexible subject, isn't it? It's cropping up in all areas of business these days — you could use it in marketing, personnel, organizational structures.'

I haven't planned to use it in a business context at all; I've been thinking about counselling, maybe advising students in a college. But I can see the appeal of running your own company.

'We make a good team,' he is saying. 'With me behind you you could go all the way.'

'I'm not sure I'd ever want you behind me, Ed,' I say. 'I'd rather have you in front where I can see what you're doing.'

He lets out a bellow of laughter as I knew he would. Then his expression changes. 'By the way,' he says, 'you better make a note of my home phone number. I'm back to the old one.' He's avoiding my gaze, knowing he's admitting some kind of defeat. I had thought, from the flurry of phone calls I had taken from Janet Reger over the last few days and his excitement when she has called, that he was moving in there. From Ed's face I suspect he had hoped so too.

'Are you back home permanently, then?'

He gives a broad grin. 'I hope not.' He stands rattling the change in his pocket, suddenly pleased with his prospects. 'Let's continue this over lunch. There's a nice little bistro I know that I think you'd like.'

The surprise of the invitation adds to the pleasure of it. But before I can reply the phone rings. I'm nearer the phone than he is and I pick it up for him. The voice purrs, she sounds like melted chocolate. I hand the receiver to Ed, noting how his face lights up and his body tenses at the sound of her voice. He takes a seat at his desk and waves me away.

I take it lunch is off.

Sam rang again last night. Suddenly he's constantly on the phone. I can't decide whether he's just plain bored, he's missing me or he's got a guilty conscience. I think it's the guilty conscience because if I had a pound for every time he's said he was sorry for not being able to get home I could afford to go out there to meet him.

It's sad that he should be coming back on Christmas Eve so that he'll miss all the shopping and wrapping. He actually enjoys all that, especially the challenge of where to hide presents from Joe's prying eyes and fingers.

Ironically, his calls are more than usually unsettling, reminding me of what I'm missing. Generally, I hardly miss the sex – it's like chocolate. If there's none in the house you barely think about it but if there's a box open in the same room you can't rest until you've pigged out. Constantly hearing his voice is making me ravenous for a nutty cluster and a walnut whip. Even more than the sex, though, I miss the closeness. I'm having to vet what I watch on TV just now. Sex and violence I can stand, but sex and love is just too painful a reminder. When you find yourself crying over a Häagen Dazs advertisement then it's time to worry.

I've never worked on a Saturday before. I'd forgotten how quiet it would be at this time in the morning – no throng to fight your way through on the pavements, no need to step into the road in the path of oncoming vehicles just to avoid the raggedy men with eager faces selling the

Big Issue. (I buy my copy from the man outside the station but how are the sellers I don't buy from to know that?) Later the Christmas shoppers will be out in force but for now there's just me.

Ed asked if I could do some overtime. The company doesn't usually allow it but what with the time and energy the mailshot has taken (it had to be rewritten due to some libellous comment Ed had included about a rival's product), we've fallen too far behind to just incorporate a long document like this into our usual workload and it has to be ready for the directors' meeting on Tuesday. Ed should have finished it last night, in readiness for me to type it up today.

'Be careful,' Tania told me, 'you don't want him to get the wrong idea. He sounds like the sort who'll try it on with anybody.'

I told her she was being daft but now I'm wondering if I'm the stupid one. I'm feeling nervous. Excited-nervous. I haven't been on my own with him before.

The office building isn't open, so I have to wait outside for Ed to arrive. The air has the crisp feel of holly berries and green spruce about it or maybe that's just the effect of the decorations I passed on the way here. A man in an overcoat passes on the other side and looks across at me, wondering what I can be waiting for. I don't know what he plans to do with the rest of the day, but whatever it is, I'm starting to wish I was doing it too. I know we'll have a laugh, but I just hope Ed hasn't read anything into the fact I said I'd come.

I walk round the corner and look in the window of the sandwich bar. It looks eerie, with its empty shelves and unlit interior. I feel like I've walked into a scene from 'The Twilight Zone'. As I stroll back, some joggers come bounding towards me and I flatten myself against the wall so as not to impede their progress. The shorter of the two, a woman, moves with the smooth co-ordination of a racehorse. Her partner, a man of a heavier build trailing behind, looks more like a racehorse owner.

It's rude to stare so I look away as they get nearer and am surprised to hear my name being called.

'Gemma. There you are.' He makes it sound as though he has been waiting for me. Ed's curls are glistening against his forehead, and now he flings himself forward from the waist panting, his sweatshirt exposing a strip of white flesh to the elements. The sandy-haired woman who stands next to him in an expensive-looking tracksuit, looks at me appraisingly, even less out of breath than I am. She doesn't return my smile of greeting; but then perhaps it doesn't look like a smile, I'm so astonished he has brought company that I may have lost control of my features. Ed, raising his head now, doesn't smile either. His brows are locked together and his head is lowered in the characteristic pose he adopts when things aren't going his way

'Maxine,' he says, 'meet Gemma. Gemma, this is Maxine. My wife.'

Chapter 11

———▶ ◀———

I hadn't realized the report I have to type would include schedules. I sit at the word processor while Ed leans over me, not too close, pointing out aspects of the document he needs to clarify and wonder if he can hear that thumping sound which is the noise of my heart hitting the floor. There are four separate charts and I have no idea how to locate a layout from the disk because I always give them to Marie. I wouldn't have come if I'd known about the schedules. I certainly wouldn't have come if I'd known about Maxine.

'How long do you think it'll take?' says Ed, straightening up. I indicate the documents and elaborate on how tricky they are, describing the complexity of devising a suitable layout, exaggerating the limitations of the computer and hoping he won't relate them to the limitations of the operator. Ed sighs and runs his fingers through his hair, and his curls bounce back, leaving no trace.

He sighs and takes a turn about the office. 'I thought we'd be finished by lunchtime. Maxine wants to go to the gym this afternoon.'

Even without the schedules I wouldn't have finished by then. I ought to feel flattered by his confidence in me but

I'm just astonished at it. You wonder where some people pick up their ideas.

'You can always take Maxine and leave me to get on. I'll be OK. You've no reason to stay, have you?' If I just ploughed ahead I'd be done by – oh, Tuesday. And if he left, I could phone Marie and get her over here to do the work for me.

Ed shakes his head and does another slow circuit of the office, kicking at the carpet as he goes. 'There's supposed to be a director in the building if other staff are here.'

'I won't tell if you won't.'

He sighs, and I notice that he's speaking to me without meeting my eyes. He's embarrassed as he damn well should be. It's like having your mother come on a date. Not that this was supposed to be a date, but you know what I mean.

I begin to type the heading and, glancing up, see Maxine in the doorway.

'I'm sure she would work a lot faster without you standing over her,' she says coolly.

'Lunchtime.' I haven't heard Maxine's approach and I jump at finding her behind me.

'I'll just stay here. I'll press on.'

'No, you must have a break. Get your coat.'

I don't want to get my coat. I want to phone Marie. A light has started flashing on the printer and I don't know what it means. I want to phone Marie and then I want to go home.

'Really, I'm OK. You and Ed go,' I say, meaning why don't you just jog off. 'I'm not hungry.'

She picks my coat up from the peg and holds it out for me making me feel like I'm a visiting niece being taken out by relatives determined to make me enjoy myself.

'This must be really boring for you,' I say as I do up my buttons, feeling under scrutiny and trying to establish some common ground.

'I don't mind,' she says, checking a chip in her nail polish. 'I like to spend time with my husband at the weekends.' I give her a half smile in case this a joke but I don't think it is.

Ed holds the door to the street open for us but he doesn't look at me as I pass through. His expression is that of a man whose chickens have come home to roost and just as he'd invested in a fresh batch. We wait for him to lock up and then he strides off ahead of us towards his car, so that we have to trot to keep up. Maxine and I are thus left together.

'He certainly seems to be in a hurry,' I say, to break the silence.

'He's in a temper,' she says unexpectedly.

'Because the report is taking so long?'

She almost smiles. 'Only partly.'

We reach the car and Ed gets in, not holding the door open for either Maxine or me, and before we have even adjusted our seat belts we roar away with a squeal of tyres.

'Slow down,' says Maxine in the weary voice of someone who has made the same comment many times before and wasn't listened to then either.

Ed toots at an elderly man in a Metro who seems to be lost.

Maxine sniffs the air in the car. 'Someone has been smoking in here. I don't let anyone smoke in my car.'

He ignores her, scowling. Desperate to lighten the

169

atmosphere, I ask, although I know the answer: 'Don't you smoke, Ed?'

'No. Never. Why?'

'Oh, it's just that you look like a man with all the vices.' Too late I realize that this isn't the ideal comment to make in front of a man's wife but Maxine turns to me with a wry smile.

'Yes,' she says, 'and he's got all the others.'

We both look at Ed and see his scowl growing deeper which is somehow satisfying. I can see Maxine thinks so too.

Ed strides ahead of us once again, going straight up to the bar, while Maxine finds a table. I say I'll go and give him a hand, meaning I'll choose what I want and pay for it myself but Maxine lays a restraining hand on my arm.

'Is lager and a ploughman's all right? We always drink lager,' she says. 'I can match him pint for pint. It's a game we play.' Seeing as Ed has to drive us back, I hope they won't be playing it today.

'So you have children?' she asks while we watch Ed place the order. I tell her about Joe and she explains that she has miscarried twice and no longer wants children. 'In any case, I don't think Ed is the paternal type, do you? He needs too much babying himself. You must have found that out already.' I'm not sure what to say to this.

'I think he may have a childish streak. But show me a man who hasn't.'

Maxine smiles at that, and I go on to tell her about Sam, emphasizing his less admirable and therefore more entertaining qualities. By the time Ed returns balancing three ploughman's lunches, Maxine and I are quite old friends. Suddenly it's her and me against him.

'I was just telling Gemma,' Maxine says as Ed settles

himself down, 'how we couldn't have children because I had enough on my plate with you already. She said she knows just what I mean.' Ed opens his packet of butter and spreads it over a roll. 'Does he ever lose his temper and throw things?' she says sweetly, addressing herself to me.

I deny it even though he has. It's not so easy for me to laugh at Ed in his presence as it is for her. She continues to catalogue his faults — pettiness, bad temper, jealousy ('You can talk,' says Ed meaningfully, the only time he has contributed to the conversation unless you count his emphatic scowl) as well as carelessness. Once when they were abroad they got lost in a blizzard. They got out of the car to ask the way and he locked the keys inside with the engine running.

But then, finishing her anecdotes at the same time as her cheese, she begins picking at Ed's food. He slaps her hand but she grabs his wrist and makes him feed her the morsel he is holding. He sighs resignedly and they smile at each other. I feel invisible.

'He has a hard life,' she says to me, patting the back of his hand. 'He has a wife who doesn't misunderstand him.' She laughs and he laughs. I finish my meal.

When Ed has finished eating — in fact slightly sooner than that, seeing as he takes his last piece of cheese with him, having playfully fought Maxine for it — he goes off to the pinball machine. We watch his back while Maxine continues with her observations on his shortcomings but I don't laugh so much now. She doesn't mean any of this, any more than I meant what I told her about Sam. Ed has told me that he no longer sleeps with Maxine but I can see that isn't true either.

Ed brings us a second lager and she regards the head on hers for a moment. Then she says, without

171

any preamble: 'He's carrying on with someone, isn't he?'

I'm so astonished that I just blink. Then I pick up my lager and sip it slowly, thoughtfully, as though I'm trying to think who the culprit might be. Suddenly Maxine laughs.

'I hope you didn't think I meant you! No, I know his type, you're all right. But he knows I'm on to him.' Ed returns to our table to ask for ten-pence pieces and Maxine hands him a couple like a mother doling out sweets. 'He feels humiliated with me being here. That's why he's in such a terrible mood today – I mean, even for him,' she continues as he walks away. 'But he likes it really. He's strong but I'm stronger.'

I nod, trying to look interested instead of entirely puzzled which is what I am. Does she really know there's nothing between Ed and me or is this her way of warning me off if there ever should be? It's not very flattering, actually, to be told that it's quite plain that a man isn't interested in you. Or has she just dressed up this intended insult in the garb of good advice?

To think Tania thought I'd be in any danger from Ed. Even if he was interested, he just doesn't have a vacancy.

Maxine abruptly drains her glass and gets to her feet. 'Drink up. We must get on.'

When we get back into the car Maxine's mood of skittishness and *bonhomie* seems to have deserted her. We drive back to the office in silence save for the odd swear word from Ed directed at weekend drivers.

When I get home, Sam phones, *again*. That's three times this week alone.

It's only a fortnight until Christmas and Christmas Eve

should be a day to look forward to. Not only is that the day of the office party, but when I get home from it I'll be having my own personal Santa coming down my chimney. Or, to put it another way, going up it.

'Six years is a long time to be together and still be hot for each other,' says Ed. It's Wednesday evening and we're unwinding over a coffee having just caught the post with a couple of urgent documents which Ed had overlooked. He is going to drop me at the station later but for now it's a relief to sit back and talk things over without the phones ringing, memos arriving and the pressure that there's something vital we ought to be doing; it's somehow provocative that the things we're talking about in this darkening office are all to do with sex. He has been telling me about his failing relationship with Maxine (and trying to cover up for her unexpected presence on Saturday by claiming she thought he'd only be half an hour. I don't know if he believes that or just wants me to). Now he is asking me about Sam and this is where our conversation has led us.

'I've always found,' says Ed, 'that the sex starts waning after the first year of living with someone.' I don't know if this a generalization or a comment on his own marriage. It's weird to find myself discussing matters sexual with my employer, someone with whom I'm in no kind of relationship, though maybe that's what makes it so easy. It feels entirely comfortable and natural. I can open up to Ed with the same ease that I can to Tania – in some respects even more so – the fact Ed doesn't know Sam makes it easier to discuss him. There are some people with whom you just have a rapport; you know that you have only to express a thought in the simplest terms and they'll understand. It's a challenge to reach his deeper side, and invigorating when you know most people would have stumbled at the obstacles in the way.

'How come you've saddled yourself with a kid and a husband? You don't seem the type?' Although I'm glad of an opportunity to talk about Sam, I need to set Ed right about the 'saddled' part.

'He isn't my husband, we live together. Or when he's home we do.' I reach into my bag for a tube of peppermints and draw out a Tampax by mistake. I shove it back hoping Ed hasn't noticed. 'He's not here enough for me to be saddled with him, and as for Joe, we wanted Joe. We wouldn't be without him.' I sound like I'm protesting too much though what I've said is perfectly true, we did want Joe, although what I don't say is that, with hindsight, I wish I'd left more of a gap between the wanting and the getting. I wasn't exactly trying for a baby but I wasn't actively trying to stop one either. Sam didn't know; he has never known. At the time I thought a baby would tie Sam in tighter. He thinks Joe was an accident.

Ed asks me what Sam looks like and how old he is and I take out the small photo of him that I carry. 'He makes me feel so old,' he says and it's hardly surprising. The camera has caught Sam's cheekbones in all their macho glory. Ed's cheekbones are buried under flesh that has given way to gravity long since though he has a rugged, earthy quality which isn't unattractive. In some ways his age is a bonus; he has a confidence and assurance that it takes younger men time to develop, and the provocative air of knowing what he wants and how to get it.

And age is only significant if you think it is. When I was first dating Sam we used to team up with the lead singer of his band and his girlfriend. Del was in his early twenties, the same as Sam, but Libby was over thirty. She had a cobweb of fine lines under her eyes and I thought she was almost as old as my mother the first time we met; by the second time we met I had ceased to consider her age at all, only that she had small neat breasts like firm lemons, was wonderfully sophisticated and exciting and I wanted to be like her.

If the band had to stay somewhere overnight, we would book into a bed and breakfast with Del and Libby. (The others would sleep in the transit or book into some dive, but Libby demanded certain minimum standards.) The first time we tried to find a hotel together there was only one room left, but it had two double beds in it and the landlord said, with an embarrassing wink, that we could have it for half price. I didn't want to have to undress in front of Libby, but even more I didn't want to say so, so when Libby asked what I thought, I acted like I was up for anything. 'Someone's enthusiastic,' said Libby, laughing.

The boys bought some whisky and grass and after the gig we went back to our room and played strip poker. I'd never played poker before but it was Libby who lost fastest; I don't think it was an accident. She usually wore half a dozen rings which should have kept her in the game longer than the rest of us, but she took her rings off before we started. Libby didn't believe in wasting time. Her breasts weren't like lemons, they were like the grapefruit my mother served as a starter on special occasions, with a glacé cherry on top. I'd thought she was a natural blonde up till then.

We all went to bed after that. Not together, though there was an uneasy moment when it could have gone that way. No, we were all very proper. Libby said we mustn't make too much noise, so we must take it in turns to make love, not all do it at the same time. So we waited while

Del and Libby had a turn, then we did. Then we all made love again, but this time Del had to hold the bedhead for us because it was banging against the wall.

The arrival of Joe put an end to that lifestyle. I wonder sometimes if Sam has ever needed someone to hold the bedhead since then.

'And this Sam – does he make you happy?'

'Of course he does. Ecstatically.'

But thinking of the fun we used to have has cast a pall and 'ecstatically' was a stupid word to use. Now Ed thinks I'm being sarcastic.

He laughs sourly. 'I know what you're saying. You fall in love with someone, chain yourself up, and then you look at all the women you could have had and you think – why did I do it?'

It maddens me to hear my relationship with Sam compared to his. Sam and I trust each other. It wouldn't occur to me to follow him around as Maxine obviously does. If Sam tells me he has to work than I know he has to work. 'I'm not saying that at all. I'm very happy if you must know, it's just with him being away so much, it's difficult to plan things and then . . .' I had no idea I was going to cry. One moment I'm gearing up to defend his implied criticism and the next, my eyes are filling up and my throat is swelling so that I think I may choke. I search blindly in my bag for a tissue, my fingers carefully avoiding the Tampax.

Ed sighs and leans closer though without touching me. 'I thought so. Has he got someone else?'

Jesus, he's as bad as Tania. Can't I just be miserable and disappointed at not seeing him without it meaning something? Sam's face, with Del just out of focus holding the bedhead, swims into my mind.

Ed takes my hand and cradles it between his own. His palms are warm and dry and to my surprise I find some of the ache in my chest running out through my fingers. He leans closer still so that our heads are almost touching. We stay sitting there, very quiet, very still. His breath, as I inhale, is like a balm. In the circumstances I half expect him to put his arm round me and kiss me but suddenly he checks his watch and gets up. 'Come on, I'll drop you at the station.'

Outside it's starting to snow which softens the traffic noise and covers the sleeping bag of a man huddled at the side of the pavement like an extra blanket.

'What will Santa be bringing you?' I ask Tania as we watch the back gardens of the London suburbs through the train window. Christmas trees and fairy lights cast a warm glow on the washing hanging in the back yards.

Tania shrugs. I'd meant it as a joke, a commentary on how the children's expectations differ from our own. There is just one thing the boys want – some awful kind of action figure models that accompany the TV series. Nothing else matters – not bikes, not rollerblades; not nothing. If Tania and I are typical, then every parent in the land is in a panic about getting the right pieces in the right colours, and resisting with all their might the temptation to buy the cheap imitations they sell in the market which to our untrained eye look identical apart from the price tag. ('Santa will have a really easy job this year,' said Joe, as Tania and I stood forlornly in Hamleys, having been told there would be no more in stock until the New Year. 'Everyone wants the same thing.') But I'd forgotten for the moment just how great the contrast was between Tania and I as regards Christmas presents. While I can expect a gift of some kind, usually quite thoughtfully chosen even if it isn't exactly what I want (as well as something small from Joe, bought by Sam on his behalf), Tania has no such source. She never hears from Jack's father, and the only presents she gets are what amount to small tokens from friends like me. Her parents do buy her something but because of Tania's state of penury their gifts tend to be things they know she needs and can hardly afford, such as a new iron, or (last year's gift) a vacuum cleaner.

'Where will you be spending Christmas?' I say hurriedly, trying to find an aspect of the Christmas experience that will be less painful for Tania, and failing. A businessman with a leather briefcase squeezes into the seat next to me. His fat thigh is unpleasantly warm against mine.

'Oh God, don't ask. Mum and Dad want us to go there as usual.'

'With your aunt and uncle?'

'Naturally.' Tania's Auntie Jean and Uncle Bob are the prickle in Tania's holly. They criticize Jack, making oblique but unfavourable comparisons with their own grandchildren. No doubt they buy Jack a decent present but there's no such consolation for Tania. Auntie Jean believes in recycling unwanted gifts, though she does have an eye for discovering the unusual in the Oxfam shop where she works as a volunteer two afternoons a week.

'You could have them to you instead. Then you needn't invite your aunt and uncle.'

'I'd still have to invite them. Mum wouldn't come if she thought they would be left on their own.'

'Why don't they go to their own children?' The businessman gets out his newspaper and opens it out, the pages brushing against my open mouth.

'They've only got Janet, my cousin. And she won't have them.'

What I will say next seems inevitable. I try to stop myself but the conversation has been leading inexorably in this direction.

'You could always come to us.' I hope Tania will appreciate the kind thought without making me live up to it. Sam and I get little enough time alone without reducing it any further.

Tania turns to me. 'Do you mean it?'

'Of course I do.' Of course, I don't.

'That would be brilliant. And Jack would love it. We can always visit my parents on Boxing Day when Auntie Jean won't be there.' She turns to grip my arm, colour rising in her wan cheeks. I'm going to get her blusher for Christmas and make sure she uses it. 'I've been dreading Christmas – you're really sure you don't mind?'

The inspector enters our carriage and we both begin to hunt for our tickets. The businessman puts his paper down and searches in his breast pocket, hitting me in the chest with his elbow but the pain I get isn't half as bad as the one in my head from wondering how I'm going to break the news to Sam.

Chapter 12

B efore I've even organized the Christmas party I know it's going to be my favourite one ever and one of the finest social gatherings ever graced by a plastic wineglass.

Well, how wrong can you be. Marie has been busy all afternoon with paper chains and tinsel and now the office looks like a bomb has gone off in the decorations section of Woolworths. (I should have known what her taste would be for overkill from her bridesmaids' dresses — not an inch of cloth without a bow or a bit of lace attached.) The men didn't want to come at all and I've had to blackmail them into it by threatening to tell Ed that they fiddle their time sheets (the effectiveness of the threat shows they obviously do).

'Hasn't Marie done a good job?' I ask Colin, just as Les opens the door from the outer office and the draught knocks the tinsel Christmas tree off the filing cabinet. He sighs irritably.

'Why do we have to have it here? There aren't enough of us.' Colin doesn't see the point of our select gathering. There will be a bigger do at our old offices but I want to cement the sense of unity we're all starting to feel (well, I am, anyway). I like it here. I like Colin, I like Piers. I even like Ed.

'Have a drink,' I say, 'If you start getting double vision it'll look more crowded.'

Actually if he gets double vision that will make six of us but the party isn't under way yet. Diane and Suzanne are going to come on after they've looked in at the official party, and will be bringing half a dozen or more of the men they work for. Brindle Sylvia is coming too. I was hoping she wouldn't get wind of it but she phoned to say she will bring her mates and some mistletoe as though this was something I would be pleased about. Diane has taken it on herself to collect money from those in her office who wish to come and passed on to them the house rules: No smoking or vomiting on the carpet.

'I think I'll just go. This really isn't my scene.'

But it isn't the scene that's upsetting Colin, he seems almost oblivious now to what's going on around us. With his hands in his pockets he has a crumpled look, not at all like him. He isn't particularly tall but now as I straighten up I realize I can see right over his head.

My ESP may have fooled me as to how good the party was likely to be but I'm willing to trust it on what's bothering Colin.

'Leave her if she's not making you happy.'

It takes him a moment to follow the new direction the conversation has taken.

'Me?' He looks bemused, as though he can't think what put that into my head. But then his jaw tightens and his expression hardens. He squares up from where he was leaning against the desk, and now he seems quite a bit taller than I am. A piece of tinsel has lodged in his turn-up and he bends to remove it.

'Considering you think you're so hot at second guessing what's going on with everyone else's love life, you seem strangely blind to your own.' Marie suddenly turns the music up so it isn't easy to catch all his words and I think I've misheard him. Then he stands back up, surprising me with his sudden aggression. 'Take a look at yourself, Gemma. Get a life. Or better still, get a mirror.' He strides away, swinging his raincoat off the umbrella stand as he passes.

I can't think what he means. I go straight down to the loos to check my make-up in case that's what he was referring to, but it looks all right to me.

It was a mistake to ask Marie to bring the music. We have a choice of Christmas songs past or her most up-to-date CD – chart hits of the year before last – but fortunately Kev has a selection of tapes in his car and brings them in. To the thumping beat of something which could be house, garage or quite possibly, portakabin music, I circulate among the party-goers. As that means Marie, Debbie, Kev and Piers, it doesn't take long. Les has gone into town to do the last of his Christmas shopping (which is probably also his first) and Roger will come if he gets back from a lunch engagement. Ed is out getting a haircut.

'Well, at least we're here,' I tell Debbie.

'Yes, well I wanted to ask. What time do you think it'll go on till? Because I'm not staying after five.' Honestly, you wonder why you bother.

By four o'clock it's dark outside and, with the red tissue paper Marie has draped over the lights, the office is cast in a warm glow. Piers, who has been indicating that he is here only on sufferance by a lame and entirely untypical attempt at filing, gives up when I requisition the top of his filing cabinet as a home for the clean wine cups.

'I hope a few more people turn up,' says Roger, clearly

regretting that he rushed back. He picks up a crisp disconsolately from the dish I'm filling.

'Oh, they will do,' I say with a forced brightness, wondering if that will include Ed. He was the only one I neglected to blackmail – ironic really, considering I'd have more on him than anyone. What's also ironic is that, somehow, if he doesn't come, the party has no point.

Ed may be a shit but I've come to realize that's what I like about him. He lives life as it comes, he's dangerous, unpredictable. He's the equivalent of wreckage you see by the roadside – you thank God you're not involved in it but you can't help watching. I don't admire him; you'd have to be a fool to get involved with a man who already has a wife and a lover – and who employs the likes of Debbie just because she points her breasts at him. But he makes me feel alive. I like the way I've got him where I want him, even with my saggy breasts that don't point at him so much as at the floor.

On the other hand, I haven't got him where I want him just at this moment. The possibility that he is in a pub somewhere with Janet Reger while I'm entertaining his ungrateful staff only adds to the dampening effect Roger is having on me.

I take the lids off some dips and arrange them on the table. They look curiously unappetizing in this light.

'We could have done with some candles,' says Roger, less impressed with the red glow than I would have hoped. Actually I meant to light some candles but I forget where I put them and I've lost the impetus to look.

Shortly before I also lose the impetus to live, Ed returns. I interrupt a fascinating anecdote of Roger's about what he once said to a policeman who pulled him up on the M25 and go to him.

With his hair newly trimmed his dark curls have sprung back. He looks like a Greek god — Bacchus probably, or someone equally licentious.

'You look very smart, Ed, you must be going somewhere.'

'I am. Away from here, as soon as I can.'

Now he reminds me not of Greek gods but of Samson, except it's not his strength he has lost with his locks but his minuscule quota of charm. A small comment on my efforts would not have gone amiss.

In silence, I lead him to the table where Marie has laid out our bottles of wine and beer and he pours himself some red, wrinkling his nose when he sees the label. 'Gemma! Is this really the best you could get?'

'No, of course it wasn't. But it's still too good for you.'

'Like you are, you mean,' he says good-naturedly. 'Don't worry, Christmas parties are always like this. It'll be fine.'

I smile, feeling foolish for looking forward to this and to his company at it. I can't understand why we're having less fun than on a normal working day.

My feelings must show in my face.

'Here,' says Ed, suddenly diving into one of the carrier bags he has brought in with him. 'This will cheer you up.' The present, rectangular with sloping sides, the shape of a box of Belgian truffles which is what I hope it is, has been wrapped by a professional, the shiny paper pulled taut with corners sharp enough to prick you. There's a bow in the middle and a rosette to match in one corner.

I know there's nothing unusual in bosses buying their secretaries presents but when you're beginning to find your boss appealing, his gift has a special resonance. I'm touched by the delicacy of the wrapping, the opulence of the decoration, ready to admit his good taste in selecting it for me. It's an acknowledgement of our special relationship. I swing round to put it down on the table while I thank him – and send the carrier bag flying, its contents tumbling to the floor with a gentle rustle of paper.

The two boxes that were in the bag are the same as mine and my exuberance trickles away as I watch Ed picking them up, their identical bows shot through with gold that twinkles tackily. For just a moment I'm disappointed to see my gift duplicated. But on the other hand, it depends on who they're for. If these are for, say, Maxine and Janet Reger, then it's an even bigger compliment.

Ed puts the boxes back in the carrier bag and hands it to me. 'I've got one each for Marie and Debbie, give them to them, will you?'

While I stand there, nonplussed, Ed sips his wine, rolling it round his tongue. 'A modest little number,' he says to Roger, 'but I think you'll be amused by its presumption.'

'Oh!' says Roger. 'I thought you were talking about Gemma.' For some reason they think this is funny.

It is with effort that I have persuaded Piers, Kev and Ed from leaving and Diane arrives with the crowd from her office not a moment too soon. Despite their protestations, it's apparent that Roger and Les would stay until whatever time the booze ran out, but the younger men ask more of a party than that. Fortunately, along with a clutch of assorted staff, Diane has brought some of the junior secretaries; as this is the aspect of a party that the younger men ask, now everyone is happy.

'Diane! You look terrific. How are you?' Now that I too am a director's secretary Diane has courted my friendship somewhat and we sometimes go shopping together at lunchtime, but we've been so busy these past weeks that

I've had to work through some of my lunch hours and although we speak regularly on the phone, I haven't seen her face to face for a while. Since I saw her last, Diane has had her hair re-styled; it's shorter at the back than the front, giving her an up-to-the-minute, voguish look and there's a shine to her eyes. Maybe it's just the effect of the red tissue paper over our wall lights.

'I feel terrific. Everything has been wonderful lately.'

'Work? Or . . .?' She got a promotion to PA to Bill, the financial director at Head Office just weeks ago.

'Oh, everything really. With all the changes, I've been involved in a lot of promotions work and I love it – setting up conferences and functions, and meeting clients, of course.' Diane was born to meet and greet, I can see she'd flourish in that sort of role. 'And, in fact, things generally . . .' She waves her hand around without signifying anything in particular.

'You sure it's not just hormonal?'

She laughs. 'Maybe that too. I don't know. It's just that everything is really good at the moment. We'll meet up after Christmas and I'll bring you up to date.'

When she has gone for a refill, I approach Suzanne. 'What is it with Diane?' Although Diane and I socialize more now, you could say our relationship is still only skin deep – especially as Diane ensures that most of our shopping trips end up at the beauty counters of various department stores.

Suzanne shrugs. 'I don't see her now.' Diane has moved up a floor and now occupies an elegant and refurbished office next to that of her new boss.

'I know, but don't you hear any news?' I don't know why I'm asking; she must be immune to gossip from the amount she picks up.

'It's different in our office without Marie – and you, I suppose. The new girls don't have as much to talk about.' I don't remember Suzanne ever talking much. 'But actually one of the girls did think Diane might have someone.'

'Does her husband know?'

'Does whose husband know?' Suzanne can be very hard work sometimes.

But we have to change the subject anyway because Diane comes sashaying over with Bill, her new boss and they, along with Debbie and Kev begin some impromptu dancing. The driving beat of the 'Honky Tonk Woman' doesn't prevent Diane draping her arms round the neck of Bill – a happily married father of two, as I recall – and swaying gently (if rather jerkily, in view of the music) against him. I recall Marie hinting that Diane might rekindle the spark with the Jed Campion, the overseas director. With Bill, it looks as though an entire bonfire is being lit.

'Look at Kev,' says Les with the sort of disgust people exhibit when they wish they could be so disgusting and get away with it.

'It's just a bit of fun,' I say as Kev's arm steals round Debbie's waist and rifles her jumper. In a corner Brindle Sylvia's meaty arms are groping Bob from Shipping.

'It's just an excuse, you mean. Kev's been waiting to get his hands on her since he started.'

'Oh, he's attentive to all the women,' I say defensively. I thought Kev had a soft spot for me. He helps me on with my coat when Colin isn't there to do it, and holds the door open when I'm struggling in with my arms full of files.

'Well, maybe,' says Les. 'But if he sucks up to you it's because you've got the ear of the boss, and if he sweet talks Marie' – does he? I didn't know that – 'then it's because he wants her to do his work first and keep quiet when he's fiddling his expenses. But with Debbie —' As we watch, Kev bends her head back and kisses her. She is running one hand down the front of his thighs. None of us says anything.

Despite having to leave by five, Debbie doesn't go until six and then she takes Kev with her. Piers has already gone, and now others begin to drift off. Diane and Bill, along with Marie, Suzanne and a few of the men have formed their own clique in the corner and are still having a good time. Ed appears at my side.

'Thank God it's over for another year.'

'Yes.' I try not to look as disappointed as I feel. Parties never live up to expectations but perhaps I expect too much. I thought Piers would dance with me, or even Les would, but they have laughed at the dancing and taken a superior attitude to office parties in general. Piers said that the only point of them was to let people who might otherwise be too shy, get drunk enough to screw each other — but that this party was a dead loss as there was nowhere to screw and no one he wanted to screw with. I thought this was a bit offensive actually.

'We better start clearing up,' says Ed, handing me a black bin-bag and tossing two plastic wine cups into it. He shoots a tray of sausage rolls in after them before I can say I was thinking of taking them home for Joe. I inspect the containers of dips before he can take them but Joe wouldn't like them. Besides, although they look as full as when they were opened, the surfaces have been dug about with crisps so the remains look unappetizing and possibly poisonous. Pretty much how I feel myself. I tip them into the sack.

As I reach for the dish that held the crisps Ed leans over for a dirty cup and we collide. He steps back, apologizing, but the hardness of his thigh against mine is unexpected and strangely exciting and leaves a trail of warmth in its wake.

At that moment Marie changes the music to 'Sitting on the Dock of the Bay' which in the prevailing atmosphere has the feel of being the last dance of the evening, and when I see her dragging on to his feet one of the men she used to work for, I see that this is the object. Thank goodness we can all go home soon. Roger draws up Suzanne, Bob sticks with Sylvia and the remaining women pair off with the available men. Suddenly everyone is in a couple but me. And Ed.

We watch the bodies begin to sway.

'Do you want to?' asks Ed, in the voice of someone prepared to grant an enormous favour.

'Not really.' I want to sound as cool as he does and he has hurt me with his duplicate presents. I'm at that stage of inebriation where the initial glow has gone and I'm beginning to feel sour and irritable especially as I, who organized all this, am having to clear up after it too. 'They look pathetic, don't they?'

Ed nods and we watch, united in our superiority. Then he takes my hand. 'Come on.'

I'm not in the mood to dance but maybe I am in the mood to feel his thigh against mine and his closeness softens my resolve. He rests his hand on my waist and we sway along with the others, but ironically so. The subtle movement of our hips, which touch lightly, may resemble the other dancers but only at first glance. A practised observer would notice our sardonic expression; we're above all this but don't wish to embarrass those who aren't by refusing to take part.

'Don't you hate office parties?' asks Ed wearily, against my hair.

'Oh, absolutely.'

'People get drunk and make prats of themselves.'

'It's just an excuse for them to grope people they wouldn't dare to if they weren't drunk.' I'm just echoing Piers but Ed's hand which has been on my waist suddenly moves up to my shoulder.

I hadn't realized it was so warm in here. As we dance, Ed's hand drifts back to my waist and it feels larger and heavier than Sam's and now I'm aware of his damp breath against my forehead. Experimentally I lie my head against his shoulder and feel him relax against me as the room begins to turn. His broad chest is warm through his shirt. The candle I was looking for earlier turns out to be in Ed's hip pocket.

'Ed . . .'

He doesn't answer but he rubs his cheek against my hair.

'Better get them the mistletoe!' says a voice, and opening my eyes, I see Sylvia waving a sprig of green leaves over our heads. People can be so stupid.

Marie helps me clear up the last of the mess when everyone has gone and we walk together across the car park to the bus stop.

'What's that?' she asks in alarm. A white BMW has silently and inexplicably started to move — not forwards but in a gentle rocking motion. My first thought is that someone is trying to start it — I've seen Sam rocking the bonnet this way when the starter motor jams. But there's no one in sight. We stand still for a moment half expecting rapists to burst forth and overpower us or extraterrestrials to beam it up. But the car just goes on rocking.

'That's Christmas parties for you,' I say and Marie nods as we walk past it giving it a wide berth. This car park is used by all the surrounding offices each of which has no doubt held a party today. So there's no reason to suppose that the feet now resting on the windscreen belong to anyone we know.

'Doesn't Ed drive a white BMW?' asks Marie.

'No,' I say. 'His is silver. But I think Bill's is white.'

We walk on slowly letting our eyes slide sideways but it's too dark to see anything.

Chapter 13

He is fumbling outside the door trying to get his key in the lock but I beat him to it, opening it from the inside.

'Sam!' His leather jacket is open revealing a glimpse of chest above his shirt and he grins his special grin that makes my stomach flip as I wait for him to pull me to him, but it's below freezing outside and he's shivering a little, unused to the cold.

'Let me in first.' He heaves in his holdall and several carrier bags and then pulls his jacket off. When we meet after a break I have to study his face, making up for the time I haven't seen him and comparing how he is in my memory (so delicious, impossibly desirable) with the reality. Today the adjustment takes longer than usual. His tan looks strange after the pale faces I'm used to but that isn't why I'm staring. He's fumbling in one of his bags, giving me time to comment.

'You've had your hair cut.'

'Don't you like it?'

It isn't a matter of whether I like it so much as why he has had it done without mentioning it to me. He knows I've always loved his shaggy hair and for me (and I thought also for him) it's always symbolized the rebel in him. But now the jaw-length locks are gone, replaced by a cut so severe he looks like he's joined the army.

'What brought this on?'

'Time for a change, babe. I've had that old look too long now. I thought you'd approve.' He looks tougher, and it brings out his cheekbones, squares his jaw. But I don't approve. How could he do this without letting me know? It's just one more reminder of how much of his life goes on without me. He ignores, or perhaps he just doesn't see, my frown and pulls me to him, laughing at what I now see is partly a joke – to surprise me with his new look – and lifts my chin. 'I'm the same guy as I was underneath all that hair.' He kisses me hard, his special way. 'See?'

'Convince me some more,' I say, with an effort to match his mood but Joe is out of bed now and comes racing down, leaping from the fourth stair straight into Sam's arms. Sam moves away from the banister and swings him round, narrowly missing me.

'How's my big boy?'

'Ready for Christmas. Got my pillow case hung up. Want to see?' Joe's cheeks are as red as if they've had lipstick smeared over them.

'Later.'

'No, now.'

Sam smiles and shrugs, leaning across Joe's shoulder to brush my lips again. He smells of cigarettes and leather.

'Have you been drinking?' he says suddenly. I've showered and smoothed my skin with perfumed body oil so I'm disappointed that it's the alcohol that he comments on.

'Office party.'

'I'll have some catching up to do then. Get me a beer, will you?'

I nod but don't do it. Instead I follow them upstairs to the threshold of Joe's bedroom. Already bumps and bangs are coming from the room, the way Sam's homecomings usually begin. He is wrestling Joe into bed but now Joe has wrestled Sam out again and is fighting him to the floor. Sam collapses, overpowered, and Joe sits on his chest threatening him with a gun Sam must have had hidden in his jacket for him, I haven't seen it before. Jesus, it's Christmas Eve, why can't he save Joe's presents for his stocking?

'Mummy! Go away!' Joe has seen me, and I slink out to hide on the landing. I love to watch Sam with Joe, there's a playfulness in their relationship I can't imitate, and an innate understanding I scarcely even understand.

Joe has handcuffed Sam to his chair and won't release him until he promises to read a story. Sam takes a long time to answer, being dead, until Joe tires of the game and gets back into bed, book at the ready. Sam reads and when he gets to the bit about the giant, he stands up and pulls his sweatshirt over his head, hunching over so his body looks deformed and hideous, and pulling a face until Joe screams.

I go back downstairs.

Over our unseasonal microwaved curry Sam tells me about the band. They've a new lead singer.

'What happened to Mark?'

'Shipped out. He's back in Birmingham pen-pushing.'

'Lucky old Mark. Have you asked about coming home yourself?'

He breaks a poppadom in half and scoops up some chutney with it. 'I haven't got an answer yet.'

'You mean you haven't asked the question.'

'Do we have to discuss this tonight?' His brow furrows into a frown.

'So, what's he like, this lead singer?'

'She's OK.'

'She?'

'Christina. Gary picked her up in a bar, but she's not bad.'

'Picked her up?'

'Met her. He heard her singing and introduced himself. Jesus, what is this?'

'I was just asking.' I reach across the table and squeeze his hand. He can be a bit tetchy sometimes after his journey.

'She writes her own songs and our manager wants us to record one of them. It's looking pretty good.'

'You've got a manager?' I let go his hand so he can take some more chutney.

'We have now.'

I smile and look enthusiastic, realizing I'm not being too convincing when Sam looks at me, concerned, and asks if I'm OK. I'm just being stupid I know, but his offhand manner, what looks to me like the playing down of major developments, is puzzling. Why hasn't he mentioned any of this in his phone calls?

'I did. She's from New York, went to the same school as me, isn't that amazing? I must have told you.'

As if I'd forget something like that. 'Did you know her then?'

'No, she was three or four years behind me. She's going back home next year.' He often refers to New York as home, although only his older sister lives there now. His mother lives just twenty miles from us.

The curry has got mixed in with the rice. It looks like those baby dinners that come in a jar which I used to feed to Joe, wondering how he could bear to eat them. It's gone cold quickly too, I forgot to warm the plates.

'So whose idea was your change of image? Christina's or your manager's?' Now I'm the one sounding tetchy.

'Darling, the only woman who ever tells me what to do is you.'

'And even then you don't do it.'

'This is true.'

I carry my plate to the bin and scrape off the remains of the curry. I feel sick, I wonder if it's something I ate at the party. I put the plate in the sink and fill the kettle ready for our coffee.

Sam turns in his seat, pointing the other half of his poppadom at me. 'Anyway, what are you getting so worked up about? Mark was terrible, you should be glad we've got someone new.' I didn't know I was getting worked up, I thought I was maintaining a sardonic air of cool detachment. (I also didn't know that Mark was terrible. Hadn't Sam told me how talented he was?) If I was feeling hot I'd put it down to the vindaloo. 'Christina's got legs like Roman pillars and a nose like Barbara Streisand, you don't have to feel jealous. Does that make you feel better?'

If I was the jealous type it might, but I'm not so it doesn't. I just don't like feeling excluded. Some Delilah I've never even heard of knows more about my man's life than I do – and has made him cut his hair.

For some reason I suddenly think of Ed's wife Maxine. I wonder how she can tell when he's having affair. Is he suddenly neglectful of her? Or does he buy her expensive gifts (I wonder what Sam has bought me for Christmas?) And – how come, when he has phoned me so often recently – that he hasn't mentioned what must have been the most exciting development with his band he has had for some time?

Sam reaches for his jacket and draws out his cigarettes. He usually only smokes when he's worried about something.

'You've been at your office party all evening but am I quizzing you on what you've been up to?'

I agree that he isn't without adding that I wish he were. A hint of jealousy from Sam wouldn't be too unbearable but he knows he doesn't have to worry about what I do when I'm out of his sight. That's one of the differences between us.

Sam wraps the last of Joe's presents – the action figure Joe would die without and which he has miraculously obtained from a contact in the toy trade, along with one for Jack – and packs it into his pillowcase on top of the other gifts, he creeps into Joe's room and positions it at the end of the bed. I watch through the open door, holding my breath at every squeak of floorboard and rustle of paper but Joe doesn't stir. Of course, this may not necessarily mean he's asleep. I well remember my dad hauling my presents up the stairs, knocking into my dressing table in the dark and swearing softly when he kicked his toe on the stool. But I was older then – probably about sixteen. My mother was always one for keeping traditions alive.

Sam tiptoes out of the room and closes Joe's door softly. He has a soft, misty-eyed look to him which I haven't seen since Sam held Joe for the first time after the birth. Emotions were drifting across his face like a breeze blowing sand – wonder, excitement, relief, disbelief. Sam doesn't cry but he almost did then and he, who is never lost for the right word, couldn't find it then. But once I came home from hospital and we got in the routine of the night feeds and crying babies, the look gradually disappeared. He has plenty of fatherly pride, but the routine of shitty nappies soon makes you forget what a miracle a new life is.

'You've done a good job with him,' he says. 'I know I should have been here more . . .' He's feeling the regret of parents who suddenly realize their children have grown up without their noticing.

'You make up for it when you're here.'

He ignores the platitude.

'How long do you think it takes a kid that age to forget you? You know, if they don't see you for a while?'

'I don't know.' I drape my arms around his neck. 'Why? You thinking of going somewhere?'

He laughs. 'I was just wondering. You don't know what goes on in their heads at this age.'

'Who knows what goes on in men's heads at any age,' I say, not realizing just how true that is.

Sam is always quicker than I am in the bathroom and on his first night home I'm always slightly longer than usual. Well, you have to make a bit of an effort. Which is why when I get into the bedroom I'm surprised to see him already undressing. I always do that for him on our first night back together. He takes my clothes off me too and we make love leaning against the bedroom wall. That is, if we haven't already made love leaning against the wall in the lounge the instant we get Joe settled for the night. But there hasn't been time for that tonight, it being Christmas Eve and everything.

'Sam! Let me.' I take hold of his remaining buttons while I nibble his neck. The smell of him makes something swell in my chest as though I've swallowed a balloon. His arms come round me and I lean against him but his embrace is less firm than usual and he isn't pulling at my clothes or worming his hand inside my dress to see which pants I'm wearing. I pull back and look him in the face. 'What's up? Are you tired?'

'Yeah. Been a long day.' He squeezes me but there's something half-hearted about it.

I've undone his shirt but now I back off, letting him ease it off himself. 'Don't you want to?'

'Yes, course I do. But maybe not right now, babe. It's late. And I'm not sure my legs are up to it.' He laughs so I laugh. 'And we're getting a bit predictable, aren't we?'

'You poor old man, you,' I say lightly, but this first-night lovemaking isn't predictable, it's a tradition. I like to keep them going too, it's a trait I got from my mother.

'Don't say you're bored with me. We're not even up to the seven-year itch yet. What are we on – the year-five hive? The year-six nettle rash?'

He shrugs again. 'I'm just tired.'

The downstairs clock chimes for midnight. Sam takes me by the shoulders and kisses me. 'Happy Christmas, babe.'

'Happy Christmas.'

I take my make-up off and when I get into bed he's already asleep.

We've had our presents and I'm just thinking about getting breakfast when the row starts. It's Joe's fault. I've been waiting for the optimum moment to mention it.

'Jack?' says Sam to Joe. 'Jack won't be coming today. It's Christmas, Joe. You can take his present round, but he won't be coming here.'

'Oh, he will,' insists Joe. 'He's bought me a car that you wind up. He told me. He's bringing it when they come.'

'Gemma! What's Joe talking about? He says Jack's coming.'

I hedge a bit, trying to imply they're just dropping in with Joe's present but I should have got Joe out of earshot first.

'They're coming to dinner aren't they? You promised.' There's a shake in his voice, he has been looking forward to he and Jack playing with their new action figures.

'Ah, well, I just said . . .' But I don't get the chance to say what I just said. It isn't that Sam doesn't like Tania but he says Tania and I gang up on him which we don't at all. I mean, not what you could call ganging up.

I tell him that Tania will be going home straight after lunch (although I have no reason for believing this) and that it will make the day so much nicer for Joe, which he can see from Joe's reaction. I say how unkind it would be to have let Tania remain alone ('She's got family, hasn't she?' he asks reasonably) and I also point out that it'll be better to have her company than either of our families. Sam disputes this and says – which I know is a lie – that he was thinking of calling on his mother this afternoon.

'You still can. You know I wouldn't have gone anyway, I hate being criticized by your mother. And patronized by Bernard.' Bernard is Sam's stepfather. He doesn't like me and usually finds urgent business to attend to on his allotment if I call.

'And I'm tired of you going on about them. I will go then.'

He bangs into the kitchen to get his own breakfast as though making a lot of noise shows he's won – while I answer the door to Tania who is coming up the path, an hour early.

'We were bored so we thought we might as well come. It doesn't make any difference to you, does it?' she says.

I'm beating the lumps out of the bread sauce when my

mother rings. She always phones Christmas morning. It takes little over an hour to reach the village where my parents now live but we don't like Christmases at their house, any more than we do at Sam's mother's, and they don't like coming to us either if it means missing some do at the golf club, which it invariably does. My mother was always one for clubs, societies, the Women's Institute. She was never at home, there was always some jumble sale, sale of work or committee meeting she had to go to.

'It's as well you didn't come,' my mother says, as though this had ever been considered, 'Dad has got a cold, we wouldn't want Joe to pick it up. And it's very icy outside, no sense in taking risks, is there?' We maintain a pretence that we would have liked to be together.

'And Joe prefers to be at home,' I say, without adding that Joe has never had the chance to try anything different.

'Yes, well he can get all his toys out, can't he? I'm glad he liked the Lego.'

Mum and Dad called in last week with all our presents; they like to preserve the idea of Father Christmas for Joe, though they had written their names on the gift tags and will expect Joe to thank them. I don't see how any child who can read can go on believing in Santa Claus. I remember, as a child, asking why my presents said 'Love from Auntie Rose', or 'Best wishes from the Baileys'. She said that everyone bought the presents and sent them to Father Christmas to deliver on Christmas Eve. Even a child doesn't need a time and motion study to calculate that this would be a waste of time. Besides, I'd been with Mum to the post office when she was posting presents, sticking the stamps on for her, and I'd never seen any addressed to Father Christmas.

'Give Sam my love,' says my mother, not wanting to speak to him in person. That's the other reason we don't meet, of course. My parents took as instant a dislike to Sam's black leather jacket as he did to their Capo da Monte and neither has ever found a reason to revise their opinions. When we meet they tell me of their friends' daughters who have got married/engaged or — increasingly — remarried (after divorces which my parents have somehow forgotten to mention). They're torn between blaming Sam for not wanting to get married, and blaming Sam for turning me into the sort of woman who (as they think) doesn't want to get married either.

I say goodbye to my mother and go to check on the turkey but Sam has already removed it from the oven and is regarding the bird thoughtfully. It looks wrinkled and rude, lying there on its back with its legs apart. 'That reminds me,' says Sam grinning at the gaping cavity between its legs, 'we didn't have sex yet.' I try to poke him with the skewer but he grabs my wrist.

'I didn't mean it about Tania, it's just I thought we'd be on our own — just the three of us. I wanted to play with Joe.' He grins, seeing my expression. 'OK, I know I'm pathetic. Of course we couldn't have let her spend Christmas by herself. We can have a drink and watch a movie on TV.'

We hug, relieved to be friends again, so I don't mention that I've looked through the TV schedules already and know that the choice is between two films that we've already seen on video; a variety programme starring comedians I'd thought were dead; or a cartoon of the Christmas story made in Finland.

'That'll be lovely,' I say.

*   *   *

203

It turns out to have been a mistake to take Tania up on her offer to bring the Christmas crackers. She got them in the sale last year, for half price as she tells me, but the snaps have got damp in her spare room and the mottoes are too grown up for the kids. In fact they're too grown up for all of us. The trouble with sale goods is that you may pay less but you get something you didn't really want.

'Listen to this,' says Sam unwrapping the motto from the cardboard cylinder of the cracker they've just pulled while Joe tries to work out how to do the puzzle that has fallen out. Sam is still laughing from Joe's red-faced effortful pulling, but his smile fades a little as he mouths the words of the motto silently to himself.

'Come on,' says Tania, waiting to pull hers.

'It's not very funny.'

'Of course they're not very funny. That's the point.'

'No, really, this one isn't even meant to be funny.' He screws it up and throws it across the table so it hits Jack.

'Come on, let's have a look,' Tania insists, scrabbling to get it from Joe.

'No, just leave it. It's stupid.'

If Sam had just read it we could have said how stupid, and forgotten the whole thing. But he seems so anxious we shouldn't read it, as though it's some big secret. Tania unfolds it and reads. '"Life is what happens while you're making plans for something more interesting".' She looks at me for a response.

'See? It's not funny, is it?' says Sam.

Jack pushes his cracker into Tania's hand and grabs the other end. The snap in their cracker comes apart, throwing Jack off balance and Tania gives him the whole cracker to unwrap.

'It reminds me of that saying – "It's later than you think". How do they know how late I think it is? I hate sayings like that, they're devised by pessimists to make the rest of us miserable.'

'That's what I told you,' says Sam, who has told us no such thing, only served to whet our curiosity so that we were guaranteed to give the motto our fullest attention.

'It's like that old Jewish saying,' I add brightly, "'If you want to make God laugh, tell him your plans".' I don't want to dwell on something so foolish yet which somehow seems to have disturbed Sam, and realize too late that the saying I've thrown in is just as bad. 'Anyway,' I go on unnecessarily, 'they're just bits of old nonsense, aren't they?' Tania nods but Sam agrees far too quickly, as though there's any possibility they might not be.

'More wine?'

'Yes, please. A lot more.' Tania says this with a glance at Sam who is flicking through the TV listings trying to find something unsuitable for the children, preferably involving car chases, bad language and nipples in soft focus (or any kind of focus). He is in a sulk again because it's almost teatime and Tania is still here and showing no signs of going. Part of me feels I should take his side but I'm enjoying Tania's company, and Christmas is a time for socializing.

Better for Sam to be miserable in our midst than for Tania to be miserable on her own at home. I fetch the corkscrew and plunge it into the cork. Only part of it comes out and I have to fish bits of cork out of Tania's glass before I hand it to her.

We've been discussing our schooldays and have got on to the subject of boyfriends. Tania wrinkles her nose trying to remember who her first proper kiss was with – or maybe it's at the memory.

'He was in the second year. Tony Mitchell. Tall, smoked Silk Cut. We used to meet up in the park in the evenings, a whole crowd of us.'

I wasn't friends with Tania during that era. When we moved to the secondary school we were put into different streams and Tania resented the slight, or I always told myself she did. Now, at the pang I get from the idea of Tania surrounded by a gang of young boys in the local park, I realize I was the jealous one. I wasn't so popular at secondary school as I'd been at primary and I never achieved the same measure of cool that Tania did. Once when I went to the cinema with my best friend, Julie Paterson, the boys sitting behind us stuck chewing gum in our hair. Up until that moment we'd thought their banter meant they fancied us. (Perhaps it did. Boys have strange ways of expressing their feelings).

I didn't have a boyfriend until I was in the fifth form, whereas Tania had several in tow from day one. Either way, we didn't meet, didn't speak, and preferred to ignore each other if we found ourselves on the same bus or passing in a school corridor.

'Who was your first kiss with?' Tania asks me in a low voice, in case this is sensitive material to be discussing in front of Sam – which seems unlikely in view of his laid-back attitude to my relations with my workmates.

'Robbie Hawkins.' Actually it was *Robin* Hawkins, he wasn't really the type to get called 'Robbie' but that's what I called him, the name making him sound more street-wise, like the sort of boy I'd have liked to date. He was tall with gangly legs and glasses and fine straight hair. He went to the Catholic school and got three grade A's at A level. I remember that because it was something my mother liked to remind me about periodically, especially after I dropped him for a boy with no O Levels who worked in the greengrocer's.

'I don't remember him.'

'He wasn't at our school, so you probably never met him.'

'What was he like?' To my surprise, I find that despite the passage of time, I don't want Tania to know exactly what he was like.

'Intelligent.'

'And a good kisser?' Well, was he? I doubted it though I wasn't sure I could tell.

'I don't know. What makes a good kisser?'

Tania considers the question. 'Someone who makes you want to do more than just kissing, I suppose.'

Sam looks up and for the briefest moment I think he is going to join in with us. But there's an ugly set to his mouth.

'Are you gonna watch this film? Or would you like me to take the TV out to the kitchen?'

Tania shoots a look at me. 'Maybe it's time I was going.'

'No, Tania. We haven't had tea yet.' I hadn't planned to invite her to stay but I'm not having Sam make my friends feel unwelcome. However, we fall silent now, Tania feigning interest in the film while I think about Robin's lank hair and damp palms.

'No, he wasn't a particularly good kisser,' I whisper, moving closer to Tania's chair. 'But he did make me want to do more than just kiss. He made me want to go out and find someone else to go out with.' We both laugh even though it's true.

Sam gets up and goes into the garden and the boys follow him wanting a game of football although it's dark outside. Through the window I see him light a cigarette.

Sam is a good kisser, by any definition. He only had to be in the same room to make me want to do more than just kiss. He's not as highly charged sexually as he used to be, but it's normal for sex to go off a bit when you've been together a while, as Ed pointed out.

'I always thought I'd marry Tony Mitchell. It's true though, isn't it? Life going on while you're making plans.'

'It's because,' I say in one of those rare flashes of insight that come after you've drunk half a bottle of wine, 'when you make your plans you envisage the other person behaving the way you want. But they don't.'

Tania picks up our nutcrackers which are in the shape of a nude lady and fits a walnut between the legs. Sam bought it when he was in Spain once and I've tried to replace it with more decorous appliances but the others don't work so well.

'You can't not make plans, though, can you? You'd never get what you wanted.' The shell breaks in two leaving the nut wedged firmly inside. 'And all the plans you've made —?' She casts a look through the window at Sam so I'll know what she's getting at, 'have you got what you wanted?'

'Yes, of course I have,' I say, somehow sounding defensive.

I go into the kitchen and make coffee which involves a lot of banging of doors and cupboards.

'At last.' Sam leans his full weight against the front door as though he's trying to keep marauders out instead of Tania. He has just walked the few yards to her front door and looks as though he resented every step. His brows are still low over his eyes. 'I thought she was never going. Why didn't you get rid of her?'

'What did you want me to say?'

'How about piss off?' It's half-past eight, Christmas Day all but over.

'It's not too late for us to have a nice time.' But it is. Sam's mood won't improve so quickly, and now there's Joe to put to bed with all the time that will take, with the reading of the story that he will no doubt still insist upon however we try to bribe him with letting him stay up late.

'Bloody great Christmas this turned out to be.'

'Sam . . . come on.' I nuzzle his neck and wind my arms round him but he shrugs me off.

'Joe! Pick those toys up, it's time for bed.' Joe gathers his new cars together with a watchful air. He doesn't often see this side of Sam and knows to keep his head down when he does.

As Sam follows Joe up the stairs he suddenly stops and turns to me where I am sweeping up some cake that has got trodden into the carpet. 'It isn't working is it?'

'What isn't?'

He has a walkie-talkie in his hand and for one joyous moment I think he just means that the batteries are faulty. But a glance at his eyes tells me I wasn't clutching at straws so much as thin air. He doesn't wait or expand on his strange words but they send a dagger of ice into my stomach.

Chapter 14

'Jesus, who's rattled your cage?' says Piers on the first day back at work, just because I've queried something on his expenses. I've got a job to do like anyone else, it's no good his complaining.

'She didn't have a good Christmas,' says Colin as though I've lost the power of speech. 'She'll soon bounce back now she's back with us.' This is supposed to be some kind of joke, Bounceback being the name of another division of our company, but I wouldn't find it funny even if I were in the mood to joke, which I'm not.

'There was nothing wrong with Christmas, if you must know, it's coming back here that's the problem. I'm just sick of people who can't give in their expenses on time, who lose their receipts and then try to make out it's somehow my fault.' I should have taken a few days off but I thought coming in to work would take my mind off things.

Piers raises an eyebrow at Colin and mouths 'PMT' which I don't find funny either. I aim at his head with the file of sales figures which is conveniently in my arms. He ducks but not fast enough and I catch him just above the ear.

Colin looks on, shocked. 'Gemma, whatever's got into

you?' But nothing has got into me though there's a ball of misery like a time bomb inside trying to get out. My anger is a disguise for keeping well-wishers at arm's length. If there's one thing I couldn't stand right now, it's sympathy.

Ed came in briefly but had to dash out for some kind of crisis meeting at Head Office and may not be back so at least I don't have him disturbing me. I shut my door and ask Marie to take my calls, saying I've got a headache. But Colin is too dense to take the hint and when I answer the tap on the door, there he is with a cup of coffee and some paracetamol. His dark eyes are wide with concern but he is also wary, doesn't want to say the wrong thing.

'It's OK, Colin, I don't bite.'

'You did earlier.'

I shrug. 'I've got a lot on at the moment.'

He takes my response as encouragement and sits down on the chair at the side of my desk but I don't want to encourage him so I start sorting through my in-tray.

'What's happened?' he says at last. 'You don't look well. Have you lost weight?' Normally I'd take such an observation as a compliment but I know he means I look haggard and drawn. It's not enough that Sam's robbed me of my confidence and my self esteem, he's also taken my fond belief that I look younger than I am.

'Nothing. I've just got a headache.' I don't look up but I can feel his eyes on me.

'Is everything all right with Joe?'

'Yes, he's fine. Santa brought him everything he wanted.'

'Even those soldier things you were panicking about?'

'Sam . . . brought some back with him.' His name sounds strange on my tongue, as though I'm talking about an imaginary friend. Until a few months ago Joe had an invisible companion, someone who had done all the naughty things Joe denied having committed himself. The friend, who had formed such a vital part of our life for the few months he was around, went away suddenly when Joe started school and hasn't been back since. If I've ever mentioned him to Joe he has looked at me as though I've asked when one of the Star Trek team was beaming down to have tea.

'And Sam's OK is he? Not ill or anything?'

I'm grateful to Colin for letting me answer so honestly. 'Sam's well. He's gone back now.'

'And it's only a headache? You don't look well. You look . . .'

If he's nice to me, I'll cry. 'I'm fine. Just tired. Christmas is a tiring time.'

I've separated out the contents of my filing tray and placed them in descending order of importance. Now I pick up the one on the top and consider what I need to do first.

'Gemma—'

'Colin, thanks for the coffee but I've a pile of stuff to do.'

He gets up, slowly, resignedly. 'I don't know what it is but—' I rustle my papers to hurry him along but he's determined to say something. 'Sometimes when bad stuff happens, it's kind of liberating. The only way to go is up.'

But it isn't. You can just keep on going down. There's no limit to how far you can fall.

I switch on my word processor and watch the screen as it lights up for action.

'Just say if you need anything.'

'If I want another coffee you'll be the first to know.'

When he's gone I get up and go over to the window. It's raining hard outside, the rainwater bouncing up from the pavement, like sea spray hitting rocks. Oh, I need something, I think, but who can get it for me?

In the train travelling home, I feel it welling up inside me, the need to spread out my pain and share it with someone. Tania knows already, of course, so I don't have to explain anything more to her, and tonight I've left work early so the children will be occupied watching their TV programmes and we can sit quietly in her kitchen before the kids need to eat.

But when I arrive Tania is in a frenzy getting ready to go out.

'I was so glad when you said you were coming home early because I want to get the kids into bed by seven. A babysitter is coming – that girl from up the road – and I don't know how good she is with them so I thought—'

I hardly listen but the gist is that Tania has a date. *Tania*! Chris Trelawny, the teacher with the hat labelled 'Teacher' and the high opinion of her teaching skills, is taking her to the local production of 'Much Ado About Nothing.' She has been experimenting with eye make-up and has tried out the mascara I bought her years ago. She must have sneezed before it was dry because she has a line of smudgy black dots along her lower lid.

I take Joe home and he's astonished that I let him watch what he likes on television all evening and don't send him to bed until almost nine o'clock.

When something affects you so deeply that you feel you're giving it out with every breath, you can scarcely

214

comprehend when others don't notice. On the other hand it can be a relief that they don't. I don't want to be questioned about it and it's humiliating, being taken in, deceived. It's like a bad dream you can't wake up from. Each morning I think I'll open my eyes and it'll all be all right again. But when I do it's to find the nightmare has just begun.

You know how it is. You think you've been so perceptive and observant, picking up the signals, seeing through the masquerade, when all the time the clues have been set for you, so you'll draw your own conclusions without the perpetrator having to say anything.

Christmas night, when Sam came down from putting Joe to bed, his mood had altered and when I asked what he meant by 'It isn't working', he shrugged and said he didn't mean anything, he was just mad because Tania had stayed and spoiled things. We made love that night but only at my instigation and it was brief and hurried, with Sam rolling away from me, hardly saying a word.

I barely slept. On Boxing Day, while Joe played with his cars in the hall, I faced him with it.

'Sam.'

'Mmmm?'

'I want to ask you something.'

'Then ask it.' He was reading his music magazine, a piece on new bands, weighing up the competition. He wasn't listening. I'd make him listen.

'Is there something going on between you and this girl singer?' I couldn't say her name.

He didn't look up, his eyes stayed hovering over the columns, then he said, 'Sorry. What?'

But he wasn't reading now. His posture hadn't altered but his neck had stiffened. And I knew, as I'd known from the moment I'd asked why he hadn't told me before about the new singer – the manager, the possibility of recording – though I'd been in denial since then, putting a gloss on what I saw, making excuses, twisting things round so they looked better.

You expect to be overcome with grief at such moments of revelation but what I felt was just a calm detachment. There would be a time for tears but now wasn't it. Besides, I also knew that once I started those tears would go on forever; even when I appeared to have stopped, they'd still be there underneath seeping away, like that leak under the sink which Sam has never managed to cure. It was like the time at school I got slapped on the shin with a hockey stick and there was a terrifying moment of calm before the pain started.

'Is it serious?'

Sam raised his face from the page slowly, mystified by my question, and certainly with no idea he'd hit me with his metaphorical hockey stick. He had laid his clues – his scorn for our usual welcome-home urgent lovemaking, his all-too-casual mention of his new female friend, his pretence that he had told me about his new prospects – but he wasn't ready for me to solve them yet. I'd caught him off guard and now the moment was upon him he was scared.

'Is what –?' He was playing for time but I was losing patience.

'This woman with the Roman nose and legs like pillars. Are you fucking her?'

It still wasn't too late. He could have leapt up, astonished – 'Where the hell has that idea come from? Gem – what's got into you? I love you!' And there was a fraction of a second when I thought he was going to – even that he had done – I saw it so vividly, the falling into each other's arms, the kisses, our faces wet with tears. A misunderstanding . . .

I've been away too long . . . I've only ever wanted you . . . I will, I'll get a job back here.

I held his gaze, willing him to tell me anything, anything at all, and I'd believe it.

His magazine slid to the floor as he leaned forward raking his hands through his hair. 'Who told you?'

He didn't realize he had told me himself; he thought he had been so subtle, but men like him understand subtlety like they understand needlework. To make things worse, he was aggrieved that I didn't sympathize with him and the great dilemma he had been facing, how hard it had been to decide. He loved me and Joe, he wanted us to go on, of course he did, but with Christina he had found . . .

Oh, he was so proud of her, my replacement. I was still his best friend – he still cared for me, so much that he wanted to share his joy with me. (I wanted to share a shot of arsenic with him.) He kept telling me how much I would like her if we met (correction, I'd like him to share a shot of arsenic with her) and trying to slip in details of her winning little ways, the magic of their first moment, how he had fallen in love with her against his better judgement (this thing was bigger than both of them? Why would I find this consoling?). The rapt expression on his face as he spoke of her brought back agonizing memories; it was a look he used to have for me. I hated him then, with his short hair, knowing who had instigated the change. He always hated short hair.

We were like two boxers – on Boxing Day of all days – circling in the ring each waiting to see who would land the first punch.

'Is it the sex that's so good?' I asked. I dreaded to know but he had skirted over that side of things.

He did the same now. 'Why do you have to bring everything down to that?'

'It's not me that's bringing it down to that, it's you. If she wasn't fucking with you, you wouldn't be interested.'

'It's not just the sex, OK? She – we – we care about each other. It's special.'

God, it was like listening to a teenager. But I knew what the attraction was. 'I'll tell you what you like. She doesn't want any kind of commitment out of you.'

He denied it but I knew it was true. She was going back to college soon; she wouldn't need him to set up home with her, to give her half his income, pay rent on a house he hardly even lives in. Most of all, she wouldn't be asking him to settle down and play mummies and daddies.

'She wants you to give up your job, give up your family, and be a professional musician.' No wonder he found her irresistible. If I were Sam I think I'd feel the same.

But I wasn't Sam and I wanted to hurt him.

'Sam. You're almost thirty. And how long have you been playing guitar?' He shrugged. 'Ten years? Fifteen?'

'Yeah. So what?'

'You've made tapes, demos, been in how many bands?'

'A few.' He raised his chin defiantly, maybe he guessed what was coming.

'Don't you think if you had *any* talent – if you were any good *at all* – someone would have noticed by now?' His eyes narrowed and the colour rose up through his face. 'You've always been crap – total, unadulterated crap – you're about as good on stage as you are in bed.' He turned to go but I wasn't finished yet. 'And you can forget about Joe. I'll go to court and tell them just what sort of father you are – the next time you see Joe he won't even recognize you. And it won't be because you've had your hair cut.'

He gave me a look of such naked loathing that I was frightened. I'd never seen him like that before.

'Fuck off, bitch,' he said. He took his jacket and slammed out.

In hurting him I'd done what I wanted, but I hadn't got what I wanted. I'd won the round but I'd lost the war. Sam didn't come back that night.

When he did, I could see I was already history. The next day I tried to get him to talk things over but every exchange that started out with the agreement that we'd remain calm and rational just turned into shouting and tears (mine, not his), and besides, he'd already changed his flight by then. There were no victors in our fights though perhaps the worst loser was Joe who sometimes tried to referee.

'Who's going to tell Joe?' I'd asked during one of our respites.

'I will,' he said.

'You won't. You say you will, but you won't. You'll leave it to me like you leave everything else.'

'I said I will.'

Of course, he didn't. But then I didn't tell Joe either, not really. I couldn't steady my voice well enough to speak of it so I just said that daddy had gone back to work as usual but he was very busy and it might be a bit longer than normal before he came home. He'd be back to see Joe as soon as he could.

Well, that much was true, wasn't it?

Sam flew back two days after Boxing Day.

Agonized, I watched him going from room to room gathering up his books, photos of Joe, things he usually left at home, waiting for a sign that he was weakening, that this was surely just play-acting. He kept raking his fingers through his close-cut hair – hair I hated as though it belonged to her not him – but he avoided my eyes, pretended I wasn't there. Joe was my best weapon for keeping Sam here and I'd have used him too but Sam knew that. He hugged Joe goodbye, chucking him under the chin the way he always did, saying he'd see him soon, same as ever, before sending him to Tania's to play.

And then the taxi came.

'Sam, no. Let's give it one more try.'

He didn't even look at me.

'Please Sam. I'm sorry. I didn't mean it.'

He picked up his walkman, shoved it into the top of his holdall, and zipped it up. Taking his plane tickets out of their wallet, he checked them over and then slid them into the inside pocket of his jacket. It was over. He was going.

Which is when I did this terrible thing, terrible for me that is, and I knew it wouldn't work even at the time but I was desperate, what choice was there, I had to do something.

I leapt at his holdall and flung myself over it, got my arms round it and held on. He tried to pull it away but I wouldn't let go. I was crying again, but as long as I held his bag in my arms, I also held him. I pressed my face against the stiff canvas and entwined my fingers round the handle.

'Gemma, get up.'

'Sam, please. Just till tomorrow.' My voice sounded raw, my words indistinct, but he wasn't listening.

He prised my fingers off it, one by one, holding my wrists away and then with his foot he kicked it out from under me and swung it from my reach before I could get up from the floor. And now he did look at me. But there was a defiance in his eyes, no softening.

'I don't love you any more,' he said.

From the window I watched him get into the taxi and as he settled back he pulled a packet of gum from his pocket and folded a piece of it into his mouth. That moment, seeing the old familiar habit for the last time, was somehow the worst of all.

Chapter 15

I stayed in bed for the next two days. On the first day, unbeknown to me, Joe knocked at Tania's door and told her I was ill. She took him in, calling round to heat up bowls of acidic tomato soup for me which I left to go cold on the bedside table. I had a bad enough pain in my chest already without adding to it with indigestion. I felt raw inside as though an ulcer was bleeding or what I imagined that would feel like; and there was something wrong with my breathing. Every inhalation caused an ache in my ribs.

'You're better off without him,' Tania said, and even if it had been true, I wasn't better off for hearing her say it.

'How will I cope on my own?' The sheer effort of staying alive seemed more than I could manage; when I had to go to the loo, I shuffled out hunched over like a pensioner who needs a zimmer frame. The prospect of ever returning to work was unimaginable; the prospect of ever getting dressed again scarcely more achievable. Underneath it all, too terrible to contemplate, was the welling realization that I had to cope with Joe alone.

Tania sat on my bed and took my hand between hers. 'You've *been* coping on your own,' she said. 'Sam's only ever been a pay packet and a voice at the end of the phone.' It's astonishing the things people will say to you when you're down. '*That* side of things won't change – I mean, he'll still take care of you money-wise, won't he? He's not like my Darryl was. Anyway, you're not on your own, you've got me. I promise you, you'll be fine.'

Intermittently, over the next few days, I would conclude she was right. I *would* be fine; depression was just a stage you went through if you'd been rejected and betrayed and I would soon be coming out the other end of it. But then I'd turn and see his trainers sticking out from under the bed, or the can of shaving foam he had left in the bathroom cabinet, and realization would crowd back in and I'd know I'd never be fine again.

On the third day I woke to find Joe at my side with a bowl of cornflakes in his hands. He lowered it on to the duvet, milk from the over-filled bowl slopping over the sides.

'You won't get better if you don't eat something,' he said, echoing the many times I'd said that to him. I lifted the spoon to my mouth and it was filled with a heavy syrup of half-dissolved sugar. Joe is limited to two teaspoons for himself but he evidently thought that as it's my sugar, I was entitled to an unlimited amount. 'Can we go out today?' he asked hopefully, leaning against the side of the bed and picking at a loose thread on my pillowcase. 'Jack's going to the swing park. I'd like to go the swing park.'

I told him I was getting up today, surprising myself with the news. It had seemed as though, if I didn't get out of bed, didn't start life without Sam, that it hadn't really happened. Sam's pillow, with the smell of his hair, was the proof of it. As long as evidence of his recent presence lingered, he might still walk in the door and we'd go on as before. But Joe, wistful and hopeful by turns, whose life had also collapsed even if he didn't know it, was a powerful antidote to all that.

'I'll look after you, Mummy,' said Joe, sounding like those doe-eyed children wheeled on in movies to tug the heartstrings of the audience because we all know the mother is dying of some terrible incurable disease and will be gone by the next scene. Despite myself, I discovered parallels between the dying woman and the child she will leave bereft and a fresh rush of tears sprung to my eyes. 'Don't cry, Mummy,' said Joe, making it worse.

In the park Tania was encouraging, and the wind on my chapped cheeks was invigorating. But by the time night came, misery had moved back in again. I lay in bed on New Year's Eve, clutching Sam's pillow and listening to Big Ben's chimes courtesy of next door's television, foreseeing all the future New Years I'd spend alone just like this one.

I'd thought that returning to work would distract me from my memories but when I wake on what should be my second day back at work, I feel ill and unable to get out of bed again, my face swollen and cheeks reddened from my damp pillow. The effort of holding my feelings in at work all yesterday has exhausted me. Whoever said time was a great healer was talking rubbish, give me Savlon and a sticking plaster any day. I've got the emotional equivalent of one of those open wounds my mother used to say had to stay uncovered to let the air get at it – with the result that I seem to keep walking into things and knocking the scab off.

Tania collects Joe for me and I bundle him out of the front door, hiding behind it so she won't see that I'm back in decline. I go back to bed, getting up only to phone the office to say I won't be in.

Later, I'm lying there with the covers over my head when the phone rings. I don't answer but it goes on and on. I get up, pull on my dressing gown, and it's still ringing.

'What's happened?'

It's a man's voice but not the one I want to hear. For a moment I don't recognize it. Despite my phone call claiming flu, Colin has told Ed I was upset about something yesterday.

'I thought I'd check on how you are seeing as I'll be away for a while. You haven't forgotten I go away tomorrow?' Ed is going skiing for a fortnight.

'I haven't forgotten.' I'm embarrassed at being unable to produce the usual banter but I can't seem to find where I keep it.

He asks a few questions, probing gently. Heartiness, positivity and encouragement of the kind which Tania has unexpectedly come out with are easy to withstand but kindness chips away at my defences, especially coming from such an unexpected source. If even Ed feels sorry for me, then things must be bad. When he asks about Sam, it all comes out in a rush that ends in sobs.

'I knew it,' he says quietly. 'Look, come into work and I'll take you to lunch. You can get it all off your chest and a few drinks will make you feel better.'

The idea that lunch and a drink will heal anything is insulting though a shoulder to cry on might be comforting. But I don't want him seeing me like this. And what's the point of feeling better temporarily? When I get back home nothing will have changed.

I fill in a few more details of what happened, hearing his voice, deep and sad for me, but his sympathy makes me feel worse, seeming to reiterate how desperate things are.

'It always ends this way for me. I loved him more than

he did me, it's how it always is.' Crying has made my chest hurt again as though someone has rubbed it inside with sandpaper.

'Sweetheart, of course it isn't.'

'It is, it is.' I cry harder now, all the bad things that have ever happened crowding in, weighing me down. Dimly through the clamour they make in my head I'm aware that he is talking.

'Gemma, listen, calm down. Look, tell me your address, I'm coming over.'

Ed — in my house? The prospect pulls me up in a way his kindness and concern never could have. I take a deep breath and feel my shoulders ease.

'Gemma, if you were feeling happy, I bet you couldn't name one thing that had ever gone wrong for you. It's just that right now your brain is in that bit of its filing system that stores those things.'

'Can't you forget work for one minute?' For a moment we're both laughing; it feels odd when your face is stiff and tight with tears. But Ed is wrong; it is always like that for me. My first boyfriend Nick, then Rudi, now Sam, not to mention the numerous also-rans. They always tire of me first.

Ed's voice is strong and positive, I've led him into thinking I'm feeling better. 'When the worst happens, nothing else can hurt you.'

He talks on, more in the same vein, not seeming to realize that it isn't only that the worst has happened but it goes on happening, a terrible ever-present cycle you can't get out of. And the pain just goes on and on like a wound that won't stop bleeding.

The next afternoon I crawl out of bed and call round on

Tania. I thought I might as well have another day at home seeing as Ed will be away anyway. I'll go back tomorrow.

This turns out to be not a good idea as Tania is very taken with Chris Trelawny and can't wait to tell me all about their date. They went for a drink after the theatre and he told her about an affair that Joe's gay headmaster is having with the janitor, and how someone told him that the trumpet teacher who comes in twice a week was seen hand in hand with Mrs McBride in a pub in Mitcham but he can't vouch for it himself. So someone even fancies Mrs McBride with her buttocks like chicken skin. It's as though there's a virus going round.

'But fortunately I'm immune to it,' I tell Tania over tea and shortbread, encouraged to hear how positive I sound. 'I'm finished with men.'

'I was finished with men, but look at me now. I never expected to feel like this again,' says Tania, flicking her hair out of her eyes. 'I feel so . . .' She doesn't find the words but I can see how she feels – younger, brighter, more vibrant. She actually has colour in her cheeks, something I haven't seen since she had the flu and a temperature of 103.

She turns to me with a pained expression. 'Oh, I'm sorry, Gem, I shouldn't be going on like this when you're . . .'

But it's good to be distracted this way from the round of my own emotions – sadness, depression, putting a brave face on it, more sadness and depression.

'How long did it take you to get over Darryl?' It's almost four years since Darryl, her husband, walked out.

'What? Oh, I don't know.' She tears the shortbread packet open wider to get at a biscuit that is hiding at the bottom. 'Not all that long. Suddenly I'm addicted to these. I was never much of a one for biscuits before.'

I top up my cup of tea, only half listening to something she is relating about the leading actor in 'Much Ado'. I know how long it took her to get over Darryl: it took her until now. It has taken a date with Chris Trelawny to exorcise the ghost.

What with Ed's skiing holiday and Christmas, I've only seen Ed for maybe five minutes in three weeks. I've been glad of the respite, time to sort myself out and get the office in order after the Christmas break but for the past few days I've been looking forward to seeing him again.

As soon as he walks in I wonder why. In my thoughts Ed is a charismatic figure, powerful and driven though flawed, like Heathcliff. But the man who drags himself into my office, surprisingly late, is just a middle-aged man with a frown on his face who could lose a little weight.

'I need you in my office. Now,' he says. No 'How are you', 'Are you feeling better?' or even, 'Have you heard from Sam?' My expression of welcome disappears as though it was a candle flame he has just blown out.

'I'm doing the expenses.'

'They can wait.'

'Accounts say they can't.'

'Accounts can say what the fuck they like. You can come into my office now or you can go straight down to the DSS and sign on but I know which is nearer.'

He turns his back on me as though he has had the last word.

'Don't waste your charm on me,' I say with heavy sarcasm. 'I'm impervious.' I'm not scared of him and even if I were, as he said, when the worst has happened, nothing else can hurt you. We glare at each other. He's a fool to forget who his friends are and for a moment I despise him.

But then the corners of his mouth start to twitch; I don't know why my anger should make him smile but it does. His mood is falling away from him as though it's a discarded shirt sliding from his shoulders to the floor. His ill humour is like his ugliness: only skin deep. I can feel a smile forming too and with it a sensation oddly akin to relief comes over me like a balm; an indigestion tablet easing heartburn.

He's such a fool. I start to laugh, and so does he.

Ed heaves himself on to the edge of my desk and his shoulders relax as he picks up my pencil and turns it over absently between his fingers, smiling a half smile. The tension is almost visibly leaking out of him and slowly his features reorder themselves and he eases back into the role I have cast him in.

'It's good to see you.' He looks at me, sad-eyed despite the smile, as though we're old friends about to part (instead of relatively new ones renewing an acquaintance) but with all the feelings of affection that implies. I'm glad he doesn't remark on how ill I'm looking, the way everyone else has been doing. 'There aren't many people who can make me laugh,' he says, holding my pencil up to the light and studying the minute print along the side, 'and God knows there's not much to laugh about right now, let's make the most of it.'

It must be trouble at home: I'm glad. We can compare notes.

'Maxine?' His brow furrows at my question as though he can't immediately recall who she is. 'No. Well, yes, Maxine's always trouble but only in the usual way. No, it's more than that.' He puts my pencil down and looks at me thoughtfully. 'Give me five minutes to get straight and we'll get started. I'll get us some coffee.'

Ed getting coffee? Things must be worse than I thought.

When I enter Ed's office he is on the phone. His coffee is on the desk; he has forgotten mine. He seems to be talking to Accounts. He isn't telling them to fuck off after all, though it's not impossible that that's what they're telling him. He is going red in the face and his jaw is fixed in a grimace in those few moments when he is listening rather than issuing denials.

Ed slams the phone down and leans forward on his elbows.

'It's bad news, I'm afraid.' He looks grave, too grave, so that I'm expecting that this is a joke; he's about to say something to make me laugh.

'They called a management meeting yesterday and I want to let everyone know before rumours start circulating.' I'm still expecting a dry, sardonic one-liner. 'Gemma, I'm not joking. They're closing us down.'

It's ironic how troubles unite you in a way that happiness never does. At the Christmas party, when our futures seemed secure, we were a motley collection of disparate individuals ready to turn on each other over a lost biro or a misplaced invoice. Now as we sit over drinks in the pub, imperceptibly inching our way towards the dole queue (or back to the agency to make my peace with Corinne, in my case), we're thick as thieves and as tight as Brindle Sylvia's new perm.

'It's just not fair,' wails Marie as though fairness ever had anything to do with anything. 'We haven't been going more than five minutes. They're not giving us a chance.'

The problem is cash flow; some funds-sapping crisis has occurred in another division and suddenly they've got cold feet about expanding so fast. We've got a month's grace but the situation isn't rosy.

'I don't know what my wife will say,' says Roger grimly, wiping the froth from his upper lip. 'She never wanted me to leave that other job.'

'I thought you said if you hadn't left they'd have sacked you,' says Les, squirting ketchup over his sausage and chips. He is the only one with an appetite.

'I turned down an offer just last week,' says Piers. 'The money was pathetic but at least they had some.'

'I've just taken on this flat,' says Kev, lighting up a cigarette. 'God knows how I'll pay for it.'

'Better ask God then,' says Ed, grinning.

Ed is more relaxed now that he has passed on the shock, as though our pale faces are somehow comforting, confirming the old saying, a trouble shared is a trouble halved (unless you judge by sheer weight of numbers in which case a trouble shared is a trouble doubled). Or maybe it's just the pint of bitter with a whisky chaser that's hitting the spot. But then he has had longer to absorb the news than we have. Laughter feels elusive to the rest of us.

Colin heads for the bar and the next round and I follow him, needing a few moments to myself. I thought the rug had been pulled out from under my feet with Sam but now with this, the whole floor has collapsed. I feel like I've fallen down a lift shaft, plummeting downwards with nothing to hold on to. Everything I grab to save myself comes away in my hands.

Colin is asking me something about crisps.

'Colin I do not give a toss about who wants crisps.' He

looks defeated; he was just trying to act normal, say what we would have said if we weren't feeling suicidal. He puts his arms round me and I wrap mine around his waist. Ed sees us but he doesn't make the sort of ribald comment I have come to expect. He knows we're just two drowning people trying to hold each other up in the water.

Don't ever let anyone tell you alcohol isn't good for you, particularly if you drink it fast on an empty stomach amongst those who are immersed as deeply in gloom as you are yourself. Within minutes our spirits have risen in direct proportion to the amount that those in our glasses have sunk.

'How was New Year, Ed?' I ask, feeling the house red bringing roses to my cheeks. New Year is history now but this is my first opportunity to ask and the only subject I can think of which isn't somehow related to work. He has already described the exorbitant expense of his winter skiing break which seems to be the main impression it has left him with and I don't want to explore that avenue any further.

'We went to Maxine's brother and his wife in Scotland for Christmas and New Year. It's always a pain, I don't know why I agreed to go. She's a terrible cook. I was in the kitchen when she was frying onions and do you know she put them in the oil before she'd even turned the gas on?' Ed prides himself on his cooking. I try to look as though I care. 'And they always feel they have to outdo everyone else with their presents – they spend a bloody fortune. I had cuff links, slippers, Calvin Klein this, Ralph Lauren that. It's obscene.' I think it sounds rather wonderful. 'What did your hubby buy you?'

I've persuaded myself that Ed hasn't asked after Sam out of tact but he has just forgotten about it, and about his own phone call which in fact made such an impression on me. I've thought about his kindness and concern several times since then but clearly it's been out of sight out of mind for him.

'He isn't my hubby.' I hate that cosy nickname, which sounds like a hybrid of huggy, cuddly and cupboard, an image which is strangely appropriate for the husbands of several people I know but in no way applied to Sam, even when he was the common-law version. In fact, Sam bought me an expensive and delicate hand-knitted sweater as well as the usual duty-free perfume which I describe for Ed, though without reminding him of the nagging pain which he also gave me and which is still the main thing on my mind, although imminent job loss is struggling to take precedence. 'A friend came over for Christmas Day, but it didn't work out,' I add, without mentioning all the other things that didn't work out either.

The festive season didn't live up to expectations for any of us. Debbie had flu and even now is still hoarse and red-eyed, unable to shake it off. Colin won't talk about it and Kev woke up on New Year's morning in the bed of a girl he had met the night before and who now thinks she is in love with him. (He confides this while Debbie is in the powder room, in the manner of an innocent asking advice, but we all know it's really to let us know how easily he can get a girl to have sex with him. As if, from a glance at his almond eyes, you couldn't work that out for yourself.)

Marie has been in deep conversation with Piers and when there's a lull in the general chat I jump in before the monster of silence can swallow us up. Sharing society with friends in trouble is one thing, but sharing a silence would be scary. 'Marie. Everyone had a terrible

Christmas and a worse New Year. Tell me yours was wonderful.'

'Mine was wonderful.'

'Oh.' I smile, trying to look pleased, though Marie's admission of gaiety feels like a lack of solidarity. 'What was so good?' I say, meaning, *what was so damn good then?*

'I had the most wonderful presents for my bottom drawer.' It emerges that Marie's definition of 'wonderful' involves becoming the owner of a frying pan with a lid and now she has one her dream has come true. Unfortunately for us, this wasn't the only dream which reached fruition and she takes her time telling us about them, drawing on a napkin for us the pattern that is on her crockery (Wedgwood. Present from her parents), and outlining the seating plan which has caused such disagreement with her future mother-in-law.

There is just one cloud without a silver lining. 'The only thing is, I've put on a bit of weight.' We all look down at her half-finished bag of peanuts but no one says anything. I consider pointing out, as consolation, that the shock of redundancy might shift a few pounds but as I mull it over it doesn't seem as consoling as all that, especially if, as I suspect, Marie heads for high-cal snack foods in times of trouble as well as celebration.

'Everyone puts on weight at Christmas,' says Ed, stretching upwards and tucking his shirt more tightly into his waistband.

'Diane didn't,' says Marie sighing. 'She lost two inches.'

'What is she now then,' I ask, 'five-foot three?'

Colin laughs but Marie treats my interruption with disdain. 'The thing is, I'm supposed to be slimming into my wedding dress, not having it let out.' I knew she would regret having ordered a size too small. In the history of

235

slimming I don't believe any woman ever fitted into a dress smaller than she was when she bought it. My mother has an entire wardrobe of designer outfits from her local 'nearly new' shop, cast-offs from women who never reached their target weight.

'Oh, if the worst happens, you can always put a safety pin in the back,' I suggest cheerily. I mean it as a joke but Marie's stricken expression suggests she has already considered it. 'Don't worry, you've got ages yet.' How long does it take to lose a stone and a half anyway?

'Will you be bringing anyone else to the wedding?' asks Marie. I haven't got anyone *to* bring which Marie surely knows. I think she's taking revenge for my unkind thoughts about her glass-topped frying pan. With Sam's long absences I'm well used to going to functions without him but there's a subtle difference between going to something alone because your partner can't come and going alone because you haven't got one.

'Are you OK, Gemma?' asks Colin leaning towards me from across the table and looking concerned.

'Yes, I'm fine. Who'd like another drink?'

Don't ever let anyone tell you alcohol doesn't do you any harm, and never, under any circumstances, partake on an empty stomach amongst those who are immersed as deeply in gloom as you are yourself.

At two-thirty Roger suggests we really ought to be getting back. The office is completely unmanned (as is Roger, from the look of him), apart from Debbie who has gone back to get some aspirins and answer the switchboard, and it's unprofessional to have no one of any seniority in the office.

'Roger,' says Ed, 'you are absolutely right. We must return to our posts without delay for, who knows, the

Managing Director may be visiting us at this very minute' – there's an uneasy moment while we all wonder if our absence could make a dire situation worse – 'and it would be very unfortunate if we were to miss the opportunity—'

'To tell him to bugger off,' says Roger.

'Absolutely,' says Ed.

But the party is over and we begin to gather our coats. There are an amazing number of glasses on the table, I can't believe we've got through so many. Maybe they hadn't cleared the table before we sat down.

'Is she all right?' I look round to see who Piers is talking about and find he's looking at me.

'Shall I get you a glass of water?' Colin is peering into my face looking concerned.

'I'm fine,' I say, speaking slowly and precisely, surprised that it's still not slow enough for my tongue to keep pace. This is odd, I've only had – I try to work out which of the glasses are mine but some of them must surely be Marie's although I'd thought she said she was sticking to fruit juice after the first one.

'Here, lean on me.' Ed takes hold of my upper arm and lifts me up and I stand up perfectly easily, I don't know why they're making so much fuss.

Outside the daylight is like being hit in the face with a wet dishcloth but not so pleasant.

Although I'm aware I'm walking rather slowly, we get back to the office in record time. One minute we're out on the street, then I close my eyes for just a moment and hey presto, the lift doors are opening and we're falling out into the lobby back at the office. Falling out is literally true, because there are too many of us to be in the lift all at once, and when the doors part I trip over Colin's foot and crash into Piers, propelling him out faster than he intended. He doesn't fall but he stumbles, looking like a stick insect with his long arms and legs and his backside topside, and as we rush to help him up, I slowly become aware of someone waiting outside to take the lift down. Someone in polished shoes and trousers with turn-ups.

'Good day to you, Mr Murray.' There's a pause broken only by a gurgle from Roger's digestive system. 'I'm glad to see that our grim situation hasn't dampened the spirits of your staff.'

It's the Managing Director, who else would materialize at the least opportune moment? We stand looking at him foolishly while I wonder if it would be indiscreet if I removed myself to the loo, the need for which is becoming more urgent by the second.

Mr Archer regards us coolly. It would be too much to ask that he should ever have visited us when I was taking minutes fit to bust, or Colin was tearing his hair out on his sales calls, or Marie was typing faster than Mr Archer can talk. No, it could only happen on the first day ever that lunch has consisted of more than a token glass of white and a prawn and mayo on brown.

'I thought it important to maintain morale,' says Ed amicably, as though the time were not almost three o'clock and his staff weren't all wearing grins as wide as wedges of Edam.

'Mr Murray, I'd be grateful if you could telephone me when it's convenient,' says Mr Archer stiffly, stepping past us into the lift and pressing the button for the ground floor.

'And I'd be grateful if you'd bugger off,' says Roger when the doors have swallowed the Managing Director and he is safely out of earshot.

'Do you think Ed is OK?' Colin asks, helping me to my

desk when I get back from the loo. Honestly, you'd think I couldn't manage. 'He seems a bit manic to me.'

But it's desperation. Behind the who-gives-a-shit grin I glimpsed panic and resignation. In the pub he was bullish and determined but now the MD has witnessed his moment of foolishness. The future of the company may hang in the balance, but Ed has surely been weighed and found wanting.

'I'll get you some black coffee,' Colin offers but, as I slump into my seat, my eyelids are too heavy for me to answer and anyway his voice could just be part of my dream, a dream constantly replaying in which Ed is pushing Sam out of the lift to where something terrible is waiting with shiny shoes to gobble him up, but we all laugh anyway.

I have a certain amount of work I need to get through this afternoon but when I try to blink my eyes stay closed and when I finally open them the light has changed and the hands of the clock have moved round so far someone must have physically altered them. Cups have been appearing on my desk, and sometimes they're full and sometimes empty though I have no memory of drinking anything.

'Gemma.' I raise my eyes and am greeted by Colin's face only inches from my own. For the briefest moment I think I've woken up with him. I pull back a little to get him into focus. 'Would you like me to take you home? It's not far out of my way.'

It's in the opposite direction, I'm not so drunk I don't know that. But I'm coming round now. This time the world isn't drifting away from me, I've got a grip on it.

'I'll be fine, Colin. Thanks for looking after me.'

'It'd be no trouble.'

'Where's Ed?'

'In his office. He was up with the MD earlier, then he came back and he's been in his office since then.' Something in his tone implies that since his return Ed has been doing deals and striking hard bargains which would be encouraging if it were true, which I doubt.

'Come on, let's get your coat.'

But I don't want to go home yet. At home, alone with Joe, I will be the only one with problems. As long as I'm here, I have people to identify with.

'Then let me get you a taxi.'

'I can get my own taxi. Look I'm fine.' I stand up, though once on my feet I don't feel quite as fine as I thought. But I'm still not going home.

Colin squeezes my shoulders and says goodbye. Everyone else has already left and when he has gone I go to Ed's door and knock. There's no answer and I knock again. 'Ed? Can I come in?'

I open the door and peer round. He is lying on the floor with his eyes closed.

'Ed! What is it?' My first thought is that he has had a heart attack. He looks pale and beneath his eyes the shadows are even darker than usual. I kneel down and turn my head on one side to listen to his breathing. It's coming steadily but he doesn't answer. 'Are you ill? Shall I call a doctor?'

'No, but you can call an Indian take-away. I'm bloody starving.' He opens his eyes slowly and grins to see me leaning over him. 'Sweetheart,' he says, 'I didn't know you cared.'

'Sweetheart,' I say, 'I don't. But if you peg out I'll have no one to write me a reference.'

He reaches out and strokes my cheek sending a feeling like warm ice cream trickling over my thighs, but the movement is too strenuous for him and he lets his arm fall back.

'When I die,' he says, sleepily, 'I want an obituary like Keats'. You know what his said?'

'No, and I don't believe you do either. You've never struck me as a great reader of poetry.'

'I don't read poetry but I do read obituaries. His says, "Here lies one whose name was writ in water." I want mine to say—'

'Here lies one whose name was writ in beer froth.'

He opens one eye and looks at me reproachfully.

'That's a little harsh.'

It's strange, holding a conversation with someone who is flat on his back. I should have moved away once I knew he was all right. Perhaps he understood why I didn't. Slowly he raises his arm and strokes the back of my neck with one finger. Then with the gentlest of pressures he pulls me towards him.

He tastes of wine and black coffee, but then so do I.

It's cold lying on the floor, I suppose the heating has gone off by now, so I get our coats from the umbrella stand and we snuggle under them.

'This isn't right,' he says but it's too late for protestations and the warmth of him is enveloping me like a healing balm. I can feel the pain seeping out of me and being neutralized in the damp heat of his body. It feels not only right but inevitable. I feel as though I've been waiting for this since that day I called him a bad penny and he laughed. We've been like two animals calling for each other in a pitch too high for the human ear, even our own. With Sam gone maybe it's time to start tuning in.

'Ed,' I say, because there's something I have to mention, even though I don't want to and this isn't the time, although on the other hand there's no other time that will be quite so appropriate: 'You've got a wife, you've got a lover, I don't see where I fit in.'

Ed runs his hand which is already growing familiar and cherished, down my side and back up between my thighs. 'No, but I can show you where I do,' he says. We both laugh.

Chapter 16

—— - ——

I'd forgotten there was any other way to have sex.

His stomach against my lips was softer than Sam's but that only reminded me of his greater maturity; his background of sexual licentiousness was in itself seductive. He had had many women but tonight I was the only one.

'I want you,' he said huskily, turning my nether regions to strawberry mousse.

He pulled my sweater over my head and when he unhooked my bra to release my breasts he brushed his tongue across first one nipple then the next, making them grow and strain towards him. It's the most powerfully erotic moment of them all, that first intimate caress, and with it the sudden blast of heat rising up through the body.

Leaning over him, I nuzzled him as I lowered his zip and loosened his trousers but he was miserly with me, clasped my hand when I tried to pull them down, and when I unbuttoned his shirt, tearing it aside to lie my face against the rough hair of his chest, he still kept it on his shoulders. He watched while I drew down my pants. And now I was completely naked and he was almost fully dressed.

We made love with me sitting astride him, his fingers

clamped hard around my nipples as though he thought I might run away. But it was I who was in charge and to be in control of this man who was so controlling, to be setting the pace and rhythm, the level of his pleasure, to hold him there in an agony of wanting was exquisite, enough to make me pant, even now, afterwards, just thinking of it.

I tell Tania I'm not in love with Ed, but I'm in something – 'In the shit,' says Tania.

What she also says is that Ed is just a displacement activity for Sam, which may be true, but as occupational therapy goes, he beats basket-weaving. I tell her what has developed between Ed and me immediately I arrive to collect Joe, stupidly imagining she will understand. I know she doesn't have a high opinion of Ed, but in the circumstances it ought to be marginally higher than the one she has of Sam. Ed – if nothing else – is doing an excellent repair job for the injury Sam caused me. Call Ed a part of damage limitation if you like.

I know Tania is in the middle of preparing a meal for Chris which probably contributes to her ill temper, but she doesn't have to be quite so hostile.

'It's crazy getting involved on the rebound like this,' she hisses, picking out potatoes from the vegetable rack.

'I'm not involved. It's just one of those things that happens.'

'You make it sound like an act of God.'

Well, maybe it was. I've been desperate these last weeks but now I feel calm and soothed and – let's not underestimate the significance of this – desirable again. The downside of getting involved with a philanderer is that you know he has been through many women. The upside is that, having had the pick, he is choosing you.

It's a compliment to you. It's like winning a contest with him as the prize.

'We were just two people in trouble who suddenly found we needed each other. And I do like him. He's strong but he's also soft.'

'Soft but strong? Don't tell me — and he soaks up stains as well. He sounds like a paper towel.'

'Tania. What's happened has restored my equilibrium. I thought you'd be pleased for me.'

She looks at me in exasperation, wiping her hands down her jeans.

'You have to give yourself time to grieve, to think things over. And supposing Sam turns up on your doorstep tomorrow, all tears and contrition, and you have to tell him you've been screwing some middle-aged bloke rigid?'

Tania can be surprisingly vulgar sometimes.

'I don't see what Ed's age has to do it. And Sam won't be turning up. But if he did, I don't have to tell him anything. I'm as capable as lying to him as he is to me.'

'You have the same rights, if that's what you mean, but capable you're not. You can't even make up an excuse for not helping out down at the school without looking as guilty as if you'd just done a murder.' Is she saying Mrs McBride has seen through all my carefully worded excuses? But there's no time to consider this now.

'I'm only doing the same as Sam.'

'Yes, but look who you're doing it with. You've told me what he's like — all these women.'

'Only two—'

'Only *two*? Oh well, *that's* all right then.' She holds the potato she has just peeled down on the chopping board and attacks it viciously with a knife. 'You're obsessed with him.'

'I am not!'

'You've been obsessed with him since you started there – you hardly talk about anything else. Ed this, Ed that. You're just infatuated and you've just jumped straight in without a second thought – not one – for where it might all lead to. You know what this is don't you? A case of premature infatuation.' She pauses briefly, somehow aware that the phrase doesn't sound quite right. Then she goes on, 'I've just been praying you'd get him out of your system before it led to anything. He's used to screwing around and you're not.' She's just making me more intransigent.

She beats some eggs viciously with a fork and when she has finished adds, unexpectedly: 'Still, it's easy to see why you're so taken with him.'

She's calmed down now and I'm relieved she's ready to concede Ed might have something to recommend him. It's like a personal compliment to have your loved one's strengths acknowledged, the more so as no one but me thinks Ed is desirable, including, quite possibly, his wife and, who knows, maybe even Janet Reger.

'Look, Tania—' I begin, warming to her now, wanting things to be right between us again.

'Yes,' she says, 'he's just like Sam, isn't he?'

He isn't at all. He's bigger built, his hair is curly, he's taller. Older.

'He's nothing like Sam.'

She looks at me with her pale, watery eyes. 'He's the same type. They could almost be related.'

But Ed is nothing like Sam. They're different entirely.

There's nothing like being told you shouldn't do a thing for spurring you on. And so what if Ed is a bad lot? What will a few more tears be among so many?

I notice Joe, standing watchful and white-faced, by the

door and lead him out of there. He hasn't seen me quarrel with Tania before. Actually, I haven't ever quarrelled with Tania before.

I sleep better than I have in a week and dream of locking us into Ed's office and undressing him slowly and against his expectations. But when I undo his shirt, there's another underneath it, and another under that one. Ed keeps laughing, especially when I get to the last one and there isn't a man inside at all, just kapok and cotton wool stuffing.

My dream is troubling at first — is my subconscious telling me that the man I've set my Dutch cap at, so to speak, has nothing inside him — no heart, no soul, no feelings? But that's not right. Then is he just a plaything — something to fill my time with? That doesn't seem right either.

The most likely explanation is that he's just someone I feel safe and warm with. The bottom line, my dream seems to be saying, is that there's no *harm* in him. He has nothing to hide.

If I told Tania this, she'd say that Ed is laughing in the dream because he knows I will think all this and that I'm deceived. But that's just typical of Tania, always twisting the truth to suit herself.

I seem to dream a lot lately which hardly seems possible considering how little I've been sleeping. The dreams are more usually of Sam, of course, even when he isn't actually in them. I'm looking for something, or chasing something, or groping for something just out of reach. The mornings are the worst. There's always a moment, just before I open my eyes, when I think it isn't really true; that it's reality which was the bad dream and that this is one of his spells at home and if I reach out I will feel his arm, or his hair

247

spread across the pillow (in my dreams Sam hasn't had his hair cut). I even smell his hot damp man smell. But the dampness is just my tears and the sweaty body belongs to Joe who has taken to crawling into my bed in the night. Anything else is just wishful thinking.

During the time I had away from work after he had gone, I took the picture of him I used to keep by my bed and locked it in the wardrobe so I wouldn't keep thinking about him. My love would be sorted away like money on deposit in a Swiss bank account: it was there until I wanted it. And if I never wanted it, no one need know. Then I gathered up his trainers that were sticking out from under the bed as usual, his music magazines, his shaving stuff and aftershaves, all the usual paraphernalia he leaves around – and shoved them into a bin bag.

But none of that stopped me thinking about him at all. In the mornings, while I got ready for work, Sam would talk to me, resting his hands on my waist as I washed up at the sink, coming up behind me and folding me in his arms as I brushed my teeth.

Now, since our coupling on the office floor, it is Ed who does all that, while Sam peers in at the window, alone and chastened, regretting he ever left, and watches us.

I've dressed with particular care today: a black close-fitting dress which swirls from the waist and sheer black tights. At the thought of seeing Ed I feel soothed and excited as though a plaster is being applied to a wound by a particularly attractive and attentive doctor.

I busy myself at the filing cabinet so he won't see my flushed face and obvious anticipation when he arrives, but will get the best vantage point for this dress which clings so provocatively to my hips. After half an hour the filing is almost finished and I'm rewarded with the sound of the door opening behind me. I catch my breath, ready to be surprised by his booming laugh or his deep voice murmuring something suitably provocative. But the voice I hear is high pitched and hoarse from the throat infection she can't quite shake off.

'There you are,' says Debbie. 'I've been looking for you. Ed's phoned in. He won't be in today. Got a migraine.'

'Did he say anything else?'

'Oh yes.'

I rally and my heart starts to beat for the cryptic message he will surely have left me.

'He says will you cancel today's meeting and sign any letters.'

Suddenly I feel foolish in my tight dress which requires me to hold my stomach in at all times and is more appropriate to a dinner date than the workplace.

Debbie pauses on her way out of the office. 'You look nice today. Going somewhere special?'

Ed doesn't arrive back to work until the following afternoon. When, unexpectedly, I find him at his desk, looking well-recovered from whatever was ailing him, my heart jumps.

'Hi! Feeling better?' I try to act natural but I forget what that feels like. I've been anticipating this moment – envisioning the way he'll kick closed the door and grasp me to him, desperate with longing. Or push me backwards across the desk or just take my face between his hands and kiss me with indescribable tenderness. Now that the moment is here I'm embarrassed in case he can read my thoughts.

'Ah, Gemma.' He leans back in his chair looking faintly surprised.

I hold his gaze, savouring the moment but then in the pause that follows the savour fades away. Ed looks uneasy but now, in the silence that follows, not as uneasy as me.

'Did anything crop up yesterday that I ought to know about?'

For a moment I think he is teasing — that that 'up' is some kind of innuendo. Or is he just shy of mentioning in broad daylight what happened here, on this floor, so very recently?

'No, nothing cropped up yesterday.' I'm feeding him a cue to answer 'But it did the day before,' but he doesn't take it so I add it myself.

He understands and now his thoughtful regard reminds me of Rudi, my lover from Corfu, as he sits there, the older man, the dominant force, always in control whatever he may lead you to think.

Ed gets up and closes the door. 'It was amazing, wasn't it? We were so pissed!' His laugh sounds almost forced. 'Are you feeling better now, about that bloke of yours?' I stand, still smiling foolishly while he adjusts a notice on his pinboard. Why is he mentioning Sam? Why is he fiddling around with his noticeboard?

But then I get it. He isn't sure how to play this. He has been expecting regrets or recriminations and is still thinking I might turn the tables on him.

'Ed?'

'Uh?' He doesn't turn round.

'Ed, it was wonderful.' He becomes very still and now he does turn.

'Yes, it was, wasn't it?' He puts his hands on my waist and pulls me to him. 'You were very sweet.'

'Sweet' wasn't quite what I was but I let it go. 'So what happens next?'

'We can do it again tonight,' he says, 'but we'd better wait until Marie's gone home, don't want to embarrass her.'

I stroke my finger down his cheek. 'No, really. What comes next?' I don't want to say her name, it having taken on a new significance now she's my rival, but what I mean is, what is he going to do about Janet Reger? His relationship with Maxine will take further consideration but there's nothing to stop him shipping Janet Reger out right this minute.

Either Ed is playing dumb — or he really is dumb. Knowing what a distorted view of personal relationships men can have, it could be either. I trace his lips with my forefinger, the way I've seen Julia Roberts do when she wants to get something out of the male lead.

'What about Janet Reger?' I ask with an effort.

He blinks. Then he takes my hand and presses his lips against my knuckles. 'Why don't we have lunch,' he says. 'Oh, not this week — I've a lot on. Maybe next Tuesday? Or Thursday?'

He strokes my cheek in a way that is paternal and painfully casual. His face implies compassion and understanding for this poor innocent who has been swept away by the tide of passion. A poor innocent who is not — and let's be clear about this — any match for Janet Reger.

There are some things which, once you've made the discovery, you never forget, such as that fire can burn you, that it always rains on Bank Holidays, or that white stilettoes are a bad idea. There are others which I find myself relearning each time I come up against them, like the fact that having sex means something different to a man; you just can't judge by what he says at the time. I remember a guy from college for whom having sex turned out to be some kind of social gaffe — I was just too *déclassé* and he backed off afterwards in case it might be catching. I've met some for whom it's like hitting a car when you're manoeuvring into a parking place: afterwards you wish you hadn't done it but not too much damage has been done — and you did want that parking space. For others it's just an opportunity they can't pass up, such as when you're given tickets to a film you don't particularly want to see but you go anyway because it's free.

Looking at Ed now I see each of those responses mirrored in his face, blending and blurring as his expression changes. How could I have been so wrong about him? How could I possibly have thought that having sex would commit him to anything? As for him not having a vacancy for me because he was already taken up with his wife and his girlfriend! There's always room in a harem for one more.

I can feel my face growing hot and now a white-hot band is tightening round my skull shrinking and tugging as though it will crack it. If I could just stab or scratch or injure Ed I would feel better and for one heart-stopping moment I think I'll explode in a fury of boiling brain cells and shattered bone if I can't do it. But now the room seems to be swaying, moving away from me, growing remote and shadowy, fading to grey.

'Are you all right?' Ed, alarmed, is approaching me from across the room.

I take a breath and close my eyes, clinging on to the desk and feeling the air cool against my cheeks. Gradually the boiling in my head subsides. When I open my eyes again the room has stilled and I'm back in control.

'I'll get back to my office.' Even though it means

confronting the old hopes I left there, that's preferable to the embarrassment I'm feeling at making such a mistake. How could I have been so stupid?

The world seems to have slowed down, my hands and arms work independently of me. I pick up the file I was carrying and turn toward the door.

'Gemma, look, don't go—' I look up at him, too quickly, relieved to have misunderstood.

But he is just snatching at what evidently appears to be a return to normality. 'I was just coming to get you actually,' he says. 'I can't find the photocopy that goes with this . . .'

Sitting up in bed I inhale deeply and the pain in my chest which I've had since Sam left, has gone. My pillow is dry and when I look in the mirror the swelling around my eyes which I've grown used to waking with, has disappeared. I feel as though I've had an operation and something has been cut out of me, but it's the part that hurt the most.

It strikes me, as I clear the detritus from last night's meal which I was too weary and desolate to do at the time, that there has been a gap in my life which it seemed no one but Ed could fill – no one who wasn't currently being bonked and bedded in some foreign land, anyway. In Ed I thought I had found a lifeline, someone to cling to among the wreckage of my life, when what I really had was just another drowning swimmer – and now he has slipped my arms from round his neck and is swimming for the shore.

It's a bit late for New Year resolutions but I make one anyway. I can't get Sam back – he has moved too far from my reach. But Ed, Ed is right here. I see Ed every day. I just have to keep swimming after him.

I close the front door and set off for work with Joe at my side hurrying to keep pace. 'Mummy,' he wails, 'don't walk so fast.'

Part Two

Chapter 17

'You will come, won't you?' says Marie, offering me the invitation. It's March, only one month away from her wedding, but this isn't what the invitation refers to. I take it from her, holding it gingerly between finger and thumb as though a tighter grip might commit me to something.

'If I can. But it's so hard to get a babysitter.' Bless you, Joe, I think.

'Diane's coming.'

'And Suzanne?'

'Well, no. It's the night she plays badminton.' And Suzanne doesn't even have a boyfriend (I've heard she has never had one) so you can hardly expect her to turn up to what a friend once referred to as a 'Knickers, knockers and nether regions night' (Marie refers to it coyly as an underwear party). 'It's not really her thing. Sylvia's coming though!'

I wouldn't have thought it was Marie's thing either, she being still at the stage where sex is represented by couples walking along the sand in soft focus. I thought these parties were for established couples for whom the first flush of love has begun to diminish, and maybe they are because it turns out it's some of Marie's married friends who have talked her into it.

'They said it's all done very nicely,' she explains with a forced enthusiasm. 'The demonstrator comes and—' she casts around for a word for what demonstrators do – 'and demonstrates everything, and you can try the basques on so it's all quite a laugh. My friend Yvonne went to one and they all had a really good time, they went on to a wine bar, even the demonstrator.' There's a brief pause, then she adds, 'And you don't have to buy anything.'

A pleading note has entered Marie's voice but she's wrong that I won't have to buy anything. I will see Marie's smile, forced and fake, when we're asked to place our orders, lest we embarrass her with our meanness in front of the party organizer and I will come home with whatever is the sex aids equivalent of a set of tupperware boxes just as I always do.

'If I can get a babysitter—'

'Please, Gemma, say you'll come.' She knows my attempts to obtain a babysitter will be minimal. 'Bring some friends if you want.'

I don't want; but when I happen to mention it to Tania, she is all for it. She says her parents will be staying that week and she is loath to miss an opportunity to go out, especially to something that's free, although the cynical might think her new boyfriend whose very mention brings a smile to her lips might have something to do with it.

Tania's mum offers to babysit Joe while her dad will look after Tania's two, so I have no good reason for not attending and by the time I think of bringing my common sense and good taste into play Tania has made the arrangements.

It's three months since Sam left; nearly two since I grappled Ed into submission on his office floor only to see him get up again as though nothing had happened. The company has had a stay of execution — we don't know yet if that's all it is — so we're all still here, even me.

I threatened to leave over the business with Ed, of course, and was so imaginative in telling him just what I thought of him that I certainly made him think I meant it. Well, you can't just let yourself be shat on and I had to do something. It frightened him that I might go and that was comforting to see. My knowledge of the business was growing daily, besides which there are too few people with whom he has a good working relationship. He couldn't afford to lose me.

'Gemma, I don't deserve to be forgiven but I'm asking anyway,' he said, striking a satisfying note of contrition. 'I took advantage, I admit it and I'm sorry. But it's not something to resign over. If anything, it's evidence of how well suited we are. And in my own way, I do care about you. I think you know that, don't you?'

There was a lot more where that came from, not all of it quite so persuasive, and I punished him a little more by making him wait for my decision. But in the end I told him I would stay, as I'd always intended.

You'd think that if you'd given the best of yourself to someone and then seen yourself betrayed and ultimately rejected, that you might form an adverse opinion of the person who had done it to you, take revenge or walk out, wanting never to see him again.

But I didn't feel that. How I saw it was that if Ed was mistaken, misguided, and didn't know his own feelings, then it was up to me to organize our relationship for him, as I organize everything else. And he's attracted to me, I see that, and that makes me feel better about myself — happier, more confident — helps me say Ya boo sucks to Sam even if Sam doesn't know it.

Rhea once said to me that rejection is a powerful aphrodisiac and I don't deny there's nothing like having someone give you the brush off for increasing his appeal. But I can see how that works both ways. When Ed thought I might leave I saw him sensing rejection too.

He tries harder with me now, dares not take me for granted. Sometimes it almost seems as though he's wooing me rather than the other way round. But there's still Janet Reger, and she will not lie down – or more likely, she lies down all too often.

Naturally, Tania has her own theory which she is only too keen to tell me as we stand with the kids in the queue for the cinema on a rainy Saturday afternoon in March. 'It's hardly surprising if you're feeling confused,' she says. 'Being rejected twice like that in such rapid succession would send anyone off the rails.' As usual, she's getting it all wrong. She won't believe that there really is something between Ed and me, it's just a matter of time before he has to acknowledge it.

What Tania really thinks I should do is to try to get Sam back. But Sam's phone calls are stiff and frosty, concerned only with Joe and whether I've got enough money. When we speak I sense his girlfriend at his side nibbling his neck or with her arms draped round his chest.

But Ed, Ed is still here. I see Ed every day.

Marie lives in a town house terrace, not dissimilar from mine but for the brass door lamp, brass door knocker and brass letter box which gleam as brightly as they did in the catalogue they were probably ordered from. I'm in a bad mood because Tania hasn't come and I wouldn't have come myself if I'd known she would drop out. She says she's ill but I think she's just in a bad mood about something.

It's probably to do with her parents staying but they go back tomorrow morning and you'd think she'd want to take the opportunity to get out rather than be sitting at home watching 'The Bill'. Actually, I wish I was home watching 'The Bill'. I wish I was home doing anything at all. Even scrubbing the kitchen floor seems appealing.

I'm half an hour late but not as late as I wish I was. Marie greets me, taking my coat and I squeeze past her brother's mountain bike in the hall and enter the living-room. Marie has arranged the chairs in a rough circle, with dining-room chairs brought in to complement the dralon three-piece suite. On the glass coffee table are bowls of peanuts and twiglets at which Brindle Sylvia is nervously picking. She had her recent and disastrous perm cut out and streaks put in; now she looks less like a Scottie dog but more like a zebra. Diane is also here and both, along with an older woman, and five or six girls in their early twenties, are making smiling effortful conversation. Two of the girls seem giggly and excitable but the others look like they're trying to keep their spirits up before undergoing some kind of ordeal, the true terrors of which they can only guess at.

Diane nods a greeting to me while wearing an expression that suggests Marie's friends don't look quite our type. I catch Marie's friends passing glances which could be saying the same about us. I perch uneasily on the end of the sofa next to Diane.

'I didn't really expect to see you here,' I whisper to Diane. 'Actually, I didn't really expect to see me here.'

'Oh, it could be quite fun,' says Diane to my surprise. 'It'll be all right once we get started.'

'Gemma,' says Marie with nervous enthusiasm, coming back into the room. 'Let me introduce you. This is my mum, and this here's Gary's mum, Judith. Judith works in a dry cleaners.'

I get up and shake Judith's bony fingers, the knuckles knobbly and swollen, the ridged fingernails painted the colour of blood clots. Her hair is an unlikely auburn and pinned in such a way as to allow a cascade of ringlets at the back. I've seen hair like this on video footage of fashions from the sixties but never in real life. And not on a woman with a neck like a turkey's either. Marie's mum is ash blonde and pencil slim, with a figure to make Marie weep (and not only Marie). Marie introduces her other friends whose names I forget instantly.

'Who's for some wine?' asks Marie's mum.

'I really shouldn't,' says Judith, holding out her glass for a refill.

The demonstrator arrives late, she had to pop into Tesco's on the way, she'd run out of batteries, and sets about arranging her goods on an occasional table in the corner, along with a rack of lingerie. It's a relief when she breezes in. Each time I whisper anything to Diane everyone looks at me.

'Well, are we all here now?' The demonstrator is a slim tall blonde with big hair. She stands and surveys the audience with the satisfaction of a politician whose small local meeting has had a good turn out. She is wearing a smart but ill-fitting red jacket with a tight black skirt, and her gold jewellery rattles as she moves. Her black tights would be sheer but for the horizontal pattern of snags up the sides of them. 'My name is Sherry with a "y"' ('Can you spell it any other way?' I ask Diane) 'and I'm your party organizer. I'm from Liverpool, you can tell from me voice, and I've been doing this job for three years now and there's nothing you can say will shock me, so there's no need for anyone to feel embarrassed. Having sex is a very natch-erel thing, we all do it, even the Queen, although she's so rich she could've paid someone to have her kids, which if I was married to Prince Philip is what I would do, oops, shouldn't have said that, and I've got a few facts here you might like to know, did you know—' She pauses to consult a scrap of paper, turning it until it is the right way up. 'Did you know that you use up more calories from a good sexy session than from a three-mile walk?' We try to look like we haven't heard this or something similar before. 'So having sex is actually a brilliant way to lose weight – I was sixteen stone before I met my husband!' Two friends of Marie's become convulsed over this and Brindle Sylvia makes a note of it on her piece of paper.

Actually the last time I heard this statistic I swear they said that making love used the same amount of calories as an *eight*-mile walk but maybe it depends on whether you're making love to Johnny Depp or Prince Philip (if it was Prince Philip I'd go for an eight-mile walk instead).

Next we play a game like consequences in which we all have to write down something dirty and pass it on. It's aimed at breaking the ice – something which I'd have thought an ice pick would have its work cut out doing but after we've finished and Diane has, inexplicably, won a small rubber ring with nobbly bits on it whose use we don't immediately comprehend, there does seem to be some semblance of party atmosphere.

Sherry gathers up our pens and papers and says she'll show us what she's got. She looks around expectantly as she says this and Sylvia obliges with, 'Oh! Saucy!'

'Now ladies. What do you think of this?' She holds up a black see-through nightie with fluffy feathers round the neck. It's the sort of thing women with peroxided hair and cigarettes in their mouths used to wear in old films. 'The feathers are hand plucked by pheasant pluckers,' she says. 'You try saying that when you've had a few.' Marie's friends haven't had a few but they try anyway and Sherry joins in showing how fast she can say it without a slip, which turns out to be not much faster than she said it already. While pairs of pants with no backs in them are passed round, Marie's mum appears with a tray of hot sausage rolls and sandwiches with the crusts cut off.

'It'd really suit you,' says Sherry to Sylvia, spotting her as the one among us most eager to join in, and holding up not just the black see-through nightie but matching pants which have a nest of feathers on the front. 'I saw someone with just your figure in one and she looked stunning. And it's just right for tickling his fancy.' Sylvia takes it and bustles upstairs to try it on, not disheartened by the fact the pants look like she'd have to wear them on one leg at a time.

No one seems keen to try on the rubber dress or a satin teddy the colour of varicose veins which, says Sherry, is because we're all after something a bit more *risqué*. She gets out a bra with cups that unclip individually, poking her finger through to show how your nipple would be suddenly revealed. She introduces it as an innovation but it's the same as one I had for breastfeeding, except mine wasn't in red lace and didn't come with a matching G-string and suspender belt.

'My husband'd go mad for that,' says one of the excitable girls.

'See if they do it in his size then,' says her friend.

'I have enough trouble keeping my bust under control without giving it an escape hatch,' says Gary's mum to Marie. 'I like harvest festivals,' she says, reprising the old joke. 'The sort of underwear where everything's safely gathered in.'

'Now listen up girls,' says Sherry with a sudden sense of urgency, possibly related to the realization that no one seems inclined to buy anything yet. 'I've got something very special for you – now how many times have you heard a man say that?' There's a general chorus of agreement from Marie's friends though the only male who has ever said it to me was Joe when he brought me a mother's day present home from play school. 'Well, for the first time in your lives, you can believe it,' says Sherry. 'Once you've got one of these, you won't need a man at all!' She gets out a vibrator with the circumference of a cucumber and begins to demonstrate its three speeds and angle of bend, running it along the underside of Marie's mum's fur rug to illustrate the rippling effect. 'Now what man can do that?' she asks.

'I'd like to see one try it on my fur rug,' says Gary's mum.

The door opens and Sylvia skips in wearing the nightie over her jumper. She spreads the skirt with her hands and curtsies, then turns and takes a bow, bending over to reveal the G-string cutting a path up the seat of her tights. I've seen more provocative sides of beef hanging in the butchers.

'Oh, that's lovely,' says Gary's mum. 'Maybe I will try something on.'

'This is much better than going to a sex shop,' says Sylvia later, as we pass round the vibrators for inspection, holding their tips against our noses as instructed.

'Is it? Why's that?' I've never been inside one myself. The blacked-out windows scare me. Who knows what might be going on in there? They might have a back entrance that was a direct route to the white slave trade and you'd be drugged up and dragged out before you could say, 'Nipple rings.'

'They're not all like that,' says Diane unexpectedly as Sylvia turns up the speed to full and tests it against the palm of her hand. It sounds like our electric toothbrush. 'The ones you see now are just like ordinary shops, with proper window displays and mannequins. The only difference is they all wear peep-hole bras.'

'There's lots of them about,' says Sylvia who seems something of an authority. 'You can just go in and buy knickers, it doesn't have to be all this kind of thing.' She cracks a plaited whip against the side of the chair but instead of the satisfying 'thwack' we're all expecting, it just flops downwards. 'Now what does that remind you of?' she says thoughtfully.

'I always feel a bit embarrassed in those shops,' says a girl with long red hair and freckles, who looks about fifteen.

'Oh, yes, this is more comfortable,' agrees Sylvia, 'being among your friends,' though I think the anonymity of total strangers would be far preferable. It's difficult, in this giggly atmosphere, to conjure the mood of sexual intensity you'd need to get your money's worth out of the black rubber bondage suit priced at £59.99.

I had had the idea that I might find something enticing to use on Ed but these artefacts seem designed for scenarios I can't imagine. They seem foolish and silly, and oddly removed from the intense pulsating experience I thought sex was supposed to be.

'You should've seen me in the shop when I was looking at one of these vibrator thingies. The assistant was a boy, couldn't have been more than twenty – terrible acne. And he kept showing me how you could use it on your neck and it put you off really, all those spots. He got them all out over the counter — not his spots!' She nudges my elbow. 'He had this one and that black Russian one and those they're looking at over there with the knobbly bits on — and people kept coming in and watching us. No, I didn't like it.'

'What did your husband say?' I ask.

'He didn't say anything. I didn't tell him.' She looks mystified at how her husband has come into the conversation.

'So did you actually buy one?'

'Well, he knocked five quid off and threw in some lubricant so you couldn't say no really.'

'There's nothing like a bargain,' I say lamely as Sylvia takes the vibrator from me and starts removing the batteries.

It looks very similar to one Sam produced from under his pillow one night as a surprise. It was a surprise too — I came in about fifteen seconds.

Diane's eyebrows threaten to reach her hairline when I tell her this.

'That must have been one for the record books.'

'Not really. It was like sneezing. It came and went and I thought "What was that?"'

'You mean it wasn't satisfying?'

'Only like when you get a tickle in your throat and then you cough and it feels better.'

'What did Sam say?'

'That he'd get me some cough linctus.'

She pokes me in the ribs causing me to kick the display table, sending a box of joyballs flying.

'Sam didn't even notice. He was still adjusting the speed on it at the time, I didn't like to say anything.'

Sylvia picks up the box of joyballs from the floor

and turns it over in her hands. 'Feel the weight of these.'

I take it from her and we laugh at the idea of our nether regions being weighed down by such things.

'I have enough to carry with the shopping,' she says.

Sherry has caught something of our conversation and comes across bringing a narrow transparent box with her. 'Have you seen the deluxe bendy version?' she asks, taking it out for us.

Diane screws up her nose. 'I don't think it's for me. And it isn't as if the average man is deluxe or bendy, is it? It has three speeds and that's not realistic either. In my experience, most men give you a choice of two: stop or go.'

Sylvia appears briefly at Sherry's elbow to ask her opinion of a rubber thing that fits round the penis for extra friction, while I consider the advance of technology over the human male.

'You want to get yerself one,' says Sherry to Diane, in a last bid to part her from her money.

'She would,' I suggest, 'but it's not like you can bring it back if you don't like it, is it?'

'She'd like it, kid, and if she didn't I'd give her her money back. Never had a dissatisfied customer yet.'

'Well, it's not the sort of thing most women would like to complain about it, is it?' says Diane. 'I think it lacks a certain something, not having any arms and legs attached. No face.'

'That's what I like about it,' says Sherry. 'It doesn't lie to you or sleep with other women when you're home minding the kids.'

'Yes, but it's poor on witty repartee,' I add.

'So was my husband. And a dildo doesn't fall asleep or drip on the sheets or lie in bed farting all night.'

'Oh, I like the sound of him,' says Sylvia, bustling over. 'Who is he?'

Later Diane discovers some thong knickers made of leather. She holds them up, between thumb and forefinger, looking as if she has just discovered something unpleasant in the U-bend.

'Have you decided what you're buying?' she asks me.

'Oh, I don't really want anything. There doesn't seem much point when you haven't got a bloke.' I don't intend mentioning Ed to Diane. And Sam would have laughed at crotchless pants and edible knickers.

'Maybe it's the way to get one,' says Diane coquettishly.

Sylvia is rooting in Sherry's box of assorted goodies and baddies. 'Anyone interested in some M & S stuff?' she calls.

Several of us look up at that. We might not make room for leather thongs in our undies drawer but you can't go wrong with a Marks & Spencer cotton gusset. I say as much to Diane.

'Not M & S — S & M,' says Diane resignedly, as Sylvia demonstrates a pair of suede-lined handcuffs.

Over coffee some of Marie's friends, along with Sylvia, try to persuade her into going to see a male stripper for her hen night do.

'My friend's one was brilliant,' says the girl with the long red hair. Far from being fifteen, she's on her second marriage. Her husband is a policeman; they use real handcuffs. I saw her turning her nose up at the suede lined ones. 'Her mum-in-law went up on stage and tied a bow on his thing. Then her aunt went up and had to undo it with her teeth — and they were false!'

'Thank God for that,' says Gary's mum. 'At least she could take them out and put them in disinfectant.'

Then another girl tells a joke about a man going for infertility treatment — he bursts into tears when the nurse who gives him a blood test says, 'Just a little prick' and then gives him a test tube marked 'sterile'.

Sylvia laughs like a drain and says 'Just a little prick' sounds like a description of her husband.

'Do you think Marie enjoyed it?' I ask Diane as we fill in our order forms.

'Oh, I should think so. Just a bit of fun, isn't it? And it'll probably give her a few ideas for her wedding night.'

I'm not sure Marie has enjoyed it. I think she was expecting less raunch and more romance. She may be saving for her bottom drawer but tonight all she has got is stuff for the back of her cupboard.

'And she'll get some sort of present too, won't she, for having the party?' says Diane.

'You mean like a lifetime's supply of nipple tassels?'

Diane giggles. 'Or all the KY jelly you can eat.'

'That reminds me,' says a friend of Marie's, joining in. 'My smear test is due.'

'Let's see what you bought,' I say to Diane as we walk to our cars. We pause under a street lamp and she holds up a pair of cream satin pants with a matching push-up bra. I hadn't seen them or I might have been tempted myself. Then she turns them round and I realize they're like the thongs we laughed at earlier.

'Bend over in them and they'll saw you in half like cheesewire.'

'They only do that if they're too small,' she says silencing me with her unexpected superior knowledge. 'What did you get?'

After all, I'd decided to take Diane's advice. 'A manual of sex tips. It's called *How to Drive Your Man Wild*.'

Diane laughs. 'That's easy if you're married to my husband. You just have to hide the remote control.'

Ed picks me up from home on an unseasonally icy morning in March and I wave goodbye to Joe who is peering out of Tania's window as we roar away from the kerb, the G-force hitting me in the back like a fist. Joe went happily to Tania's to be taken to school as usual, but seeing me swept away in a shiny silver BMW instead of battling my way to the station in the rain is more than he can bear. He raises his hand in a forlorn wave and mercifully we screech away before I have to witness the trembling lip.

Ed has to visit our Birmingham office and has asked me along. He says he wants me to meet someone but a more likely reason is that he thinks it will please me to have a day out of the office. These days, in his small way, Ed tries to keep on the right side of me.

'Are you warm enough?' asks Ed with an uncharacteristic show of concern. I nod but he turns the heater up anyway.

We're more wary of each other these days and avoid some of the old banter — sexual innuendo isn't quite so titillating once you've had sex with the person — but I see in his little attentions that our relationship is moving forward. It's beginning to relax again; to change into something more comfortable, as you might say.

'Do you think you'll get back together with that guy of yours?' Ed asks, pushing a cassette into the tape deck. We haven't discussed anything this personal since we had our falling out but the enforced intimacy of a car is like the confessional, allowing you to say all kinds of things you wouldn't otherwise.

'I don't know. Sometimes I'm so sure of it I expect

to turn round and see him walking in the door. Other times . . .'

Ed turns to me with a sympathetic smile. 'Other times you hope like hell that never happens!' He finishes off my sentence for me and gets it wrong but I don't feel like correcting him. Other times I know Sam's gone forever and that it has just been Joe holding us together. All those extended contracts and cancellations of leave, that's what they were about.

'Why do you ask, Ed?'

'Just wondering. We're both in the same boat really, aren't we? Alone and fancy free.'

'You're not fancy free.'

'I'm married to Maxine. That's almost the same thing.' He laughs, though actually it was his girlfriend I was referring to. But he makes me laugh anyway; I know he believes it.

Later Ed says, apropos of nothing, 'Tell me, are you permanently wedded to Treadz?' The question, coming not so long after the one about Sam, makes me think they're connected for a moment.

'No,' I say, 'I'm not wedded at all, but I might consider the odd affair.' He looks surprised to hear what he assumes is the old innuendo, but it isn't, it's just a joke.

'I've got something for you. It's on the backseat.'

I turn, half expecting to find something small and gift-wrapped with him in his present mood, but all I can see on the back seat is a sheaf of papers. 'What am I looking for?'

'It's there behind you. You can't miss it. Have a look.'

I reach behind his seat with an effort and after much grappling, pull the papers towards me. I look at the cover which has Ed's name on it but I can't see why he wants me to read it.

He's smiling to himself, savouring my confusion. 'It's my business plan. Welcome to the firm.'

I resist the old temptation to say, 'The firm what?' and open it at the section on predicted sales figures.

'Looks good doesn't it?' he asks. I nod as though I'm impressed, which I might be if these were achieved targets rather than some figure Ed has dreamt up and then doubled, or quite possibly trebled. 'And we should be able to reach that easily, I've made very conservative estimates.'

A car speeds past us in a spray of foam, and Ed curses. I've realized he was planning something over the last few weeks but I hadn't imagined it would be anything quite as extreme as setting up his own company. A finger of anxiety jabs at my heart. I don't want him to leave.

'Haven't you noticed anything?' asks Ed at length. Apprehension makes me irritable. I hate it when people ask that – does he mean have I noticed he's driving too fast, that he has cut himself shaving, or that he's being more than usually smug?

'What should I have noticed?'

'Look at the staff list.'

Maxine is there as partner, Roger as Financial Director, and as Sales and Marketing Manager there is – me. *Sales and Marketing Manager?* Until I started working for Ed my sole experience of sales and marketing was a Saturday job I had in Boots when I was sixteen.

'Surprised?'

Bloody astonished.

'There are a couple of courses I can send you on, but even without them you're three times as good as the competition.' He pauses. 'You will come, won't you? The

273

money won't be terrific but I can give you more than you're on here — well, you'll be doing more.'

So this is why he has brought me along today. He wanted to be away from the office where we would have plenty of time to talk it over.

The remains of frost on the houses we pass are suddenly caught in a ray of early morning sun giving them a shimmering iridescence as though they're excited about something.

The tape comes to a halt with a click and Ed sorts through his tape collection while I swallow the anticipation that's rising into my throat. Ed discovers a 'Best of' Doors album and slots it into place. It's a favourite of Sam's as it happens, and in other circumstances I might feel uncomfortable, here with Ed, remembering the times I've lain with Sam while 'Light my Fire' thumped out through the floorboards. But for now I hold the business plan in my hand and Sam's memories can not touch me.

'How many staff would I be managing?' I ask, eager to put a number on it. ('Tania, I'll have *four/six/ten!* people under me.')

'Oh well, obviously it's a status title initially, it'll be just us to start with, but in the fullness of time . . .' The warm shiver of delight which has started in my neck has cooled by the time it reaches my feet. How come that I have forgotten so soon that Ed is a salesman? It's his job to make you want what he wants you to want. I turn the business plan over in my hands while phrases like *total bullshit* and *I'm a complete idiot* spring to mind.

On the other hand, what would I do if Ed left? I need him. Life is what's happening while you're making plans. You can't always take your time when you want to get something.

On the subject of which: 'Why is Maxine involved?' I don't like to see her name associated with Ed's as though she's a permanent fixture.

'She's just a sleeping partner. Although I don't actually sleep with this one.'

'You're sure she is a sleeping partner — and not completely comatose?' This all needs careful consideration. I don't like the idea of Maxine being involved, but even less would I like the idea of her not being involved. She's more reliable and steady than Eddie. If she's putting money into it then it can't be such a risky prospect.

'Gemma, you're such a worrier,' he shoots me a sympathetic smile, not answering my question but managing to make me feel better anyway, a skill I've sometimes seen him use on clients. 'We've got the best of all worlds: you, me and Maxine's business acumen but without her interference.' Maxine lectures in business studies and ran a small concern of her own at one time.

Ed raises one eyebrow conspiratorially before braking to avoid a maniac who has cut in. He thumps the horn hissing, 'Prat!' and then goes on as though he's continuing something he had already begun, 'I'll tell you why the whole company is going down the tubes. The directors won't look ahead, there's a gap in the market and they just can't see it. Well, I can. We'll take over their trainer business and expand into other sports accessories. The market is phenomenal.'

His enthusiasm is infectious. I see us in our suite of offices with a view of the city while clients phone begging us to do business with them and the financial pages of the broadsheets wonder at our overnight success.

'It'll be another couple of months before you'd need to join us,' Ed is saying, as he slows down for the motorway exit. 'And don't forget they could pull the plug on Treadz any time and you'd be left with nothing anyway.'

'Oh, and your company couldn't?'

He throws me a reproachful look while changing gear. I'll be sorry to give up my comfortable office with Colin and Marie wandering in and out providing light relief. But part of what I admire in Ed is his individuality and adventurous spirit. It's no good my complaining when he demonstrates it.

'It's a tremendous opportunity, you know,' Ed says, as we pull up outside our Birmingham office. 'For all of us.'

It is, and especially for anyone who wants to consolidate her relationship with the new Managing Director.

'I'll have to think about it,' I lie, getting out of the car.

I wander off to a coffee shop while Ed goes in to the meeting which is to provide an alibi for the real purpose of our visit. Within the hour he is back to pick me up. 'I told them I had to get away for another meeting,' he says. 'Well, it's the truth isn't it?'

Don Ashby, manager of a sports and leisure complex just outside Warwick, is short and stout, resembling the pint pot that probably helped him get that way, and looks as though his idea of a good suit is any that are cut to do up over his belly. He is the reason we have come today. Ed had intended I should go into the meeting with him but Don who is the type of man who thinks a woman's place is at the hairdresser's, insists there is much I can learn from a tour of their leisure facilities and entrusts me to the care of his under manager, a thin reedy boy who is trying to grow a moustache (with less success than some of the women I know). I admire the sauna and squash courts, and grow enthusiastic about the weight training room so that he won't guess that the only exercise I ever get is running up bills.

'We've just got our first customer,' says Ed happily when we're back in the car, the meeting over and with us both having enjoyed, if that's the word, a lunch of withered salad courtesy of the sports centre cafeteria.

I know that Don Ashby has been with Galaxy Leisure, our holding company, a long time. 'How did you pull that off?'

'I think "poaching" is the technical term,' he says, switching the engine on. But before we pull away, he turns to me. 'Look, I don't feel like going straight back, do you? We could wander round the town or something.'

I have the feeling that this has always been on the agenda. He's seducing me lest I turn down the marvellous opportunity that is his new company, but I'm game for anything that involves shopping.

'I know what you'd like.' He lets the clutch in and turns the wheel hard, sending a spray of gravel towards a woman in a jogging suit the colour of oysters.

I don't know why Ed thought I'd like Warwick Castle more than a wander round the shops – I don't want postcards or oven mitts and I've already got a ruler with the kings and queens of England on it.

I'd been to the castle once as a child when we stayed with relatives. We came for a day out. My mother brought sandwiches and hard-boiled eggs and we ate them in the grounds pretending the castle was our house and this was our garden. Well, my brother and I pretended. I don't suppose my mother, the doyenne of the Round Table, joined in.

Twenty years ago a stately home was a dry and dusty

learning experience. Now it's history as entertainment; history as a theme park with an entrance fee as befits it.

'Do you like history?' I ask as we make our way past a waxwork dummy of Richard Neville who lived in the fifteenth century, the guidebook informs us, and who is better known to history as Warwick the Kingmaker. He may be known to history, but personally I've never heard of him.

Ed pauses to look at the dummy, the skin of which looks as lifelike as his own while the mouth has the same determined set.

'No, I can't say I do. History is something that's over and done with. The people it happened to are all dead, so I can't see the point of it.' I'm a bit astonished by such a philistine attitude and don't immediately respond but Ed retrieves himself just in time. 'But on the other hand, it's comforting to realize that life goes on. However bad things get, it's all happened to someone before and they survived.'

'Or else they didn't,' I say with a nod to the long-dead Richard Neville.

'What do you want to look at?' asks Ed, referring to the timetable of events we were handed with our tickets. 'You can hear a talk on battles or watch a medieval knight being dressed in armour.'

I'd rather see a medieval knight being undressed but that isn't on the itinerary. We make our way across the courtyard and Ed pauses to look up at the castle walls and speculate on the sights they must have witnessed. It rained before lunch but the watery sun that is peering over the battlements isn't strong enough to dry the ground which boasts puddles at irregular intervals.

'Do you really want to see this knight thing?' asks

Ed, implying that he doesn't. 'We've only got an hour or two and wandering about would probably be just as interesting.'

'The dungeons are over there. Shall we have a look?'

'Oh yes, can't miss the dungeons.' He turns towards them acting the gleeful schoolboy and leads me down the steep stone steps. The small room at the bottom is damp, dark and cruelly cold. I know that's what dungeons are supposed to be like but all the same I shiver and it's not just with the drop in temperature. On the walls are the remains of manacles and some sort of metal harness is suspended from the ceiling, though 'ceiling' is too civilized a word for the bare blackened stone we have here.

There are few visitors to the castle today and with just the two of us alone in this dismal place, the atmosphere is especially oppressive. I can feel the hopelessness of those who died here. Some words are scratched on one of the walls and I strain to make out the letters.

I'm aware of Ed behind me, peering over my shoulder. 'Ed, can you read—' I don't get any further. He has pulled my scarf away from my neck and is blowing down my neck, a long warm blow that caresses my back and goes on working all the way down to my toes. He doesn't speak and despite myself I lean imperceptibly towards him so that my head meets his shoulder. Feeling him so close makes my scalp prickle. Sharp points of heat dart down my cheeks. He runs his tongue round the rim of my ear and the air turns to frost around it.

'Come on dad, come *on* dad!' Two boys and presumably their father, are making their way down the steps behind us. I move away from Ed smartly managing to step on his toe as I do so. That will teach him, thinking he can wipe the slate clean just by offering me some poxy job. I may want him but not like this, not here, and not at his bidding while Janet Reger is still on the scene. She still rings quite regularly. We've even had a chat once or twice.

'Ed, have you seen that?'

'Seen what?' There's a note of frustration in his voice which I'm pleased to hear.

Set into the floor is a small hole topped by a grille. A prisoner would be lowered into it, with scarcely room to breathe and that's where he would stay. I kneel down to look more closely as an involuntary shudder takes hold of me.

'Ed,' I whisper, suddenly overcome for the men who have suffered here. 'The things men do to each other.'

He bends down to look over my shoulder. 'That's nothing,' he says, 'you should see some of the things women can do.'

'In your case, you probably had it coming,' I say, not realizing quite how true this would turn out to be.

We follow the boy and the dad up the steps out of the dungeons and a couple waiting to come down stand aside to let us pass. For a moment I don't recognize the woman with her severe but fashionable haircut.

'Gemma!' says Diane.

'Bill!' says Ed to our financial director. Immediately we adopt the expression of people delighted at running into old friends and come out with variations on 'Fancy meeting you here,' right on cue and as though we're pleased about it.

Chapter 18

––––– ––

'Where have you been?' says Tania accusingly, opening the door to me and checking her watch.

'You know where I've been.'

'I was expecting you hours ago. Joe has got a temperature and he's been irritable all afternoon. He won't eat any tea.'

I don't want to talk about Joe's ailments, or for him to have any ailments, and I don't want Tania to be cross with me. I want to tell her about my job offer, and Warwick and who we saw there.

I feel Joe's forehead and he continues watching 'East Enders' listlessly without acknowledging my arrival. I can never judge from touching him whether he has a temperature or not but it's what mothers do.

'He'll probably be all right once he gets home. It's been a long day for him.'

'It's been a long day for all of us.' Ouch. 'I just hope whatever it is isn't catching.' Tania is exhibiting an unusual lack of sympathy. 'Sophie has already had flu this year, I don't want her getting anything else.'

'I'm sure it's nothing,' I reply trying not to sound tetchy in response. It's not my fault if Joe has got a bug. It's probably the cold Tania has anyway. 'There's always something going round. Joe usually shakes anything off in a day or two.'

'Yes, but Sophie doesn't. Once she's down she stays down.' This is so unlike Tania, and she isn't meeting my eyes. There's a sullen twist to her mouth which I don't recognize either.

'Tania, is something wrong?'

'No, what could possibly be wrong?' This is what I used to say myself to Sam prior to a row. I don my kid gloves to deal with her.

'I'm sorry I was so late, such a nuisance for you, especially with Joe not being well.' A little crawling never hurt anyone. 'The meeting at the leisure centre went on forever.' Damn, now I've lied to her. I can't mention Warwick now or she'll guess why I was late.

Usually Tania stops to hear about my day and to tell me what has been happening down at the school. Today she is clattering the tea plates and loading them into the sink, with much sighing as she sweeps crumbs off the table and into her hand. She's probably just worn down with having had her parents to stay.

'You look tired, why don't you sit down and I'll clear up for you? I've been sitting down most of the day.'

'And drinking.'

'What?'

'You've been drinking. I can always tell.'

We did stop at a pub on the way back but that was primarily because I'd wanted a loo.

'Well, I am old enough.' I cast about for where I could have been drinking that won't imply pubs or wine bars. 'It was someone's birthday. They brought some wine in.' Now I'm lying to her again. She sounds like my mother.

'I don't care if they brought in the bloody crown jewels, I'm sick of minding your child while you're out at some jolly.'

I don't know how to handle this. I've never seen Tania so intractable. 'Look, Tania, I'm sorry about whatever has happened to upset you. But don't take it out on me, I wasn't even here.' Before I've finished the sentence I can see it was the wrong thing to say.

'Yes, precisely. You're never here. Off at the crack of dawn, back God-knows-when, with some tale about the train being late or the buses not running.' Those things have been true. Evidently I'm no more convincing when I'm telling the truth than when I lie. This row isn't just about tonight then, it's the culmination of resentments she has been harbouring. 'I could just about cope when you were temping – it wasn't every day and it wasn't every week. Now you expect me to take Joe every single day, holidays too.' My heart sinks a little further. We haven't discussed the holidays but I'd certainly been hoping she would take him over Easter. 'I've put up with it because you needed a job and Joe and Jack get along, but right now they're not getting along or maybe you haven't noticed—' She says this with heavy sarcasm and in fact I haven't noticed '—but even then I've soldiered on because you're supposed to be my friend – ' Supposed to be? What's with 'supposed to be'? '– but I've had enough. You take me for granted. All you think about is that godawful jerk you work for. Ed this, Ed that, Ed the fucking other. It's time you took a look at yourself. You're obsessed with him.' She has said this before and it's beginning to get to me. Indignation brings a rush of blood to my face and my neck prickles with anger. My kid gloves are off.

'You're jealous. You can't bear to see me with a new bloke.'

Tania shuts the kitchen door to block out the faces of our children who are finding our contretemps more stimulating than 'EastEnders'.

'Jealous? Of you and him? I saw him this morning – he's years older than you.'

'Only twelve years.'

'He must be getting younger. You told me fifteen.'

'Anyway, what does it matter?'

'It matters if you're late because he was testing your commitment to your work – at some hotel somewhere.'

Friendships rely on a mutual trust and a readiness to believe what you tell each other. When your friends stop believing what you tell them – even if what you tell them isn't the whole truth – there's nowhere for the friendship to go.

'You're wrong, Tania.'

'I don't believe you. You're sleeping with him.'

'I'm not!'

'Then you intend to.'

'I can do what I damn well like without asking your permission.'

'Then you can do it while someone else is looking after your bad-mannered brat.'

'*What*?' I thought she liked Joe! 'Don't start taking it out on Joe. You're nothing but a jealous cow.'

'*Me*? Jealous of you and a man like the stupid jerks you pick up with? I thought Sam was bad enough! Ed must be so busy watching his back it's a wonder his head doesn't come unscrewed.'

'Oh, and you've got such a prize in Chris.'

Tania becomes very still and she lowers her chin as

though she's about to headbutt me. 'Just shut up and get out.'

'Don't worry, I'm going. Joe! Get your coat.' I scrabble about amongst a pile of shoes by the back door trying to find a pair that match.

'Joe!'

He comes to me, offering one socked foot at a time and waiting with an anxious, watchful air while I lace his shoes. Tania waits, holding the door open for us. I stand up and take his hand and my eyes meet Tania's.

'Tania—'

'Try Carla Reynolds,' she says sullenly. 'She does childminding.'

As I come downstairs from settling Joe and dosing him with Calpol the phone starts to ring.

'Hi. It's . . . me.'

The fact Sam thinks I might not know who it is is a salutary reminder of how far things have gone.

'How are you?'

'OK. And you?'

'Yes, fine.' I've had more intimate conversations with the men who phone selling fitted kitchens.

The phone has disturbed Joe who rallies on hearing it's Sam and comes to speak to him, demonstrating impressive though garbled recall of my quarrel with Tania and telling Sam he won't be going there any more and is to have a new childminder. Then I speak to Sam again, who has more sense than to ask what the row was about or perhaps just isn't interested, and now finally gets round to telling me why he has rung. He's going to his mother's the week after Easter, which falls late this year, at the end of April, and he wants to know if Joe could stay for a few days. In the light of what has just transpired with Tania, this will be ideal. He sounds as though he's hoping we won't run into each other although we'll surely have to start sorting things out by then. We can't just let things drift on indefinitely.

There's an awkward pause while I, and maybe Sam too, wonder if there's anything else we should say. What I really want to ask is if the girl with the legs like pillars is making him unhappy, as I hope. And to drop into the conversation the fact that Ed is totally besotted with me and loves me more with every passing day, so it had better work out with Miss Big Nose because it's too late to come back here.

But when I speak it's just to say: 'The washing-machine has packed up but the man's coming out to fix it on Tuesday.' And yes, I have got enough money to cover it.

When I go back upstairs Joe has put himself back to bed. He stirs restlessly but he feels cooler to the touch and his face is less livid a colour. I tiptoe from the room leaving the door ajar so I can hear if he wakes.

I'm just getting ready for bed myself when the phone rings again.

'So who's a dark horse then?' says Diane.

'You are from the looks of it.' I'm in no mood for girl talk but she is and she giggles like a teenager about to trade secrets. Bill told us that he was visiting the Birmingham branch and took Diane along to meet some of the staff she has contact with; his meeting finished earlier than he expected so they decided to visit the castle. Ed and I said what a coincidence, that's what had happened to us.

She's angling for me to open up about Ed but what's to tell? That I still fancy him like crazy — and that he returns my feelings with such ardour that I'm placed as high as third in his affections? Our relationship may sound like a joke but that's no reason for treating it like one.

I hedge and suddenly find myself telling her about my row with Tania. It's upset me more than I want to admit.

'I shouldn't worry,' Diane says consolingly when I've told her the details and she has come down firmly on my side of the argument as I knew she would with only my side to go by. 'These things always blow over. Why don't you give her a ring to clear the air?' I've thought of ringing her but it wouldn't be to clear the air — I want to tell her what a cow she is being and how she ought to be ashamed of herself. Now she's got a man of her own, she doesn't care about anyone else. I've said something of this to Diane but I go over it again in my head, embellishing it with especially stinging remarks while Diane is waffling on. 'I had a similar problem once,' she says and talks for ten minutes about some stupid tiff she had with someone a decade ago. Then she says, 'There's something else isn't there? What else is bothering you?'

'I'm fine.'

'It's Ed isn't it?' I suppose it's her own history with Jed Campion, Bill and God knows who else, that gives her psychic powers in this area and probably running into us together outside the office may have provided a small clue. She ought to be the perfect one for me to share my mixed feelings for Ed with, but we've never discussed anything that really matters; prior to the knickers party, the most she had confided was that she once bought a perfume she hated just to get the free towelling dressing gown that went with it.

I sense the slightest change in her breathing. She can

smell the intrigue. 'It's always a problem if you start mixing business with your personal life.'

'Has it happened to you then?' I don't want to talk about what's happened to me, but I've no objection to hearing what's happened to her. And it's a relief to stop dwelling on Tania.

'Well, no, not personally.' Diane evidently has the same reservations about opening up to me as I do to her. 'But I've seen it happen several times. A friend of mine got herself involved with someone she worked with and it was very messy. And she felt humiliated you know, thinking people might know even though they probably didn't.'

'Did he love her?' If he loves you then it'd all be worthwhile.

'What? Oh well, probably, yes, at the time. But these things can end quite suddenly, you know how fickle men can be. It was quite difficult in many ways. I mean, it ended up perfectly satisfactorily, better than she could have anticipated, but initially it was very awkward because she had to stay in the same job — she couldn't afford to go anywhere else.'

'What happened to her in the end?'

'Oh, she's fine now.' I'm about to ask a more probing question about her 'friend's' new man, but Diane suddenly changes direction. 'You're not having an affair with Ed, are you?'

'No, of course I'm not.' I don't believe it! Diane caught me so off guard with her question that I've just denied the very thing I was preparing to discuss with her. I can hardly take it back ('Sorry — I'd like an affair but he's too tied up with his wife and his girlfriend. We did have sex on his office floor but that probably doesn't count does it?') So now I find myself telling her about Ed's job proposition — well,

I have to say something. I pretend that this is what's on my mind, skating over the details, and omitting all mention of Don Ashby but emphasizing my new role as sales and marketing supremo and kicking myself the whole time.

'If Treadz folds then by all means take his offer,' Diane says thoughtfully, 'but don't give up what you're doing now for the sake of some prospects that may never materialize. And you know his history. I take it you've seen his CV?'

'No, but he has worked for some very prestigious companies.' He hasn't said which but this has been my impression.

'Oh, I know, he's worked everywhere. But only for months at a time. Either he doesn't stay or companies don't keep him, I don't know which, though quite frankly I can guess, but I can tell you the directors had a lot of doubts about taking him on. If they hadn't been able to get him on the cheap they'd have picked someone else.'

This is just Diane's own prejudice coming through. Hasn't Roger testified to his abilities?

'What you also have to consider,' she goes on, 'if, you know, you *did* have an affair at some time – and I'm not making any assumptions but I know you get on well and these things can escalate – then if he owns the company he could just make it untenable for you to stay.'

'Oh, I wouldn't risk getting in too deep with someone like that – he's such a womaniser!' As I say this, I feel a swelling of pride, as though this is indeed the stance I've taken and I believe what I'm saying.

'Well, I'll tell you frankly, Gemma, I'm really pleased to hear you say that. I was quite worried when I saw the two of you together today – I always thought you were far too sensible to get involved with a man like him.'

'Oh absolutely,' I say, my heart sinking further. Not

only will I not be able to tell Diane what I feel about him tonight, now I never will.

'The best approach is to do exactly what you're doing – keep him on the hook thinking you might be interested. My friend said to me once, keep them thinking you might, you know, make love with them at any time but never actually do it.'

After all, I'm glad that I haven't told her. I laugh but it doesn't sound like a laugh and I turn it into a cough.

'Because once you let them,' Diane goes on, 'they've got the upper hand.'

I thank Diane for her help and we chat on for a few minutes about what we'll be wearing to Marie's wedding. But I wish she hadn't phoned. I still haven't been able to tell anyone about the warmth of Ed's breath on my ear or the naked desire in his eyes when I turned to him in the castle dungeon.

On Thursday morning Joe wakes as right as rain. When I say that, bear in mind that rain isn't as pure and health-giving as it used to be, but overall he isn't as bad as I had expected. It takes us longer than usual to walk to the doctor's because we have to walk the opposite way round the block from usual so that I can avoid passing Tania's house. I'm not sure if we're on speaking terms and I don't feel like finding out just now.

The doctor diagnoses an ear infection, not too serious, and after we have collected the antibiotics from the chemist I take him round to Carla whose childminding capabilities Tania was so keen to recommend.

I know Carla as well as you know anyone you have sat next to at a school nativity and with whom you've exchanged admiring words about the paintings on the wall on parents' night, but her smile when she opens the door to me is as welcoming as if I'm a teacher arrived to tell her her child is top of the class.

'I hope you don't mind me calling round like this. But Tania said you might be able to take Joe after school and as he is off today, I thought—'

She draws the door wider open, stepping sideways to block the path of a three year old intent on hurling himself out of the front door, and we follow her into her living-room. The room is marginally bigger than Tania's or mine, and bright with a number of pushalong toys strewn about the floor and a children's video playing. Joe crouches down to watch, ignoring the three year old who tries to engage him in doing cooking in the toy kitchen.

'I can take him any day, I've got a vacancy just come up – do you know Valerie? Tall, lives in one of those detached houses past the school? Well, she's on maternity leave so she has taken her eldest back off me—'

Carla makes coffee and we sit on hard chairs by a table in the corner so she can keep an eye on the little ones. She is in her forties with thick long hair, almost to her waist, too long for a woman her age and yet perfect for a woman her type, with her brown leather sandals, the full skirt and long cardigan. She has a narrow face with a long prominent nose, features which her long straight hair emphasize, but the overall effect is one of warmth and wholesomeness with just a touch of the crusader perhaps. I don't know that she ever went to Greenham Common but she's got the outfit.

A little girl comes running up to show her a necklace she has made from plastic beads the size of hen's eggs and Carla exclaims over it, bending her lanky frame down to the child and putting her arm round her, holding the necklace in place from where it threatens to fall to the child's waist. This is what you want in a childminder, not someone like me who daren't get too close to a child in case she snags your tights or makes you chip your nail varnish (or who, like Tania, makes disparaging and unfounded remarks about your dates). Carla isn't wearing tights and you wouldn't want to draw attention to those square stubby fingernails.

'I know what you're thinking,' she says, sending sparks of alarm through me in case she really does. 'You're wondering if I'll have time for Joe among all these little ones. But they're only here until lunchtime. Then I pick up the bigger children, there are two of them, one is in Joe's class so it isn't as if he won't know anyone. Joe—'

'Yes?'

He answers without turning his face from the screen.

'Do you know William Clayton, in your class?'

'No,' he says and Carla laughs as though she thinks Joe is teasing her. 'He does,' she tells me. 'I've seen them in the playground together.'

She asks about my job and a little about why Tania can no longer have Joe, which I skate over giving Tania commitments, responsibilities and shortcomings she would be surprised to hear of, and then we leave. Joe has to be dragged away from the video and only stops struggling when Carla tells him he can watch it when she collects him from school tomorrow.

In the afternoon, I call in to Sainsbury's and have to hide in the detergents aisle until Tania has gone through the checkout. I could hit her, seeing her chatting away to the assistant and laughing as though everything is the same as ever. She'll be sorry. Chris Trelawny will drop her and she'll need me and then she'll be sorry.

Later, watching children's television with Joe, I notice a sense of unease in the pit of my stomach, something between sickness, hunger and longing. Tracing it back to see when it started I remember the sickness began last night, with my row with Tania. I feel so isolated. What's wrong with me that everyone wants to abandon me? All the little normalities and securities of my life seem to be falling away. Then there was Sam's phone call, the memory of which is like a highlighter pen, underlying everything that's going wrong and the impossibility of turning the clock back. Is this strange, disconnected sense of longing just my wish to be reunited with him? But watching inwardly as the thought takes shape I realize that isn't right. The sickness is still for Sam; what I feel about Tania is just a pale imitation, and it's tied up with resentment, bitterness and sheer fury. But the longing . . .

Joe yelps with delight as one cartoon animal hits another cartoon animal with a frying pan, but I am back at Warwick Castle with my knight in shining *amour*. Ed is a bit like a roller-coaster ride – exhilarating, intoxicating, you can't wait to take your turn. It takes you out of yourself, is an escape, a total release, from all life's problems. The fact you can see you'd get hurt if you fell out is just a risk you have to take.

Chapter 19

——— —

And then, a week later, everything changed.

A rail strike has made me late in to work but still not as late as Ed. It's almost ten o'clock before he comes striding in. He has his head down, never a good sign.

'Good-morning, Ed.' He grunts, throws open his office door so that it reverberates against the wall, then slams it shut.

'Ah,' says Colin, who has been hovering with a letter he wants Ed to see. Other than the one time he was drunk, Ed's door is kept open, it has become a matter of principle with him and now the outer office looks different, as though it has one eye shut.

'I thought Ed looked a bit preoccupied when I passed him in the car park,' says Piers, coming over. 'Is it bad news about the company?' It's three months since we were warned we might have to close but we'd been given a stay of execution and have begun to hope that we might keep going indefinitely.

But I don't think it's the company. 'Preoccupied' is just another example of Piers' gift for understatement. Ed looked haggard and drawn, his face grey and his hair spikey and unkempt as though he had forgotten to comb it. His tie was askew too as though he had dressed in a hurry or without due attention.

I wonder if he has trouble at home.

I bang on his door and as he doesn't answer, open it and peer round. 'Want some coffee?' Well, I had to say something.

'No.'

'I'll bring some anyway.'

'I don't want it.' But I'm walking away by now so I pretend not to hear.

'Do you think I can go in?' asks Colin, looking anxiously at the letter he's holding. I like Colin but he can be a terrible wimp and now Marie has come to join us. Standing there in a huddle they look like they've come to the hospital to visit the sick but are scared they might catch something.

'I don't think he's well,' I say, the image providing me with an excuse for him. 'Leave that letter with me, Colin, I'll give it to him in a minute.' Colin looks at me with profound admiration and affection as though I've said I'm going outside and I may be some time.

I take Ed his coffee and close the door behind me. He's sitting with his head in his hands and my first thought is that there has been a death in the family. It couldn't be his parents, they died when he was a teenager. Then he shifts slightly in his seat, drawing his fingers through his hair and I just know.

'She's left you.'

'Yes.' We aren't talking about his wife.

'I went round there last night and she told me the good news.' I thought he was being sarcastic and he is in a way. 'She's pregnant.'

'Is it yours?' I'd asked too quickly and see from the

tremor that passes across his features that I've hurt him with my lack of tact.

'Yes, it's mine.' It's terrible when someone is so destroyed by a situation and you're so delighted by it. I've been scheming for ways to oust Janet Reger but it hadn't occurred to me that she might oust Ed. When you want someone you assume everyone else does too. 'My only child, and she won't let me get involved.'

'It seems very sudden.' Although she hasn't phoned for a week or so, now I come to think of it, or not when I've been around to witness it. 'You didn't see it coming?'

'No. I thought . . .' He sighs and leans back in his chair, doodling with a pen on the white leather-bound blotter. 'I don't know. I wonder if maybe she used me, you know, because she wanted a baby. I always knew she did but I thought I was part of it . . . that's what she meant me to think. I keep going over it, I was so sure . . .'

I wonder if Maxine knows. She can't help but notice the state he's in.

'Maxine is in Belgium, thank God. Won't be back until Monday. She'll be glad won't she, now she's got my full attention. I've been a bastard, do you know that?'

I don't imagine he really wants an answer so I just straighten a few things on his desk and get up to go. If he's going to get morose he'll be better left alone, or anyway I will; I've exhausted my small fund of counselling skills. (I wonder why I ever thought this was something I should make a career of, I'm useless at it.)

As I rise to leave he says, bemused, 'And guess what. I saw my specialist yesterday. He told me I've got some kind of liver damage, you know. I was distraught when he told me. But it doesn't matter now, does it?'

He looks so lost and helpless, as though he can't believe

the turn his life has taken. I know that feeling too well; the sense of dislocation, of going through the motions of living as though you're watching yourself from a distance. It's less painful that way, to watch your distress rather than experience it.

'It matters to me,' I say. I feel that this is what he means me to say but I'm glad to oblige all the same.

I almost skip out of his office. This is so different from our usual conversations about Janet Reger. And it's even less like what he said in his office three months ago when I told him I was going to leave.

'Let's be grown up about this,' he had said. 'We like each other and I'm very attracted to you, you can see that.' He pulled his drawer out as though he was looking for something but he just wanted something to do with his hands. 'But what happened was a mistake. I love someone else. I can't give you what you want.'

It had been brutal of him to say that and I couldn't keep the pain it gave me from showing in my face, but fortunately he didn't see, he was staring straight ahead towards the window where the red roof of a double decker was just visible. His chin was tilted up, determined, this is a far, far better thing that I do, than I have ever done etc., etc.

But now he doesn't have anyone else. Now we can start to move forward together.

Yes, I know there's still Maxine. But she isn't a problem. There's a line of Byron I remember from school which sums up what their relationship is. Something about the chains that bound them together being so loose they just never bothered to break them.

Chapter 20

It's true that trouble can unite you. There's nothing physical between us, but there's everything between us. Ed and I identify with each other's pain. A cord ties us together; tight as piano wire it reverberates when we stand close. Strange, how what was a mild interest has grown to take up the whole of my life but he grows more attractive to me by the day. When he comes and leans on the door frame of my office to ask me something, head on one side scratching at the paintwork with his fingernail, I notice the way his shirt is taut across his chest, how his Adam's apple bobs above the collar. His hair curls like that on Greek statues. I wonder why I once thought I could see the start of jowls; his jawline is firm and square, with a humorous lift to one side of his mouth. I find myself concentrating on how he looks as though I expect to be tested on it. I wish I sat where Marie does, outside his office. To look at him she just has to turn her head.

It's three weeks since the news of Janet Reger. Now most days Ed will wander into my office to sit, one leg hooked over the corner of my desk, and discuss this or that and sometimes, provocatively, the other though without reference to what once happened on his office floor. He prefers to pretend now that it never occurred (may even believe it. He told me how faithful he had been to Janet Reger and looked abashed at my waspish retort). Colin, Piers and Kev no longer bring their grievances about the boss to me. They know I still have, as Colin used to say, the ear of the boss, but now they're not sure how much else I might have too.

Ed even looks different, has lost a little weight, tightened up around the middle. He's playing squash three times a week and weight training and already it shows. Finally the shadows have gone from round his eyes which allows their colour to shine out, a dusky smokey green that changes to grey with the light. He has taken to heart his doctor's advice regarding his health and has cut down on his drinking and altered his eating pattern. Out has gone his regular eleven o'clock order for bacon sandwiches which Debbie would collect from the sandwich bar down the street; out go the two spoons of sugar in his coffee. In come Sweet and Low, decaff, pre-packed salads and chicken sandwiches.

He has bought a new suit too, a soft grey wool and pale shirts with button-down collars that caress his neck like a woman's fingers. Marie says his weight loss is probably depression at losing his love, and his improved appearance is his attempt to woo her back. But what I see, as he leans against the window sill in my office, discussing the slowly improving sales figures, is a man rebuilding his life. He is someone to whom the worst has happened but who has found, after all, that the worst wasn't so bad. Salvation was closer at hand than he had appreciated.

Diane called in this week to meet me for lunch and said, 'What's Ed done to himself? He's looking quite . . .' She didn't say what and she didn't have to, I know what that lift of her chin means. I hustled her out of there before she could give Ed the benefit of her coquetry (Ed is mine now, but why confuse him by offering competition?) I told her that the change in him is due to his new health regime, his exercise and reformed diet, but it isn't. It's down to me.

I still haven't made things up with Tania. I thought she'd have called round on some pretext and we'd have been all right again but that hasn't happened and Joe has made a new friend at Carla's so he's no longer so keen to spend his Saturdays with Jack. She needn't think I'm going to be the one to make it up with her.

For a while I had that feeling of something missing, like when you go out without your handbag. I missed having someone to talk to. I suppose that now Tania has a boyfriend she thinks she doesn't need me, but that cuts both ways; now I'm growing closer to Ed I don't need her either.

'Gemma! Have you heard the news!' It's rare to see Colin so animated, without that hunted look he gets when Ed is on his tail. For a sinking moment I think he has got a job somewhere else. I set my features into something suggesting pleasurable expectancy and lock it in place so as not to reveal any imminent disappointment. 'We've had a reprieve.'

'Who has?'

'Us. The company. The sales figures have shot right up. Repeat after me: I – will – not – lose – my – job.' He speaks slowly and clearly, seeing the doubt in my face.

'Oh. Terrific!' Colin's quizzical expression shows me I haven't sounded as convincing as I'd hoped. If Treadz prospers Ed won't find a market – maybe he won't even want to if things are looking up here — and I won't get the new career direction I've been looking forward to.

Anyway, I can't see why Colin is getting so excited. 'It won't make much difference to you, will it? I thought you wanted to leave?'

He shrugs. 'There's a difference between jumping and getting pushed. I want to find something in my own time — I don't want to risk ending up somewhere like this again.'

I nod as though I agree though, of course, I want to end up somewhere almost exactly like this.

He wanders over to my window and gazes down at the traffic below. It's April, and sunny today with a feeling of spring in the air, and Colin, in a new beige suit, looks ready for it. He must be a perfect off-the-peg size; the sharp square of the shoulders makes it look as though it was made for him. His shoes are highly polished and expensive looking, the kind Sam would scoff to own. When he turns round I notice that his tie seems to swell out beneath the knot, the way male models wear them. I must be looking at him too hard because he shifts uncomfortably, rattling the change in his pocket.

'What is it? Don't you like this tie?'

'It's a terrific tie. I was just admiring it.' He smiles, relieved: perfect white teeth against the dark skin.

'Nina doesn't like it but I thought it went well with this suit.'

'Nina doesn't know what she's talking about. So how are things with her now?'

His smile stays in place yet something changes behind it. 'Fine. She's fine.'

'So she's stopped trying to change you?'

'Oh, I don't think it's that exactly.' He pulls up a chair and sits down, spreading his legs wide as he leans back.

'We get on fine most of the time. But well, sometimes I start to wonder . . .'

I never get to hear his answer because at that moment Ed comes bursting in. 'Who's had that bloody Spencer file. It's gone again.' He heads straight for the filing cabinet shooting Colin a threatening look *en route* and raising the temperature in the room by several degrees – at least the bit of it where I'm sitting. Suddenly I feel like I'm wearing centrally heated pants.

'Haven't you got work to do, Baxter?'

'He was just checking something with me,' I answer hurriedly, knowing Ed will let it go if he thinks I'm involved, but Colin has gone before I finish speaking. In any case, Ed is too wound up in his search to give Colin the full benefit of his ire.

'Ed, calm down.'

'I'm perfectly calm,' he says, and as he turns his face to look at a file he has pulled out, the frown lines on his forehead form a perfect V. It spoils his features, those lines will have formed into deep ridges in another few years. I've noticed how his normally hot temper has become even more combustible; now the smallest spark will ignite it. I think he hasn't quite got over Janet Reger and I remember how, when Sam left – sometimes, even now – his face would loom into my inner vision at unexpected and disconcerting moments, just when I'd begun to think how well I was doing.

Ed needs to relax, find a way of letting the tension ease out of his body. He ought to try aromatherapy or go for a massage.

Or maybe he just needs something to take his mind off things.

Glancing into the outer office, I see that the men have

303

all gone out, only Colin is left at the other end searching for the file Ed has misplaced. Marie is covering reception while Debbie is making coffee.

My filing cabinet is behind my office door. He's leaning over the middle drawer now, still sorting through it and muttering under his breath.

I push the door closed quietly and take a breath. This is stupid. He is definitely not in a receptive mood. There will be other times, better times.

There will be no better time.

Noiselessly, I move behind him. He is still huffing and puffing over the cabinet, leafing through a manilla folder and mumbling. I inhale quietly and lean against him, my back against his back. He stiffens slightly, straightening up, and I bend my knees slowly so that my backside slides down to rest against the back of his thighs, then I straighten my legs and rise up on to my toes so my buttocks are sliding up over his. Then back down again. The muscles of his legs are hard and pleasing against my softer flesh. He shifts, uncertain what I want him to do. But I don't want him to do anything, just be still while I rub against him like a cat.

'Stay where you are,' I say. 'No moving,' and I press back hard against him, sliding my hands along the outside of his thighs, across the front of his legs and then gently, slowly, between them. It's intensely erotic to have him here, at my disposal, vulnerable, uncertain but clearly willing.

'Gemma . . .' His voice is low and vibrant with anticipation as he struggles to reach behind to touch me.

'Got it, Ed!' The door flies open; it's Colin, holding out the file Ed's been looking for. I leap away and Ed swings round sending the filing drawer shut with a shudder.

*　　*　　*

Piers opens the doors to each of the kitchen cabinets and surveys the empty shelves with disappointment. 'No biscuits? Not even a lone Jaffa cake?' We never have biscuits but Piers, who never makes the coffee, must have fondly imagined our small office kitchen to be as well-stocked as his mother's. 'Are you sure it's on?' He fiddles with the plug connection to the kettle making the light go off, and I slap his wrist and move him aside.

'Why don't you get the cups out and I'll make the coffee.' I know that if you don't let them do it themselves, they'll never learn, but sometimes the teaching process is just too painful. Besides, Piers isn't really here to make coffee; he's here because this is one of the few places it's possible to have a private chat secure in the knowledge that anyone of any seniority is unlikely to interrupt. He wants to tell me about his new job.

'I'm not giving my notice in until I get it in writing, but it sounds excellent. An extra five thousand on what I'm getting here, and lots of travel.'

'You deserve it, I'm very pleased for you.'

'I thought I hadn't got it because at the interview—' He tells me about various *faux pas* and indiscretions which make a good tale but which I don't really believe. There can't be many holes he couldn't dig himself out of, emerging smelling sweeter than before he fell in. Then he says, 'And I hear Ed may be on the move too.'

'What?'

'He's setting up some company. Don't tell me you didn't know – he tells you everything, doesn't he? I thought you'd be bound to be in on it – Debbie always said there was something going on with you two.'

'Debbie? Well, she'd know, she's all over Kevin like the measles.' It's a bit of a giveaway to reveal my greater

305

sensitivity to an implied personal relationship rather than a business one, but fortunately Piers is too excited by the prospect of Kevin and Debbie to notice.

'Kev and Debbie? But I thought he was shagging that girl he met at Christmas?'

'The one doesn't necessarily preclude the other, does it? He's a man, isn't he?' I feel flustered and it's making me sarcastic.

'I thought he and Debs were just pals these days.'

'You've led too sheltered a life,' I say, pouring boiling water on to Nescafé. I've no idea whether Kev is seeing someone in addition to Debs, but it will be out of character if he isn't, and I can't imagine how Piers can have observed Debbie arriving and leaving with Kevin each day, rubbing herself against him whenever they think they're alone, without drawing the obvious conclusion.

'Well, I wouldn't have guessed that,' grins Piers.

'Wouldn't have guessed what?' asks Colin, appearing from out of nowhere which seems to be becoming a habit. Piers tells him the Kevin story which of course Colin, being a sensitive and observant man and quite unlike his male colleague, had sussed out long ago. Slightly miffed perhaps, Piers returns to his earlier comment.

'So will you be leaving?'

'You're leaving?' Colin ignores my protestations and puts his cup down, looking reproachful that I hadn't told him first.

'Of course I'm not. It's just some stupid story Piers has come up with.'

'You can tell us, you know, it won't go any further.' Piers adopts an irritatingly knowing expression.

'There's nothing to go any further.'

They exchange glances over my head as though I'm blind

or not even present, an impression Colin reinforces by asking Piers where he heard the rumour.

'I was just talking to Diane on the phone earlier. She reckons Ed is setting up some little venture of his own on the side.'

Colin gives a low whistle. 'I hope she watches who she tells about it.'

Flecks of limescale are floating on the top of my coffee and I tip it down the sink, splashing my sweater as snippets of my conversation with Diane come drifting back. Just what did I say to her?

Piers opens a drawer and pokes about among the cutlery. 'So it wasn't you who told Diane, then?' he says, perusing a fork with a bent tine. 'I thought she said it was.'

'How could it be? This is the first I've heard of it.' I start washing the cups while Piers and Colin begin a discussion of how soon Ed might leave.

I feel sick. How could I have been so stupid as to tell Diane? She's not even a proper friend, there are a dozen people in this company she is closer to than to me. But because she rang me at home — and what with my focus being on Ed the lover rather than Ed the wheeler dealer — I was thinking of her amorous connections not her business ones. I just wasn't thinking of the sensitivity of what I was saying. Who else might she tell? What have I done?

When I'm back in my office, Ed suddenly appears at the door looking rugged and mean. His eyes have a half-closed long-lashed look, an expression I haven't seen before. 'I enjoyed our little interchange earlier. But check no one's in the vicinity next time.' His voice is gruff, scarcely audible, and he gives me a sly half grin. If he came any closer I'd be obliged to do it again but he doesn't and I sense he knows he's teasing me by maintaining his distance.

Then he says, checking there's no one in earshot, 'That little matter we discussed when we went to see Don Ashby in Warwick.' He raises one eyebrow as though this might clarify what he's talking about. 'It's all looking good. I'm getting a lot of interest. But obviously we need to keep quiet about it for a while yet.'

'Oh, obviously.' I give him my sincerest smile, secure in the knowledge that we discussed many little matters that day, most of which I have mentioned to no one at all, but my stomach lurches and heaves with foreboding.

I reach under my bed and pull out the book I bought at Marie's sex-aids party. I had hidden it away from Joe immediately I got home but last week I was rooting through the wardrobe looking for my grey sweatshirt, and there it was, hidden among my jumpers.

Skipping over the chapter on sexual positions, I turn to the section on attracting your man. 'Be unexpected,' it says. 'Talk dirty. Think about what pleases him.'

It also says, 'Surprise him by wearing no underwear,' but this morning there was frost on the ground outside. You have to draw the line somewhere.

The book keeps me awake and I spend a largely sleepless night in which bare-chested men with buttocks of steel pass among the shadows.

'I was just going out for a sandwich but we could get something at the pub. Fancy coming?' Ed's eyes are sea green today, reflecting the colour of the shirt he wears.

I check my watch for no reason other than to slow down

the speed of my response but the eagerness still shows in my voice.

'I don't mind if I do.'

'I don't mind if you do either.'

Once outside Ed leads us not in the direction of the pub but to a small upstairs room at Emilio's, the trattoria where I had come so long ago with Diane, Marie and Suzanne. The waiter shows us to a table by the door but Ed says something in Italian and the waiter laughs and indicates one in the corner by the window. The morning's sunny skies have yielded to a sudden downpour and, looking down, my view is of the tops of black umbrellas and men running with newspapers held over their heads. We arrived just in time. I'm never at my best with my hair in rat's tails and mascara cascading down my cheeks.

Ed orders poussins for us both, saving me from myself. I'd been about to order spaghetti carbonara forgetting that I don't look my best with strands of pasta trailing down my chin either. The waiter waits, quietly tapping his pencil on his pad while Ed takes his time over the wine list dwelling on the relative merits of a Cotes du this and a Cabernet that – not to be compared to the incomparable Châteauneuf-du-Pape he sampled just last week – while I try to look as though I care.

'We've got a lot in common, haven't we?' he says, just as I am starting to doubt it. 'We're going to make a good team.' Ed takes a breadstick and snaps it between his fingers. 'You've got a lot of potential.'

'Well, thank you. I think you have too, even if you do try to hide it.'

'Do you think so?' He looks at me, head on one side, as though I've paid him a great compliment instead of just echoed the one he paid me. He looks thoughtful while he chews, clearly pleased with my comment, not realizing I meant it to be tongue-in-cheek and that I'm leading up to something.

'I do think so. Which is why I find it so puzzling that you're such a bully.'

'Me?' He looks almost hurt.

'Why do you like everyone to be scared of you?'

He decides to drop the pose of injured innocent and his eyes are smiling as they meet mine over a breadstick. 'It's the only way to get things done.'

'I get things done without being scared.'

'You're different. Most of them need a boot up the backside to get them moving.'

'You know that isn't true. Why don't you try more carrot and less stick?'

'And why don't you try less cajoling and more bread-sticks.' He leans towards me and offers me the end of his to bite. 'If you don't like my management style, you know what you can do.'

'I do know — and I'm doing it.'

He laughs at that but I let the subject drop, seeing he's going to grow tetchy if I pursue it. I don't believe that he really thinks that shouting and storming about the office is the best way to motivate people; it's that, without a show of strength, he believes people will think he's weak and somehow that frightens him. It's a form of insecurity.

It touches me to observe this flaw in him, and the disastrous way in which he has tried to conceal it.

'You've gone very quiet,' he says, just in time to prevent our companionable silence growing awkward. He reaches for another breadstick at the same time as me and inadvertently our fingers touch. He strokes the side of my hand before retracting his own.

'Where do you see yourself in ten years' time?' He has asked me this before and I have the impression it's something he always says when there's a gap in the conversation.

'Oh, I don't know.' I search the rain-washed street for inspiration. 'In a senior position somewhere, in a hierarchy. Where I can see what the next step is.'

'I meant on the personal front, not career-wise.'

'Oh, I see.' I feel the rush of embarrassment that strikes you when you have misunderstood a perfectly simple question even when, like this one, it was reasonable enough to do so. 'I'd like to be in a settled relationship again. Married preferably. Living in a bigger house than we have now and with—' The wine arrives and the waiter pours a little for Ed to try. He nods appreciatively. One day I'll hear someone say *This is pond water, take it away.* But not today. The waiter pours some more and I sip, glad of the interruption. Ed had begun to look bored. In fact, I'm chastened to realize just how pedestrian and uninspired my ambitions are. 'Marriage' and 'exciting life full of incident and adventure' aren't images that readily go together yet it's just that combination I've been looking for. I thought that as long as I (fascinating and remarkable individual that I am) was one of the marriage partners, then I could have all that – and the mortgage and a settled existence would somehow dovetail into it. No wonder Sam fought so hard against it. It's disturbing to discover your entire gameplan has been based on a misconception.

The silence that has fallen is growing too long for comfort. 'So. Your turn. What do you think you'll be doing in ten years' time?'

He leans back in his chair and holds his wineglass up to the light. 'Sitting here with you.' A wave of heat bursts over me, as though the sun has burst out through the clouds and is burning through the window. It must be the alcohol opening up my blood vessels.

I open my mouth to speak but he goes on, 'Or someone like you. Someone young, enthusiastic . . . sexy.' He leans towards me over the table and reaches for my hand but I back off.

'Someone like me? Someone *like* me?' I'm a unique and mysterious individual. What does he mean — someone *like* me?

'OK, OK.' He's amused to find me so sensitive. 'With you then.' He's smiling, wondering why it matters to me, and I'm embarrassed yet again to have given myself away. But what he means is in ten years' time he hopes he can still make some woman younger than him want to have sex with him. *Any* woman.

By the time our meal arrives, when he has refilled my wineglass and proposed a toast to the future — 'To *our* future,' — he has started to make me laugh again and I'm already forgiving him his clumsy attentions and his charm is covering me like a cloak of warm bearnaise.

I sprinkle some salt over my plate and when I offer the salt cellar to Ed, he takes it from me and places it down, taking my hand between both of his. His palm is as warm and dry as autumn leaves that have lain in the sun.

'It's been a dream of mine, to run a business with . . . people I really get on with. People I can trust.' Over his poussin his eyes are saying, People I want to make love to. 'So you wouldn't have to think: this is work, this is play. You'd just think, This is life, let's do it.'

Beneath the table my foot is held between his. I always thought footsie was just for inhibited lovers too repressed to do anything else. But now I'm exhilarated by the very properness of our behaviour while, with all four hands above the table, Ed sends tongues of fire licking up towards my groin.

I lean towards him conspiratorially and he edges forward to hear. 'Let's do it,' I say.

He laughs huskily, his eyes narrowed to slits.

'OK, but let's wait till we get back to the office. Don't want to embarrass the chef.'

He thinks he's joking.

Back in the office, the afternoon is interminable. Ed has gone to a meeting, and without him the day loses its meaning, like being on holiday when the sun isn't shining. I have a list of phone calls to make but I can't concentrate. All I can think of is him. Sitting opposite him in the trattoria, the need to reach out and touch him was exquisite, all the more so for it being almost impossible to act on.

Not that it was entirely impossible. I ordered profiteroles and, dipping my finger into the chocolate sauce, reached across the table, offering Ed my finger to suck. His mouth was warm and yielding. He held my fingertip between his teeth and circled his tongue round it.

In the lift going up to the office we stood opposite each other. I looked at him, the way his hair curls across his brow, at his shirt stretched tight against the rise of his chest, and at his dark and glittering eyes.

'You're melting my socks,' he said, smiling. I waited to be kissed but he looked down at his watch and tapped the face as though it wasn't working. 'Got to be out by three,' he said.

I'm deep in an erotic scenario starring Ed and an uninhibited and provocative me when I hear the door bang in reception and Ed strides past my office door without looking in. I hurry in to him to find out why he's back so early from his meeting.

'Cancelled,' he says abruptly in reply. 'The director was taken ill at lunchtime.' He spits the words out as though this is a feeble excuse designed to annoy.

'Come on—' My voice sounds gentle and tender to my ears. The word 'darling' forms in my throat but I swallow it back. 'Come on, Ed,' I say with an effort to sound businesslike, 'you only lost an hour and you were moaning about having to go anyway. It's a chance to get on with your other stuff.'

He sighs and slumps into his chair, looking up at me, his face free of its public expression. 'What would I do without you?' he says simply. His eyes are softer, wider, the lids somehow heavy with things unsaid.

'Ed—'

'I still think about her, you know. Stupid isn't it?'

What's stupid is that I keep imagining he's thinking about me.

His phone rings and I leave him to answer it.

Back in my office I close the door and take a seat behind my desk. I'm irritated with Ed for bringing Janet Reger's unwelcome memory along to the aftermath of our entirely satisfying lunch and I take it out on the keyboard, hammering it hard and fast so that the letters appear on my screen in a jumble of unpronounceable consonants.

Maybe it's anger or jealousy that acts as a trigger. Maybe it's the idea, however much I want to avoid it, of Ed and her together. Perhaps it's the red wine and sitting so close to Ed while it took effect, or maybe it's all or none of these. Whatever, suddenly my mind is full of the sex manual I read last night and the dreams that followed it. The pictures, the positions, the suggestions. And Ed is the man I see in the illustrations.

An electric current is running up through the seat of my chair to my nipples. It's hot in here; too hot, but these windows don't open.

I undo the top buttons of my blouse thinking of him, his dark glittering eyes, intense behind their closed lids, as they would surely be; his buttocks hard as I gripped and ground against his thighs. His chest hair would rub against my breasts, teasing my nipples, unbearably erect. His lips are parted and sucking, sipping, biting.

I come against my fingers, thinking of him. From my desk, one hand still gripped between my thighs, I buzz him and tell him all this. I hear him swallow, down the phone. 'My office. Now,' he says huskily.

He kicks the door shut with his foot and the room shrinks around us, there's hardly room to breathe, the walls are squeezing the breath out of me. 'So,' he says, and his face is heavy with desire. He takes a step towards me, and now the room has grown, it will take a decade to cross to where he is. He opens his arms and suddenly I'm lying against his chest wondering how I got there.

'Is this what you wanted?' he asks.

Ed wedges a chair against the door and takes his jacket off.

'Someone will hear,' I say, suddenly anxious.

'Then you'd better keep quiet.' He sits on the chair and pulls me to stand in front of him, undoing the zip on my skirt, pulling it down roughly and then slides his thumbs under the waistband of my tights. He slides them off with an ease I've never managed myself and when I lose my balance as I raise my foot to take them off, he catches me, pulling me upright again to stand in front of him and leans

forward to nuzzle me through my pants. His breath is hot
and I cup his face in my hands but he pulls them away and
now, his hands on my hips, he pushes me backwards to the
desk and turns me round to face it, undoing his trousers as
he does so. I lean over his desk, pushing his files to one
side with care, but with a single movement he brushes
everything on to the floor. There's a swish of papers and
clang of the filing tray, and another clang as he kicks the
tray aside with a whispered curse.

'Ed . . .?'

'Be quiet.' He's fumbling in his pocket and I realize it's
a condom he's unwrapping; I've no sooner seen it than he's
holding my hips, I didn't expect it like this, I want to look
at him, kiss him, but there's no time to say so and soon I've
forgotten that I wanted to and now he's inside me, burning,
and such an ache and he reaches forward, fingering me with
one hand, teasing my breast with the other, squeezing,
pushing, I feel him against the back of my thighs and the
soft weight of his balls like a rhythmic caress.

He comes with a groan, leaning forwards, his chest on my
back while I push back against him, holding his powerful
hands against me.

Afterwards, dressed again but with me still perched on
Ed's lap, we sit silent as though a tidal wave has washed
over us, leaving us bruised and shocked yet incomparably
cleansed.

He's such a big man, his biceps hard through his shirt.
I wipe a smudge of lipstick from his cheek as though he's
a child yet feeling like a child in his arms. He looks
up at me and his face is different; serene, gentle. The
words well up in me and I try not to but I can't hold
them in.

He puts his fingers over my lips and holds me to him. I

nestle against him, burying my face in his neck, inhaling his special smell.

While Ed picks up the items he swept to the floor I move the chairs back in place. 'I do like the way office chairs have wheels,' I remark, sliding his chair back behind the desk. 'It does facilitate matters.' Ed looks bemused and I describe a fantasy I have of kneeling, hidden, under his desk while he takes phone calls, issues orders, deals with visitors. With just a shove I could push him back from the desk so there'd be room for me to manoeuvre under it, in front of him.

'Well, I'm free tomorrow afternoon,' he says.

On Wednesday night, I've just collected Joe from Carla's and am hurrying home with him, clutching his hand, when I see a strange car parked outside our house. As I get nearer a woman gets out and comes to meet me.

'I hope it's not inconvenient,' says Diane.

Chapter 21

———— —

While I get pizzas out of the freezer, Diane listens to Joe read in that flat halting tone that all new readers seem to start with. I didn't want to let her in at all — not after she had repeated all that stuff about Ed's new company to Piers — but what can you say when someone follows you up your own path and assumes you're pleased to see her? And I didn't want to make too much of it, make her more suspicious.

I feel obliged to offer something to eat and wish I had something more wholesome to offer: a home-made casserole or a meat pie with pastry I'd made myself. Joe won't actually eat casseroles and there's no point in cooking something different for myself when there are just the two of us but I'd prefer her not to witness the way we live. It's much more important to impress your enemies with your standards than your friends. Friends make allowances. Why did Diane have to call in anyway? Couldn't we have met up at work? I haven't vacuumed in a fortnight and Joe has drawn a picture in the dust on the television.

'He reads very well,' Diane says to me, as I settle Joe in front of the television with his tea. 'He's bright, isn't he? He'll do well.' She knows nothing at all about Joe but I glow at the compliment. It's what I believe myself.

Diane has declined the pizza but opens the bottle of wine she has brought. 'I hope you don't mind my calling like this, but I just needed to talk and somehow it was you I kept thinking of.' She smiles showing her even teeth, their whiteness emphasized by her scarlet lips, and managing to imply that she's paying me another compliment by being here. Although on the face of it, we get along quite well, I don't really like Diane. But she seems to feel we're kindred spirits, united by our uncertain love lives.

She carries the wineglasses into the dining-room while I switch on the gas fire and clear a mess of papers off the table so we can sit down at it. She's wearing a slinky dress that swings as she walks, its sheen caught in the dim glow cast by the wall light in which only one bulb seems to be working. With her long neck she reminds me suddenly of a snake.

'Nothing's wrong, is there?' I ask, hoping there is (why else has she called?). But now I look at her she seems too happy for that to be the case. She looks younger and there's a brightness about her eyes; she has developed a jauntiness about the jawline. 'Has something happened at work?'

She tucks a strand of jet black hair behind one ear as she considers her answer. 'Yes and no.' She lowers herself elegantly on to the rickety chair and cups her face in her hands. She looks about fifteen. 'Bill has asked me to marry him.'

I pause in cutting up my pizza and play for time. 'Bill? Your boss?'

Her smile is radiant. 'We always liked each other and then when we started working together things just took off. I went away with him for a weekend in

February.' She lowers her eyes coyly. 'Now he's left his wife and moved into a flat and he wants me to join him.'

I want to say, 'Didn't you have an affair with the overseas sales director once?' to remind her that her record in personal relationships is not sound — and more to the point to embarrass her by the fact that I *know*. But my mouth is full of pizza and by the time I've swallowed it I've changed my mind.

'Are you keen on him?' What I mean is 'Do you love him?' but I'm not always sure that other people mean the same by 'love' as I do. Increasingly, I'm not sure what I mean by it myself.

She nods, getting a faraway look in her eyes. 'That isn't the problem. It's Ray. I don't know want to hurt him but—' She sighs, and looks down into her wineglass, tipping it this way and that.

'What about your daughter?'

'She's eighteen. She'd stay with Ray for convenience. All she wants is somewhere with a bed and a well-stocked fridge, you know what teenagers are like.' I nod though I have no idea. 'The only thing she'll miss is having me to do her washing.'

From the corner of my eye I see the dining-room door opening slowly. Joe's face peeps round the edge, shy of entering. 'You can come in Joe, she won't bite.'

He doesn't and in fact he steps back a little pulling the door with him so that Diane can't see him. He's whispering something but I can't quite hear it.

'He wants an ice cream,' says Diane helpfully.

Oh lord, I think. Pizza and ice cream. Working mothers. 'What about a yoghurt, Joe? Or an apple?'

Joe looks astonished. I don't think he has eaten an apple

since I bought them puréed in jars from Boots when he was still in his high chair.

'There aren't any yoghurts left, I looked,' he says, petulantly.

'Have there been problems between you and Ray?' I ask when Joe has gone to get a choc ice from the freezer. Diane sighs and checks the state of her manicure. 'He's a good man but we were married too young.'

She met Ray when she was still at school. He was a car mechanic and she was swept off her feet by a beau who wasn't a schoolboy but a real man with a car, a wage and dirt under his fingernails. Her parents who had sacrificed family holidays to pay her school fees were horrified and their disapproval cemented the union. Then Diane fell pregnant and Ray did what seemed like the decent thing at the time and married her.

'But you have been happy? You've been together a long time.' If Caroline is eighteen then Diane must be only about thirty-five. Her air of authority has always made her seem older than that.

'He'd do anything for me, I can't complain about him. But we don't like the same things. He doesn't read or like the theatre or anything, he'd rather be at the races.' I'd never taken Diane to be much of a reader unless it was of fashion magazines. 'We were never very alike and we've just grown apart down the years.'

She has made her mind up; she doesn't want to talk things over with me, just to hear her decision expressed aloud and to have it witnessed. I've never met Ray but I feel sad for him: he has his own workshop now and a thriving business but Diane isn't interested in the success of a blue collar worker. She wants a rising young executive with a company car and an expense account. I feel sad for

Diane too. When she's snuggled up in bed at night with her expense account, will she be any happier?

Bill has sandy hair and a paunch, and the unhealthy pallor of a man carrying too much weight. I don't know Ray but I prefer the sound of him.

'Maybe you should let things ride for a while. It could all blow over, couldn't it? I don't mean give Bill up,' I add hurriedly, seeing her about to protest. 'But defer any decision you might regret later.'

Diane pulls a face and leans forward slightly. 'I know I can trust you not to say anything.' Oh yes, like I can trust her. 'But Bill isn't the first. He's the best obviously – it is special this time. But there were others.'

I look dutifully surprised in the expectation of hearing some fascinating sexual anecdotes relating to the overseas sales director. She disappoints me. 'It's hopeless, isn't it? But no one can say I haven't tried.'

'Perhaps if you went for marriage counselling, tried to find out what's precipitated all these affairs . . .'

Diane starts to laugh and empties the bottle into my glass. 'I've told you what's precipitated them,' she says, laughing. 'I don't see how marriage counselling is going to make him develop an interest in opera.'

The conversation drifts back to Bill and how wonderful he is and then on to Marie's wedding and via that to the office. Then following a pause she asks, almost as though it's for something to say, 'How's the infamous Mr Murray?'

I've been awaiting the question but now it's here it takes me by surprise.

'Gemma, you're blushing!'

'Actually,' I say, a little stiffly, so she'll see this is no laughing matter, 'I'm very fond of him.'

'Fond? What are you saying?'

'What do you think I'm saying?' I collect our glasses and my plate on to a tray.

She looks shocked, almost alarmed, which is disconcerting. I'd expected some moral support after what I'd just heard from her. 'Are you sure you know what you're doing?'

'Yes – why? Aren't you?' We face each other across the table. A draught blows in from the open dining-room door sending a chill through the room.

'Oh, I'm sorry, Gemma. It's just not what I'd imagined. I know you get on well but when you told me there was nothing going on I believed you.'

I shrug. 'There wasn't then. Things change.'

She looks at me, uncomprehending. 'Look, I have to go. Bill knows I was going to make a decision tonight and he'll be on tenterhooks until I call him. Thanks for your help.'

'I don't think I gave you any help. You'd made your decision before you arrived.'

'No, really, you have. You've made me see things more clearly. You're right, sometimes you have to acknowledge a thing is over and be ready to move on, whatever the cost.'

I don't think I said anything like that but Diane has heard what she wanted to.

As she pulls on her coat, I snatch the opportunity to set things straight about what she'd told Piers.

'Diane, you remember I told you once about some scheme Ed had for setting up a new business?'

She pauses with one arm in her coat. 'Yes?'

'It was all just pie in the sky and it's fallen through now. You won't mention it to anyone will you? I know you told Piers, but he won't let it go any further.'

She searches in her pockets for her gloves, not looking at me.

'No, of course not. Look, I have to dash. Bye.'

She runs down the path, waving to me without turning round and leaving me with an inexplicably cold, heavy feeling in my stomach.

'Tania! How are you?' From my astonished tones you'd think she lived on the other side of the ocean rather than just two doors away but I can't contain my relief at being friends again. She has phoned on the pretext of asking Joe to play with Jack – they have made up whatever quarrel they had had – and now she wants to do the same with me by asking me to dinner. But my initial relief gives way to a self-righteous petulance. I'm still hurt at the way she laid into me and she hasn't apologized. Maybe I shouldn't sound too keen.

'I'm not quite sure I can make it, it depends if I can get a sitter.' She will know that I'm just stalling for time but it's the first delaying tactic that springs to mind. 'Who else have you asked?'

'Just you. And Chris of course. I want you to get to know each other.'

I don't want to get to know Chris with his wobbly teacher hat. I think he's a fool and Tania is making a big mistake. (What is it with everyone just now, pairing themselves off with these no-hopers?) But she leaves me no choice.

'I've already asked Sandy if she'd be able to sit for you and she can.' Sandy is a girl who lives down the road.

'Oh. Thanks.' Damn.

'You can bring someone if you want to. Do you want to bring Ed?'

If I didn't know it wasn't in Tania's nature to be catty this is what I'd think. In fact, this is her way of apologizing but Ed and Tania in one room isn't a happy thought. Ed would look askance at the mess Tania lives in and say so to me if not to her, while Tania would see all Ed's faults and shortcomings and say nothing, which would be worse, denying me the chance to defend him to her.

'Ed's away at the moment,' I lie.

'Well, what about that other bloke you work with, he always sounded nice.'

'Colin? He's got a girlfriend.'

'That doesn't usually stop you.' It's meant to be a joke, referring to Ed and Janet Reger but I don't think it's funny and there's an awkward moment when we both realize that our friendship has not recovered sufficiently for comments like this to be made. But I make myself laugh, healing things over, like stitches on a wound.

I have no intention of asking Colin. But two days later he arrives at work and tells me that he and Nina have just split up. He looks so miserable that I ask him and Colin says he would love to come.

I like shopping in Sainsbury's on a Saturday. The branch I use isn't their biggest, being only about the size of Leicestershire but I like the anonymity and if you come in the afternoon it's surprisingly quiet. It can be a bit exasperating if I have to bring Joe, who is too big to sit in the trolley and wanders off at regular intervals, but today he is playing at a friend's so I can roam the aisles at my leisure.

I've decided on the wine I'll take to Tania's tonight and am looking at the Easter eggs – wondering whether to get Joe a big one out of generosity or a small one out of consideration for his teeth – when I hear a familiar voice.

'Darling! How are you?'

I turn, recognizing the long painted nails and dangly earrings before I see the face.

'Corinne. Hello.' She is at her most stylish today, slim and elegant in black jodhpurs and a waisted jacket in hot pink, short enough to reveal a few inches of firm buttock. I'm still in the baggy leggings and sweatshirt I've been wearing while I cleaned the house and I haven't washed my hair yet, intending to do that tonight before I go out. She makes me feel like a bag lady.

'I didn't know you shopped here,' she says. I didn't know she did either. I'd assumed she lived close to the branch of the temping agency she manages.

It emerges that we live only a few miles apart. I wonder that we haven't bumped into each other before and we talk about this astonishing and fascinating coincidence as though it's comparable with finding life on Mars. Then she says, 'As you haven't been back to me, I assume you're still with the magnificent Mr Murray.'

'Yes, it's worked out very well.'

'You see? What did I tell you? You thought I'd set you up sending you there, but I could see you were the one to handle him. I know you think I just sit back and count my commission all day but I take note of what employers tell me, and I could tell you were good with people. I'm glad it's worked out, well done.'

I'm disappointed to find there's more depth to Corinne than I'd thought. I like to think I'm a good judge of character despite the mounting evidence to the contrary.

'And how are things for you? Still with the same bloke?'

LYNN PETERS

Her boyfriend is the agency's area manager. He's the one I
used to fantasize about.

'Yes, it's been nine months now – the longest I've been
out with anyone in years. But I'm a bit sick of the job, to
tell you the truth, all this interference from Head Office.
Some days I think I'd like to be an area manager myself,
other days I wish I could just run the whole show.'

I adjust Corinne's character profile a second time. I
hadn't seen her as a businesswoman though I wonder why
when I recall her assistant telling me how their branch did
the most trade in the entire company.

Corinne knows nothing of my relationship with Sam but
I find myself telling her all about it anyway. She sighs and
shakes her head in dismay making her earrings jangle when
I tell her that Sam is, in fact, coming back in two weeks,
after Easter, but that it's just to see Joe.

'I'll bet you he comes crawling back.'

'No, not now.'

'He will. It's what they all do. We go through life
thinking we can't do without them but when it comes
down to it, they can't do without us. Either this woman
will get bored of him or she'll start asking the same things
of him as you did. He'll be back.'

She thinks she is offering consolation and encouragement
so I'm obliged to tell her why the prospect of getting Sam
back is no longer high on my list of priorities – or even on it.
When I say not only that I have a new man but that the man
is Ed Murray – making it sound a slightly more established
relationship than perhaps it is – she hoots with laughter.

'You dark horse! When I said you could handle him I
never expected you to take it literally.' She tears open a
packet of Lion Bars and hands me one, a kind of mini feast
in celebration of my great coup.

Freed of the constraints of coercion and negotiation, the usual tenor of our relationship when I was temping, Corinne is almost human. She has to dash off when she remembers she only has ten minutes left on her car-park ticket but we part agreeing to meet up for a drink sometime soon. And obviously if I'm ever in need of work I'll give her a call.

Placing Joe's Easter egg in my trolley – the larger egg of the two since meeting Corinne has inexplicably put me in a good mood – I reflect on the fact that I can't see me needing her services again in the very near future but it was fun to run into her all the same.

'We've met before, haven't we?' says Chris stepping out of Tania's small kitchen and handing me a glass of wine. 'Tania said we had but I couldn't place you.'

I'm not sure whether I'm relieved he has forgotten my débâcle with the reception cookery class, or insulted that I made no impression on him. He pours beer for Colin and then retreats to the kitchen to stir something in a large pot on the hob.

'Chris is a really good cook,' says Tania, giving him a look that could only be called admiring (unless you'd prefer to call it stomach-curdling, as I do). 'He's done the casserole so I only had to make the pud.' I smile, trying to look enthusiastic as Chris passes the admiring look back to her. Couples. 'Do you cook, Colin?'

'Nearly all the time, my girlfriend hated to cook. I'm not keen on desserts, what I really enjoy is casseroles and curries. Lamb especially.'

'Chris is vegetarian,' says Tania hurriedly. He would be. 'I used to think vegetarian food took a lot of preparation but it's surprising . . .' She witters on, failing to surprise me at all except by being so easily converted back to men.

329

LYNN PETERS

After all the things she used to say. When I get her on her own I'm going to ask if they're sleeping together. I mean, at least I don't do it where Joe might be affected.

When we sit down to table, Chris serves us with a mess of vegetable casserole and jacket potatoes. When he stands next to Tania to ladle hers on to her plate she reaches up surreptitiously and strokes the back of his thigh.

'So, how long is it that you two have known each other?' asks Tania. She knows how long it is and I glare at her lest she be casting herself in the role of matchmaker. She should be called Titania, falling in love with the first man she set eyes on, as she has. In her present frame of mind she's quite capable of thinking I'll do the same. I must be growing cynical because falling for Ed hasn't produced this romantic glow in me. Couples are like swimmers, always calling, 'Come on in, the water's fine,' wanting everybody else to get their costumes wet just because they have.

Colin talks a little about our office and then confides something of his regret that Nina is moving out. She has fallen for a steward on the airline where she works. I think he should be pleased.

For some reason, Chris does too. 'Sorry to hear that,' he says cheerily, holding his wineglass up to the light. 'There's a chip in this one, Tan. Did you know?' *Tan*? Since when has she been Tan?

'No need to be sorry, it's time for both of us. It's just run its course, like for Gemma and Sam.'

Tania tops up Colin's glass, an action designed to soften the fact she is about to disagree. 'Oh, I don't think things have run their course with Sam, have they Gemma? He's just a wandering spirit, he could be back at any time.'

'Some men are just like that,' says Chris, backing her

330

up. 'It's just how they are. Never understood it myself, but it's not that uncommon.'

There's the briefest pause in which Colin jumps in to agree that certainly Sam could be back at any time, despite what he just said. I drain my wine and refill it immediately, wondering why everyone is so keen to convince me he's coming back – even Corinne who had never even heard of him before today. I can't think why they all imagine they know more about him than I do.

Thinking of Sam throws me off balance, souring my mood and the rest of the evening doesn't go well. The other three concentrate on drawing me out and raising my spirits but I refuse any more wine and resist all attempts at levity.

'Can I come in for a coffee while I wait for a cab?' asks Colin when we get to my gate. I guess he must have been waiting for me to offer or he'd have asked before.

'Why didn't you call a cab from Tania's?'

'I thought I should see you home.'

'I only live two doors away!'

He sighs and turns away, frustrated. 'Where's a call box?'

'Oh, don't be silly.' I open the front door and he follows me in. I switch the kettle on while he telephones but the taxi will be here in five minutes so there isn't time for him to have a coffee. I make one for myself anyway.

'Gemma—'

'What?' I dig the spoon hard into the coffee jar, sending a spray of granules on to the worktop.

'I'm sorry if I upset you with what I said about you and Sam. But I thought it was over, what with you and Ed.'

'It is over. And what about Ed?'

LYNN PETERS

'All these rumours for one thing.'

'What kind of rumours?'

'The usual kind.'

The kettle has been hissing and bubbling but now it switches itself off leaving us in sudden silence.

'If you're bothered about me seeing Ed, then how come you came tonight?'

'You asked me.'

'And you do everything people ask you, do you?' Before he can answer, I go on, 'You probably do actually, you're that soft. Your middle name must be Axminister — you lie down and let everyone walk all over you.'

Colin doesn't answer, but a muscle twitches in his jaw. I didn't mean to hurt him — at least I did, but now I wish I could take it back — but I wanted to lash out at someone and there's only Colin here.

'I'll tell you why I came. Because I like you, and you can do better than him.'

'Oh, like with you, you mean?' It's only as I answer and see his stricken face that I really understand what he has said. He becomes very still.

'Why did you ask me if that's all you think of me?'

I start to say that of course I like him, that he's a kind man but it's too late and anyway I'm not saying the thing he wants to hear. His voice is barely audible as he goes on, echoing something I had thought myself earlier, 'I've always been a bad judge of character — but if you think Ed is a decent guy, then you're an even worse judge than I am.'

The doorbell rings then, for the taxi, and Colin leaves before I can add that I'm a worse example of everything than he is.

*   *   *

332

Over the weekend one of my fillings comes out and though I get to my dentist's emergency surgery as early as I can on Monday morning, by the time I arrive at our offices it's almost lunchtime.

Immediately I walk in, I know something is wrong. It's unnaturally quiet, and Debbie looks strangely cowed as she sits behind her desk in reception chipping off bits of black nail varnish. When she looks up and sees it's me she looks delighted. That's unusual too.

'Gemma! You're back!'

I take my coat off and hang it on the rack in the corner. 'I had to go to the dentist. I've been waiting there since eight o'clock and there wasn't a phone.'

'So you haven't been up with Mr Archer?'

'Mr Archer? Why, does he want to see me?' I've only spoken to our MD once and that was only to thank him for holding a door open for me.

Marie creeps silently in from the outer office having heard our voices. She looks harassed and miserable. Kevin follows her but he looks excited and it is Kevin who speaks first.

'Gemma! Any news?'

'News about what?'

My first thought is that there has been an accident and I search the faces now joining Marie to see which of us isn't here — there's Piers, Les, Colin. No sign of Roger. Or Ed. They wouldn't expect me to have news of Roger. But Ed . . .

'Is Ed all right?' My face feels tight, as though my jaw is frozen. Perhaps that's just the effect of the injection the dentist gave me.

Marie looks at Debbie before she speaks as though she

isn't sure she should be the one to tell me. In fact it's Piers who speaks.

'Ed's been sacked,' he says.

Chapter 22

The phones are busy this afternoon but between times I sit quietly, trying to control my breathing. I've been into Ed's office, scouring it like a forensic scientist, hoping for some trace of his presence, but all I find is a shirt button which may not even be his. I sort through the wastepaper bin for clues but I don't know what I'm looking for. The walls are bare, the noticeboard has been stripped, and removable items have disappeared – his stapler, hole punch, and half a dozen lined A4 pads that were awaiting use on his window sill. It's no longer Ed's office, the engine room of our company, the walls echoing with his husky voice and deep laugh; it's just a room with cheap furniture.

Apparently after Ed arrived this morning, he was called up to the boardroom. He was only gone twenty minutes; when he came back he just cleared his desk and left. Debbie was the only one he spoke to and that was just to say he was leaving and to direct any personal calls to his home number. I have phoned it repeatedly but it's on answerphone and his mobile phone is switched off.

I really don't know what to do. Suppose it has something to do with what I told Diane? I know it probably hasn't, anything could have happened. And he's had his card marked with the MD since he saw Ed's entire staff falling out of the lift drunk that day. But even so.

I dial again and leave another message on the answerphone, hanging on for a few moments in case he is home and should answer when he hears it's me. He doesn't.

A little after two Roger arrives, looking tight-lipped and grim, the bags under his eyes more than usually prominent. Everyone gathers round him, the way they did me this morning.

'Roger, what have you heard?' asks Marie.

He leans back on the reception desk and considers his shoes. Then he tells us. He has been with the directors, it emerges, since being called in from his sick bed this morning. They wanted to know how much he knew of Ed's activities, and being finally convinced of his, Roger's, innocence, involved him in the discussion of how Treadz is to proceed without a leader. It has been decided that in the interim Bill, the financial director, is to move here from Head Office while they advertise for a replacement although it's not impossible that they may just close our enterprise altogether. It seems this is just one blip too many.

The hisses of disdain that accompanied the news that Bill is to be billeted on us are hushed by news of possible closure. You could have heard a pin drop; you could even have heard someone thinking of hearing a pin drop.

'What did Ed do?' asks Marie at last, breaking the silence.

I've never seen Roger angry before. 'Nothing at all. But someone blabbed,' he says.

'What about?' My mouth is still a little numb on one side which is no doubt why my voice sounds odd.

'That company he was planning,' he says to me, and then turning to the others and adding by way of explanation, 'He was thinking of setting up on his own. Nothing definite, he'd just drawn up a few plans for if they put Galaxy Leisure into liquidation.' He shrugs and rubs the bridge of his nose with thumb and forefinger. 'Somehow the board found out – dunno how, we thought there was only you—' to me, '—and me that knew.' He looks up at me suddenly, 'You didn't tell anyone?'

I hold his gaze, no guilty looking away. 'No, of course not.' He sighs. 'No, well, they got wind of it somehow, you never know with these things. But the upshot is, they accused him of planning to take business away from here, and of doing his own stuff on the firm's time. And a load more where that came from, all balls, but what can you do?'

Roger rocks on his heels, hands in pockets. Kevin and Colin begin to move away and then Piers says, 'It wasn't as secret as all that.' We all stand rooted to the spot as though someone has said, 'Freeze.'

'Oh?' Roger looks up, tight-lipped.

'Diane knew a week or so ago because she told me.'

'Diane? Who would tell Diane?' He gazes into space thoughtfully. Then his mouth forms a mirthless smile and his eyes focus on me. I get up from the chair I've been sitting on and prepare to wander back to my office as though this new information is irrelevant. I can feel Roger's eyes drilling into me.

'You're friends with Diane, aren't you?'

And then before I can answer, Marie says, 'Bill will have told her.'

We all look at Marie, not quite following. 'Bill and Diane are having an affair. You needn't look so shocked—' She says this to Roger, although I don't think it's the affair which has shocked him. 'So obviously Bill found out from somewhere and told Diane, and she told Piers.'

'She never could keep a secret,' says Debbie. 'She's known for it.'

The meeting begins to break up with this logical explanation which seems to have obscured the fact to everyone other than me that it might have been Diane who told Bill, rather than the other way about.

The day after Ed's sacking, Debbie takes a call for me. 'It's some foreign bloke,' she says. 'Got an accent thick as a ham sandwich.'

She puts the call through and I wait, hoping, knowing, who it will be, my heart racing in case I'm wrong. 'Ed! Where have you been?'

'Out and about. Ducking and diving.' I'm so relieved to hear him in such buoyant mood, his old self, ebullient and effervescent as though nothing has happened that I could cry.

'You had Debbie entirely confused with that voice.'

'That's not as hard as it sounds, is it?'

We both laugh and my life, which seems to have been on hold for the last twenty-four hours, starts up again.

'So you're still there then?'

My delight at hearing his voice is tempered just slightly by what I perceive as implied criticism. Perhaps I should have walked out myself, on principle? I've been so busy waiting to hear from him and wondering what has happened that I haven't thought of it. A twinge of guilt nips at me and makes me snappish.

'Of course, I'm still here. Where else is there for me to

go?' If I'm on the defensive, it's also because I want him to confirm his earlier job offer.

He laughs gruffly. 'I hope you'll soon be moving in with me.' I savour the ambiguity as it hangs in the air.

He goes on to tell me that he has found some offices, and has just got confirmation of the financial backing. Everything is going according to plan; no, better than that.

'So you're really all right, Ed?' I can't entirely keep the throb out of my voice. It's odd how, with someone you hardly know, that question is at the head of the conversation. But when you mean it, when you really care how they are, it falls much later.

'Considering I've been dumped on from a great height, I feel extremely well. In fact, they've done me a favour. If I hadn't been pushed I might have sat around for months plucking up the courage to go it alone.'

I feel my shoulders drop with relief and realize how tensely I've been holding them. So after all, things aren't as grim as I've feared.

Then he says, 'Still I'd like to find out what bastard blew the whistle on me. I don't suppose you've found out?'

I tell him I haven't and he asks if I could finish work early the following day so he can show me over the premises he's thinking of taking.

I put the phone down from him feeling my thighs turning to water just thinking about him.

The prospect of being with Ed every day, just the two of us, keeps me in a state of constant moist excitement. Just as everything King Midas touched turned to gold, now whatever I look at turns into an aphrodisiac. The great outdoors has become just a collection of hard and soft surfaces with potential for having sex on, against or under; so has the great indoors, come to that. Food is suggestively soft to suck or erotically hard to bite, the juices sharp or sour. Everyone I speak to seems to be thinking of sex, or looking as though they are.

I go to sleep with the sex manual under my pillow, dreaming of Ed, sensual and teasing, in provocative and tantalizing degrees of undress.

The offices are in a big old house with oak panelling in the hall, the sort of premises that private doctors often seem to favour. Even in its unfurnished state, it breathes opulence and good taste. When Ed has shown me round them and we've discussed where we'll sit, where the photocopier will go and how many filing cabinets we'll need, we go shopping for office furniture at a nearby office supplies centre. I choose a red chair which will look rather fine against the pale grey carpet of our small office suite and a desk with a particularly convenient arrangement of drawers – shallow ones for holding different kinds of paper, and a deeper one for files. Ed doesn't have the money to get them today but he makes a note of the styles and reference numbers.

When we've decided on what we'll need, like a young couple setting up home, Ed turns to me with a smile of satisfaction. 'I think we'll be very happy together, don't you?' he says, picking up my thoughts.

Marie gets married on Saturday but I don't believe she is looking forward half as eagerly to getting her guy to herself as I am to getting mine.

Easter is late this year, falling right at the end of April. The wedding is on Easter Saturday which could mean even heavier traffic than usual so when Colin says he will drive me to Marie's reception I offer only token resistance. It takes him miles out of his way, but we've hardly spoken in the weeks since Tania's dinner party and his offer is by way of an olive branch.

'Do you think Marie will like the wedding present?' Colin turns to me as the car sits idling at traffic lights, glancing down at my legs in their shiny black tights and my patent dominatrix stilettoes which, needless to say, I'm not wearing for his benefit.

I'm meeting Ed at the reception; Maxine won't be coming. This will be our first public appearance together marred only by having to arrive separately. But Ed is so busy with the new company, he wouldn't have had time to collect me.

Colin smells of woodsmoke and pine and his silk tie is a moody pattern of crimson and purple. His dark skin has a matt, cool look; he has the superclean air of having just stepped from the shower (unlike me, who with my ruby lips and heavily mascara'd lashes, have the look of having just stepped from a bordello. But this is a look Ed will like). I hope he won't upstage the groom. The way I'm feeling, I could well upstage the bride.

'She should like it, it was on her wedding list. You could buy half the contents of my house with what those glasses cost.' There was a general office collection which paid for a bone china tureen I swear she'll never use, but Diane, Suzanne and I wanted to give something just from us.

'She has good taste,' Colin admits sagely.

'She has expensive taste. That's not necessarily the same thing.' Her dress cost hundreds of pounds and in the drawing she did of it for me it looked like something one of the Ugly Sisters might wear.

Fortunately for me in view of my income, I don't have expensive taste. Judging from the look on Carla's face when I dropped Joe off at her house where he is to stay the night and she saw my dress, she doesn't think I have good taste either. She told me I looked 'Very nice' but her expression added, 'if you want to look like a hooker.' But with her arty beads and scruffy sweaters, what would she know. I think she's just jealous of my figure in this shimmery black lycra. Colin's opinion is far more valuable. When he came to the door he greeted me as though I was this week's lottery jackpot and he'd got the winning ticket.

The problem with arriving at an evening reception when there's a free bar and more valued guests have been there since mid-afternoon is that you're stone cold sober and they're so drunk they can hardly stand up. To be fair, this doesn't apply to all Marie's guests, but the best man is red-faced and staggering and a group of ten or twelve people in an advanced state of inebriation are throwing crisps at each other. Some of the men have taken off their jackets and ties and one has undone his shirt to the navel. It's a less salubrious gathering than I'd imagined; they probably think dressing for dinner means putting your vest back on.

Marie and Gary have been too busy toasting and hosting to do any serious drinking and when I arrive they look as fresh as if the day has just begun.

'This is Gary,' says Marie with pride. She's wearing a fluffy lacy off-the-shoulder creation which shows off her ample cleavage to advantage, the skirt gathered at intervals to reveal a peach underskirt and with a broad sash at the waist. Being full length the dress conceals her heavy calves and thick ankles (Marie is pretty and vivacious but her powers of attraction diminish towards ground level). Her hair is pulled up in a series of loops and waves, and a headdress of beads, ribbons and flowers is entwined among it. She doesn't look at all like an Ugly Sister, more like

Little Bo Peep (a glance at Gary suggests to cast him as the sheep would be typecasting).

Gary is just slightly taller than Marie, though of a smaller build with light red hair and freckles. His morning suit is generous about the shoulders as though he's borrowed it from a bigger brother and his pale lashes, and clear blue eyes are almost lost behind gold-rimmed glasses. He looks abashed at finding himself the centre of attention and as though he doesn't deserve it. He grasps my hand between his and shakes it vigorously, seeming overcome by emotion. I have to strain to hear his voice.

'Gemma, I'm so glad you could come. Marie's told me all about you.' It always makes me nervous when people say this, in case the person in question really has, but Gary relieves my anxiety when he adds, 'She really thinks a lot of you.' I clasp his hand tightly in return, touched by his comment, and then he adds. 'Which part of the Lake District is it where your dad's got his cottage?' He thinks I'm Suzanne.

Colin introduces himself and Gary grins, shaking his hand. 'Eh, Colin. I thought you were my rival for a bit there.' Colin looks at him blankly and this time Marie steps in looking aggravated.

'Oh Gary, not Colin, that was Conrad. He left last year, I told you.' She elbows Gary aside and kisses Colin's cheek telling him to take no notice, Gary's a bit thick sometimes.

Colin smiles wanly and Marie directs us to where the others are sitting. We head towards them, threading our way between drinkers and dancers. Brindle Sylvia is here in an electric blue two piece with sequins round the neck, and sitting next to her is her husband. He has the same stocky frame as Sylvia but with a narrow face and mean pinched mouth. They are looking in opposite directions as though they've had a row. At the adjacent table sits Diane in a sheath dress of white and silver. Next to her sits Bill.

As I approach Diane stands to welcome me over. I try to pretend I haven't seen her but Colin takes my elbow and propels me to her. 'Gemma, there's Diane. Over there.' Diane gets up to kiss me on the cheek, but I duck away as though I haven't noticed. Bill also rises to shake my hand, blocking my path, and asks me if I'm well, raising his voice over the beat of the disco. I take his pudgy hand politely in view of the fact he's the boss now, but I don't answer. I had forgotten they would be here and a flame of anger rises up to my throat. I can't say anything here, in front of everyone, but I fix Diane with a glare to let her know that I know.

Diane knits her brows at me but decides to ignore my coolness. 'And this is Sylvia's husband, Terry,' she says. I don't want to meet Terry, I want to get Diane in a corner and lay into her but Terry's eyes have homed in on mine. He leans forward to shake my hand without enthusiasm. He has stubby fingers, square at the tips, and the skin is red and rough. I take a seat, turning my back on Diane with a flourish but unfortunately this seats me facing Terry.

'So you're the one went to university?' he says accusingly.

'Yes, I did go to university,' I say, raising my voice so that Diane will hear. Diane didn't go to university.

It's odd what people consider to be your distinguishing characteristics but Terry has his own agenda.

'My son's at university.' He looks at me expectantly as though his son and I might know each other. 'He's at Newcastle. Proper university that is, not one of them new ones. Rubbish they are. Where did you go?'

I did my degree at what used to be a polytechnic and is

now one of them new rubbish ones. He makes me feel I've been passing myself off as an imposter. 'It was in London,' I say vaguely, hoping he won't press me any further.

'You're not one of them stuck-up Cambridge lot then?'

'Er, no.'

Sylvia has been observing this exchange with mild interest. Now she digs him with her elbow. 'Pipe down you miserable bugger.' She leans forward and touches my arm, 'Ignore him, he's in a temper because I've made him keep his tie on.'

Colin, who has been speaking to Bill, comes to sit next to me and now we turn to look at the dance floor where Piers and Suzanne are engaged in uncoordinated and jerky movements almost but not quite in time to the music. Kevin and Debbie are also dancing, with more style though less movement. Les and Roger haven't come. I look around but there's no sign of Ed.

Brindle Sylvia leans across and calls to Colin, 'On your own then? No girlfriend tonight?'

'Nina and I split up,' he says, repeating it a second time to ensure Sylvia has heard. She nods understandingly.

'Not you and all. First Gemma, now you. But what can you expect with your girlfriend working away all the time. I said it'd happen, didn't I, Terry?' Terry takes a swig from his pint without responding. And then, with one hand to her mouth to conceal her words from Terry − though still yelling them at the top of her voice − 'Mind you, I wish this one would work away more often.'

Colin smiles, looking embarrassed.

'But you're all right, are you?' Sylvia looks at him, suddenly concerned.

He meets my eyes but turns away. 'Yes I'm fine,' says Colin.

*   *   *

After the buffet I move to a seat at the furthest end of the table from Sylvia and Diane but as soon as Sylvia has finished eating she plonks herself next to me and strikes up conversation. 'I think Terry has taken a shine to you,' she says conspiratorially.

'Oh?' I wonder what he's like with people he doesn't like. She goes on, 'They're a funny lot though, aren't they, men? I told Marie, don't believe what they tell you before you're married. There's only one thing my husband said that turned out to be true.'

'And what was that?' I ask, seeing that I'm expected to say something.

'He said he wasn't good enough for me!' She laughs, almost choking on the cocktail cherry she was sucking. Terry leans across and slaps her on the back more roughly than is necessary. I don't have a high opinion of Sylvia but I think she may be right.

Looking up I see Diane *en route* to the toilets. She is taking little pigeon steps in her too-tight dress but the effect is to make her wiggle which is attracting the attention of some of the men present.

'Excuse me,' I say to Sylvia. 'I have to go to the loo.'

Diane is leaning over a washbasin looking into the mirror. When she sees me enter she pauses with the lipstick still in her hand. 'That dress really suits you, Gemma.'

She wants to be my friend again but what I want is to see her head on a stick. 'Yours doesn't suit you,' I say. 'You slither like a snake in that dress.'

A woman who is spraying herself with perfume at the far end of the bank of washbasins sees my expression and thrusts her atomizer back into her bag to make a hasty retreat.

Diane gives my reflection a half smile, thinking I'm surely joking. Then she says, 'Has something upset you?'

'No. Why should having my boss sacked upset me?'

She draws back from the mirror and sighs. 'I'm sorry, I should have realized. It's awful, isn't it?'

I don't answer directly. 'Why did you do it?'

'Do what?'

'Oh, don't play the innocent. I suppose it's because you've always been jealous of me. You didn't like me being made a director's secretary when I'd only just come into the company, you didn't like me being put on the same money as you—' I try to think of a third reason to round my accusations off – surprising myself with how many reasons she might have for resenting me – and find one. 'And you don't like the fact I'm getting ahead and you're going to be a secretary forever.'

'Gemma?' She looks astonished and mystified. But she's injured Ed with her rumours and I fully intend to hurt her as much as I can.

'They laugh at you, didn't you know that? Marie and Suzanne, even Sylvia. All of them. With your hoity-toity ways and your pretentiousness.'

I didn't realize she was such a good actress. She looks as though she's about to cry.

'Why are you saying all this? I thought we were friends.'

I snort at that and turn to the mirror myself, trying to calm myself down by brushing my hair but the bristles pull a strand into knots which increases my anger.

'I thought we were friends too – that's why I told you about Ed's plans. Which just shows how stupid *I* am. I should have known you couldn't wait to scoot up to the fifth floor to let them know – was there a bonus in it

347

for you? Or did you do it out of undying love for Bill Whatshisface out there?' I yank at my scalp in temper and a tangle of hair comes away with the brush.

'Oh, I get it.' Diane's eyes have stopped welling with tears and developed a hard sparkle. 'You pathetic little bitch. You think I even *believed* that cock and bull tale you told me about his pie in the sky company and that wonderful new job he was supposed to be giving you? Let alone that I'd repeat it to anyone!'

'You repeated it to Piers.'

'Yes, as a joke. We were talking about how smitten you were with Ed — so much that you believed any tale he came out with. I couldn't believe it when it turned out to be true! If you want to know how the other directors found out, I'll tell you.' She says it with a degree of satisfaction. Straightening up, she faces me, her lipstick pointing at me as though suddenly she's the accuser. 'That feeble-minded idiot of yours went to Don Ashby. Don Ashby! He's been a customer for years!'

'Don't kid me that Don Ashby just rang up and blew the whistle.'

'He didn't have to. Bill was on the phone to him and Don mentioned Ed had been in — which surprised Bill because when we saw you in Warwick Ed didn't say a word about it. Bill's a clever man. It didn't take him too long to find out a few facts. Ed thinks he's such a hot shot but he's not as smart as he thinks.' She replaces the cap on her lipstick and zips it into her evening bag. 'And neither are you.' She turns towards the door, her tight skirt impeding the dramatic exit she would like to make. As she opens it, she turns back. 'I can't believe what you've just said to me. What did I ever do to you?'

'Diane—'

'He's a two-faced bastard and you know what? I think you make the perfect couple.' She sweeps out.

A group of four musicians take their places on the rostrum and the singer taps the microphone and says one-two, turning to look at his colleagues as he does so. There's some twanging of strings and experimental banging of the drums and then with a sudden one-two-three-four they launch into a surprisingly impressive rendering of 'Brown Sugar.' They must be well into their forties, but I suppose this must have been their era first time round. They're all greying except for the drummer who has hardly any hair at all.

'Come on Gemma. Let's have a dance.' Colin had disappeared to the bar earlier and now he materializes unexpectedly by my side. I could hardly be in less of a dancing mood, what with my row with Diane — she has moved tables and is sitting with her back pointedly in my direction — and there being no sign of Ed, but Colin did bring me here. Besides, a turn on the dance floor will show Diane that she hasn't upset me as much as she would have liked. Even though she has.

'Yes, why not?'

I follow him picking my way between the closely placed tables, looking for a space on the small dance floor between the even more tightly packed couples. The band has prompted half the audience to get to its feet and I'm jostled and pushed as we worm our way through to the front. But once in our small space, directly in front of one of the speakers, the heat and the music alters my mood. We dance for several numbers, grinning at each other stupidly, unable to speak over the noise, but when the tempo changes for the quieter 'Lady in Red', Colin moves closer and draws me to him for a smooch.

'I'm glad we're friends again,' he whispers. I can still barely make out the words but I get the general meaning and smile my encouragement. I'm glad too. What with Diane and my recent row with Tania, I need all the friends I can get.

'Maybe we could be a bit more than friends.'

He speaks during the singer's brief pause in his throaty impersonation of Chris De Burgh and his words come through all too clearly. I draw back a little so that I'm no longer leaning against him in that companionable way and loosen my grip on his shoulder. Why does he have to spoil it? Why can't we just go on as we used to be? He's attractive but he's too nice. He just isn't my type.

As I look over his shoulder, wondering how to put this tactfully, there's a sudden lurch in my stomach. Standing by the entrance leaning against the wall, with what I guess is a spritzer in his hand, is someone else who isn't my type, though his being too nice isn't the reason.

Colin has noticed I've stopped moving and turns to follow my gaze.

'Come on, Gemma, you can see Ed later.' But I think, no, Colin. I can dance with you later.

'Ed! You said you'd be here at eight-thirty.'

'I was here at eight-thirty.'

'You were not. I was worried.'

He looks down at his glass and then draws me to one side to avoid a gang of teenagers who are trying to push past. 'So I wasn't here. So what? Don't start getting possessive, you sound like my bloody wife.'

He has wrong-footed me and I nod foolishly, like Joe

does when he wants to keep on the right side of me so I'll still let him stay up and watch television.

'Anyway I did look in earlier but you were sitting with Bill. I didn't feel like passing the time of day with him or the rest of them from that hell hole. If you must know, I wouldn't have come at all if you hadn't seduced me with your sexy bum and the free bar.' I start to laugh and he adds, running his hand down the curve of my bottom, 'It's not every day you can get a free bar.'

It emerges that actually Ed has been here some time, taking full advantage of the free bar and talking to Marie's dad. 'Decent bloke, it must be breaking his heart to see his daughter settling for a wimp like the groom.'

'Gary seems very nice.'

Ed laughs and aims a mock punch at my jaw. 'You little hypocrite! I don't see you settling for some guy who's "very nice". If anyone ever says that about me I'll sue for slander.'

'Yes, well it's a good thing we don't all want the same thing in a partner.' I take his drink from him and sip from it, wanting my lips to rest where his have.

'And what is it you want, Gemma?' He leans towards me and his mouth brushes my ear provocatively, daring me to say 'I want you to make love to me,' or something.

The crowd of teenagers come pushing back, almost knocking Ed's glass from his hand. He swears at their retreating heads.

'Right now, Ed, I want to dance.'

'Oh no, anything but that. Ask Piers. Ask Kevin.'

I place his empty glass on a side table. 'I'm asking you.'

He groans and turns his head away from the dancers and towards the bar as though rescuers might be arriving from that direction at any moment. But I pull on his reluctant hand and lead him on to the floor under the steady gaze of Marie, Diane and Piers and the openly hostile frown of Colin. When we've pushed our way through I turn towards him and link my arms round his waist. I can still feel the pressure of Colin's hand against me, but the memory is extinguished immediately by the rougher grasp of Ed. I don't feel as comfortable and relaxed as when I stood by Colin just minutes before, but instead I feel tremulous and enlivened, and there's a sudden surge in my power supply. Before we start to dance he kisses me.

We dance two dances, except that we're not dancing just pressing against each other and then he bites my earlobe. A shower of sparks scatters down my side.

'I've got an urgent need to press myself against you,' he says.

'I thought you were.'

'I've barely started.'

'All right, go on then.'

He laughs, mouthing, 'Not here,' over the sudden upturn in the volume of the music.

Ed takes my hand and leads me through the throng of heaving bodies out into the corridor. Several passageways lead off to either side but we pass these only stopping when we come to a wide staircase at the end. Ed looks either way like someone following the Green Cross Code and then climbs the stairs. From the landing he leads me down another corridor and now the doors have room numbers on them.

With a thrill, I realize where he's taking me. 'Have you booked a room?' The spontaneity of the discovery is fabulously erotic; I clasp his hand tighter, feeling something reverberate deep inside, like a guitar string being twanged. Why didn't I guess he would do this?

'Not exactly booked it, no.'

So we must be borrowing someone else's. Well, that's OK, I didn't come prepared to stay the night and I wouldn't like going down to breakfast in the morning in last night's knickers.

We walk down the length of this corridor and come out on to another landing. Ed tries the handle of the door facing us. I'm surprised to see that the door doesn't have a number on it. He pulls it open and looks inside. Then he looks around to see we're not observed. 'Quick, in here.'

It's dark inside but he switches the light on. It's a conference room. In the centre is a long dark mahogany table.

'Brilliant,' says Ed. 'It's perfect.' He turns to me expectantly and sees that he has disappointed me, though if that's all he sees then he needs glasses. I could hit him.

How is it that the likes of Marie get to consummate their love with champagne and silk sheets and I celebrate mine repeatedly amongst filing trays and office furniture?

'What were you expecting?' says Ed, amused. 'The honeymoon suite?'

Well, why not? This would have been the perfect opportunity to have sweet, leisurely sex instead of yet another quickie.

'Sweetheart ...' He tips my chin up and kisses my lips, a slow, warm kiss to which nevertheless I don't respond. 'Don't you want to? This is living – taking your opportunities where you find them – acting on the spur of the moment. Where's your spirit of adventure? Don't tell me that what you want out of life is everything booked six months in advance – and with a horsedrawn carriage and six white mice like Cinderella down there?'

He reminds me of something Sam used to say though I can't quite remember what. I don't answer, pushing my lip out in a sulk the way Joe does. Looking down at my shoes I see the toe of the right one has got a fleck of mayonnaise on it and I wipe it off on the carpet.

He takes me by the shoulders, I can feel his fingers digging into my flesh. 'Have you seen the shine on that table? I can't wait to see your backside reflected in it.'

For just a moment doubt flickers through me. Much as I want Ed, I don't want our relationship to be only about sex. Suppose he thinks I'm just a blow-up doll with attitude?

He must note a change in my demeanour because he loosens his grip and takes a step back. 'Don't you want to?'

I do, but . . . He runs a finger down my face reflectively, making the skin glow under the light pressure.

'I can't help it. I just want you all the time. But we can wait if you like. It's only a matter of weeks and we'll be together all the time.' His voice is husky and tender, his expression so gentle and concerned it makes me want to cry. 'If you don't want to, sweetheart, we can go back downstairs.'

He lets go of my shoulders and moves towards the door, giving the awful possibility of not having him some substance.

The strains of 'Hotel California' drift up from downstairs. I hold my arms out to him and he slams the door closed behind us.

When Ed goes to the bar Marie comes sweeping over. Her hair has fallen out of its pins now, giving her a saucy drunken air which is more appropriate than I immediately realize.

'Gemma! I wouldn't have thought you had it in you.'

I wonder if she's caught Sylvia's penchant for the *double entendre*. But surely she wouldn't be smiling at me if she knew I'd just desecrated the conference facilities. 'What are you getting at?'

'You and Ed.'

'Me and——?'

'Getting it together. *You* know. You can't deny it, we've all seen you.'

I glance around, playing for time. But there was no one on that corridor, we'd have seen them and the window of the conference room looked out on hotel roofs, as I'd noted at one stage when Ed was pressing my buttocks up against it.

'I thought it was odd, him not bringing his wife with him. Then once you started kissing! I think it's really upset Colin.'

'Oh.' I can't think what to say.

'Come on. Tell me all about it. Have you been going out with him just since he left or was it before? Because some people did say some things, before he left, but I said they were wrong because I used to sit right outside his office and I'd have known if anything was going on with the two of you.'

'We got together after he left,' I say, this reply requiring least explanation.

'So is he getting a divorce now?'

'Oh yes.'

The imperceptible move of her head shows that this is new information which she can't wait to tell Diane. It would be news to Ed too; I hope no one repeats it within his earshot. But it's only a matter of time. There's an urgency between us which is too strong to be ignored.

'I can't believe it. You and him. Or any woman and him. Don't you remember what we used to say about Janet Reger — whatever did she see in him?' I thank Marie for reminding me with a sarcasm of which she is oblivious. 'What happened to her anyway?'

'She backed off,' I say. 'Had to get out of the kitchen.'

'Why?' Marie looks momentarily confused.

'She couldn't stand the heat,' I explain but Marie looks none the wiser. 'The competition was too much for her.'

'For who?' says Ed, coming up behind me, fortunately not waiting for an answer. 'Marie, you're not drinking, let me get you something.'

But I'm not as fortunate as all that and clearly she has been drinking because she goes on, 'No, it's all right, I was saying to Gemma, maybe she'll be next.'

I try to butt in but Ed interrupts me. 'Next to do what?'

She twirls round by way of explanation, her dress ballooning out like a cream puff. 'You should've been here when I threw my bouquet, I'd have made sure you caught it.' She directs this at me, excited at the prospect of one more couple joining her in her blissful married state.

Some guests are hovering wanting to make their farewells and Marie hurries over to them.

'How come she thinks you and Sam could still get married?' says Ed, mystified. 'Haven't you told her he's gone?'

Sometimes you have to be grateful that men are always one step behind in the conversation.

'Where's your little boy tonight?' asks Ed as we queue for our coats, feeling in his jacket for his cloakroom ticket.

'He's staying with a friend.' For a small fee, Carla will

keep children overnight, to be collected first thing in the morning. She has been a real find. She's as good with Joe as Tania, but with the added advantage of not quizzing Joe's mother on her sex life.

'You mean you're free tonight? Why didn't you say so?'

Now that we're standing so close we could be joined at the hip, I wonder myself, but I know not to take Ed for granted. I wouldn't want to make extensive plans and then find he's taken a better offer at the last moment. When you've faced rejection once you're very careful not to set yourself up for it again but anyway I assumed he had to get back for Maxine, though evidently she's away for a few days. There is something deeper between us, I know, but it would still be all too easy to scare him off. For all his size he's like the hedgehog Joe found in the garden. We had to woo it with morsels of bread and milk and then it stayed with us all last winter, but if we'd ran up to it every time it appeared it would have scuttled away.

'Gemma, what were you thinking about? We could have stayed the night here instead of messing about in that poxy boardroom.'

'You said you preferred spontaneity and the spirit of adventure.'

'Sometimes I wonder about you, Gemma,' he says resignedly.

'So what's it to be, my place or yours?' asks Ed as we stand outside the double doors looking at the night.

In the same way you always wish you could win on the Premium Bonds but without expecting your wish to come true, I've been so desperate for us to spend the night together, that I thought it was sure not to happen. Seeing as things never turn out how you plan, I've been scared to imagine it too vividly, in case that somehow prevented it happening.

'Maxine's away, you can come to mine if you want.'

I'd like to see where Ed lives but I've met Maxine and there are strict limits beyond which I will not betray a person. I'll borrow her man, as another woman borrowed mine, but not her bed. It's bad enough that I may be adding to Maxine's stock of unhappiness without also adding to her laundry.

Anyway, I have to collect Joe at nine-thirty so it will be more convenient to be at my house. As I say, I haven't planned for this. But it does just happen that the bedroom is tidy and I put fresh sheets on the bed only this morning.

Chapter 23

When we arrive home a party is in progress at one of the neighbour's and there's nowhere to park so Ed leaves the car at the end of the road and we walk. He feels different from Sam, his hips brush mine at a higher point and his stride is wider so that I have to do a little hop periodically to keep up with him. It's disorientating to feel his arm round my waist after the many times I've walked down this same street thinking of him. It's as though a movie star has stepped off the screen and into real life.

He stands back from the front door while I unlock it, perusing the frontage thoughtfully. Once in the hall, he does the same, making me aware of the scuff marks on the paintwork and the place where Joe picks at the wallpaper. But perhaps he is just resting his gaze while he thinks of something else entirely: as I close the door he grabs me round the waist, swinging me round in his arms to face him. He kisses me hard.

Ed draws out of the kiss and looks at my face making me feel even more self-conscious than I did about the scuff marks. I wait expectantly for him to kiss me again but he says, 'So – aren't you going to offer me a drink?'

I don't usually keep alcohol in the house, and anyway

I'd have thought he had drunk enough, but there's a little whisky left and a bottle of wine left over from Christmas.

He asks for wine and while I open it wanders into the living-room and begins riffling through the few CDs left me. He switches the CD player on and 'All Right Now' booms out. I hurry back in to him, the wine bottle in my hand.

'Ed! This is a terrace. The neighbours will be banging on the wall.' I lean over to turn the sound down. 'The neighbours won't be the only ones,' he says, coming up behind me, pulling me upright against him and running his hands down my thighs.

He takes the bottle from my hand, placing it on the floor and moves against me in time to the music, unbuttoning me slowly.

'Don't you want the wine?'

'We'll drink it later,' he says, brushing his lips across my brow. 'I might try sipping it out of your navel.'

'God, I hope not. There're enough stains on my mattress already.' But Ed doesn't seem to be listening. His face is growing heavy, his mouth full and dark.

I undo his shirt, pushing it off his shoulders and sliding his trousers down for him to step out of. He has changed from the man I met six or more months ago; gone is the loose flesh of a man who has lived not wisely but too well, to be replaced by a young man's body, the belly muscled and strong, firm to my fingers. I leave him in his tight black pants; they contrast with the hard bulk of his thighs, emphasize the line of hair that rises above them to join with the T of curls on his chest where I now lay my cheek. It's the first time we have been like this together, skin against skin, without the pressure of time and potential observers.

I run the edge of my fingernail down his chest, down his loins and then gently between his legs; not so gently back up his length. He's hard and protruding now above his pants.

Taking hold of his hand, I lead him upstairs as he did me earlier, his free hand curving round my bottom as I climb.

In bed I push him on to his back and lie flat on top of him, my breasts against his chest and my legs balanced on his. His skin is rough against mine, his smell unfamiliar in these surroundings. With each breath he takes my body is lifted up a little. I draw my head back to look at him, wanting to stay like this, to savour the moment, this moment when I have him just where I want him.

But he also wants me. Laughing, he rears up suddenly, rolling over so that I slide off him, then he turns swiftly and pins me on my back holding my wrists. His kisses on my face are like the brush of a moth's wing, and on down my neck to my stomach. Tantalizingly, he misses out my breasts. I think I may die of wanting. He fetches the wine and drips it on to my nipples.

I didn't know that he would be so tender. Though shouldn't I have guessed from his concerned phone call after Sam had left me? From his quiet sympathy the time we sat in his office and he held my hand so gently, asking for nothing in return? Ed adopts a forceful, macho persona but he overplays his role and what people see is a harsh abrasiveness. But beneath the fake exterior lies a fine sensibility he tries to hide and I have found it. Lying here in the crook of his shoulder, it comes to me that, though we have had sex before, this is the time that counts. I wonder now that I could have been so blind to the fact he cares for me, that I didn't predict that tears would spring to his eyes or how his body would shake with emotion. When he recovered he said he was sorry, as though it wasn't this very involuntary outburst which gave his shuddering climax its poignancy.

Afterwards I cried too, though ironically that was because, as the white heat tore through me, I heard Sam's name in the rush of air. But that was just habit, the way when you rearrange the cutlery drawer you still go back to the old place when you want a knife. I didn't tell Ed, of course, and we clung together like two children wondering at the power of what they have unleashed.

We're standing on the edge of a precipice, hand in hand, wondering whether to jump. Looking at his face, the muscles relaxed and softened making him faintly unfamiliar, I realize just how long I've been waiting for this moment.

'I love you,' I whisper against his cheek. He draws back and looks at me, his eyes entirely free of their usual hard glitter. He doesn't have to tell me, I know already, but he does anyway. 'I love you, too,' he says.

'Shall we have a shower?' says Ed. I am dozing, cocooned in the damp fug of contentment, preparing to drift into the cloudy weightlessness of a sweet sleep. I do not want a shower.

I try to say, 'I'm tired.' It comes out uh-uhuh.

He shakes his shoulder free of me and sits up abruptly swinging his legs from the bed. 'Come on, the night's still young. You can sleep all day tomorrow.'

He has forgotten about Joe who must be collected by nine-thirty. I curl into a ball and pull the duvet over my head, exhaling deeply to warm up the space immediately before my face and drawing my feet up even closer. He prods me through the duvet, making me grasp it tighter but at once it's pulled from my fingers sending a gust of cool air sweeping over my legs. Ed pulls the duvet on to the floor and then leans over me, giving my bottom a resounding whack.

'Ed!' I sit up at once, furious. I have no sense of humour when I'm tired. But he just laughs.

'Up now, madam. Or the hairdo gets it.' Looking up I see he is holding the glass of water I keep by the bed. It is tilted dangerously over my head. He's such a child.

Once in the shower I discover Ed was right, I'm not tired at all. Nestling against his skin as the hot water runs down is a particular kind of bliss, the more exquisite for the knowledge of what has gone before and what is to come after. His body hair turns to silk under the soap and it is intimate and erotic to explore his body this way in the confined and steamy space.

'You've got a scar.' My fingers have found a seam in the skin across his stomach. 'Appendix. I was just a kid.' I kneel and press my lips against it, tasting soap and warm water. The idea of his having suffered is painful and a wave of emotion floods over me as he lathers my hair.

'Ed?' I press my face against his stomach, my arms clasped around his legs. 'Is it just sex with us? Or is there more?'

The steam seems to cast a hush while I await his answer.

'There's certainly more sex.'

'No, what I mean is—' He knows what I mean but I have to pursue it. 'Would you ever leave Maxine?'

'For you, you mean?'

Not to put too fine a point on it, yes. But he's embarrassed by our recent closeness and what he has revealed about himself, and is seeking to distance himself emotionally. I alter my angle of approach. 'Is it something you think you'll finally get around to?'

He has stopped massaging my scalp but now he starts again. 'I'd leave her at the drop of a hat, quite honestly. But I need her know-how for the new business.'

I don't care to acknowledge Ed's more Machiavellian traits and I pass swiftly on. 'But before, when you were with Janet Reger, you didn't need Maxine then. Why did you stay with her?' I need to know if he still has feelings for her. If he's only with her out of practical considerations, then I can start to plan our future – not the boring, secure expectations of his 'n' hers hand towels and carriage clocks that Marie and her ilk pine for – but a future of unpredictable fun and immeasurable love and laughter. I can make him happy again. Oh, I know that with a man like Ed you can't assume anything will be forever. But who wants to live forever? The foreseeable future will do just fine.

'It was complicated. Janet Reger, as you call her, didn't want me to leave Maxine.'

'Why ever not? Is she married herself?'

There's a long pause while I wait for his answer but when it comes it's tinged with exasperation. 'Do we have to talk about this now?'

He raises me up by my elbows, holding my head back under the stream of water to rinse my hair, then kisses me on the mouth. He's right, there's too much else we could be doing to get bogged down in a question and answer session. And if I want to know how he feels, I only have to ask myself: who is it he's making love to in the shower?

We finish just as the hot water is beginning to run out. 'I hope you left the towels where you can reach them,' says Ed, turning off the taps. He doesn't do it quickly enough and a stream of cold water sprays over us before he can stop it.

Laughing, I turn to the shower door and am about to push it open when I stop. Didn't I close the bathroom door when we came in? It's difficult to see through the frosted glass of the shower but I was sure I had because I didn't want to lose the warm air into the draughty hall. Light from the landing is flooding in, yet not through the whole of the doorway. Is it just the glass distorting my vision?

'Ed?' He doesn't answer but I know from his sudden stillness that he has seen something too. And now the figure, and it surely is a figure, in the doorway begins to loom nearer. It's dark and shadowy, silent in its movements. I lean back to press myself against Ed, feeling him move back too but there's nowhere to go in the tiny cubicle.

Suddenly the door opens and a bath towel is thrust towards me. 'You can come out now,' says Sam.

Chapter 24

— —

I take the towel from Sam and step from the shower. He's ashen, for all his bitter smile, lounging against the door frame. He's cool, in charge of the situation, but his mouth twitches and his cold stare can't quite conceal his pain. I don't know how long he has been standing there but long enough for him to master his immediate emotions and plan how he wants to play it.

I hand the towel to Ed who is hovering uncertainly and reach for another for myself.

'What's this?' says Sam. 'A bit of tit—' he looks Ed up and down with distaste '—for tat? A bit of "anything you can do I can do in the shower"?'

I don't answer, wanting to get a towel round myself first and finding the one I've picked up won't cover both my breasts and my bottom. I can't believe that he would just wander back in and talk to me like this – and on the first night I've got Ed to myself. But I need time myself to decide how to play this.

Ed is on top of things already. Looking as relaxed as though he meets partners of his lovers in their bathrooms every day of his life (and maybe he has); he tucks the ends of his towel in place and steps out of the shower, standing his ground.

'I'm Ed Murray. Who are you?'

Sam straightens up from the door frame and stands appraising Ed, legs apart as though he's about to go for his guns. He doesn't reply to Ed, turning instead to me. 'Gemma, will you ask him to go? We need to talk.'

Ed raises his chin a little, his signal that he isn't intimidated. 'Do you want me to go?' He's still looking at Sam but the slightest tilt of his head makes it clear he is addressing me. 'It might be better if I stay.'

For an instant I see myself being fought over, obliged to marry the victor. In a duel, who would I root for? Sam, father of my child, friend and lover of so many years — who has betrayed and abandoned me? As I look at him I see a woman draped around his neck, her hands unzipping his fly, see him kissing her, undressing her as he used to do me. Ed, who has cried tears against my neck only an hour before looks impressive, standing out against him.

'I'm OK, Ed. I'll call you tomorrow,' I say, not for Ed's benefit but for Sam's. It's important that he should know that this affair is not some cheap sexual episode, like his own, but that we have a relationship, and of the sort where you show how much you care by phoning each other frequently. I put my arms round Ed and kiss him.

As Ed brushes by Sam he says to me, as though in passing, 'Call if you need anything. I can be here in minutes.' He means it as a warning to Sam but Sam wouldn't hurt me. I mean, not now, in any way you could see.

I try to read Sam's expression. He's got his features under control but he's angry and, I guess, frustrated that he has no right to give vent to it. He's hardly in a position to criticize me. He seems smaller; diminished in some way. It could be just by comparison with Ed but I don't think it's only that.

Ed dresses swiftly and when he emerges from the bedroom Sam and I still haven't moved. Perhaps neither of us is sure what will happen next. Maybe he thinks I'll collapse on to his neck crying and he'll forgive what he has just witnessed — and I him? Will he fall to his knees, begging me to take him back? Could we, perhaps, run to each other and, all debts paid, heal our hurts with tears and lovemaking? There's the briefest moment, in which old hopes prod at my memory, like friends you never expected to see again, when any one of these scenarios seems a possibility. But as the front door slams Sam resumes his all-American guy slouch against the door frame and takes out a packet of gum from his pocket, and then it's too late.

I begin drying my legs and speak without looking at him, trying hard to match him in coolness. 'So. What brings you back?'

He unwraps the gum and folds it into his mouth, his jaws beginning to work slowly in that old familiar way.

'Wanted to surprise you,' he says.

When I've dried myself I put on my dressing gown and go downstairs where Sam is in the lounge drinking whisky. He has poured me one which I don't want but, once I sit down, I'm grateful to have something to hold. I take a gulp and feel the fumes hit the back of my nose.

'Who is he?' says Sam abruptly.

'You know who he is. I work with him. I told you about him and you said it was fine to have sex in the stationery cupboard as long as it was on work time.'

'And was it?'

'Sometimes.' Our attempt to smooth over the situation with flippancy doesn't work. After this exchange it's still

369

just him and me and a silence big enough to fill the Albert Hall.

'Where's Joe?' he asks at last.

I tell him and he nods, not really listening. He has looked in his room and would have guessed he must be at the house of friends. 'Does Joe like this bloke?' I realize with a jolt that it's not just the idea of me and Ed that is weighing on Sam but also of Joe and Ed.

I fudge my answer, seeing as they haven't even met yet. Sam draws what seems to be the obvious conclusion from this.

'So it isn't serious?'

'It is, actually. Joe won't be a problem. Ed loves kids.' Wow, what a lie, he told me himself how he'd have liked to murder his nephews when they visited recently, but then they answered back and had fed sandwiches into his video player. Anyone would feel the same. I certainly did when Joe did that to ours.

'He's *my* son,' says Sam with a hint of belligerence.

'Yes – and where have you been all his life?'

'Well, someone had to earn a living—'

'Not overseas, you didn't. You could have worked back here if you'd wanted, don't deny it.' I can't maintain my cool detachment and at once I go for the throat. 'It's suited you too well, acting fast and loose over there and coming back here when you wanted a rest. The reason you never wanted to get married and settle down was because you wanted to stay single and live it up.'

He could never match me in argument and my sudden outburst has taken him by surprise, though he should have seen it coming. Now he sinks into the sofa, perceptibly dwindling.

'Gemma, we need to talk.'

'So talk.' They say it's wrong to kick a man when he's down but sometimes that's the only chance you get.

His eyes roam the room while his brain searches for appropriate phrases and fails to find any. Finally he says, 'You're right. Everything you said is true. I've been selfish, I've been stupid. I've made mistakes. But the point is, I see that now and I'm sorry.'

I don't know that that is the point but he looks at me with Joe's eyes, dark and soft, asking to be forgiven.

Suddenly I realize what this is all about. 'Has she left you.'

He looks uncomfortable. He hadn't wanted to come to that just yet.

'Yes. But that's not the reason—'

'The reason that what?'

'That I—' He hasn't wanted to get to this bit yet either, has anticipated being on firmer ground by now. 'That I want you back.' Now he has said it and the words hang in the air like a mobile slowly turning, with Sam seeing it from one angle and me from another. 'I realized a while ago that I'd made one hell of a mistake. But I didn't know what to do, I'd done everything wrong – tonight I just thought if we talked, and you saw how I've changed . . .'

He has changed too. His hair is starting to grow back now, hinting at its old shaggy unkempt appearance, the way I used to love it. But now it just seems untidy.

I don't answer and perhaps he finds my silence encouraging because he takes a sip from his glass and then goes over the main points of the news again. 'I'm sorry. Christina was a *big* mistake.' Something in his emphasis on 'big' makes me think he means from his own personal point of view more than mine. I wonder just what went on there. 'Nothing like it is ever gonna happen again, that I can promise you.

371

Which is why . . .' He takes a breath and his eyes meet mine on the exhalation. 'I want to come home. I want you back.'

And I want to savour this moment. I hold my glass up, watching the amber liquid, the colour of a traffic light. How ironic, to be offered what I'd always wanted so soon after I stopped wanting it.

'It's a kind of rough justice,' he continues in his slow drawl, 'walking in on you like that.' He eases back against the sofa and I can see the whisky is starting to take effect. 'It was a shock, I can tell you that much, I never imagined . . .' The pain of the moment of discovery revisits him and he takes another sip of whisky and rolls it round his mouth. He has visualized me sitting at home by the fireside weeping gently these past months. I'm glad he didn't arrive back on one of the evenings when I was doing just that. 'I would have wished it didn't happen and it's gonna take me a while to get over it. But when you think it over, it's the best way it could happen, isn't it?'

The whisky is making me feel a little sick and my mind has begun to drift during his self justifications but now he has my full attention. I don't see what he's getting at.

I say as much and he elaborates. 'It means we're even. I've had someone. You've had someone. We haven't burned our bridges. We can start over.'

The difficult thing with bridges is knowing which ones to cross, which to burn and which to build but on this occasion I've already started striking matches. 'Everything I care about is back here,' he adds, waving his arm around to include me, Joe, the CD player.

He should have quit while he was ahead, played the 'I love you so much' card, the 'I didn't realize how much I needed you,' hand, trumped it with, 'You're the only one

I've ever really loved.' But all he has said is that he wants to come back because he's found he can't do any better. He doesn't think that's what he's saying but it seems to me that that's at the heart of it.

'Gemma?' His face takes on a strained look, even more than it has already, as though he's going to say something that's really difficult for him. 'Gemma, will you marry me?'

So *that* was the trump card. But the game has been over long since, before he even arrived. Besides, the idea of getting married no longer impresses me. I can't recall where the attraction once lay in a long dress you could never wear again, or in a phenomenally expensive bun fight for the benefit of guests who don't care a toss for you and would just have sex with each other on mahogany conference tables. Sam's declaration counts for little set against Ed's recent closeness, his own confession that he loved me, and his rising to my defence in that way that made me feel so cherished and protected. These were never at risk from Sam's poor performance.

As for his saying we are even – Sam might have fallen in love and out again, but I am only just starting with Ed. Why should I give it all up for a man who has left me once already and could do so again as soon as the opportunity afforded itself whatever he might say now, seduced by the comfort of his own home and a bottle of whisky? After what Ed and I have shared tonight, it's only a matter of time before he'll leave Maxine. I know that's what women always say but this time it's true.

'I'm going to bed,' I say, getting up. 'I take it you'll be driving back to your mother's.' Presumably it's her car that he has borrowed to get here.

'Can't I stay — I could sleep in Joe's bed?' he adds hurriedly.

'No, you can't.' He rakes his fingers through his hair while I stand looking at him, wondering if there's anything else to say. He gets to his feet and comes towards me but I hold my glass in front of me like a barrier.

'I do love you.' His eyes are wide and scared, his voice almost inaudible. But it's too soon after hearing these same words from Ed, too big a contrast with the way my body had ached and responded to them. Now I just feel tired. I take his glass from his hand and carry it out to the kitchen.

Chapter 25

T ania is wearing make-up. Well, mascara and lipstick
anyway, and her hair has been newly trimmed ridding
it of the wispy, uneven ends. It has a new shine as though
she has used a colour rinse but that would be taking things
too far. She is mixing up lard and nuts for some kind of
cake you feed the birds; she must have been watching those
wildlife programmes again. When it's ready the children,
who are currently quarrelling over which nose should be
put on Mr Potato Head, will stuff it into a net and hang it
up outside for the birds to peck.

'You're looking very nice, Tania.'

She looks pleased and tucks a strand of hair behind one
ear with a finger that still has lard on it.

'Chris said he might call in after school.' She pauses in
kneading the dough. 'You know that old cliché – "your
other half"? You meet someone and you see yourself
reflected back? Well Chris is mine.'

I'm cynical of such romantic imagery. Sam was more
like an odd piece of jigsaw I was trying to force into place.
Ed, who seems to engulf me, is like the hard chocolate
on a Rolo and I'm the soft toffee in the middle. Tania's
satisfaction is somehow irritating and I turn on the kids,

threatening to confiscate Mr Potato Head if they don't stop arguing.

'Actually, I've got something to tell you.' Tania's words send a tremor through me; when people have news you're going to like they don't say they're going to tell you, they just do. On the plus side, if she's getting married at least I can wear the outfit I got for Marie's wedding.

'Chris is moving in,' she says. It's not as bad as her getting married but almost, and without the compensation of being able to wear my lycra dress. Inevitably his arrival will distance us. I say this.

'Well, yes,' says Tania, determined to present things in a positive light. 'But if you get together with Ed then you won't need me for moral support in the same way will you? We'll be like all those women we used to make jokes about in the queue in Tesco's, moaning about their husbands.' We've always done that anyway, that isn't the side of things I expect to change.

'This is all very soon, isn't it?' I'm not in the mood to look on the bright side, I'd rather darken it.

'It is too soon, we've both said the same thing. But we're going to do it anyway.' We, we, we. I liked it when Tania was 'I'. 'It just feels right. And even though we've only recently started seeing each other, it's not like I've only just met him. It's mostly been his classes I've helped out in down at the school.' I search the space on the wall over Tania's dusty dresser for a further objection but she goes on, 'And like with you and Ed, if you've worked together it does mean you've seen the other side of them. If you just date someone it's much easier for them to put on an act.' She wipes her hands on her jeans and goes over to the sink to wash them.

I'm not happy to hear Ed compared with Chris. Not only

does my tantalizing relationship with Ed bear no similarity whatsoever to her pedestrian one, but I don't want us to be presented as a *fait accompli*. We're still some way from being a couple in the accepted sense and there's something *risqué* and exhilarating about that. What's so good about social conventions anyway?

Perhaps Tania senses my hostility because she changes the subject. 'So, when is Joe coming back?'

Sam has taken him to his mother's for the week while he's on leave. This contract has another month or so to run, then he's got a transfer back here. I don't know what arrangements we'll come to about the house but I've made it clear he's not moving back in.

'I suppose you'll be seeing him to discuss everything, then?' Tania pauses in filling the kettle and looks at me hopefully.

'You needn't think we'll be getting back together,' I say, reading her thoughts. 'He was bad enough when he thought I was chaste and innocent – now he knows I'm as bad as him, there'd be no stopping him.'

'You know he's talked to me?' She says this shyly, clearly aware that I didn't know. She must have been waiting for the right moment to tell me.

'What did he say?' I'm surprised to feel my heart beating faster. A shout of anguish goes up from Sophie who has had Mr Potato Head wrested from her grasp. Instead of stepping into the dining-room to settle the altercation in her usual way, Tania closes the door on them.

'He wants to come back.'

'Well, of course he does, he told me that much himself.' Sam's girlfriend has gone back to the USA and got engaged to an old flame. Poor old Sam, left high and dry without either a lover or a lead singer.

'You know why he turned up unannounced like that?' asks Tania.

'Who knows why men do anything.'

'He was going to creep in and just get into bed with you. You'd wake up with his arm around you and he'd ask you to take him back.'

'*What*?' Blood rushes to my face in anger with the speed of an express train that isn't stopping at this station.

'I suppose he thought it would be romantic. And that actions would speak louder than words – you always said he was no good at talking about how he felt.'

I take a spoon and prod at the birdfeed Tania has made.

'He seems to have had a good stab at it with you.'

'He was desperate, Gemma. And who else could he talk to?'

'I'd have thought he had plenty of people,' I answer, not adding that I wouldn't have expected Tania to be numbered among them. He must have gone to her to find out about Ed.

Tania pours boiling water into the teapot and while the tea brews, takes a dishcloth and begins rubbing at the fingermarks on one of the cupboards. When did she get to be so houseproud?

'What did you say about Ed?'

'Oh, not much.' She looks embarrassed. 'That you work together . . . That you like him . . .'

'That he's married?' I have told Sam a little but this fact seemed irrelevant.

'I don't remember.'

'So Sam thinks it's doomed to failure and that I'll take him back when it's all over.'

'No, I don't know he thinks that at all.' She looks

exasperated. 'But it's not impossible, is it? Before this happened you never even looked at anyone besides Sam.' She takes a step towards me and lays a comforting hand on my arm. 'Get this out of your system and see how you feel then.'

She looks at me from her pale eyes, their rims smudgey from where she has forgotten the coating of mascara and rubbed them and I think of lying in bed with Ed, his body trembling over mine.

'How would you feel,' I ask, 'if I described Chris as "someone you have to get out of your system"?' She draws her hand back as though I've burned her. 'Anyway, I've given my notice in at Treadz. I start work with Ed in two weeks.'

She sighs, exasperated with me, just as there's a particularly plaintive cry from Sophie in the other room. Tania grabs the door handle and yanks it open. 'Shut *up!*' she shouts at a volume none of us knew she could reach.

Chapter 26

——— —

Corinne used to be fond of saying that starting a new job was a bit like making love, but one of her temps had a different version: 'The difference between starting a new job and having sex is that when you start a new job you wish you hadn't come, and when you have sex you wish you had.'

What I'm thinking as I make my way from the station on my first day, is that sometimes starting a job and having sex are the same thing. It's the first really warm day we've had this spring and as I stroll along feeling the sun on my face, a song keeps playing in my head: 'I'm mad about the boy. There's something of the cad about the boy.' I heard it on the radio this morning and immediately it made me think of Ed. But then everything makes me think of Ed.

Our offices are on the third floor with, Ed has told me, a breathtaking view without saying of what. These rooms are not, in the end, the ones he showed me initially; somehow that all fell through — someone he knew heard of premises that were better and this is the first time I will have seen them — but the element of surprise and mystery only adds to my excitement.

People say it's unwise to work with someone you're in

a relationship with, but I can't see that. If you get on in one area of your life then why not in another? And if you love someone you want to be with him every minute.

It has been a strange courtship, if you can call it that. There's been a lot of passion considering how little time we've ever spent alone – but there's been little chance for our relationship to mellow. I'm looking forward to changing all that. Ed has been like something you see in a shop window and keep going back to look at, wondering if you should have it. The fact you have to wait until you can afford it only increases its value.

Well, I've been very patient, saved hard, I'm about ready to make my investment. I don't think it will be long before Ed is asking to move in.

The reception area is wide and airy, the walls hung tastefully with reproduction Van Goghs, though I'm disappointed that the desk in the first office I look into isn't the one I'd recommended – this arrangement of drawers isn't nearly so convenient as the model I'd pointed out with its narrow paper trays. Maybe these were better value.

There seems to be no one around but then as I approach the fourth door leading off this outer office Ed steps out from it. He's soaking wet, his shirt plastered to him and water is dripping from his chin. He's drying his hair on a tea towel.

Perhaps it's the memory of Ed in the shower; maybe it's that there's something indefinably erotic about a body dripping with water. His shirt has turned transparent, outlining the swell of his chest and hinting at the shadow of his dark hair on his pectorals. He looks so vulnerable and exposed, caught unexpectedly like this; it seems an age since we were together though it's only a few days since he called to see me at home. I want to study his face, memorize the slope of cheek, the rise of his forehead, imprint them on my memory so they're always with me when we're apart.

I move towards him but he laughs and holds an arm up to protect me from him.

'The damn tap. It was dripping and I thought I could fix it — it's soaked me.'

The water has increased the curl of his hair and its dark sheen; his eyes are brilliant in this light. From a safe, dry, distance I lean towards him and our lips meet with a spark of static electricity that makes us bounce back from each other with a laugh. It seems prophetic and entirely appropriate that the sexually charged air should also be charged with electricity. This may not be exactly the time to consummate our new partnership but hopefully there'll be many occasions when it will be the place.

'Just let me get this tap fixed. I want it finished before Maxine gets here.' He turns back towards the small kitchen.

'Maxine?' The sound of her name makes me feel as though I'm the one who has just been sprayed with cold water.

'She's just giving us a hand.' I hope he'll soon be giving *her* the boot. It must have been Maxine who chose the furniture.

'What was wrong with the equipment we looked at originally?' I've also noticed an electronic typewriter which won't do what a PC would.

He leans over the sink and turns the tap on gingerly.

'Finances, sweetheart. We'll get you what you want as soon as the cash starts flowing. But I took advice from a friend who thought that would do the job as well in the short term.'

A small knife cuts into my chest and begins scraping at my ribs. 'What was wrong with the advice I gave?'

'It was wonderful advice. But this person has experience with new companies – it was she who found us these premises.'

He looks up at me, suddenly concerned and sensing the chill in the air. 'That's not a problem, is it? It was a matter of expediency, that's all.'

'No, of course not.' Cow. I hate her whoever she is.

He gives me a sympathetic smile, making me feel like a new wife complaining about the housekeeping. 'Once we're on our feet you'll have *carte blanche* to order what you like.'

The tap seems to be working satisfactorily now and Ed gives me a smile of victory, oblivious of my change of mood.

'We're going to have such good times here.'

'Are we?'

'I can guarantee it.'

His closeness neutralizes my anger. Ignoring his wetness, I pull his shirt open with difficulty, the buttons slippery and resistant, and lay my face against his damp chest. His arms come round me hesitantly, suddenly cold through my blouse. This is what I want, I think, companionable intimacy and trust.

Well, not only that, naturally.

Ed is at his desk, telephone in hand shouting at a twenty-four hour plumber who can't come till Thursday, while I make name tags for the filing cabinet, when the door flies open with a thud against the wall, and there stands Maxine.

She blinks at Ed's wet shirt but doesn't ask. She beams on seeing me, however, and pushes her way in holding a bottle of champagne and a box of wine flutes.

'Give me a hand, Gemma. I nearly dropped these in reception. That door swung back and almost hit me.'

I relieve her of her load and she stands, arms akimbo, looking round with satisfaction.

'What do you think?' she asks me.

I'm already envisaging our small rooms filled with the ringing of telephones from eager clients placing orders, while secretaries run back and forth with mail and faxes, and the salesmen hurry in to collect samples before dashing off again.

'It's going to be terrific.'

She cocks her head in the direction of Ed who has so far ignored her arrival. 'Don't tell me he's been washing his dirty linen in public again.' She laughs at her own joke which I try to join in with though I think she should be more sympathetic.

I try to keep the combative note out of my voice. 'He was trying to fix a leak.'

'Ed fix a leak? He can't always *take* a leak without assistance. If you'd seen the state of my pedestal mat, you'd know what I mean.' She fetches the tea towel Ed dried his hair on earlier and begins wiping the glasses she has brought.

'The next time anything goes wrong, ring a plumber or a carpenter or whoever it is you need. He always ends up having to get one in the end anyway, he's useless.'

These last words would have forced me to spring to his defence but Ed has put the phone down in time to catch them and as he lets it pass I'm obliged to do the same.

'Ah, you got the champers, good girl. Let's get it

open.' He begins to pull off the foil but Maxine stops him.

'You can't open it yet, Miriam isn't here.'

He looks at Maxine in faint surprise. 'Is she coming?'

'Of course she is. She had to go to the doctor's first thing but she said she'd be along afterwards.' She turns to me and adds by way of explanation. 'She's going to do the books until Roger can join us. He had to give longer notice than you did.' She says this in a tone of voice that suggests Roger has been somehow remiss.

She goes into the kitchen and potters about, reminding me that the cupboards will want a wipe over before we use them, and reeling off a list of items we will need as though I'm her assitant, not Ed's. Then, while I resume the making of labels for the files, she begins some long tale about a contact she has who is going to put lots of business our way, dwelling rather more on the circumstances of how she met him than the business actually, and making me wonder if she is saying all this for Ed's benefit rather than mine.

She is still in mid flow when I hear a deep 'Hello' from Ed who has been doing something in reception.

'That'll be her,' says Maxine. Picking up the champagne and carrying it through.

The woman is taller than Maxine, and younger with a jaunty playful air about her. Her shoulder-length auburn hair is piled up on top with tendrils hanging loose and casual, as though she caught it up hurriedly before getting into her bath and then forgot to let it down again. She looks like she'd be fun in other circumstances and I hope she soon finds other circumstances to go and have it in. I don't want this sort of competition.

'Mimi, meet Gemma,' says Maxine. The woman holds her hand out to me while Ed takes the champagne bottle, removing the last of its foil cap. She has long elegant fingers, free of rings. 'I'm so glad to meet you at last.' She turns away and starts unbuttoning her coat. 'I hope you like the furniture. I think it looks rather impressive myself.'

I nod politely. So this is the person who chose it. She has a voice like bitter chocolate. Black satin. Silk underwear. And, despite myself, it conjures up a subliminal image of she and Ed making love on a leopard skin rug before a raging fire.

As her coat falls open, I realize that she is pregnant.

'So how do you all know each other?' I ask Mimi, breathing slowly to keep control of my voice, but it is Maxine who answers.

'How do I know her? Can't you see the likeness? She's my little sister! I thought Ed would have told you. *Men!* You can't rely on them to tell you anything.'

She takes the champagne bottle from Ed and forces the cork off as Janet Reger takes off her coat and hangs it on the peg over my jacket.

Chapter 27

——— ——

Corinne lays a caramel toffee on my desk and gives me a pleading look. 'You're sure you don't mind if I nip out for a couple of hours? Stylists can be so temperamental, can't they, and you know what Clyde's like if you're late.' I don't know at all, but I nod and take the application forms to the two women hovering inside the door. Housewives and mothers returning to work, at a guess. They look faded and wan, like Tania used to (she starts her teacher training in September. Chris says she's a natural). Their hair is in need of cutting and their skirts were fashionable five years ago.

I hand them the forms and they exchange nervous glances, like schoolgirls waiting outside the head's study. They'll feel even more like that once I get them to do the typing tests, standing over them with a stopwatch. They wish they had my job (they would also wish for my sporty little car if they could see it. The same jeans-clad boys who rushed to clean Corinne's windscreen now dash to do mine). And I see from their expressions that they imagine I get a vicarious pleasure from treating them this way, not realizing that I'm both forewarning the strong of what their temping future holds, and protecting the weak by making them drop out now, before the Eds of this world can get to them.

Though they may hate me, Corinne admires me for my sharp way with employers who are slow to pay, and employees who dare let us down in any of a variety of ways. I'm particularly quick to spot temps being taken on in some deal designed to avoid the fee due to us, the way Ed poached me from Corinne. My abrasive manner with the temps sorts the wheat from the chaff: those who can't stand the heat don't come anywhere near our kitchen.

Corinne and I set up the agency, 'Top Temps', three months ago, and it's going very well. I knew she had always wanted to be her own boss and when I walked in looking for work we got talking and the idea just grew – we're planning to run an agency for nannies alongside it once we're on our feet. Childcare arrangements are always a problem for working women and there's an obvious gap in the market – which would have been plugged already if most businesses weren't run by men who leave all the childcare arrangements to the women.

I haven't seen Ed since that day at his offices. It was odd, drinking to our futures when I knew that mine was over already. I knocked back the bubbly in the hope things would look different through an alcoholic haze but there was no mistaking that body language (how had Maxine remained so oblivious?). I saw how he still loved her in the way he helped her on with her coat when she left, arranging her hair so carefully about her neck so that it didn't catch in her collar, the way I would do for Joe.

'Sweetheart,' he began, after they had gone and I told him that I knew. 'You've got it all wrong. It's all over between Mimi and me. Ask yourself – if it wasn't, would I really risk you meeting each other? I'd have to be crazy.'

And somehow, hearing him say how crazy it would be, I knew it was true and what was worse, that it had happened by design not accident. It was something he was getting off on in his fantasies, a future where Mimi and I — and who knows, maybe even Maxine — worked alongside each other; when it wouldn't be just me, alone, acknowledging the undoubted advantages of wheels on his office chair.

Tania was right, of course, I was obsessed with him. I'd seen him as a challenge but really I was consumed. I fed off Ed — for confidence, stimulus, self esteem — as though these were things that only he could get for me. But my time with him wasn't entirely wasted. I saw in his look of panic when I said I was leaving that he didn't only want me for recreation. For the first time I realized I was good at what I do.

Perhaps I was obsessed by something else too — the idea that I couldn't survive without a man of one sort or another. It's only now I see that the men I clung to so desperately were those who couldn't survive without a woman.

I still see Sam. He rents a flat just a few miles away so he can see Joe as often as he wants. He works flexi-time now, which is ironic; he's always calling in, gets on my nerves. I'm still fond of him, but that sheer animal magnetism that was so exhilarating and exhausting seems to have gone. I look at him now and see not some sex god but just a sweet guy with a tight butt and loose morals (not to be confused with Ed who, fifteen years older, has a sagging butt and no morals. I always told Tania they were nothing alike — though they had one thing in common: they both thought being committed to a relationship was the same as being committed to prison). It was Sam's elusiveness that was part of his charm; the fact I couldn't have him — or Ed,

or, now I come to think about it, Rudi – entirely, just made
them the more desirable. When I see Sam now, I remember
what loving him was like but it's like looking at an old
photograph when you can't ever believe you wore clothes
like that and thought you looked nice in them.

Corinne comes back just before closing with her hair the
colour of carrots. It was black when she went out.

'What do you think?'

Her usual colours are reds and pinks, I can't see even her
carrying this combination off. But the new shade alters the
effect of her skin tones and the shadows under her eyes seem
to have disappeared. Actually she looks rather wonderful.
'I think you'll need a whole new wardrobe.'

'A whole new wardrobe is exactly what I want. I can
always rely on you, darling, to say the right thing.' She
looks happier than she has in a week as she dials a number
with a scarlet painted fingernail. Her boyfriend, who used
to be our area manager, dumped her just last Thursday
and this change of colour is her act of defiance. I've heard
that song about washing that man right outa your hair –
if I'd tried that a year ago I might never have got involved
with Ed.

'Look,' she says, changing her mind in mid dial and
putting the phone down. 'I'm going to that new comedy
club tonight, there's a crowd of us going. Why don't you
come? Bring a bloke if you want.'

There's only Colin but I wouldn't want to bring him.
I've spent some time with him recently and now Corinne
thinks we may be becoming an item but I was only helping
him decide what college course to go for.

'OK,' she says, 'then what about Sam?' Corinne has met
Sam once or twice when he has called in with Joe. 'He

looks good fun.' I don't respond and she flicks a carroty lock from her forehead, giving me the flirtatious look she usually reserves for potential customers. 'I could always take him off your hands.'

I'd like to go but I don't see the need to bring a man at all. I'm enjoying being by myself. At last I'm making a success of my life, doing what I want to do and if there's one thing I don't need it's another albatross round my neck. Men are such needy creatures. They let you think they're taking on responsibilities but you end up doing everything for them. They don't want lovers and partners, they want someone to take care of them. I'd blame the mothers if I wasn't one myself.

But Corinne's words have sent the smallest flutter shivering through me. It's probably just some old residue of protectiveness at the idea of her scraping Sam's back with those vicious manicured talons but even so . . . Sam may just have loose morals and a tight butt but not let's underestimate the value of a tight butt. I don't want him back, but one day I may want something. On my own terms. Who knows. And he is Joe's dad.

A woman who has damaged her chances with us by arriving in a tracksuit, hands her application form to me and I check it over. 'I may give him a ring,' I say to Corinne over my shoulder. 'But I'm not committing myself.'